# MONKEY MAN

# MONKEY MAN

## STEPHEN PRICE

NEW
ISLAND

Copyright © 2005 Stephen Price

MONKEY MAN
First published 2005
by New Island
2 Brookside
Dundrum Road
Dublin 14

This edition published 2006

The author has asserted his moral rights.

ISBN 1 905494 22 X

British Library Cataloguing in Publication Data.
A CIP catalogue record for this book is available
from the British Library.

Typeset by New Island
Cover design by Fidelma Slattery @ New Island
Printed in the UK by Cox & Wyman, Reading, Berks

10 9 8 7 6 5 4 3 2 1

*'Anyone who hasn't experienced the ecstasy of betrayal knows nothing about ecstasy at all'*

*Jean Genet*, Prisoner of Love

*'I am not Lee, thou art not he, and the rest are not important'*

*My most heartfelt thanks to everyone who helped with this book – you know who you are.*
*And to Sarah, for her patience.*

# 1

## VIAGRA

I think that the Monkey Man still loved me when he sent me to fetch his Viagra. That is to say, I think he still *trusted* me, because you'd need to bloody well trust someone, wouldn't you, to let them in on a secret like that? Imagine if his enemies in the press got a hold of it: EXCLUSIVE! CHAT SHOW HOST CAN'T SCREW PEOPLE!

If only.

The Monkey Man had certainly told me he loved me, coked off his balls in nightclubs, kissing my hand, on bended knee. Of course, at the time, I was no stranger to chemicals myself. Proper stuff, though, not old man's mickey-fixer. When he sent me to fetch his Viagra, I'd been up all night, pilling it. Talking endless shite with my monged-out friends. That was bad, because I shouldn't have been at the Class As, not on a Thursday. Back then I, of all people, seriously needed my shit together on Friday. But hey – somehow the party always tracked me down and forced me to join in.

One of the things about working with the Monkey Man was every time I thought, 'This is the insanest shit I've ever had to deal with', subsequent events would invariably prove me wrong. The other things about working with him were the money, the drugs, and the vicarious fame of it all. Rubbing shoulders with celebrities, on a par. Part of the business, a player in the game. I was his producer, so that made me somebody. The general perception was that if I could handle *him*, then I must have been a pretty clever young fellow. Of course, in boom Ireland perceptions were everything.

So I'm late, floating into work, my head adrift from its moorings. I've had precisely two hours' sleep. I glide into the air-conditioned chill of the TV Ireland building, escaping the soggy heat of a Dublin summer that refuses to die. People nod and wave as I waft through reception … well, hello and *hello*. I'm as cool as a breeze, getting away with it.

Then, up ahead, the door to our production office opens, and out hops the Monkey Man. He glances up at me and quietly pulls the door shut behind him, like he's trying not to wake a baby. The corridors are carpeted but somehow the little bastard can always sense when I'm close, on his monkey radar. He scampers towards me, grabs my naked forearms with his dry, clutching paws, and fixes me with that meat-skewer stare from deep beneath a pair of unfeasibly bushy eyebrows. I brace. A bollocking, for sure. ('You're late, do you know what fucking day it is? There's no free rides around here, baby!')

But why sneak out of the office and pass up a perfectly good chance to scream at me in front of the others? Loves a good row on a Friday does the star of *The Kevin Carver Show*. Fridays are made for fighting – great, big, public displays. He'll shriek, throw a few chairs around, jump up and down like a demented chimpanzee with a banana stuck up its arse. Friday is programme night, so he's always stressed to the max. Nerves. Hyper. I have to say, he certainly *looks* mental. Almost ready for his weekly convulsion, but, as it turns out, not quite.

Instead, he dips a paw into the pocket of that silly sports jacket he wears and slips me a scrunched-up piece of paper. For a bizarre instant, I think he's passing me a wrap. But he whispers, as only he whispers (so as the entire building can hear):

'Teach! You gotta go get this for me! Please! I can't! You know ... get it myself! I would if I could! I know it's not an errand worthy of a senior producer, but will ya, Teach? Yeah? Yeah?'

Teach. That's me. As if I could teach Kevin Carver anything.

'What is this?'

'Shhhhh!' A passing floor manager looks up at his jet-engine hiss. Her smile of deference unacknowledged, she wisely keeps on walking until she reaches the studio, pushing the heavy door. Rehearsals have started, then. Good. Other people are functioning,

3

even if I'm not. I study the proffered scrap, and stifle a laugh.

'Jesus! I didn't know you ...'

He shakes me by both arms. 'Shhhhh! I'm invited down the country after the show tonight! Milton's place! Party! Don't tell the others, will ya?'

Don't tell the others, my arse. I know he himself will have already told the others all about Milton's party, because he can never resist an opportunity to boast about his mega-rich friends. Carver is the least discreet person I've ever met. But he's also the vainest, and therefore evidently not keen to advertise his little something for the weekend. That wouldn't fit with the image of alpha monkey, head of the troop, leader of the gang. I reckon by now I know all his dark habits, so I'm a bit surprised. Flattered, though. Trusted. Loved, even. That crooked, complicit grin. The eyes, like shiny bullet-holes shot into a shrivelled coconut. When he's like that with you, you can't help but grin back. I stick the prescription in my pocket.

'Anne, poor woman. She won't be able to piss straight if you swallow all that.'

Anne Stutz, formerly Anna Thema, of the long-defunct Jersey City Sluts. Don't worry, I'd never heard of them either. Carver likes to tell everyone that he met Anne on tour, the same year as Sid met Nancy. Been together ever since – just like Sid and Nancy, you could say, only not as dead. Anne talks Noo Yawk real loud, bears more than a passing resemblance to Ziggy Stardust, and towers head and shoulders above her diminutive partner. I often

4

wonder how she and Kevin kiss. Maybe he kicks her legs and climbs up the bruises.

'Who says Anne's coming to the party?' Carver half-pats, half-slaps my face, then emits a yowling, simian cackle as he pretend-clutches his stomach and stamps a small foot in filthy mirth. I shake my head as he slides back into the office, closing the door so the others can't see me go.

I don't like shopping centres at the best of times and I hate them when I've been up all night. Too many normal people, doing too many normal things, under too much artificial light. I stagger into Boots the Chemist, present Carver's prescription, and the squat, middle-aged wagon behind the counter glares as if I've handed her excrement instead. 'Assumpta', her badge flatly states. Assumpta studies me, studies the prescription, then utters Carver's name out loud, followed by the name of the drug. Only in Ireland, I swear. The daft cow either can't, or won't, get it into her head that I'm picking the stuff up for somebody else, somebody quite famous, so please shut up. The other customers at the counter glance over, expecting to see a TV celebrity buying Viagra. Instead, they see me.

I've been losing weight lately, what with all the pills and late nights, and fuck food when your stomach doesn't want it. Ecstasy, hash, vodka, and fags – my re-tox diet. Plus, I'm sweating. Pill sweat. Always worse when you find yourself jerked out of context, having to handle the unexpected. Then I twig. This store-front genius has decided that I've been robbing pre-scriptions. In Assumpta's lexicon of the depraved, I'm a photo-fit scumbag who'll mug unborn children to finance his next hit. I look nothing like Carver, so she obviously thinks I've broken into his car and rifled the glove compartment, or burgled his doctor's surgery, or some shagging thing. What if she calls the cops? No longer cool and wafting, I remember that I have a nugget of hash nestling in my pocket, and probably a few crumbled half-pills as well. Ah, to hell with Carver and the rotten things you end up doing for him! Listen, lady, I may *look* a mess, but I'm actually the most highly paid TV producer in Ireland, okay? I don't *need* to steal drugs. I can buy them like chewing-gum. What's wrong with you? Can't you *tell* I'm a person of substance?

Evidently not. I'm wearing an olive T-shirt with a black helicopter on it and matching combats. Now, why in the name of Christ am I wearing olive combats? I nearly always wear tight black stuff on Fridays, the universal uniform of the television élite. I just wanted to crawl into work and skulk around the studio, where it's cold and dark. Supervise rehearsals, let the researchers take care of any last-minute shit. They know where to find me if they need a decision. See, if you haven't got the big stuff set up well before show day, you're kinda screwed. So, Fridays I count on being able to lurk, maybe go meet a few guests in the early evening, buy them a drink, schmooze. Then throw them to the tender mercies of Kevin Carver and six cameras. Live humiliation. You can't beat it.

But not for me, not here in a shop, not in the middle of the mundane afternoon. I feel weak. I can't cope. I have work to do, and this woman is about to summon security, I just know it. Bugger, blast, bollockstitwank! Never expect people who wear their glasses on chains around their necks to grasp anything more complex than their own fat arses. You can explain nothing to them. One last try.

'Look, Assumpta, it's not for me. Can't you understand why this ... *person* ... would send me to pick up this vital medicine, instead of coming here himself?'

Assumpta's face now bears the expression of a bulldog licking piss off a nettle, so I take that as a 'no'. I can feel myself reaching an executive decision, which is to grab the prescription and run, when a girl my age appears at my shoulder, neatly snatches it from Assumpta's clasp, and shoots me an amused look.

'This will take a few minutes, why don't you have a seat?'

Her badge says 'Therese', and, in spite of my distress, I can't help noticing that she carries a large carton of prophylactics under one arm.

'Hey, you can't ...' the older woman starts, but Therese is already at the far end of the counter, handing the prescription directly to the pharmacists.

My nemesis follows her with a filthy stare, then mutters and moves off to serve another customer. I sneak off behind the family-planning display to try to stop sweating.

Feeling at a loss, I whip my phone out and text the Creature. Texting is the heaven-sent answer to all our redundant moments. You never have to appear unimportant when you can be frowning into a mobile phone. The Creature, or Stella, as she prefers not to be called, is my flatmate. Our relationship is platonic – most of the time. After last night's session, I bet she's still in bed, and I know for a fact that several web designers, minor journalists, and trainee architects will still be flopped around my living-room, lying where I left them, maybe rolling the first joint of the day, calling their respective places of work, and throwing sickies. Out of all our druggy little circle, I'm the only one who absolutely, one hundred per cent, has to be on their feet on a Friday, come hell or high water. Broadcasting: it ain't life or death, it's more important than that.

AM BUYING VIAGRA, U NEVER GUESS WHO 4

Short delay, then beep-beep.

U GOT OLLY REED ON SHOW 2NITE?

NO FUCKWIT HE DEAD. R 4 CARVER!

Almost instant beep-beep. Stella has the fastest thumb in Ireland.

GR8! I SELL STORY 2 PAPERS 4 MONEY!

FUCK U. NEVER TRIED VIAGRA. RU UP 4 IT?

Beep-beep.

BIGTIME!

'Your prescription, sir.' Therese, as if from no-where, extends a small paper bag towards my face.

'Eh … uh … thanks.' She treats me to an ironic curtsy, then begins placing boxes of condoms on the shelf beside my head. With her arm extended, and slightly on tiptoes, there's something sensuous and exposed about her shop-uniform-clad body. I find myself thinking about buttered toast. When did I last eat?

'Excuse me,' and Therese stands directly in front of me, the way girls do when they want to be hugged. Hugs are good. 'You're in my way.'

Coming to with a jerk, I step out of her personal space, but not too far. 'Hey, thanks for that. You saved my life.'

Therese stacks more condoms and quickly looks me up and down. 'The patron saint of lost causes – that's me all right.' She breaks into a lop-sided smile. Slightly irregular teeth, very white. Her face is round, brown. She has a pointy nose, dark, heavy eyebrows and pale blue eyes.

'These aren't for me, you know.' Lord, what a gormless thing to say.

'Yes, I gathered that.' Her accent isn't Dublin, but slow, deliberate. From over west, Kerry maybe; almost a drawl.

'Right.' And I turn to go, before I start sweating under a woman's gaze again. She could have let me leave then, just another weirdo at the prescription counter, but instead she stops stacking.

'You don't look so hot yourself. Are you okay?'

'Yes,' and I turn back towards her, lying. 'I'm fine. Late night, that's all.'

9

'A *very* late night, I'd say,' and we both laugh.

'Listen … Therese,' and she pouts mock-dolefully at her badge, but I deliberately don't look down in case she thinks I'm weighing up her promising, medium-sized breasts. 'That was an uncommon act of kindness.'

'We aim to please.' The lop-sided smile again.

'Look, you probably think I'm talking shite, but have you ever thought about working in television? You see, that's kinda what I do …'

'I gathered that, too.'

'Well, we always need runners, and if you ever wanted to go for a pint and a chat …'

'No, I would not like to work in television, thank you.' She draws out the word 'television' as if it were a new invention.

'What, you like it here in Boots?'

'My job is not my life.' Something in her eyes tells me I'm being a wanker.

'My job isn't *my* life, either.' Hell and damn. Normally I'm better than this, I swear.

'If you say so,' and she starts shelving the condoms again. Great. I've really blown this one, no bother to me. Usually, tantalising talk of telly-land works well enough to get potential playmates into a pub, where I can further lay my scintillating personality upon them. I've never thought of myself as seedy, but suddenly, before this mere shop-girl, that's exactly how I feel.

'Sorry. I guess I owe you one, that's all.' Having channelled as much gratitude and humility into my face as I can muster, again I step away.

10

'The one thing I *don't* like about my job,' and she frowns at the shelves, 'is having to wear my name pinned to my tits. It puts me at a disadvantage, don't you think?' And, God, do I love the length of time it takes her to say 'disadvantage'.

'Lee.' I extend a hand. 'Next time, I promise I'll wear my badge, too.'

Outside in the car-park, I suddenly feel dizzy and sit heavily on the edge of a large concrete plant-pot full of parched heathers. I can see my car, a silver Alfa GTV, but it may as well be halfway across the Gobi Desert in this hateful heat. Global warming, I swear. Whatever happened to autumn? When I was little, I seem to remember Ireland being a cold place. What am I doing, stuck in this suburban nowhere, when I have a two-hour chat-show to put out? Why can't I stop sweating, and why am I drooling over strange girls in shops?

'Drugs. I've got to stop it with the Class As, at least during the week.' I'm not sure whether I think this or say it out loud, but Dublin's full of junkies mumbling to themselves, so it doesn't terribly matter. Speaking of drugs, I feel a professional curiosity about the Viagra because I've never seen any before. I delve into the bag. Instead of the brown plastic bottle I had envisaged, Viagra comes in strips, like headache tablets. So, I pop four of the little blue diamonds out of the plastic, and stuff them into that tight hip pocket where people keep small things they don't want to lose. Sweeties for the boys and girls. There's no way Carver will need twelve

11

whole tabs, not in one weekend. Call it sharing, call it payment, call it what you like, he's not exactly in a position to complain, is he?

Who says Anne's coming, indeed! Wonder who will be? Coming. Ugh! The sudden mental image of a naked Monkey Man strutting, Caligula-like, around some country-house bedroom with a small but inextinguishable erection ... I nearly wet myself laughing as I stagger towards my car, like something out of *Ice Cold in Alex*. I stick my shades on, crank the aircon and the CD player up to full. A Strokes song pumps cold air at me. I drive fast, back towards TV Ireland. By degrees, I chill. God is in his heaven, the sun is in the sky, and I'm in my dinky, refrigerated sports car. I laugh at the violated Viagra packet, curled up beside me on the passenger seat. The things you do for love, eh?

# 2

## BEING MASSIVE

Back in the office, Carver is acting strangely. I amble
through the door, my head in a happier place, and
usually it's, 'Hiya, Teach', and, 'How's it goin'?' But
instead, the others have their heads bent forward, each
with pens poised over pieces of A4 paper, like students
doing an exam. My antennae stiffen immediately. This
is a busy production office, on transmission day. These
people are meant to be running around shouting at
each other, not hunched, cowed, and silent at their
desks. The atmosphere is nervous, wrong.

'The band here yet?'

I throw this out by way of a standard inquiry as I
make for the water cooler, trying to guess what's
caused this horrible vibe. You wouldn't believe the
amount of rehearsal time that gets eaten up by
directors wanting to be shot-perfect on whatever

trendy act we have booked. 'It's only a chat-show, not a shagging music video!' I don't know how many times I've uttered that line, only to be greeted by a cold silence from the gallery. Then the tannoy, 'Okay, everyone, can we get back into position, we'll take that from the top ... '

No one looks up, so I repeat the question. Only then do I notice Carver, in a far corner bent double over Charlotte's shoulder. Charlotte is a runner, Kildare horsy stock, and one of Carver's charity cases. She's so outrageously stupid that she wouldn't be working with us if little Kevin hadn't offered her a job for sucking up to him in a nightclub one fine evening six years ago. He likes posh accents, especially when they beg.

With a quick sideways movement, he slides over beside Dervla, one of the researchers. Sucks on a cigarette wedged in his paw. Frowns at what she's writing. Purses his mouth. Transfers his negligible weight from one foot to the other, folds his arms. The tension in the room is palpable, as if he's about to assault someone. Or sack them, perhaps. Even Scally, an emaciated inner-city kid that Carver keeps around the place purely for his own amusement – a kind of Monkey Man's monkey – is labouring over this mysterious task, concentrating so hard he has his tongue practically stuck up his nose. My assistant producer, Kate, shoots a disturbed glance up at me, but immediately returns to her task when Carver spots her treachery. He scurries behind her and scowls.

'Sit down, Teach, we're almost done!'

'The fuck is going on?'

'Teach! As senior producer, you are excused from this exercise! You don't have to do it! Just sit down!'

I remain standing. 'Do what? What *is* everyone doing?'

Carver has his bully mask on. That flinty, fascistic face that demands complete compliance with whatever madness he's perpetrating, under pain of a nasty explosion, with shrapnel, in your direction.

'You're going to be massive in the game, all of you, one day! Huge! You're gonna be real players!' I nod. Of course we are. Just like you, Kevin. 'But in order to be massive, first you gotta learn! It's all about good journalism, and good journalism is about instinct, a feel for the story!' He encompasses the room with a violent sweep of the hand, 'So, I'm giving the team a lesson in editing! Editing the show!' Pulls hard on the fag, primate eyes scanning mine for signs of dissent. By now, I've perfected the art of keeping my expression totally blank, my voice neutral.

'We *have* a show set up for tonight, and these people should be busy making it happen. Can we not do this some other time? You need to get yourself to studio for rehearsals.'

'I don't need to rehearse, Teach! It's all up here, in my head!' And he slaps a paw off his narrow, creased forehead, in case I'm in any doubt as to its precise location. He looks mad. He *smells* mad. His brain obviously lost contact with ground control shortly after I departed on my noble errand. But I keep my tone even, until I get a feeling for this particular trajectory.

15

'Still, the director's gonna want to get a look at you, check the autocue is working okay …'

'We're nearly finished, Teach, nearly finished.' He addresses the room, harshly. 'Now. Has everyone completed their wish-list?' He stubs his fag out in the tray of the water cooler. Carver uses everything as an ashtray, except ashtrays. The rest of the team sullenly set down their pens.

'I've told them each to compile a list, Teach! A list of all the people they think should be on the show! Now, we're going to go through these lists, one by one, and I'm going to explain exactly what's wrong with them! All of the names, and why they will never set foot in our studio! I'm not thinking about me: I'm thinking about you guys! You have to learn the game, and a big part of learning the game is avoiding the no-nos!'

The no-nos. The nonentities, the non-persons. In other words, every politician, every journalist, every actor, every writer, every sportsman – everyone in the world that Kevin Carver dislikes or disagrees with. We could be here a long time. This is the kind of thing that happens when Carver short-circuits – one of his master-classes in journalism. He collects the lists and clutches them to his face. Shakes with disbelief, then starts slapping his head again.

'Whaaaat? What the fuck? Who wrote this? Scally! You wanker! What makes you think I'd ever have Roddy fucking Doyle on this show?'

'Err … because he's Ireland's best-selling writer?'

True, and a mortal crime in Carver's eyes. He

himself wrote a book once, but Doyle is in a different league, and is therefore a ...

'... fuckdog and a mediocrity! Ireland's official scribbler! A talent-free zone! And what's this? What *the fuck* is this?' He's staring at another list now. Charlotte's, judging by the outsized writing.

'Mary Robinson? *Mary Fucking Robinson?*' He takes a kick at a swivel chair, which spins but fails to fall over, so he pulls it aside and slams it into a wall with both hands. 'Mary Robinson' is a very bad answer. A lefty lawyer who became president, then blagged a job as UN Commissioner for Human Rights, 'Mary Robinson' is a very bad answer, because:

1) The Monkey Man detests the liberal intelligentsia, as he knows they look down upon him.

2) He has not yet been invited to rule a country, himself.

3) He has absolutely no time for human rights.

So, Mary Robinson is a ...

'... university-educated prat! A self-serving pox! The doyenne of the chattering classes!' With one hand, he crumples the list up and flings it at Charlotte's head. Good shot, because it bounces off her crown and onto the floor, but not a great shot, because it misses her wide-open mouth. Next.

'Glen *Dara*? Who the fuck is Glen Dara?' Carver's eyebrows rocket ceiling-wards in a symbol of exaggerated puzzlement.

Kate coughs nervously. 'It's a place, not a person. You know, the road protestors, down in Wicklow.

They're blocking the new motorway through that glen. I mean, valley.'

Carver's voice arcs even higher than his eyebrows, before exploding on the expletive. '*Protestors?* Why the *fuck* would I want a bunch of smelly hippies in *my* studio?'

'They're not all hippies. Apparently there're lots of archaeological remains down there.' Kate reddens but ploughs on, even though this particular furrow is doomed to turn up nothing but misery for her. 'I heard a report on local radio a few months ago, and some of them were very ... articulate. We could always,' and her already thin, timid voice starts to expire at this point, 'ask them on to ... put ... their ... case ...'

Carver sticks his fist in the air, holding Kate's list. 'This,' he barks, 'is why you will always be an *assistant* producer! Because you know fuck-all about fuck-all! Our viewers drive cars, every single one of them, and they don't give a shit about a bunch of hippies chaining themselves to trees! Stupid cunts, come winter they'll be gone! This country *needs* roads, not arkey-fucking-bollocks-ology!'

He sags, like a soldier taking a bullet, and puts his hands up to his face. I make a move for my computer, switching it on, but what I'm really doing is entering his space, to show that I'm not afraid. Anything to break the spell over those pale faces, rapt at his performance.

'I have no ego,' he bangs on. 'Really. I don't!' He seizes my arm, stares up at me through those beetle

18

brows, waving the remaining lists. 'All these people have egos, but I don't! I just want what's best for the show! We have to keep raising the bar, Teach! No Mickey Mouse stories! No resting on our laurels! None of this C-list celebrity shite! Mediocrity is inimical to proper journalism!'

This has gone on for long enough. Diversion tactics are clearly called for. 'I have your stuff,' I mutter so only he can hear. He tightens his grip, his expression changing instantly from that of Stalin ordering a purge to Clinton enjoying a blow-job. Big grin, showing his long, yellow teeth to their full. Eyes burning in their pits. He drops the lists.

'Really?' His louder-than-loud whisper. Gone is the darting, angst-ridden editor, troubled by the profound imperfection of all around him. Now he's naughty monkey, show-me-yours monkey. He drags me out into the corridor and pulls the door shut.

'I had to pay for them myself. Expensive, these things.'

'Ooooh!' he giggles, examining the foil packet. 'When you get to my age, Teach, they're worth every penny. I wonder do they work?'

'This your first time, then, love?'

He frowns. 'I have no cash on me,' and he pats his pockets, dramatically. He never has any cash on him. Only a gold credit card, to lose in nightclubs. The rest, he borrows off us.

'We're cool, I took a few, okay?'

Carver laughs, crosses his eyes, and does this thing where he sticks his long, brown tongue out of the side

19

of his mouth, raises a knee to his stomach, and balls his little fists, like a grotesque parody of disco-dancing. This is body language for 'I've just been up to some extreme devilment', or 'I'm about to get up to some extreme devilment'. The office door opens, and he drops the pose. Charlotte the Charity Case. Big, shit-eating grin on her.

'Phone, boss!'

Some yuppie magazine. He takes it. They want him to model male underwear. Stand around, looking hard, in his nags. Photo-shoot next week. He demands a stupid fee. They agree to it. Send a limo and he'll be there, he says. No problem. His outburst forgotten, Carver summons a taxi and scurries off to the lobby to meet it. Every afternoon of his life, without fail, he crawls off home, drops a few Diazepam, and, journalistic integrity intact, enjoys a little snooze.

The office breathes a collective sigh of relief as soon as he leaves. I look around. I'm half-inclined to berate them for indulging the little fuck like that, but I can see the embarrassment in their eyes, and anyway, they'll report back every word I say to curry favour with him. Ireland has a long and honourable tradition of informing to despised masters.

So I stroll over to the studio, which is an oasis of calm compared to our office. Rehearsals are chugging along. I watch from high up in the semi-circular audience stand. The band, a bunch of polite, good-looking, middle-class college kids, turn up bang on time. Ne Plus Ultra they call themselves, going for the art-house vibe. The Ultras are fast becoming fashionable, but have not yet entered the prima-donna phase. Give it just a little more time. Their song, about the emptiness of existence, is on CD, so they mime it over and over for an hour, and then happily bugger off to the green room for a bite to eat. What pros. The director's ecstatic. Scally is playing stand-in on the presenter's chair while the cameras take a look. Autocue's fine.

Scally bears little resemblance to his lord and master. He's about half-a-head taller, built like a pencil, and has a shock of spiky blond hair. His distinguishing feature is a large birthmark splashed across his left cheek. Accented by the upright hair, Scally always looks as if he's just had a glass of shiraz thrown in his face. However, he does a fair impersonation of Carver reading his links and, every so often, pretends to masturbate, which gets the crew going. The girls and boys on the cameras find the combined concepts of 'Monkey Man' and 'sex' as laughable as I do. If only they knew. Christ – it occurs to me that some of them might. None of them would be that stupid, would they?

'Hello, Lee.'

Ugh. That bumptious voice, that egregious presence, that seeping oil-slick of fake gravitas. It makes me feel filthy, but punch the surface and there's nothing underneath. Who else but Dickie Vaughan, Head of Programmes, TV Ireland? He's crept up in the dark, noiselessly, like one of those fleshy fish you see in documentaries about the bottom of the sea. Well, imagine a cross between a bottom-feeding fish, a dwarf, Elvis Presley, and Kim Jong-il, and you'd be close to picturing Dickie Vaughan. He sits down beside me, and my skin doesn't so much crawl as try to bolt. Dickie doesn't know our nicknames, and if he did, he wouldn't use them. That would be a touch too informal; much better the brittle falseness he's learned from his *How to Be a Better Middle Manager* books. In fairness, we don't use his nickname to his face, either. One of the sound-ops has an uncle who went to the same school as Dickie, where apparently the big boys used to physically pick him up and use him to clean the blackboard. Hence, 'Duster'.

'Everything okay for tonight?' He peers at me through a pair of heavy, hilariously rectangular designer glasses. Media people wear the worst glasses in the world.

'Looking good.'

'What's the bang?' Every show has to have a 'bang', in Duster-speak. It's all part of his 'helicopter view'.

'Archbishop's out for the first time on the child-abuse scandal.' This being Ireland, it's never hard to find something depraved or corrupt enough to headline with. 'Then we have the Minister for Finance debating poverty with a few lefties ...'

'Can I just stop you there, Lee? Poverty. Yes. Very worthy, but wearing my producer's hat, I wonder if that won't turn people off.' Duster has so many imaginary hats, he ought to open an imaginary fucking millinery.

'Not the way we're going to do it.'

'Convince me, then. Sell it to me. Imagine I'm a punter in a pub, and you're trying to get me to drink up, go home, and watch tonight's show. Go for it.'

'Duster, if you were a punter in a pub, I'd fucking well leave and go elsewhere, but not before throwing a petrol-bomb through the window to burn you to a crisp and put an end to your pathetic second-hand psycho-babble. I don't *need* to sell you shite. People will watch this show, one of the highest-rating shows in the country, because they know, at some stage, Kevin Carver will start a fight. The Irish love a nice, juicy, public scrap, and that's why they love this show. Carver could start a war in an empty broom-closet, let alone in a TV studio full of handpicked targets, in front of millions of people to admire how big and clever he is. Now, bugger off back to your big, tidy office instead of trying to tell me my job, you arsewipe.'

No. I don't say that. I want to say it, but I don't. The man is, after all, technically my boss. What I really say is:

'Look around you. Ireland has gone from being a third-world basket-case to a first-class economy in just a few short years. We've had a fantastic boom, and the mood is good. This Minister for Finance is a hero, because his tax cuts have put money back into the pockets of the middle class, and these days, everyone thinks they're middle class, particularly our viewers. But the charity sector has been hounding the minister since the last budget, whining about poor people. They say that the boom has been squandered and that the less fortunate have lost out. So, we're getting a couple of bleeding hearts on to let them make their case. Then, Kevin is going to side with the minister and give those lefties a whipping. Blood on the floor. The charity industry. Careers that depend on creating problems. Our audience will love it.'

'Hmm. I just don't think that poor people are very sexy.' Stupid fucker hasn't understood a single word I've said.

'Come back next week. We're going to deny there's such a thing as racism in Ireland.' He shoots me a look to see if I'm taking the piss, but I keep it blank. Annoyed that he can't tell, he picks himself up and wobbles off to act self-important elsewhere.

Allow me to point out a very basic mistake that I'm making here. Management, in most sections of the media, is crammed to overflowing with morons like Duster. You see, people who can make programmes, people who can write, present, direct, people who can create product, generally aren't interested in becoming managers. Why would you want to do that when you can do the real thing?

No, the ones who get promoted up the pole are generally the clueless twats who compensate for their lack of creativity by perfecting their office politics. The piggyback merchants who attach themselves to successful projects in a marginal way, then claim all the credit. They rise spectacularly from nowhere, ass-kissing their way to positions of power, whilst the rest us sit back and go, 'Jesus, how did so-and-so do that? He's useless!'

So, what mistake am I making? I'm letting Duster know that I know he's useless. One day, I'm gonna pay for that.

# 3

## FUN TIME

The interview with the Archbishop is quite easily the most fawning piece of television that *The Kevin Carver Show* has done to date. And *The Kevin Carver Show* is not meant to do fawning. The phone lines are going mad. The four phone-bunnies are hunched over a bank of flashing lights, pressing random buttons on the switch, listening for a few seconds, then saying things like, 'Yes, sir, I know, but I only take the phone calls, I don't make the *decisions* round here ... no, you *cannot* talk to the producer, the show is on air. Yes, I *know* that child abuse is a very serious matter, but all I can do is take your comment, your name, and your number ... yes, if you want to complain to the broadcasting authority you are, of course, *entitled* to do that ...'

Fucking hell. The Arch-bish has been dodging the media for weeks, as yet more of his paedophile priests have their Church-constructed cover blown by proper, working journalists. While he hid, I had several meetings with his people and agreed to give him a relatively easy ride in order to land him as a guest. A tricky situation, as every outlet that didn't get him will be watching us like hawks. Big Boys can nearly always negotiate the terms under which they give interviews when there's a story in the air. It's the price of their co-operation, and if you get too hung up on what amounts to partial self-censorship, they simply go elsewhere. Of course, the professional trick, having done a pre-interview deal, is to make it look as if you haven't. One of the accepted methods is for the interviewer to ask a few choreographed 'difficult' questions when someone has a controversial position to defend. If you don't do this, you look like a stooge. So, in conjunction with his press officer, I'd carefully negotiated the Archbishop's interview, point-by-point, in such a way that neither party would look overly craven. But so far tonight no blows have been landed, not even a few token slaps. Carver has gone way off-script; instead he's treating the Arch-bish to an extended tongue-bath. A wonderful man, in trying times. Was it hard for you, Archbishop, when you read in the newspapers about your colleagues screwing kids? Was that *upsetting* for you?

I dash from my control booth during an ad break to collate a few of the choicer slices of public fury from the phone-bunnies, scribble them onto a clipboard, and thrust it into the hands of a waiting floor manager, who runs across the studio to Carver. I'm back in the booth, already. I hit talkback.

'You cool?'

Carver grins into camera 2. He's cool. He's reading the clipboard, and his grin broadens.

'You're not a bit thirsty, after all that licking? Jesus! You haven't asked him *any* of the questions on our list! What's wrong with you? Can't you hear me?'

Carver winces and waves a little paw around his left ear. This is monkey sign-language for, 'Don't distract me, I'm trying to concentrate on something so incredibly complex, only I can understand it.' Balls. Eyes bright with amusement, he leans over to the Archbishop, showing him the comments on the clipboard with a smile.

The Arch-bish resembles a large, black pyramid with a mournful white head. His eyes are watery behind a pair of steel-rimmed glasses. Studio audiences are usually as compliant as dough, but this one is talking out loud during the break, mostly in annoyance. The Arch-bish can plainly feel the hostile vibe, as his face has become stern and obdurate, the natural reaction of the old-school authoritarian Catholic towards a disgruntled flock. Carver, however, appears to be enjoying himself.

'Back in ten, nine, eight ...'

The director, on open talkback, which Carver point-blank refuses to use. 'Why the fuck would I want to hear what that big ponce has to say?' as he so elegantly put it. On air, we've wired it so he only gets me in his ear. But the rest of us can all hear one other.

'Okay, coming to you, still on camera 2. And try to salvage something here, please! Standby.' Roll VT, a five-second promo, which pushes the show's phone-in number. I wish you luck getting through, you poor, angry sods.

'You're on!' Red light on camera 2.

The smile is clean gone, evaporated like urine off a bonfire. He's looking down at the clipboard, mouth pursed. Frowning. You can hear the chatter of the audience dying slowly away as, one after another, they realise we're live again. We even catch a floor manager at the back of shot, making that two-handed downward wave which means, 'Shut the fuck up, please, we're back on air!' Carver keeps his head down, mock-studiously, until he has everyone's attention. It seems a long time. Silence. A few coughs from the audience. Then slowly, he lifts his face and addresses his camera, from deep beneath those mountainous eyebrows.

'Welcome back to the programme. I'm going to take a moment to read some of your comments. Most of you do not ... *approve* of the way I'm conducting the interview in progress here tonight.' Lifts the clipboard, and an eyebrow. 'Des, in the midlands, wants to know why I'm being so *easy* on the Archbishop. Angela, in Dublin, says that I haven't asked the *hard* questions. Well, *Des.* Well, *Angela.*' The names spat out, like sour chewing-gum. 'What would you like me to do? Perhaps you'd like me to *head-butt* the Archbishop, is that it?' Cranes his neck and turns his head sideways, in query, like a bird listening for a worm.

A quick cut to the Arch-bish shows him looking uncomfortable. Senior churchmen dislike television, or indeed any other situation they can't totally control. Carver has played dead nice so far. But I can see the Arch-bish think, 'Is this where I get bitten?' By Christ, I hope so. Carver glares at the camera.

'Angela. Des. Perhaps you'd like me to act the hard man, kick the Archbishop around a bit? Show him who's boss?' The Arch-bish now looks distinctly alarmed. Utter, utter silence in the studio. Even the sparks are listening, their big gloved hands hanging at one length. 'Are you suggesting, *Angela* ... or *Des* ... are you suggesting, for one instant, that I, or indeed the Archbishop, *approve* of what's been happening, in churches, in children's homes, in parochial houses, over the past thirty years?' Carver gives his bully stare, then shakes his head in mock-sorrow, turning away from the camera. His voice loses the aggressive edge.

'Your Grace, these must be very distressing ... very *dark* times for you. I know that, from what you've said to me privately.'

The Archbishop takes a moment to respond, as if ascertaining that he is not about to be head-butted. Eventually, he rumbles to life.

'Yes. Thank you for your understanding. These are indeed dark days. When such terrible things are alleged, of course Mother Church will always try to deal with it in her own way ...'

I hit his talkback. 'What, by sweeping it under the sacristy carpet?'

A minor shake of the head tells me that Carver isn't taking my question. Fuck him, anyway! The Arch-bish trundles on.

'... and of course we must remember the clear separation that exists between Canon Law and temporal law. That is to say, the Church has different *procedures* for dealing with such delicate matters.'

'Yeah, they transfer dirty priests to another parish!' Ignored, again.

'Your Eminence, this is an ongoing issue, and obviously you cannot comment on cases that are active, but for victims who have had their abuse proven, perhaps there *is* something that you can say?' What's this? A feeder line, if ever there was one! The Arch-bish coughs and looks into the camera. This has been rehearsed, I can tell. But not by me.

'Yes. To all those who have suffered at the hands of a small number of misguided individuals, who were clearly unwell in themselves, on behalf of the Church, I would like to issue a formal apology.'

Carver nods, as if rapt, but of course he's acting. He knew this was coming. A murmur goes round the studio audience.

'But I would also ask everyone to consider the damage that these ... *allegations* are doing to Mother Church and to bear that in mind, going forward.'

The Archbishop sits back, set piece delivered. An apology, qualified. Carver turns to the camera. He begins.

'Child abuse is an *abomination*.' Pause. Frown. Purse mouth. 'It is, in my opinion and, I'm quite certain, in the opinion of most of you, an abomination made ... *exponentially* worse, when it is perpetrated by those whom we trust, by the very people who administer the spiritual needs of this country. Perpetrated by priests, by nuns. It has been made worse still by the *reluctance* of the Church to acknowledge this awful *hurt*.' Quite a few murmurs of assent at that. 'But I would like to think we've gone some way towards lancing that boil tonight.' Pause. Frown deepens. 'Terrible things happened, things that we knew nothing about, things that are only now coming to light.'

Light. Fuck. Open talkback. 'Cathal!' Cathal is somewhere twenty feet above my head, manipulating the studio lights through a kitchen-sized desk. 'Take the set right down and throw a spot on your man! Now!' As the vast room darkens and Kevin Carver morphs into a hard-shadowed, vengeful little god, I half-expect a whinge from the director, having trodden on his toes. But he's pulling camera 2 closer instead, completely with me on this one. Carver fills our screens, the crags and valleys of his face hewn in black and white.

'On this programme, you've heard the most senior representative of the Catholic Church in Ireland apologise for some of that suffering. And the plain people of this country are no strangers to suffering. My own mother and father ...' he continues, and heaven help me, is that moisture welling up in the darkened gouges where his eyes are? '... my own mother, and my father, were hard-working, simple people, with huge hearts and broad backs. God knows they'd have needed broad backs for the times they grew up in.' Pause. Looks down. He seems to stop his voice from cracking and gathers himself. Looks up again. 'But my mother and father also had their faith, and their faith gave them great strength. Their faith gave them the strength to endure a cruel life, a life of endless work and self-sacrifice.' Stops again. Pinches his eyes with a forefinger and thumb, sniffs slightly. I realise that I'm watching my monitor through a mesh of fingers, my own. There is, of course, absolutely no logical connection between this folksy snapshot of his family and his love-in with the Arch-bish, but false emotion, sincerely expressed, is what the media is all about.

'So in memory of the good people my parents were, and for the sake of many thousands of ordinary, decent people like them, people who still draw enormous comfort and succour from their faith, let me just say this: in spite of what we now know about a small ... about a *tiny* minority of the clergy, I believe that this Archbishop is a good man, that we should acknowledge his sincerity and wish him well in the days to come.'

I look at the phone lines. Dead. Every one. They're all watching, I can smell it. They don't want to miss this, so they've hung up.

'Those who have suffered abuse at the hands of the Church have endured pain. Unimaginable pain ...' and his softness has gone, now. He's deploying his flinty, fascistic stare, tearing into the lens, into the electronic guts of the camera, beaming out into every home in the land. He makes a show of glancing at his clipboard. '... but *Des* in the midlands, and *Angela* in

Dublin ... do either of you *seriously* believe that *I* am going to *cure* that pain, that *I* am going to *lessen* that suffering, by being *hard* on the very man who's had the moral courage to come on to my show tonight, to publicly *address* it?'

Cue applause. Slowly, at first, then building. Tumultuous applause. Not quite thunderous, but getting there. We Irish are suckers for an apology: it works every time. Ah, sure give the poor bastard another chance. It fits perfectly with our psyche; confession plus penance equals clean slate. And next time you dirty your slate, you can always confess again – marvellous system. Carver nods humbly towards the studio audience and slumps back in his seat, as if exhausted.

'We'll have some music, now,' he says, quietly and sincerely.

Lights up, guitar chords hammer from the monitors. Cue Ne Plus Ultra, miming about the emptiness of existence. The cameras, having loved Kevin Carver, leave him.

Right now, I do *not* love Carver. Something happened tonight that I wasn't part of, on my show. My chest tightens. That would be fury, I guess. I have an assistant producer right by my side who watched while I was blatantly ignored on talkback. Everyone else on the programme heard my prompts and saw Carver dismiss them. I feel exactly as I did when pleading for his Viagra this morning – stupid and impotent. But it really wouldn't do to show emotion right now, say for example by smashing the talkback

34

box whilst pretending it's Carver's head, so I step out of the booth and into the corridor to take a few deep breaths. We're still live, we've another fifteen minutes to go. Now is not the time. Charlotte bustles past, ushering the Minister for Finance and the two sacrificial lefties in through the studio door. A runner emerges, guiding the Arch-bish. I follow him into his dressing-room. His people, a woman and two men in sober, efficient suits, greet him with sober, efficient smiles.

'Well done, your Grace. You came across well. Delivered the message.'

The Archbishop snorts like a bull seal. 'Well, it's out there, now. Let them make of it what they will.'

Incongruously, across the pristine make-up counter, lies a half-chewed mess of microwaveable pork ribs in brown goo sauce, the kind that Carver invariably demands and devours before every show. The meal before battle. Ah. Here's the evidence. The Monkey Man must have been in here with the Holy Man on the run-up to air. So, that's when the final deal went down. Why, I can almost see him sucking on a rib, his make-up bib hanging out over his suit, telling the Archbishop not to worry about fielding awkward questions.

'Even better than we agreed, Lee. Thanks for that.' One of the Archbishop's people steps forward, with a sober, efficient handshake.

With superhuman calm, I refrain from spitting. His boss has just been made to look like a hero, in exchange for a platitudinous apology. We'll be slaughtered for letting him away with it. I can see the headlines already. In their arrogance, these people can't. Indifferent, the Archbishop turns, inspects my clothes, and proffers me a hand, which he withdraws, lightly and automatically, as soon as I touch it.

'How did we do?' he asks, sonorously.

'Fucking great!' I blurt, before I can stop myself.

I stomp back to the booth, and Carver is really giving it some. He's interviewed the Minister for Finance about the prospects for the economy (all fantastic, apparently) and the token lefties who were invited on to tackle the Minister find themselves on the receiving end of a few of Carver's dirty tackles instead. He calls one of them 'a fucker'. The man goes pale and crumples in disbelief. The phone lines light up again.

One sure sign of a successful television chat-show is a packed and frantic green room afterwards. Free drink and a chance to glad-hand the Big Boys are both powerful lures. Tonight is unusual, because amongst the throng of black-clad bodies there are two competing alpha groups, whereas normally, by definition, there'd only be the one. The first alpha group is centred, as always, around Carver. That's how it should be. Everyone I know watches your show, Kevin! So, this is what it's *like*, backstage. How *interesting*. The Arch-bish has, surprisingly, hung back for a natter, and is cradling a balloon-glass of red wine. His people mill around him. He ignores them for an anecdote about some drunken politician, which the Minister for Finance recounts and Carver acts out. Mutual friend of theirs, presumably. Our director and our plugged-author-of-the-week look on, smiling vaguely at Carver's antics. Duster stands at the edge of this group, along with the rest of the assembled station suits, laughing far too hard.

The competing alpha group is younger and larger. It's more of an alpha crowd and has formed around the college-kid band, lounging on a sofa. In their handsome, laid-back way, the musicians soak up a lot of fawning from their entourage, the station staff, and the ever-present PR brigade. Fucking marketing people. They're like a manicured, pert-breasted disease, taking over the planet. I clock Carver glancing at the gorgeous swarm surrounding the band, his expression hard to read. I should, and could, be in the middle of one of those groups, getting my bum kissed. It's highly important to let other people know how highly important you are, at every available opportunity. Modesty can be very damaging to your career. But tonight I feel tired and cross, so I just stand in a corner and watch. Oh, here we go.

'I have an announcement to make! I have an announcement! Silence, please!' Carver, standing on a coffee table, rapping his glass with a fork.

'Could the band please shut the fuck up? I mean, I know you're young and good-looking and you're all going to get laid tonight,' and the band plus hangers-on laugh, whistle, and clap, 'but you're forgetting who's the celebrity here! Me!'

The entire room, including the Arch-bish, is

seized with unexpected hilarity, as Carver stabs a paw at his own little chest. He does his knee-up, tongue-out, balled-fist disco dance, acting the maggot. What a great guy. So famous, yet still able to poke fun at himself. Of course, everyone's attention is now precisely where Carver thinks it ought to be.

'I'd just like to thank the people who made tonight's programme happen, including my wonderful team!' That's us. Faint applause. 'I'd like to thank these young men for playing their music!' More applause, whistles, and cheers from the musicians plus hangers-on. 'At least, my producer assures me it's music, and that you guys are on the brink of success.' Laughter. 'That's great news, because we love success on this show, don't we folks?' Big shout from all around the room. The band know they're being publicly insulted, but are smart enough to smile. 'We certainly enjoy being successful, and I'm glad to hear that you hope, one day, to join us! As most of you know, I've already done the rock-'n'-roll circuit myself, and it ain't all it's cracked up to be! I have a walk-in wardrobe full of those particular T-shirts!' Public humiliation. You can't beat it. You can only join it.

'On a sincere note, folks, I'd like everyone to thank the Archbishop and the Minister for Finance for coming on our show. They're great men, and we owe them a lot, more than most people realise. What these men do is so often a thankless task.' Lots of whistles and a few sarcastic jeers, but the Big Boys look suitably pleased with themselves.

'I said I was making an announcement, ladies and gentlemen, and here it is: I'm going OUT!' A massive roar of approval. He opens his monkey arms. 'Who's coming with me?' Another deafening roar, bottles held in the air. I have sixty seconds to escape, starting now.

# 4

OUT

Coke. I hate coke. I hate coke because it promises so much and delivers so little. And I hate it because, although I'm acutely aware of cocaine's utter pointlessness, like most people, I'm incapable of turning it down. That first hit of the evening is always sublime; I exit the cubicle, check I've no white flecks on my face, and sashay back to the table. Command, conquer, control. I'll feel better than God for half an hour. Then, when the acrid chemical numbness stops trickling down my throat, I'll want more. A night on coke is like watching *Apocalypse Now*. Twenty minutes in, you have that amazing scene where Robert Duvall destroys the village to the strains of Wagner. He loves the smell of napalm in the morning. Then you spend the next three hours wondering when the film is going to get so good again, and it never does.

There was no escaping the post-show posse into town. There never is. I'd quietly slipped away from the green room to the control booth to grab my car-keys, while everyone else converged to slap Carver's back. Well done, Kevin, great show. Not exactly how I feel about tonight's performance, but I really ought to wait until I get him on his own. I thought I'd made my getaway but he intercepted me in the station lobby, one arm stretched up around that grinning fool Charlotte's neck, the other arm wrapped round a requisitioned champagne bottle, glass in hand. Like I say, the little bastard always seems to know exactly where I am, on his monkey radar.

'Come on, Teach, you're in my car! That crappy band can follow, if they can keep up! Scally! Scally! Get over here, you pox-doctor's clerk!' Scally, the company clown, always ready to leap to his master's voice.

'I thought you had a prior engagement? Or were you just pretending to be popular?'

'Baby, I'm as popular as powder at a pyjama party!'

'As opposed to little blue pills?' His eyes widened, and he clutched at his breast pocket. Grin. Tongue out. They were still there.

'Will you call Milton for me, Teach? Tell him to catch up? I'm in no hurry to go to the sticks, not before we do town, good and proper. I'm on a buzz. Fuck that country-house shit, it can wait. Tell him to come and pick me up when I'm good and ready, yeah? Yeah?'

I have most of Carver's rich buddies programmed into my mobile. He's always losing their numbers, in the form of little scraps of paper which he secretes about his person, until they drop away like flecks of old skin.

'Oh, and order some ...' and he wiped a little monkey paw under his nose, snorting. Several times. Everyone looked, everyone knew, everyone was meant to know. And yes, I have those numbers programmed into my mobile, too. I called Milton from the taxi. When we reached the nightclub, I hung back outside whilst the others piled in, and, after a bit of thought, made a few more calls, of the kind that are best not overheard.

'To the Teacher! Here's to my Teach! Come here, you big fuck! Without my producer, I'd be finished! I'd have no career!' Carver has his glass up. He drags me down onto the sofa beside him, and I let myself be dragged, mainly to annoy the headlamp-eyed PR girl who, tonight, reckons she's his new best friend.

We're in The Terrapin Club, the first of a succession of media-circuit dives that will become increasingly dire as the night unfolds. In the beginning, when we were winning, I couldn't get enough of these places. Media slut. How I loved to swan around, soak up the gossip, savour the envy. But now the novelty has gone, and I could write the script for exactly what's going to happen, who we're going to meet, what they're going to say, everything, for the next four hours. Coke. The movie you've watched a thousand times, strapped to your chair.

Around the table: Carver, 'the team', the director, this week's plugged author, assorted PR mannequins, and two of the Ultras, along for the spectacle. I don't blame them. Young, virgin company can get quite taken with Carver, because he's so old, yet balls-out crazy. The first time they encounter him people often follow in fascination, just to see what will happen next. Right now everyone's getting fuelled up, tripping back and forward to the toilets.

'I love you, Teach, you're great.' Arm around my neck. 'Good show tonight. You wouldn't believe the feedback I'm getting. It's amazing. Everyone loves our show.'

'We're gonna get murdered in the press for that Archbishop interview. The hell were you playing at?' So much for waiting. That first hit of gak has put my tongue temporarily beyond control.

Mock-pained monkey. He withdraws the arm. 'Teach, Teach, you're still learning the game! You're a good producer, but you're not sneaky enough!'

'Hey, Mister Selective Memory, I *know* we did a deal to get the Archbishop on. It was me who did it, remember? But I don't remember promising to kiss his hairy ring! There was no need to go that far. And you ignored my talkback. Why did you do that?'

'I was pulling a move there, you obviously didn't spot it. I gave him a blow-job, so he issued his big apology on our show – bingo! We have to think ahead! It's all about how we position ourselves in the game!'

'Sorry, I thought we were "the intelligent, rock-and-roll show that doesn't tolerate bullshit". I thought that was our position, in the game?' But he doesn't remotely recall the quote, from his own lips, six years previously. He sparks a fag and throws me a weird little look, one that I've never seen before.

'I run my show by my own lights.'

'*Your* show? Excuse me?'

The look lasts a few more beats, then he shakes his head, smiling. He half-pats, half-slaps me on the face. 'Teach, we have to start thinking long-term. We have to be smart.'

I'm listening. For an instant, I'm ready to be saved, ready to be convinced all over again, ready to buy whatever line he's peddling, ready for my belief, for my love, to be re-ignited and blaze like a Kuwaiti oilfield. But suddenly, the PR girl makes her lunge and pulls at his sports jacket, interrupting us. She jerks her head in the direction of the toilets. Subtle.

Now, what I ought to do here is slap her stupid hand away, grab Carver by the lapels, and scream, '*No!* Finish this discussion, it's *important*! This is about you and me, about *our* show!'

There was a time when I would have done that. A producer-presenter relationship should be like a marriage, and ours was, once. A proper marriage, with trust and the best kind of love, based on the most solid of foundations – mutual need. Of course, no marriage would be complete without fights, and ours had plenty. Epic fights. Fuck you, fuck you, and fuck you. I'm one of the few people I know who's not afraid of him, and because of that, we were always able to bawl each other out of it, then kiss and make up within the hour. So confrontation is not a problem. But lately, I have a feeling in my tummy that I'm turning from a clever lover into a nagging housewife, and that's not the part I auditioned for. So, instead of grabbing him, I do something else.

Carver has a paw outstretched. He didn't drag me down beside him for nothing. I slip him the nice, bulky wrap that I specially prepared during my visit to the jacks. It goes into his breast pocket, along with the rest. There's your gear, baby. Hope it does the business for you. Then, he's on his feet, grinning his dirty-monkey grin at the rest of the table, waving his glass, and allowing himself to be led away by Miss Pert. Bet she doesn't even have any snort and just wants some of his. All fur coat and no drugs, these PR types.

I slide down into the sofa. Watch Charlotte braying empty nonsense at the musicians, her big balloon head held back, equine teeth on full show. I watch the director and the plugged author, all pretence at intellectual superiority now gone, as they get lashed into Kate, the researchers, and a few of the runners who've tagged along. Middle-aged men always smile too much when they're trying to pull girls half their age. If only they could see how feral it makes them look, like old dogs begging for scraps. Scally uses Carver's absence to get the table laughing at yet another impersonation. I know the routine, off by heart. One of these days, Scally will get a job *being* Kevin Carver, of this I'm sure.

Beep-beep.

WHAT'S THE STORY, HUN?

The Creature.

STUCK WITH CARVER. U?

Beep-beep.

STONED!

WHERE U ALL GOING?

Beep-beep.

7TH CIRCLE THEN MCLOONE'S

U BETTER KEEP ME SUM PILLS, OK?

Beep-beep.

U ALREADY HAVE SUM!

SOD VIAGRA, NEED PILL PILLS!

'Good show tonight, well done. An object lesson in defending the indefensible.' Smooth, rich voice, leaning over my shoulder from behind the sofa – smooth, rich Milton. His smirk could be a genuine greeting, or he could have been reading my phone. With Milton, I honestly don't mind. Milton is medium height, well built, sallow skin, with a Gallic nose, big brown eyes, and short dark hair. Looks a damn sight younger than he deserves to, the swine. His Dorian Grey face comes from his French mother, and from having an awful lot of money. The casual suit he's wearing probably cost more than my car.

'What are you doing there, organising the rest of your boss's night out?'

'He's not my boss, and I thought *you* were going to whisk him away from all this beastliness and give me the evening off.'

'I thought so too. Thanks for ringing me. Where is my little house-guest, anyway?'

'Guess.'

Milton looks around the table and grins. 'Shall I order us some shots, then?'

'I'll sort the shots, you go sort yourself.' I slip Milton some gak and head for the bar while he heads for the jacks.

Most millionaires I know are thoroughly decent people. It doesn't really matter how they made their millions, whether it's hard work, good luck, or sheer robbery. Celebrity millionaires are the exception that proves the rule, though. These are invariably fearsome cunts, because to be a big celebrity, you've got be a cunt, and money merely reinforces a cunt-ish disposition. Milton is very much in the 'anonymous' millionaire category. In boom Ireland, where any fool with a few quid can live his life through the gossip columns, Milton eschews publicity and is rarely photographed. Daddy was a publisher; Mummy was an artist from Toulouse. Back in the seventies, Milton rebelled against his haute-culture upbringing by shaving off all his hair and starting an indie record label. One of his many acts was Kevin's old band, Carver and the Nutters. The two of them go all the way back to the punk wars, although to look at Milton, you would never think it.

Then, the way he tells it, in the early eighties, Milton realised that he hadn't rebelled at all. He'd merely followed his father into publishing, albeit in another medium. Dads, eh? The harder we try to run away from them, the more we find ourselves turning into them. So, he buggered off to San Francisco, hung out for half a decade, thought about life, the universe, and everything, and came to a conclusion. And his conclusion was that the next big thing in publishing was not going to be clapped-out punks or books, but software. He returned to Ireland, sold his record label, and got into software before anyone else in the country, employing geeks fresh out of college. For a while, he did better than okay, but then, in the late nineties, he went totally nuclear on the back of the tech-sector explosion. Christ only knows what kind of software he actually sold – he'd attempted to explain it to me many times, but always when we were twisted. As far as I could understand, big corporations and government departments used it to make all their other myriad systems talk to one another.

Whatever about that, Milton had gone from rich to ridiculously rich in just a couple of years. Now, he spends most of his time trying to figure out what to do with his spare cash. Fair play to him, I say. Sometimes, in direct contrast to their celebrity counterparts, ordinary millionaires develop a deep-seated need to prove they're just as decent as the rest of us. Look! Wealth hasn't changed me, see? I'm still a good guy! Well, with Milton, it's not an act: he genuinely is one of the good guys. In my book, anyway. Needless to say, any millionaires I know, I've met through Carver. Carver knows everyone.

So I'm at the bar, accepting delivery of a tray of B52s, when Carver stumbles out of the jacks, dragging Milton by the arm. Miss Pert follows behind, red and flushed. She staggers into a wall, clutching her hand to her mouth, then runs back into the toilets. Oh, dear. Carver pays her no notice.

'You fuck-dogs!' he declaims, in the direction of our table, but most of the club's clientele is looking on. 'You university-educated fucks! I want you all to meet Milton McMahon! Milton is my friend! He's the Irish Bill Gates! Obscenely rich, but I knew him when the arse was hanging out of his trousers! So, I don't want you to treat him any differently because of his money! He's not the reliable sort, anyway!'

'I'm as reliable as you are, you scabby little chancer. Dragging me into town when you're meant to be at my party ...'

'Oooh!' Carver clutches his heart, as if he's been shot through it. 'Ooohhh!' and he stamps a tiny foot on the floor. Then he raises his glass to the side of his face. One of Kevin's many affectations is what I call 'the soundproof glass'. He has this habit of shielding the side of his mouth with whatever vessel he's drinking from, as if that renders the person beside him automatically deaf.

'The last thing you need to know about Milton is, he's a woofter! So, ladies, that's another reason you won't get a penny from him!' Big laugh at that, and Carver squeezes Milton's neck with his arm. Milton goes slightly pink and smiles gracefully, then detaches the arm and joins me at the bar. Milton is indeed, as it happens, gay, but like everything else in his life, he tends not to advertise. He surveys the tray of shots.

'It's going to be that kind of night, Milton.' I neck one. Milton necks one.

'It's going to be that kind of weekend, Lee.' We order another tray.

'Come on, you fucks! Come on! We're leaving!' Carver is pulling at us. The others are already on their feet.

'But I've only just arrived,' protests Milton.

'Fuck you! We're leaving! I want to sing!'

We invade a nightclub called Verdana. The place is more like a restaurant that's seen better days, and it has a piano that's definitely seen much better days. Big, round tables draped in thick linen. Candles. Pretty Eastern European waitresses working under a permanently rat-arsed Irish matriarch who sits at the counter quaffing brandy, gossiping with customers. Carver walks straight through the door, grabs the mike from the pianist, and launches into a truly dreadful version of 'Hey, Jude'. Even after all these years, I still can't tell if he's trying to parody it, destroy it, or do it justice. I suspect the latter, which is why I've never asked. I mean, I hate The Beatles, but they don't deserve this.

Our posse is spread across two tables. Champagne. Gin and tonics all round. I order vodka, large, with ice and a glass of water. The trips to the toilet begin almost immediately. More coke. A lot more coke. The rest of the clientele reacts with amused horror. We, the entourage, may be loud and obnoxious, but we pale in the shadow of our Dear Leader. He has a microphone, he's famous, and he's prancing around the piano like an orang-utan with showbiz pretensions. Mostly, the punters just gawp, but one bald guy, sitting up the back with a young woman, makes the dreadful mistake of assuming that the money he's paid for his table entitles him to a bit of peace and privacy. Wrong. Carver spots him trying to talk to his date above the death by a thousand moans he's inflicting on the rest of us. A dissenter. A heretic. He must be sacrificed. Halfway through a rendition of 'Should I Stay or Should I Go?' (which sounds worse, if such a thing is possible, than the original), Carver breaks off singing, but gestures at the pianist to keep playing.

'Hey, Baldy! Da doo-be da-be doo be-doo ... hey, Baldy!' The man looks up. 'Yes you, Baldy, I'm talking to you! Should I stay or should I ... hey, Baldy! What's the matter? You don't like the music?' The man gestures with his hand. Piss off. Not interested. Can't blame him – I never liked The Clash either. The piano stops abruptly. Carver's head has gone purple through the effort of singing, although that wrap I gave him earlier may also have had something to do with it. He has the mike lead wrapped round his hand, like a knuckle-duster.

'Hey, look, everybody! Look at Baldy! Baldy is *having an affair*, right under our noses! And he *dares* to criticise *me*?' Cheers. Jeers. People turn round, leaning their elbows on the backs of their chairs, to stare at the target table. 'I mean, why else would a pretty young thing like her be smooching with *Baldy*? In a shit-hole like this? They must be having an affair! Aren'tcha, Baldy? Are ya givin' her one? Are ya? Are ya *givin'* her one?' Most of us are laughing, but Carver's voice has taken on a nasty edge. It disintegrates slightly, becomes guttural. 'Hey, Baldy, is the wife at home, wonderin' where ya are? While you're *givin'* this girl one? Is this baby your *chicken?* Is she? Well, is she?' Baldy makes as if to stand up, but his young partner grabs his arm and pleads with him to sit down. 'Yeah! Wise move, baby! Sit down or fuck off! Hey! What do ya do for a livin', Baldy? I bet you're in Accounts!' Carver turns towards us. 'Hey, everybody! Baldy from Accounts is a bit of a hammer-man, by all accounts! He must be, because he's slipping it to Heidi from Personnel! How are ya, Heidi? Could you not get a boyfriend your own age? Baldy has two point four children living in the suburbs, did he not tell ya about that? And he doesn't like our singing! Do ya, Baldy? Well, fuck *you,* baby! I'm the most highly paid presenter in Ireland, and I'm here to sing a song for *you!*' Moans. '*Maaa ... gic mo ... ments, when two hearts are shaaaring ...*' Scally jumps up to join the sick serenade, arm around his Führer's shoulder. It would be kinder to pull Baldy from his chair and kick him across the floor.

Seems like we've only just arrived, but an hour later we're back in the street outside Verdana.

'Come on, Lee! Get in!' Voices summon me from the back of Milton's gargantuan black Merc. 'Come on! It'll be good fun!' Pavement. Dark. Wind. The door of the Merc lying open. From within:

'Teach! As your celebrity presenter, I order you to either piss or get off the pot! You're keeping me back from my three-ball! Or maybe a four-ball, if I get lucky!' Cue assorted sounds of mirth and disgust from the warm leather cave.

'Come to the party, Lee. It looks like everyone else is.' Milton, standing beside me, ponders his crowded car as if reluctant to climb aboard. I don't want to go to Milton's party because I've dropped half a pill. Instead, I want to go find the Creature, my druggy friends, and relative sanity. Now is definitely a good time to flee.

'Look, dude, thanks, but I'm knackered.'

'Ah, come on, sure you never know who you might meet.' Milton makes a direct appeal to my networking instincts.

From the back seat, Carver barks at Milton's driver. 'Take us to your master's place in the country! Just leave him and my hotshot producer here in the street – I have an orgy to attend!' Cue an assortment of giggles. 'And would some fucker roll a spliff? You young bastards know how to roll spliffs, don'tcha?' The car door slams shut. Milton's driver doesn't move, except to wind down a window, awaiting further instructions. Just as I'm thinking how much I hate these pavement-outside-the-nightclub dilemmas, the two Ultras tumble out, demanding to know what's next.

'Your boss told us there was a party,' one of them informs me, belligerently.

'He's not my boss, and it's not my party.'

Milton checks his watch. A mini-crowd of hangers-on and PR trash has formed around us. Everyone's oh-so-beautiful, oh-so-gakked, and oh-so-up-for-more. Miss Pert, eyes wild with stimulants, demands to know where Carver is.

'In there,' and I maliciously point at Milton's car.

She claws her way through the door, like a weasel diving down a rabbit-hole.

'What the *fuck*?' I hear Carver whine from within. Milton sighs, then opens the front passenger door, and ushers one of the musicians into the vacant seat.

'Take them to the house, we'll follow.'

As the expressionless driver moves the Merc away, Milton waves to a waiting taxi. Having hesitated, I'm lost. For the second time tonight, I have failed to escape. It would be really goddamn rude now not to allow myself to be hustled aboard with Milton, a Miss Pert Mark 2, Charlotte, and the other musician, upon whom Charlotte evidently has a notion to prey, Jurassic Park-style. So near, yet so far-gone. Must inform the Creature.

HEY, LOOKS LIKE I'M FUCKED.

Beep-beep.

SO WHAT'S NEW, HUN??

HAVE BEEN KIDNAPPED BY A MILLIONAIRE.

Beep-beep.

YOUR DREAM COME TRUE!

BOLLOCKSTITWANK

Beep-beep.

HAVE U TOLD HIM UR ALREADY MARRIED – 2 YR JOB?

UP YRS. CU BACK @ FLAT?

Beep-beep.

WILL HAVE YOUR COCOA AND SLIPPERS STANDING BY!

'Not keeping you from something, am I, Lee?' Milton's face is under-lit by the glow from my phone display. I feel my body warm up. I feel the pattern in the cheap fabric of the car seat through my top. I feel Milton's leg against mine and Miss Pert Mark 2's breath against my cheek. She's been drinking something made of strawberry-flavoured chemicals and her lips are wet. Milton gives the taxi driver directions. Charlotte babbles about how great it is, working for Kevin Carver. He's great, she's great, we're all great. Fan-dabby-doozy. I relax between the bodies and watch the lights go by. This doesn't feel right. But I must admit, I quite like being driven, watching from car windows, when I'm coming up.

# 5

## E G O

To the south, the Wicklow Mountains form a barrier against which the tide of Dublin breaks. To the north and east, the slovenly city seeps fitfully into a drab agricultural plain. But at Killiney Head a line of brawny blue-grey mounds emerges out of the Irish Sea, stretching inland to repel the seething wash of housing estates. As the land sharply rises, flat urban carriageways disappear, mutating into a maze of secretive, narrow ribbons of tarmac climbing into the valleys beyond.

Past a set of iron gates, across the rattle of a cattle grid, the taxi headlights follow a single-track road through a thick pine planting. After a few minutes, I ask Milton whether all this is his property, and he smiles his rich smile. I bet he counts to himself, working out the average time it takes for that specific query to arise.

Even Charlotte's vapid yakking dries up as the trees give way to an open hillside. Perched at the top, an impossibly wide cantilevered window projects over the slope. Silhouetted knots of people standing within the house appear suspended some twenty feet above the ground, encased in a rectangular, cream glow. The taxi deposits us in a circular drive, crammed with anonymous black Mercs like Milton's, an assortment of silver jeeps, and a smattering of wedge-shaped sports cars no higher than my waist. My eye lights on a single, much older-looking car, parked proudly amongst the sea of bland metal. A Bristol, if I'm not mistaken. Milton turns me around, arm over my shoulder, pointing back the way we came.

'Well, what do you think?'

Below, about fifteen miles distant, Dublin lies in her bay. She wears her orange jewels, set against a black velvet dress. Away from the heat of her, the night up here is cold and clear, as stars pulsate high beyond her skyward glow. The mountain air strokes the down on my arm, and for a moment I feel almost as perfect as the view.

'Will you give me all these things if I fall down and worship you?' I pat Milton's hand, to show I'm not jealous. It's most un-Irish, but really, I'm not. Someone ought to own this. He chortles in my ear.

'The devil got to you long before I did, Lee.' I turn, but can't read his eyes in the dark. He steers me towards a set of broad, low steps. 'Party's this way ...'

Milton has studied his Frank Lloyd Wright, all right. And his Le Corbusier. And his Mies van der

Rohe. Long hallways. Ruthlessly open-plan layout, suspended stairways, internal balconies. Surprise vertical spaces set against split horizontal planes, liberal but tasteful use of concrete, glass, and wood. The modernist dream that never fades. This house is so well-judged, it could date from the thirties, the fifties, the seventies, or just last year – which turns out to be the case.

'I hired a specialist firm of builders in from Germany and put them up while they did the work,' explains Milton, whilst I coo.

'That explains why the entire fucking house hasn't tumbled down the hillside, then.'

Milton's immense cantilevered lounge is even more spectacular from within. Several clusters of timeless furniture, of the kind that only real money can buy, are spread apparently casually, yet deeply formally, across the elegant space. At key points, a subtle mixture of classical and modern statuary surveys the human company. As a result of the room's sheer size, the gathering seems disjointed, with some fifty individuals bunched in prides, separated by open savannahs of pale-grey carpet. Mostly, it's bitingly expensive casual wear for the men, and a toss-up between Miyake and Chanel for the women. Not a cheap Prada dress in sight. Yes, it's that kind of party, and here's me in my scrappy two-day-old combats and T-shirt. I begin to suspect that maybe it's me who's disjointed, and not the party.

Carver's chattering cry issues from the alpha group, which in this case consists of a well-known radio DJ, his wife, two top politicos, their wives or women or whatever, a moderately famous actor, and a couple of big-business bods whom I should probably recognise but don't. Gavin Kelly, a gossip columnist for *The Sunday Reporter,* hovers around the alpha fringe. Carver has half-a-shirt hanging out over his trousers and is in the process of giving a wildly exaggerated account of his mauling of the two sacrificial lefties on tonight's show, which by now seems a stellar age ago. Most of his audience is still relatively sober, even at this late hour – I can tell by the way they guffaw just that little bit falsely, then glance furtively at one another as the laughter subsides. Kevin Carver is clearly not sober and must seem disproportionately excited to the non-drugged. The word 'fucker' echoes over, with greater frequency than I recall it being deployed on air. Miss Pert clings grimly to Carver's side, eyeballing the company to which she is clearly superfluous with silent, hostile intent. She looks like she's about to fall over. Milton strides forward, with diplomatic rescue obviously in mind.

The musicians, assorted PR mannequins, and the rest of the trash we brought with us from town flounce untidily along a wall of outsized abstract canvases, snatching drinks from the tray of a small Spanish-looking woman wearing a house-coat, Japanese trousers, and black slippers. Having barely entered the room, I mutter something to Charlotte about needing a piss and wander back down the stone-floored hallway in search of a bathroom. Best get it over with now. I locate a luxury toilet in the depths of a large, discreet cloakroom and bolt myself in. I do a generous line of gak, plus my last half-pill, excavated from the fluff of my pocket. I know the coke will make no difference whatsoever; the abuse is merely symbolic at this stage. Hence the need for another half-pill. I'll stop it with the Class As on Monday, I swear to Christ I will. I check for white flecks, then it's time to get back out there and watch.

First, I follow the Spanish servant to a bottle-bedecked cabinet below the giant paintings, where I politely insist on mixing my own vodka and water, with ice. At least, I try to be polite towards her but, judging by the look on her face, instead come across as impertinent and weird.

'Ah, jayziz! It's yourself!' Marty Pelham, one of Milton's corporate press-officers-cum-gophers, his ginger chubbiness stuffed into a silver-grey suit so sharp it could cut slate. On the surface, it may seem odd for someone who shuns publicity the way Milton does to employ any press officers at all. But that is to misunderstand the nature of the job. When they work for a small outfit, the press officer's role is to generate attention, this is true. But when they work for a big outfit, like Milton's, their role is to channel or deflect it.

'This is Catriona. Catriona, this is Lee.' Catriona is crimped, painted, and poised to perfection, her Wonderbraed chest pushed up to her throat. She smiles like an air hostess, as she reaches her plum-varnished nails in my direction. 'Are you here with your boss?' Pelham's little V-shaped smile, wedged between two apple-red cheeks.

'No. You here with yours?'

Pelham laughs and bends backwards on his knees. 'Ah, well, you know yourself, these things have to be endured. He's in a fair old state, all the same!' And Pelham flicks his head in Carver's direction.

'You should go over and say hello. I'm sure he'd be glad to see you again.'

Pelham bends backwards even further and hoots, as if I've just told him the funniest joke in the world. Marty Pelham was mixed up in a big legal case that Carver took against his former band-mates six years ago and lost. Catriona smiles cluelessly, displaying advert-white teeth. I step forward, put my face up to hers, hold her gently by one shoulder, and run the tip of my tongue over the edge of her incisors.

No. Christ. Fuck. No. I don't do that, but I want to. Must be that second half-pill, coming on hard and fast. Am I sweating a bit? Has my face gone flushed? Do my eyes look big in this? Or am I pale, alert, and interesting? Through my largest shit-eating grin, I claim I'll return once I've delivered my vodka to an imaginary recipient at the far side of the room, and make an unconvincing escape. Pelham is the last person I feel like talking to right now.

Tastefully arrayed along the length of the super-sized window is the advertising-stroke-fashion brigade, all nodding delicately at one another. I head straight for their ranks and, once swallowed up, stop casually by the glass, feigning contemplation of the night. Instead, I study faces in the reflected room and sample a quick cross-section of the all-pervading guff.

'... yes, it's really about results-orientation, at the end of the day. Going forward, I think you'll find that brand credibility is reinforced by a sustained outdoor campaign, coupled with an optimised direct marketing solution. Anyway, that's how we're steering our premium client accounts ...'

'... new kitchen in that little place, you know, at the top of the village. Superb display, you can walk in and it's like, you're there. Brushed aluminium, stainless steel, and American maple, I've told Michael I simply won't rest until we have ours done that way. Portuguese limestone tiles, and you know those wonderful magnetic strips they use to display the knives ...'

'... third investment property, in the Wooden Building at the edge of Temple Bar. Yes, Rocha has a place there. Melissa says she's seen him on the balcony. At least she *thinks* it's him, anyway ...'

'... all those clicks convert to page impressions. Stickiness, that's what I told them. That's your problem, I said, your site isn't sticky enough. It's a question of driving traffic. Content is *king* ...'

Boom Ireland and her bastard children, making a virtue of the blinding obvious. As if we are the first, as if nobody else in human history has ever had money before now. Truly, this is our finest hour. If I stand amongst these neo-trendies for another five seconds, I'm liable to start a fight – it's the Monkey Man in me. So I disengage from the herd to assume my watching brief from elsewhere. I feel like a sniper, caught in the open. Got to find cover, focus my sights. Sit. Be calm, and let the ecstasy work through. There's a few scruffy, local-looking types smoking and talking on a backless L-shaped sofa, huddled under a hanging stairway opposite the main doorway. Everyone appears oblivious to their presence, so I slither onto a low footstool in the shadows close by them. That way, I won't appear to be alone, attracting strays who'll talk endless shite to my slack, uncomprehending face. I skin up, my back to the window, to admire the choreography of status.

The trash faction establishes a raucous territory around two black leather sofas close to the generous bar cabinet. Finding their squiffy bearings after an uncertain entrance, the musicians, Charlotte, and assembled PR mannequins become joyously sloppy, the object of raised eyebrows and patronising smiles. Some are snogging, others bray incongruously, competing crassly with the aching sophistication of the rest of the room.

The alpha group dominates the centre of the floor. Milton has managed to spread the conversation a bit, and I can see Carver grow restless as he scans the room in search of fresh attention. Having established his importance amongst the People Who Matter, his interest, I can tell, will gravitate quickly back towards the trash faction. At least they appear to be having a good time. People Who Matter tend to be grindingly dull, especially when gathered in shoals.

I should be back in my own flat by now, chilling with my friends, safe, soaking up ambient sounds, not stuck up a distant mountain in this hugely expensive glass-and-concrete box with all these goddamn posers. But is this a valid emotion of my own making, a burst of prescience, or just plain coke paranoia?

Why the fuck am I here?

I realise that mankind has been asking this particular question for quite some time, but I'm in the mood for speculation, so here goes. I'm here because of Carver, that much is clear. Without him, I wouldn't know people like Milton. This is how the upper ten per cent of the other half lives. I don't belong here, but here is the place I've been elevated to. Carver doesn't belong here either – in fact, he's the complete antithesis of here. But everyone wants a part of him these days, and, by extension, a part of me. The fame rubs off. If I wasn't so monged, I'd seize my social rights and strike a few poses too. 'Yes, I produce *The Kevin Carver Show*, you know. Oh, you watch it? How nice of you to say so! And what do you do, like I give a toss?'

Charlotte slips off the arm of a sofa and lands on her generous arse. Cue a raucous burst of applause from the trash faction. A tall, slender, balding fellow in a grey polo neck helps her to her feet. That, if I'm not mistaken, would be Milton's live-in boyfriend. I've vaguely met him elsewhere. Charlotte accepts another drink, to cheers. Why the hell did Milton feel compelled to introduce Carver's semi-wild sub-set into this delicate milieu? Why wreck an otherwise perfectly tedious party?

Because, because, because ... because a brace of coked-up media industry wretches will lend colour to any occasion. Milton knows this to be true.

No. That's not it. Colour is one thing, but empty, howling fluorescence is quite another. I know: Milton invited us all up here because he's coked off his balls, he wasn't thinking straight, and allowed the craic in Verdana to carry him away.

No. That's not it, either. Milton didn't invite this rent-a-mob to his party at all – Carver did. Milton left the piano bar chatting to me, by which time Carver had dived ahead and crammed Milton's chauffeur-driven car with a brace of hangers-on. Milton could have turfed them all back out onto the street, but he's way too polite for that. Ah. I see it all now.

'Fuck that country-house shit, it can wait.' Carver knew not to come here early, sober, and alone. He knew he'd have been bored beyond belief, swapping sweet nothings with Milton's moneyed mates. So instead, he imposed his own frenzied reality on Milton's subtle scene, skewing the situation to suit his own ends, as he invariably does. Clever monkey. Coked monkey. Unleashed, in your living-room. Doesn't matter that Milton and he go way back, Carver plays it his own way, all of the time. He couldn't give a toss for other people's plans – in fact, he derives enormous pleasure from wanking all over them. I'm here, simply because Kevin Carver is chaos theory, personified. I'm just a small fragment of the chaos that trails in his wake, wherever he chaotically roams. I am nothing without him. Nothing. I laugh as I think this all through, although coherent thought is rapidly becoming a major challenge. What the fuck is Milton going to *do* with all these people? Let them crash on the couch?

Or maybe ... maybe ... maybe I'm wrong about all that, and Milton is a closet degenerate. Maybe, any minute now, his refined guests are going to pull their clothes off and fall on us newcomers like a pack of randy wolves. Maybe we've been brought here as victims, as fresh young meat (well, most of us) for a big swingers' sandwich. Maybe these people have orgies every Friday night, to give themselves something to talk about on the golf course of a Saturday morning. Yes, that has to be it. Any minute now, those Chanel dresses will slip from slim shoulders, revealing a welter of diet-flattened breasts and concave gym tummies, then the men will remove their ties and belts, flexing them between their fists, as they encircle us wide-eyed trespassers with broad, meaningful smiles. I glance towards the hallway, and, sure enough, there's a man in a dinner jacket holding a woman bent over a metal banister, his balled fist shoving her cocktail dress roughly up her back, as he gives her one from behind. She groans, clutching the rail, shaking her head, then looks back along the corridor towards me. When she sees me watching, she smiles.

Wait. I don't see that at all. The long stone hallway is in fact empty, apart from a few coats draped over the banister, and the atmosphere in the outsized lounge is boring, utterly devoid of menace. Everyone is talking languidly, affecting mild ennui, just as before. I'm in that place where it's hard to tell whether my mind is dictating to the drugs or the drugs are dictating to my mind. Focus on something, don't let the head wander.

What's Carver doing? If I feel this far gone, how must *he* feel? I see that he's defected from the alpha group back to the trash faction, as predicted. He flings off his jacket, does his mad disco pose, and they roar their bollocks off at whatever he's just said. He has his back to the rest of the room now, and the rest of the room abandons all pretence and watches his back. Everybody *knows* he's on something.

'... same as it ever was. Still the same old gig. Some people never change, man, and he *is* some people. Little Kevin. He's like, you know, a sort of modern satyr.'

'He's beyond satire, man.'

'No, *satyr*, t-y-r. You know, half-goat, half-human. Randy gobshite from Greek mythology.'

'Roman mythology, you mean. Satyrs were Roman, I think. Mad bastards, prancing round the olive groves, fucking everything that moves.'

'Greek, Roman, whatever. It's all Latin to me.' Cue throaty chuckles.

I realise that the three locals I'm using for cover are watching Carver, too. The one in the middle evidently knows him. Compact, funny hair, late forties. It takes me a few more seconds to recognise him without his sunglasses, which he's rarely seen without, even indoors, at night. Fuck me ... it's *not*, is it? Guy to the left, long dirty-blond hair. Guy to the right, black hair, crew-cut, quite good-looking in a square-faced kind of way. And the one in the middle. It *is* him, shit! I'm staring, and, as always happens when I stare, I get caught. The guy in the middle clocks me, skulking within earshot. This is Ireland's most famous export, after Guinness. A certain rock star: let's call him Ego. He likes Latin names, that's why his mates laughed. Their little joke.

I've always had mixed feelings about Ego. My big brothers played his records non-stop in the eighties. Used to drive my father mad – he couldn't figure why they didn't dig Led Zeppelin instead. Maybe I was on the cusp of the generation switchback, but I always sided with my father on that score. I also had the distinct impression that Ego thought he was Jesus, and, as a committed atheist, that kind of left me cold. But then, he always stuck up for poor people, using his stardom to niggle constantly at Western guilt. And Ego is a big commodity throughout the Western world. Unlike Sting, Ego appeared to mean something. He could have sat in his mansion, perfecting his tantric sex, or like many other stars, he could have used the world's starving for a cheap, one-off publicity stunt. But he kept at it: Aids, famine, third-world debt – no cause has been too great for Ego to tackle, the clear implication being that these problems are almost as big as he is. Personally, if I had Ego's money, I'd spend the rest of my life dropping pills on a private island at the edge of the Atlantic shelf. I'd give the odd million to charity in order to salve my drugged-up conscience and blow the rest improving my view, my library, and my wine cellar. Ergo, Ego is probably a better person than I am. But then, that wouldn't be hard, would it? Good old Milton, full of surprises, eh? I remember the Bristol parked outside: bet you that's his car. I'd say they cruised up here from super-rich Killiney to crouch quietly at a comfortable party; a bit of random late-night relief.

In these situations, one invariably imagines oneself full of wit, knocking the international celebrity dead on his ass with a cracking one-liner. Instead, the best I can manage is, 'I know him, too.'

Ego peers over at me, totally neutral. He speaks.

'You, too? You know who, too?'

'The person you're talking about. The Monkey Man. I'm his producer.'

'The Monkey Man? Is that what they're calling him these days? I see where you're coming from, man. He *is* a total animal.'

Shit. I've let slip my private name for Carver. Hell and damnation, I wish I hadn't taken that second half-pill. Ego glances back towards the trash faction and I follow his eyes. Whoops, Carver is striding across the room, straight at us. Straight at me. Shirt half-open, eyes half-crazed. Face flushed like he needs to sweat but can't.

'Teach. Teach.' Takes my hand, kisses it. Leers at my joint, reaches out, appropriates it. Yes, he *is* even more fucked-up than I am. 'Teach. Have you any stuff left? Come on, you pox, don't hold out, gimme what you got! I need it, so fucking give it to me! It's *mine*!' He stands, swaying on an axis running through both ankles. Technically, he's wrong. I paid for this shit – he only ordered it. The gak is mine. But he's more than welcome to more. I fish another special wrap out of my combats.

'Bless you, Teach! I love you!' Carver half-pats, half-slaps my face. As he does, he clocks Ego and his mini-entourage following our warm exchange. The air turns chilly all of a sudden. Very chilly indeed. No further words. Carver just frowns, purses his mouth, turns on his heel, and weaves back towards the trash faction, where he waves my wrap before one of the sofas. Miss Pert and one of the Ultras leap up to join him. The three link arms and head for the hallway. Ego returns his gaze to me, speculatively.

'Well, he's certainly got you exactly where he wants you,' and his eyes penetrate mine.

'And where's that, would you say?'

Ego keeps the gaze well-fixed. 'Just one thing, kid. Don't fall into his evil ways.'

Sometimes in life good advice comes from the most unlikely quarters. For free. And sometimes in life, one is utterly incapable of recognising good advice solely for what it is.

'I'm only here because of him,' I blurt. 'And anyway, what did he ever do to you?' Over the years, I've lost count of the number of times I've requested Ego for our show. And never had a response, just silence.

'Ah, he wrote a shagging book …' From the depths of my addled mind, I remember that Carver's single stab at literature was a personal overview of the Irish punk-rock scene. Ancient history, so I've never been arsed to read it.

'… I'm just saying to you … well, you heard what I said, okay?' Ego's face is not unfriendly.

'I think, in some ways, I'm worse than he is.'

'I severely fucking doubt that.'

'I make my living from him, and I know full well what he is. So what does that make me?'

'It makes you a person with choices. You have a lot to lose, before you lose your right to choose.'

'Is that from one of your songs, or did you just make that up there now?'

Wrong, wrong, wrong. Stupid, cheap, nasty, and wrong. Coke sarcasm, very bad. Ego stares a moment longer, then shakes his head and returns to his huddle. This conversation is over, baby.

At a loss to retrieve the situation, I feign indifference by skinning up a joint to replace the stolen one. I have a daft notion that I'll pass it to one of Ego's friends, to light as a token peace offering, but as I reach the completed number out they're on their feet, moving across the room, patting Milton on the back, heading for the hallway. A babble encircles the room; the other guests belatedly realise who's been sitting quietly in their midst. Oh, no! The alpha group was really only a beta group all along! Milton follows the three men out, and they're gone. I watch the lights of the old car as they tilt down the driveway and disappear into the trees. The rest of the party gathers at the window to contemplate the departure of unannounced nobility.

'You all right?' Milton sits down beside me. Shit. How did he get back here so quickly?

'Sure. Hey, I hope you don't think I had anything to do with them leaving. I wasn't hassling them or anything. I didn't even cop who it was, until a few minutes ago.'

'Relax, he pops in sometimes, but never stays more than an hour. I told you, didn't I, you wouldn't know who you might meet if you came to my party?'

'Milton, you're such a big fucking show-off, but what pisses me off is you're so good at it.'

He blesses me with his smooth, rich smile, hugs my shoulders, and reaches for the spliff. Miss Pert stumbles out of the hallway and into the room. She makes for the trash faction, flops onto a sofa, and shoves her face into her hands. Is she crying? Or is she about to throw up again? Or both? No more drugs for that woman. Milton returns the spliff and takes to his feet to try to prevent a soiled carpet. Some of Milton's 'proper' guests tut-tut openly. Then, the musician comes running into the room, glancing backwards over his shoulder as if he's fleeing from something scary. He spots me and strides over.

'I don't believe ...' he starts, and in the distance I can see Carver coming down the hallway. He doesn't look right. 'I don't believe your f-fucking boss ...' the musician stammers.

'He's not my boss,' but I'm distracted, peering over his shoulder. Carver has reached the doorway. He is shirtless.

'Your boss called that girl a worthless piece of sh-shit, just because ...'

Most of the room stops talking, and Milton, attending to Miss Pert, looks up to see a half-naked Monkey Man hanging in the doorway, arms spread, paws clinging to the jambs, like some obscene crucifixion. Correctly assuming that this could spell infinitely more trouble than some PR bimbo puking on his rug, Milton abandons Miss Pert and makes towards Carver, who by now is leering into the room the way Johnny Rotten used to leer at his audience.

'... and then she ran off, and he like, started shouting at me ...' but the musician has absolutely none of my attention now.

'Get away from me, you *cunt*!'

Carver practically bends double with the effort of roaring this last word, at which all remaining conversation in the room ceases, and Milton halts in mid-stride. Everyone's attention is now exactly where Carver thinks it ought to be. The sockets of his eyes are deep in shadow, the lip-less skin drawn back from his yellow teeth. He sticks his crimson head forward on his neck and juts his jaw, staring venomously at poor, shocked Milton.

'Get away from me, you university-educated *cunt*!' he repeats, somewhat superfluously, as Milton has already taken a step back, hands up, palms outward.

'Jesus, Kevin, are you *all right*? What's wrong with you? What happened?'

'You're such a big fucking *man*, aren'tcha? Big man about town!'

Milton shakes his head, at a total loss. His assembled guests share his stare at the bogeyman, execrating into the room. If Osama himself had burst in and threatened to suicide-bomb the first person who moved, they couldn't be more silent or still. Milton's statuary gazes on, in sympathy.

'What are you talking about?'

73

'Oh, *I'm* such a big man about town,' and Carver alters his pose, striding into the room with a stage-comic walk, his bare pigeon chest extended, thumbs hooked in the pockets of an imaginary waistcoat. 'I'm so big and fucking clever. I own lots of people and computers and stuff. I'm Milton the millionaire, would anyone like to suck my *prick*?' Milton's grey-jumpered partner takes a quick step forward, but Milton grabs him by the arm. Carver breaks his Dick Van Dyke strut and eyeballs the couple from a few feet away.

'What's your pal gonna do, Milton? Does he fancy his fucking chances? Does he? Well *does* he? Come on, Mister Bum-chum!'

'Look, I've no idea what this is all about, but you should ...'

'I should fucking *what*? Stand here and wait for *you* to sort me out? I'd be waiting a long time, wouldn't I?'

Carver cocks his head at Milton, then does his Dick Van Dyke strut again as far as a glass coffee table, which he springs up onto. He denounces the assembly, screaming.

'You're all a shower of *cunts*! I'm Ireland's most highly paid presenter, and in my professional opinion, you're nothing but a crowd of fucking *cunts*! I earn more than all of you put together!' This last statement, in present company, is patently untrue, but Carver rarely allows the facts to get in the way of a great performance. Porky Pelham, I notice, has manoeuvred as far from the epicentre as he can get, leaving Catriona alone, frozen and puzzled. Even the formerly rowdy trash faction gawps in disbelief. Charlotte wisely sits where she is, motionless and pale, her arm round the sobbing, vomiting Miss Pert. Then Kelly, the gossip columnist, emerges from the cringing herd. Someone always has to act the hero.

'Look at the shape of you!' He gesticulates angrily at Carver. 'You're just a jumped-up little arsehole. Do you really think that fronting a fatuous TV show gives you the right to behave like this?'

Carver shrieks and jumps up and down on his soapbox. 'Quite frankly, YES! Yes, I do! And who the fuck are *you* to be talking to *me*? You're a fucking no-no! A nobody! You're *toast*, that's what you are! Toast! Brown bread! Dead!' The table cracks under his stamping feet and then gives way altogether, tossing him to the ground in a costly mixture of glass and twisted chrome. Milton and his partner rush forward, lifting him by the arms, but he wrestles them off, tiny cubes of glass falling from his elbows and the naked skin of his back.

This has gone on for long enough. Diversion tactics are clearly called for. I leave my hidey-hole in the corner and stroll into the empty space surrounding my celebrity presenter. Alerted by movement, Carver turns on me, poised, with a demonic glare. Wild monkey, ready to bite. See how it postures, how it threatens. His face looks ready to explode. If I try to be reasonable, he'll chew me like another piece of diplomatic dog-food. There is no neutral territory here. There's only him and us. You're either for, or against. So I put my hands loosely in the air, in surrender mode, then return them to my hips.

'Hey, you're right. It's a shit party, anyway.'

Carver looks around at all the staring faces. His head darts back towards me, then he starts to laugh. A big, forced, red-faced laugh, pushed heavily through his lungs and hurled like a missile at the hushed assembly. I brush past him, making for the hallway. I know that if I look back, all is lost. I'm halfway down the corridor before he catches up with me, paws on my arm, eyes wide, beseeching.

'You saw what he did, Teach, didn't ya? I mean, am I supposed to stand there and *take* that sort of abuse?'

I keep walking. 'Absolutely not.'

'That prick! "Scabby little chancer!" Did you hear that? Calling me a "chancer", in front of all those people in the club! Having a go! Making it clear to everyone, right from the start, who was the big man, and who was the little man! Me!'

We reach the bathroom. His shirt is rolled up in a ball on the floor. I unravel it, and a flange of foil-coated plastic drops out, the kind they use for tablets. I pick it up; he's too busy scowling at the mirror to notice. Crazy little bastard popped two Viagra. I wonder when? In Milton's car on the way up, I'll bet. Jesus. I didn't think he'd get round to those so soon. Give the blue diamonds about forty minutes to kick in, and that times it just about right. On top of the wraps I'd given him – no wonder he's detonating. I pocket the tablets, then hold his shirt open and say nothing, while he puts it on.

'There was no need for that! I'd forgiven him, Teach, for what he did! Really! I had! I was cool as a breeze, up until tonight!' Jesus, here we go. More ancient history. His primal snarl echoes off the Scandinavian tiles. 'But I'm telling you, Milton only has one thing in mind! Humiliation! He let me down once, now he's at it again! Dragging me all the way up here, to take the piss in front of his stuck-up friends! They think they're *better* than me! A better class of person! And that arse from *The Sunday Reporter*! What's *he* doing here? Part of the set-up; I bet he's phoning his copy in right now! Fatuous, am I? What the fuck is "fatuous", anyway?'

I withhold the definition for the sake of peace. It isn't hard to figure out what happened in here. Carver, Miss Pert, and the musician had hoovered up a fair portion of my generous wrap. The extra dose pushed Carver's brains beyond boiling point and released the inner monster. Feed the monster with a few insecurities and old paranoias, and we have lift off. I recall the anodyne banter when Milton first arrived at The Terrapin Club. So, that's the hook that the evening's disgrace will be hung on, tonight's *casus belli*. Of course, the real culprit lies in powdered swathes across the cistern. Everything your mother ever told you about drugs is true. If you take enough, you *will* make a total fool of yourself.

We emerge from the toilet. Milton and his boyfriend head up a huddle of onlookers, which prudently remains halfway down the hallway. Milton steps forward, holding out Carver's jacket, face angry and tight. I take the garment, saying nothing, in case Carver thinks I'm siding with the enemy. I throw Milton a look to indicate that my rudeness is merely a tactical necessity, but his eyes remain hard and bright.

'My driver will take you back into town.'

There's enough middle-class sensibility left in me to want to fall at Milton's feet, apologising profusely, but whilst perhaps fitting, that would not be wise, so I keep my head up and a small, supercilious smile fixed on my face whilst I bundle a muttering Carver outside, into the waiting black Merc. A delegation of shame gathers on the steps of the impossibly beautiful house as the car moves off. Suddenly, Carver jerks out of his torpor and lunges for the internal door handle, pushing it open.

'You're nothing but a bunch of fucking sausage jockeys!' he shrieks. I throw myself across him, tugging the door shut. He falls back in the seat, laughing, and fumbles in his pocket for fags. He lights up, sucking hungrily. I can see the driver's eyes in the rear- view mirror. He'd happily drag Carver from the car and kick him to death at the side of the road. If Carver wasn't worth eight grand a month to me, I'd happily help.

'You did the right thing there, Teach, well spotted. Shower of cunts! As long as you back me up, you'll always be okay. I know exactly how to handle situations like that. I could tell, right from the very start, what that bad bastard was up to. He has nothing but contempt for me, for the show, for our public … I got us out of there just in time!'

'What, you think they intended to gang-rape us?' The car bumps down the mountainside, the driver deliberately braking late into corners, hurling it around.

'It was the moral equivalent of gang-rape, Teach! Milton had those fuckers lined up, ready to have a go. It was a set-up! That bastard you were talking to!'

'Fatty Pelham?'

'Nao, nao, he's only a minor bastard! I mean the major bastard!'

'Oh, *him*! He says *you're* a major bastard!'

'Ha! I exposed him in my book!'

'Yes, he mentioned something about a book. What did you write about him?'

'I said he was no fun.'

'Harsh words ...' I know I'm risking it with the sarcasm, but I can't help it, at this stage.

'And that pox-dog of a columnist! I know him from the old days, from that disaster of a newspaper!'

'Who?'

'That arsehole Gavin Kelly. A real no-no, beaten docket. Busted flush. He's the kind of mediocrity who would hate us for what we've achieved. That crowd at *The Sunday Reporter* would *love* to bring me down!'

'Jesus, everyone has it in for you tonight, don't they?'

'Teach! That was definitely a set-up! Trust me! I can spot these things a mile off! Thank Christ I insisted on having you along! I just *knew* I'd need some strategic support, before the night was through!'

'I'm *so* glad I was able to be there for you ...' The driver throws the car around another corner, the sideways momentum pushing us together on the seat. Twenty minutes later, he dumps us unceremoniously in the centre of town. As it happens, we're within staggering distance of Dolce Vita. Dolce Vita would be the last nightclub open in hell, if hell had nightclubs. Carver descends the iron steps and hammers on the bolted door with both fists.

'They won't let you in! It's the wrong side of three o'clock!'

'You're a fucking fader, Teach! Don't you leave me now! What's wrong with you? The night is but a pup!'

I call down the steps. 'Later! Manyana! Good luck!' He breaks off belting the door to bid me goodnight.

'That's right, fuck off, you fucking fuck!'

Noun, adjective, and verb, all in one sentence. Not bad. The door is yanked violently open and Carver falls inside. I wander off to find my flat, wherever they put it.

I land home to find about a dozen people, only some of whom I know, lying monged around my living-room. Goldfrapp burbles from the stereo. The kitchen counter is a mess of bottles, grass, pills crushed for snorting, and hash-ash. I don't like being home alone, which is just as well, because the Creature never turns guests away, at any hour, and my flat has become Party Central. She makes a show of giving me a big hug, pops a spliff in my mouth, and wrestles me onto my designer sofa. At twenty-eight, Stella is two years younger than me. She DJs for pocket money and does the odd waitressing job, but never lasts long in any gig before storming out or getting sacked. She doesn't pay rent. She just sort of arrived during a post-club party – rather like the one we appear to be having this morning – and stayed, like a cat. Neither of us is certain when this happened exactly, but we think it was just before the millennium. I strongly dislike the term, but I guess you could say that we're fuck-buddies. In our defence, I'd like to make it clear that we only sleep with each other when we've got absolutely nothing better to do. And sleeping with other people, getting wasted, stacking the dishwasher, and going clubbing all constitute 'better things to do'.

Miraculously, there's plenty of pills left, so I take one. We all take one. Soon, I have everyone laughing their bollocks off, telling them the tale of Milton's party. People love Monkey Man stories. He's the favourite topic of conversation amongst all who know him personally, and those who only know him from the TV enjoy the celebrity bullshit anyway.

The pills kick in. Next thing you know, there's bodies in the living-room, bodies in the bedrooms, bodies in the bathroom, a couple in the shower. My balcony doors are wide open, and someone's cranked up the music. These are good pills, old-style Doves, pure and strong. Hard to find these days, not cut with speed. Soon, the talking stops. Warm skin, slippy with sweat. Tops up, navels, tummy-muscles, tickle. Touch. Be touched. Hug. Smoke more. Zips down. Murmur. Kiss. Hair. Eyes. Music. Another half-pill; like I need it. My throat contracts, refusing to swallow, but I force

81

it down with a swig of vodka. No-one's watching; everyone's doing. Clothes off, half-dressed. An ankle-length boot under a glass table covered with spilt wine and the overflow from a big chrome ashtray. Hand on me, now on you. The down standing upright on my arm, stroked by the cool mountain air outside Milton's house, the lights of Dublin in the distance, fading far away.

# 6

## THE ASSISTANT HEAD KEEPER

Beep-beep.

A girl I don't know walks down the corridor wearing only knickers, and puts her mouth to the kitchen tap.

Beep-beep.

She glugs furiously at the lukewarm city water, sucking it, spitting it down herself. She sticks her head in the sink, beats water around her hair, face, shoulders, and breasts.

Beep-beep.

She walks back up the corridor towards my bedroom, dripping. Why is she in my bedroom and not me? Because I'm on my sofa with Stella's head in my lap. Where the fuck are my trousers?

Beep-beep.

Grey dawn-light around the balcony doors. My guests have pulled cushions to the floor to sleep;

they're stretched out in rows, like victims in a makeshift morgue after a massacre.

Beep-beep.

Cold. I pull my T-shirt back down over my exposed torso, try to sit up. Stella swears in her sleep and readjusts herself on the sofa.

Beep-beep.

I scrabble for my combats, somewhere on the floor.

Beep-beep.

It fucking can't be, it can't, aw fuck it *is*. Green light on my phone display pulses cheerily away. In the name of sweet divine. Time on the phone says quarter past six.

Beep-beep.

Fucking leave it. Whatever it is, it can't be good.

Beep-Beep.

Aw, bollockstitfuckwank. I press the button and try to say 'Yes?' but all that comes out is a little croak. Swallow. Cough.

'Yes?' Barely a whisper.

'Can I speak to Lee Lovecraft, please?' Man's voice, country twang, loud, sober, neutral. Now, why would the bank be calling to remonstrate about my overdraft at this time on a Saturday morning?

'Speaking.'

'Guard Anthony O'Mahony from Store Street Garda station. Are you Lee Lovecraft, the producer?'

Cops. Fuck. What have I done? Did I crash my car again last night and leave it? Say this: 'I'm really glad you rang, officer, I was actually lifting the phone to you. I've just come up from my underground car-park and I'd like to report that my vehicle has been stolen by teenage junkie fucks.' No, wait. They never contact you that quickly over a mere car wreck, and anyway, my car's out at TV Ireland. Left it there, last night. Last fucking night. What is it? What's *wrong*? I know. My father's been found alone and dead. No – it can't be that either: my father would never make life that easy for us. It's me. It has to be me. I've done something incredibly, badly wrong, and I just don't remember what it is. Shit! I know! Fuckers are outside the flat, about to burst in on a drugs swoop! Hell fucking drugs! One of our dealers has been busted and pointed the finger, to get himself off. But why would they ring? Usually they just kick the door down, don't they? At least, they do on TV ...

'It's Guard Anthony O'Mahony here, from ...'

'Yes, yes, sorry, Guard, that's me. Whassamatter?'

'Well, we have a certain television personality in one of the cells down here. We can't raise his partner, so now he's asking for you. He gave us your number.'

'Gave you my number?'

'Well, he screamed your number out loud over and over: that would be a better description of the situation down here. He says he was with you last night. Do you have any idea how he got like this?'

'Got like what?' Deny, deny.

'Look, are you able to come down here, at all?'

'*What?*' I don't like the sound of 'down here' one bit.

'It would be very helpful to us if you could come in.'

'Why, have I done something wrong?'

Slight pause, then, 'No.'

Ah, shit, shit, shit! I can barely speak – how am I going to handle a shagging police station at six in the morning? That filthy monkey! What if they've found something on him and he's told them who supplied it? Like I say, every time I think, 'Right, this is the insanest motherfucking shit I've ever had to deal with', the little bastard invariably proves me wrong.

'Er, what's happened to him? What's he done? Is he hurt?' That's better, Lee. Move the subject away from yourself. Now you're thinking.

'Any damage, he's done to himself. He's very worked up, and we're ringing you because he asked for you. Because of who he is, we've made the call. That's all.'

'Ah, sweet divine *Jesus.*'

'Will I tell him that's a "no", so?'

'No, no, sorry, Guard, sorry. I'm just a bit, you know, I've just woken up, tell him … look, give me twenty minutes, and I'll be there, okay?'

I hate police stations, on drugs. They always know, you know. They can tell just by looking at you. That's why I hold my combats upside down and empty every pocket before putting them on. That's why I get the taxi to drop me four blocks away and walk the rest. Bit of air. I have a great belief in being polite to cops at all times. Start with the attitude and they'll do you. Especially Dublin cops, who eat crack-happy council-estate crazies for breakfast.

Cop-shop receptions remind me of public toilets. Guard Anthony O'Mahony looks me over impassively, mentally slots me into the 'middle-class waster' category, and lets me into the bowels of the station through a reinforced metal door. I can hear the Monkey Man's shrieks all the way down the corridor. Demanding his human rights, citing the Geneva convention, telling them they're all fucked, that he knows the Minister for Justice and he'll have them all sacked, that this is brutality against a working journalist, it's police corruption, they'll be exposed to the light of public scrutiny, et fucking cetera. He wants to call his lawyer, call Anne, call Lee, call a priest, call a doctor, call parliament, call the United Nations. Call Mary Robinson. Jesus. A veritable litany of coked-up grievances. He must have taken more of the wrap I gave him at Milton's. Or maybe it was Happy Hour in the jacks at Dolce Vita. He's definitely had a lot more of something. At each fresh outburst, tides of laughter emerge from the surrounding cells.

O'Mahony lets me peep through the door-flap, and there he is, curled up on the floor, fully clothed, an embryo of hideous, unmitigated rage. He's lying with his back to the door, so I can't see if he's been hit. He's kicking his feet, as if on an imaginary bicycle, his arms tightly folded up to his chest. The noise is tremendous, a rasping, adult version of a full-blown infant strop. The policeman closes the flap and leans against the door, in no hurry. I'm in no hurry to go in there, either.

'What's he taken, d'you know? You better tell us, so we can call in the doctor.'

So they've searched him and found nothing.

They've brought me down here hoping I'll blab and drop him in the shit. Even so, they still can't do him without finding gear on his person; it's probably just the gossip value they want now. Not a few cops pick up bucks on the side, feeding stuff to the tabloids.

'I don't think he's taken anything. A crowd of us went drinking, after the show. We always do. He's had champagne, quite a bit. I left him at the door of Dolce Vita just after three. I went straight home to bed.' Okay, stop there, Lee, those are your lines, as rehearsed.

'A lot of people drink champagne in Dublin these days. Ya don't see 'em get *this* wankered. Come on, now, you must have seen him at somethin' else!'

'We were in several different places and I wasn't holding his hand the whole time, know what I mean? Look, you asked me to come down, so here I am. What happened? Did someone smack him? Was there a fight?' Always move the subject away from yourself.

'Did he take any substance that was illicit?'

'Not that I saw.'

'Tell me all the nightclubs youse were in.' And I list them, off by heart. 'And were youse at any parties?' O'Mahony looks away from me as he asks this, and my crumpled antennae stiffen immediately. Always, always beware when a cop asks you a straight yes/no question that he's had an opportunity to verify elsewhere. I make a judgement call, and thank fuck it's the right one.

'We went to a private party in Wicklow, couldn't have stayed more than an hour.'

'Did he take drugs there? Look at the shape of him, he's definitely on something! Now, stop messing me around!'

'I'm not messing with you! Look, Carver is a pretty highly strung individual at the best of times ...'

'Whereabouts in Wicklow were you?'

Keep Milton out of this. Poor bastard's suffered enough.

'Someone's house, up in the mountains. I've no idea where. It was dark. Spur-of-the-moment thing, some guy we met in The Terrapin Club. Brought us to his party. That happens a lot, with Carver. Bunch of us shared a taxi, but it was boring, so we didn't stay. Nothing happened. Like I say, I was home in bed around half-three, end of story. Where did you find him? I saw him through the door of Dolce Vita, and that's as much as I can tell you. Has he been fighting?'

O'Mahony gives me a long look, then shrugs.

'A few of the lads went into Dolce Vita to tell them to close. We do it most mornings: people know to just drink up and get out. You get the odd awkward bastard. But doesn't this one,' and he taps the cell door with a fist the size of a football, 'doesn't this one start tellin' the boys to eff off. Because of who he is, the boys put him out on the pavement and tell him to go home, but he starts again, so they stick him in the back of the van. He's been roarin' his head off ever since, stuff about some big drugs party down in Wicklow. Says the real criminals are out there, and why don't we go get them and leave poor, decent people like him alone. He says you were with him, said that you'd back him up. Jayziz, you'd think it was the Hellfire Club he was at.'

'Officer, if the party had been that much fun, we'd both still be at it. But it was all bow-ties and evening gowns, definitely no, uh, illicit substances. The party was crap, so we came back into town.'

Carver erupts into a fresh barrage of gibbering shrieks. O'Mahony can see he's getting nowhere with me.

'Go on then. Fucking take him with you.'

'What?'

'I said, take him home. You can have him.'

'Now, wait a minute ...'

The cop affects disinterest, but really what he's doing is putting it up to me, for stonewalling.

'If you're so sure he doesn't need medical assistance, then take him!'

'But why do I have to ...?'

Trying hard not to smile, O'Mahony moves to unlock the cell. 'He's all yours. The morning shift is coming on and it's one less hassle for me if you take him with you now.' He pushes the door open. Carver is too busy bellowing at the floor to notice. Evil bastard cop. There's no way I'm walking into that cell, not without chest armour. And how the hell am I meant to get that crazy bastard home? In a shopping trolley?

'Where is he? What have you done to him? We're gonna sue the fuckin' asses offa you guys, you hear me?'

We turn. A tall, big-limbed figure strides along the corridor towards us. With a flowing leather coat, knee-length boots and a bright red mullet, Anne Stutz looks like something off the cover of a Lou Reed album. Androgynous, but not in a good way. She looks through me as if I'm not there, glaring at O'Mahony with laser-guided eyes.

'What the fuck have you done to him? Do you realise who he is?'

Praise Jesus. With impeccable timing, the Head Keeper has finally arrived. My presence is no longer required, so I slip off, unacknowledged. Anne's nasal, turbo-charged whine mounts steadily behind me, and, in spite of his pettiness, I feel a sudden wave of sympathy for Guard Anthony O'Mahony, and indeed for the entire Irish police force, as a body. Thankless fucking task.

Outside the station, I make a quick call on my mobile, then immediately wish I hadn't. Perhaps I'm pushing things a bit too far. I feel rattled, unclean, in need of normality. And I know I won't get anything remotely resembling normality at the place I call 'home'. But where the hell can I go at seven o'clock on a Saturday morning? Church? The gym? On a sudden, delusional whim, I hail a taxi to the most normal place I can think of in my shattered condition – the shopping centre where I bought Carver's Viagra … when, yesterday? Feels like fifteen centuries ago.

Most of the big units aren't open yet, but a small coffee-shop is. I buy a few newspapers and sit at a window table with as much espresso as I can persuade the girl at the counter to put in one cup. The creeping horror of my surroundings is superseded by the contents of newspapers, all of which carry front-page pictures lifted from our show.

ARCHBISHOP APOLOGISES, BUT ONLY JUST, says one headline. Another is more direct:

CARVER LETS ARCHBISHOP OFF THE HOOK

By Staff Reporter

*In an extraordinary appearance on* The Kevin Carver Show *last night, Archbishop James McQuillan issued a formal apology to the victims of paedophile priests, but requested that viewers 'consider the damage that these [abuse] allegations are doing to Mother Church'. Chat-show host Kevin Carver strongly backed the Archbishop's position, remonstrating sharply with callers who complained that he gave his guest 'an easy ride' on such a controversial issue. Donal Kelleher, a spokesman for the Network for Victims of Ecclesiastical Abuse (NVEA), condemned both the Archbishop and the programme saying, 'Today, hundreds of abuse victims will feel sidelined by this mealy-mouthed, partial apology.'*

And on it goes, dissecting the interview and giving us a well-deserved hammering into the bargain. There's nothing more scathing than a journalist counting the holes in a rival's story, and last night's show had more holes than a string vest after an airstrike. The reviews are universally negative, and a few papers also cite Carver calling the sacrificial lefty 'a fucker' as further evidence of our show's awfulness. Suddenly, I feel very, very tired. The chemical tow rope that's been keeping my brain aloft for the past thirty-six hours has fallen away. Under normal circumstances, I'd be straight on the phone to Carver over any headlines we generate, good or bad, but today, I can't think of anything to say, except, 'I told you so'. Anyway, Anne will have him tucked up in bed by now, sedated.

Just then, I see what I knew I'd see if I got here early enough – Therese turning up for work. Her brown hair bounces round her head like a mop. She's wearing a long, red raincoat of undecided vintage, a pair of sandals, and carries a straw shopping-bag with a large yellow sunflower woven into the side of it. I rap on the coffee-shop window and her round eyes widen with surprise. I gesture at her to come inside and she does, wearing a cautious smile.

'Well, what's this?' she drawls, keeping her distance from the table. 'Are you stalking me?'

'I've been out all night.'

She runs her eyes over me. 'I'd never have guessed.'

I stand and show her an imaginary badge on my chest. 'Lee Lovecraft. Messenger boy and mashed person.' She approaches gingerly and perches on the edge of the chair across the table, as if ready to dash for the door should I make any sudden movements.

'So, what does your boss need now? Run out of condoms, has he?'

'Run out of … ugh! No! He's not my … no, I'm here to see you, actually.' She raises an eyebrow. 'Can I buy you a coffee, please?'

'Some of us have to work on Saturdays, you know.'

'I've just come from work'

'Hard day at the office, so?'

'I've had a bit of a mad one and I can't go home because my flat is full of dead bodies. I need to talk to someone normal.'

'And what makes you think I'm normal? Because I work in Boots?'

'I don't know. By "normal", I meant "nice".'

'Oh, so I'm *nice* too, am I? Don't tell me, you want a cool, sympathetic hand to mop your fevered brow, something like that?'

'Well, if you're offering …' and I smile ruefully, to show that I fully applaud her right to be as cheeky as she likes towards me. I refrain from adding that I badly want to fall asleep in her arms. I fetch her a coffee from the counter.

'Doesn't it bother you, some of the things you get up to in television?' She's looking down at the newspaper headlines when I return to the table, her faint smile gone. 'I watched your show last night, out of curiosity. I normally wouldn't be arsed, but I know it's popular.'

'And?'

'I thought it was disgusting. Not only the way Kevin Carver sucked up to that horrible priest, but he also called Charlie Morrison "a fucker" on national television. That was totally uncalled for. I happen to know Charlie. He's a very decent man who does a lot of hard work for homeless people, and he didn't deserve to be treated like that. He's got a family. I bet they were all watching.' So, the sacrificial lefty had a name.

'You're right,' I blurt, for once not just telling someone what I think they want to hear. 'The entire

94

show was a piece of shit from start to finish, and I'm actually not a runner: believe it or not I'm the fucking producer, so I guess that makes me a pretty bad person, eh?'

She pauses, perhaps diplomatically. Then, 'It's the media's job to reinforce the status quo – to be honest, I wouldn't expect anything else.'

I look down into the ringed stains of my cup. Jesus, I'm in bits. 'It wasn't always like this; we used to do some really good stuff on that show.'

'You *used* to? Well, why don't you any more?'

I have no answer to her question, at least not a short one. What am I going to do, tell her all about the Monkey Man and how I'm watching myself turn into him? So I just shake my head. Therese stands up.

'Look, wonderful to see you again and all that, but I'm late for work.'

'Can we go for a drink some evening when you finish?'

'I can't.'

'Ah. Boyfriend. Sorry. I shouldn't be so …'

'It's not that. I stay quite far out of town.'

'I have a car. That is, unless you're ideologically opposed to cars, as well as television.' I give her a wry smile, and she shoots me a look.

'If only you knew what you've just said.'

'What did I say?'

'Never mind. If you really must, here's my mobile number.' She takes a cheap biro from her pocket and scribbles on the back of a napkin. 'Ring me some time and maybe we'll see, but I've got a lot on at the moment. Now, go home to your bed, you big feckin' eejit.'

I nearly fall asleep in the taxi on the way back to my flat, which, as predicted, is still jammed with catatonic corpses. Stella has stretched herself over the entire length of the sofa, one thin, pale arm pointing in evidence at the collective, snoring carnage on the living-room floor. With a smash of lipstick exaggerating the size of her mouth, she could be an elegant murder victim. I can't face sitting here, waiting for this lot to gain consciousness and start skinning up breakfast joints. I can't handle this monged morning nonsense: my head feels like a bunker buster. So, I leave again and take a taxi to TV Ireland, where I collect my car. I'm so fucked, I'm practically hallucinating. I switch off my mobile and drive out to Howth Head, where I park at the summit and sit on a wall, staring down at the sea. I stay there, watching the water for what seems like an awfully long time.

# 7

## SETTING THE AGENDA

Back in the office, Carver is acting strangely. It's the following Tuesday, the start of another glorious week in commercial television, and it's like bloody well *déjà vu*. Once again, I walk into the office, and once again, nobody says 'hello'. The atmosphere is tense and grim. I'm clean-shaven and quietly dressed in a blue shirt, jeans, and jacket.

'Ah. My producer. There you are. Sit down. We need to talk about the direction of this show.'

Carver is sitting in his place at the head of the room, with his hard, flinty face on. His swivel head, pursed mouth, and meat-skewer stare monitor me as far as my chair. The others are quiet, sitting to attention, like neophyte cult-members awaiting some exotic decree. Supine fuckers. Why is it always my job to face him down? Tuesday is our first working day of the week, a time to bandy ideas about, have a chat and a laugh, catch up on all the gossip from the weekend. That's the way a good show works; plenty of give and take, an agreed sense of what's going on in the world and what to say about it. But not today. He tilts his craggy face at me.

'I've been trying to phone you all weekend.'

Lie. 'Sorry, some fucker nicked my charger, and my battery ran down. You okay now?' And I wonder whether Anne has told him I was at the police station when she arrived. Charlotte flicks me a glance, but quickly looks away when I meet it.

'I'm okay. I'm more than okay. I've been doing a lot of thinking and I've come to the conclusion that *I'm* okay, but everything else is *not* okay!' The air smells of burnt electricity. Obviously, the question is going to be left hanging, until I ask it.

'What's not okay?'

'This *show* is not okay, and as the producer, I want to know what *you're* going to do about it!'

And it's like I'm in a car that lurches into a sudden, nasty skid. Any normal person might be expected to experience a bit of humility after the events of Saturday morning. Instead, Carver is spoiling for another fight. I can handle his day-to-day tantrums – that comes with the territory. Working with celebrities, you've got to know when to give ground, but also when to stick up for yourself. It's a balance. Do too much of either, and you're fucked. However, by stating in front of the team that there's a problem with the show, he's backing me into a corner. As the producer, I can't not deal with this. Usually, when either of us has a genuine grievance, we talk privately in the studio, man to monkey. In fact, on the way in I'd been debating whether to take him down there and have it out with him about ignoring my talkback on Friday night. I'd been hoping to find him contrite enough to do that, but here he is in pre-emptive strike mode. Jesus. Where does he get the energy? As if I don't know. Okay, calculate fast. He has that acrid aroma; reason will be anathema. The madness of the weekend is still upon him. Worse, the Archbishop débâcle has made him look stupid, so now he wants a scapegoat. Me. I've committed the cardinal sin of having been right. However, if I let him humiliate me in front of the others, I'm fucked. On another level, there's also a growing part of me that wants to jab him in the eyeballs with a plastic fork.

I lean back in my seat, fold my arms, stretch my legs out, and face him full-on.

'What's not okay about the show, then?'

And he's straight in with, 'Well you tell me, you're the producer! What did you mean when you said on Friday night, in front of all those people, that you weren't happy with our major interview? In the club. Before Milton arrived. You were *part* of that, weren'tcha?'

'Part of ... *what*, exactly?'

'Part of what was going on. You were there, weren'tcha? I think I'm *right* in saying that you were with me, in the club, or am I going *completely* mad?'

'I remember I said something about the Archbishop. I said I thought you were too soft on him. Look, is this really about the show, or just about me?'

'It's about both, Lee.' Uh-oh. He only uses my proper name when he's *really* pissed off. 'As my producer, you thought one of my interviews was too soft. Why didn't you say so at the appropriate time, when we were on air?'

I let out a half-laugh, half-snort. 'I *did* say so, at the appropriate time. Thing called talkback, goes in your ear.'

'I don't remember you saying anything on talkback!'

'Well, I did. It's open talkback for everyone in the studio apart from you. Gallery, cameras, lights, sound, they all heard me intervene, and they all saw you ignore me. Kate,' and I nod in her direction, 'was sitting right beside me.' Kate studies her fingernails with intense absorption. 'Made me look really good, thanks for that.'

'With all due cunting respect, this show is about making *me* look good, not *you*! It's called *The Kevin Carver Show*! The name "Lee Lovecraft" does not appear in the title! At least, not the last time I checked!' The dirty little fuck. Our show. *Our* show. I swallow the rising bile.

'Look, we were live. Heat of the moment and all that. We both knew that the price of getting the Archbishop on was that we couldn't savage him. I just felt you were too easy on him, that's all. For some reason,' and I allow myself a mini-sneer, 'the line of questioning I agreed with his people went out the window. Maybe you could explain that? Or maybe having the Archbishop on was a bad call, in the first place.' And I know it's coming now, so I brace.

'Can I take it, then, if you're such a genius producer, that you saw the papers at the weekend?'

'Most of them, yes.'

'And what did you make of *that*?' All of a sudden, he's on his feet, roaring. He lifts one of the guilty publications and flings it into the middle of the floor. CARVER LETS ARCHBISHOP OFF THE HOOK. The rest of the team stare at it like it's a meteorite just come through the ceiling. I stay seated, give it a few beats, and keep the voice one hundred per cent steady. But I have a tight feeling, like an iron band, squeezing slowly around my chest.

'I told you we'd get killed, and we did. It's not the first time the press has had a pop at us: it's part of the price of success. We take the hit and move on.'

'*No!*' he roars. '*Nao!* We do *not* move on! Those bastards in the papers, they don't understand what I'm trying to do! They're deliberately misconstruing the interview! They're out to *get* me!'

'Well, maybe you could call a few more guests "fuckers", live on air? That should boost the ratings ...'

'Shut *up*, you bad fuck! You know what I'm talking about! You saw that little toe-rag at Milton's, fucking *waiting* for me!'

'I seem to recall several toe-rags, a bunch of bastards, a few no-nos, a smattering of fuck-dogs, and at least one shower of cunts. Which particular toe-rag did you have in mind?'

'That fucking columnist! The one who had a go! Fatuous! That's what he said! Fatuous! I'll give *them* fatuous! You and your big pal Milton, setting me up to make me look bad! I'm a scabby little chancer, am I? That's not the first time Milton has dropped me in the shit! But you were part of this one, right from the start, weren'tcha? Fucking at me in the club, wrecking my head about the fucking Archbishop, before Milton even arrived!'

Right, that's it. Chest too tight now. Therese, looking at me across a coffee-shop table with eyes that won't bear lies.

'You paranoid *fuck*!' And now it's me on my feet, me roaring. I'm out of my chair like a whip, pointing my arm across the room, aiming right between his monkey eyes. I have my father's temper, which I hate, because it's a filthy, violent temper that took me many years to get under control. 'You paranoid little *fuck*! Number one, Milton is *your* friend, and if you want to bitch-slap him, be my guest! Or better still, be *his* guest, I'm sure he'd *love* to have you back in his home again! Number two, I'm not part of anything, except for this fucking show! You went on a solo run with that cunting Archbishop, and everyone in this room knows it! You admitted as much in the club, so stop trying to pin it on me! You want to talk about the show, we can talk about the show! You want to talk about what happened on Friday night, we can do that too! But I'll tell you one thing, you definitely want to get your fucking head straight, or next you'll be seeing fairies!'

There's a moment when it could definitely go either way. The two of us, bolt upright, at opposite ends of the room. The team, like spectators at deuce in some nightmare tennis match. The crumpled face of the Archbishop, peering up from the floor. I can see Carver make the mental calculation. He's squeezed me and reduced me to his level, playground-bully style. But how much more will I say, if he squeezes any harder? Surely, surely, Anne has told him that I was there, at the cop-shop? He grunts and gives a sudden small smile. Flick channels, change of mood. I'm right, she must have told him.

'There were too many fucking fairies out and about on Friday night, I think that was part of the problem.'

That's the peace flag, a minor conspiratorial gesture of equanimity restored. I sit back down and turn on my computer, to give me something to look at apart from his gnarly face. He slopes over to me and seizes my shoulder, while that fucking Windows start-up noise, the signature-tune of the damned, wooshes all around me.

'The Archbishop, Teach, we gotta do *more* of that sort of thing, not less. Move the show on, bring in the mainstream audience. Do the Big Boys. I don't give a fuck what the papers say, fuck them. If we're upsetting those bastards we must be doing *something* right. Bad publicity, good publicity, yeah?'

I pretend to check my e-mail. 'So, what *would* you like to do on this week's show? Can we talk about that, now?' The leaden sarcasm goes unnoticed, or at least unchallenged.

'We need to toughen up, start setting a few agendas. I've had an idea, Teach, a good one – police brutality!' He smacks the desk. 'Police brutality! They're fucking abusers; they'll set you up, for no reason! Bad bastards! I think that police brutality will resonate with our viewers! That's the kind of issue I have in mind!'

I give him my big eyes, my open, honest face. 'Police brutality? What's the hook?'

The answer comes just a bit too quickly. 'Nao, no hook, I, uh, just think it's a good topic, and we should do it right away, yeah?'

He starts barking orders at Scally, Kate, and the rest. Ring so-and-so, get this, get that, try the other. The rest of the team start scribbling and reach for their phones, grateful for something self-effacing to do. So, he's a reconstructed civil libertarian now? Yes, ladies and gentlemen, viewers at home: out of the blue, police brutality has, for no particular reason, become an urgent matter of social concern, a horrendous injustice that Kevin Carver, the people's presenter, society's weathervane, is set to expose forthwith. Jesus. For this relationship to work, increasingly I have to swallow my balls, hide behind my acolyte mask, and try not to let it slip. Can he see it slipping? I keep my face jammed into my computer screen lest it betray me. Instead of speaking my mind, I delete reams of junk mail from corporate PR whores, trying to push their ludicrous clients onto our show.

'Scally, you dog. What's the number of *The Sunday Reporter*? It's so long since I've had to answer to those poxes, I can't remember.'

Scally calls the number out and Carver spends the next five minutes yelping into his receiver at some features editor, giving out shit about the paper's gossip columnist, Gavin Kelly. Kelly is a dishonest mediocrity who writes fatuous nonsense that nobody believes. As long as this appalling, unprofessional, scabby little chancer is working for *The Sunday Reporter*, there is no prospect that any other journalist from that fatuous newspaper will be invited onto *The Kevin Carver Show*. Goodbye, and fuck you.

That little confrontation momentarily quenches the simian blood lust, and he noses his way through the day's tabloids, quiet for a while, like a baboon picking through his fur. Then he lets out a yowl.

'Fuck me! Listen to this!' The team snap to instant attention. I can't say who I'm beginning to despise more, them or him. 'Larry fucking King has just signed a new contract for twelve million dollars! Twelve fucking million, and his own private jet!'

He whistles, shaking his head at the disparity between rates of pay for American pundits and Irish ones. My phone goes. Reception. A limo has arrived to take Carver to a photo shoot.

'What photo shoot?' he demands, indignant. 'Who arranged that?'

I'm at a loss. What am I, his fucking diary? Dervla, one of the researchers, coughs.

'That magazine. Remember. You were going to model ...' she stops, goes puce. We all look at her. Carver, in particular, seems stunned.

'What?' he demands.

'You were going to model ... *male underwear.*'
Dervla is from a part of the country where men
probably don't wear *male underwear.* It's all I can do
not to wet my own pants. I can't help it, really, I can't.
I'm busting my hole laughing.

'Well, you said you wanted a new direction for the
show ...'

'Fuck YOU!' Carver shrieks, and buries his face in
his paws. Shaking his head, he fetches his sports
jacket and storms out the door. 'Remember, you
cunts! Police brutality! Earn your fucking wages and
book me an item!'

We experience a rare moment of team laughter as
soon as he's out of earshot. But my mirth is short-
lived. A minute later, my phone goes again. Internal
number. Dickie Vaughan, Head of Programmes, TV
Ireland. He will have had reception inform him of
Carver's departure. He wouldn't dare ring the office
otherwise.

'Hello, Lee. Have you got a minute?'

Right now, an audience with Duster is just what I
need. His top-floor office is adorned with posed
photographs of himself, mainly taken in the green
room, with famous guests from our show over the
years. There's even one of him with Gary Glitter,
which he's obviously forgotten to take down. His
shelves creak with golfing trophies, of varying degrees
of hideousness. Today, Duster is wearing a tight black
polo-neck, which, along with his bouffant hair, serves
to emphasise his diminutive rotundity.

'I take it you've seen some of this?' Duster has all

the bad-news stories from the weekend papers cut into clippings and slotted into clear plastic folders. He also has the neatest, least cluttered desk I've ever seen. If Ireland ever holds a Tidy Desk competition, Duster will win the gold medal.

'Yes, I *have* seen them, and I've already had this discussion with our celebrity presenter. He knows he fucked up.'

'And?'

'And, you may have overheard parts of our discussion, through your floor.'

'Indeed.' Far be it from Duster to confront Carver himself. He leaves all that to me. 'It was that sort of discussion, so?'

'I made my feelings clear to him.'

I'm about to hand back his portfolio of clippings, which I've lifted to peruse like I give a fuck, when I notice one that I hadn't read at the weekend. I deliberately didn't buy the Sunday papers. Instead, I'd slept until late afternoon, then driven back out to Howth Head again, to walk by the sea some more, to think about Stella, about Therese, about the Monkey Man, about my father, about Class As, about life, the universe, and shagging well everything.

The item is short. One paragraph, no photo, byline Gavin Kelly of *The Sunday Reporter*.

*Who's a naughty boy, then? Word reaches us that a certain television presenter has been hitting the Diet Coke as of late. Clue: this fellow's personality is much bigger than he is. Piece of advice: keep your shirt on, you silly little man, the whole town is talking about you. Don't*

*expect any invites to posh parties in the near future, but*
*the boys in blue send their fond regards and look forward*
*to having you back real soon. Ta-ra!*

Duster watches me closely, as I read. 'Does that newspaper article mean anything to you, Lee?'

I think carefully before answering. Duster is stupid, but nature compensates stupid people by endowing them with rat-like cunning. For certain, he would have seen me leave the station with Carver on Friday night. Beyond that, Christ knows who's told him what. Dublin is a small town that only thinks it's a big city. When in doubt, always answer a question with a question.

'Dickie, am I my brother's keeper?'

This next bit is obviously rehearsed. It's too articulate for that not to be the case. Duster turns his fingers into a podgy little steeple.

'Lee, we pay you to produce good television. And you do. But on another level, we also pay you to supervise, on an ongoing basis, what I would call "a creatively volatile situation". We must manage our talent. That, more than anything, is your true value to this station.'

Without saying a word in reply, I lift what I judge to be the heaviest of Duster's golf trophies down from its shelf – a big, tacky, cut-crystal vase on a large wooden base – and, much to his surprise, beat him to death with it.

First, I smash it sideways into his spazzy designer glasses with a lovely back-hander, then, as he screams, I bring it down two-handed on top of his Elvis hairdo, sending a thick ribbon of blood splattering across his desk. That shuts him up, apart from a low groan. As his eyeballs roll upwards in his sockets, I land a final forearm swipe smack in the middle of his podgy, annoying face. His head snaps back on his neck, and the solid edge of the trophy-base peels most of his nose up onto his forehead. Several shades of blood spatter onto his polo-neck, from dark through to bright. Then, with a gurgle, he slumps lifelessly onto his not-very-tidy-any more desk. I hurl the trophy over my shoulder, wipe his hot, smelly liquid from my own face, and yell at his misshapen head, 'Fuck you, Duster! If it wasn't for me, you wouldn't *have* a fucking station!' And I storm out of the room, slamming the door behind me.

Of course, I don't do or say anything of the kind. I'd really like to, and I probably should, but I don't. Instead, I shrug and make to leave quietly.

'Lee!'

I turn. Don't push your luck, Duster. Your golf trophy whispers to me.

*Do it, Lee! Do it! Do it! Do it!*

'Anything you know about our little celebrity's – how shall I put this – *erratic* behaviour; any problems, any fights, anything at all – I want you to communicate to me, right away. In total confidence, of course.'

*Pick me up, Lee! Go on! Kill the fucker!*

I spin on my heel. Hearing murderous voices coming from golf trophies is not a positive development. Nonetheless, I force myself to walk slowly down the length of Duster's big office. I feel his beady eyes drill into my spine, as I exit.

That night, alone in my flat, I roll a spliff and flop into a leather recliner by the open balcony doors. Stella is out, probably spinning vinyl somewhere. Or dancing to it, or getting it on, collecting another pubic scalp to add to her collection. Hope she doesn't bring anyone home; I'm not in the mood. My cleaner has been around and sorted the place out after Friday night's drug-orgy. Glass and wood smell of polish, a miniature edition of Milton's heaven in the hills. I watch a cargo ship mooring across the River Liffey. I like to spend time looking out across the water; it has a calming effect, helps me think. My sports car squats in the underground car-park, safe far beneath me, engine clicking as it cools. This is my fee. This is what I earn, in exchange for what I do. Or, more correctly, my flat and my car are the physical expression of the enormous debt that my earnings entitle me to. Of course, there's also all the stuff that's gone up my nose and down my throat in the past six years. That costs money, too. My show. My lifestyle. My sanity. My self-respect. I've managed to stay off the Class As since Saturday morning – that's nearly three whole days.

One by one, I fish my credit cards out of my wallet and lick along their edges. I feel my tongue go numb.

# 8

## REWIND

I spend a lot of time watching the water these days. You go to any seaside town and you'll see car after car of old couples, parked, facing the waves. They drive down to the sea, stare at it, and then fall asleep with their heads thrown back and their mouths wide open, as if they've been shot. Why do they do that? Because retirement is boring? Because water always changes, because it's never the same, from one instant to the next? Or is it because the sea is where we crawled out of, millions of years ago? Is watching the water a form of evolutionary nostalgia? Are they merely homesick?

Sometimes, I think I should write about my time with Kevin Carver, but a lot of it is so completely insane, people would think I was making it up. I even went through a phase of hanging around the National Library, reading old press clippings, just to see what I could add to my knowledge of his background. The earliest piece I found was from an old magazine called *Sounds Around*, dated September 1979. At that time, I would have just turned seven years old. It was a concert review, for Carver and the Nutters. There he was, in the old, heavily inked photo, surprisingly unchanged apart from a bad seventies haircut, clutching a microphone, howling into the audience.

The article mentioned the band's current single, the conservatively titled 'All Politicians Are Bastards'. The reviewer gave Carver passing praise as a charismatic lead singer, but concentrated more on the band's guitarists, a pair of twins called Maggie and Vinnie O'Gorman. Much punk-ethos amusement was derived from the fact that the pair actually had an older brother, Brian, who, in 1979, was an up-and-coming politician. As it happens, Brian O'Gorman went on to do quite well for himself.

A piece from *The Daily Enquirer*, dated December 1980, profiled Carver himself on the happy occasion of him joining that paper as a columnist. By that time The Nutters had disbanded. Carver said that the band had 'served its purpose'. He would carry on the good fight, but in different ways. He promised that his column would 'challenge the corrupt and vanquish the venal'. His hatred of the establishment stemmed, he said, 'from a poor upbringing, where we had nothing. No opportunities, no possessions, no future.' A statement which, incidentally, could be applied to three-quarters of Irish society from the beginning of recorded history until the mid-nineties, when the country's first-ever boom kicked in. But in the media, poverty plus pluck equals profile. Angst has to come from somewhere.

The thing is, for all their anti-authoritarian posturing, punks were right little media whores, never missing a chance to do an interview, play on TV, push themselves across every available outlet. Like every other 'youth phenomenon', from teddy-boys through to mods, rockers and eventually rave, punk truly rose to prominence in the public mind precisely through media manipulation. Mutual exploitation. Shock, horror! Here's the younger generation – aren't they *awful?* Come air your grievances, kids – and let's sell some product while we're at it.

But in reality, many punks had fabricated their working-class credentials, and were in fact suburban smart-arses who'd already guessed a secret – that anyone with enough push, ego, and cynicism can make a decent living out of the media. So when the movement started dying, there was a mass-migration of refugees into the more profitable pastures of the fourth estate. If you don't believe me, go to the offices of any newspaper, radio, or television station full of balding forty-somethings, throw a stone, and you're guaranteed to hit an old punk. Or someone who says they were a punk: same difference.

Carver's progress becomes easier to follow via his stuff for *The Daily Enquirer*. Some of it makes amusing reading. He followed that tried and tested journalistic technique of sucking up to those whom he admired and kicking the shit out of those whom he did not. Nine pieces out of ten were of the shit-kicking variety.

Conflict sells, consensus is dull. He set himself up in the role of professional contrarian, a sort of hired Antichrist. His writing had two distinct strands to it. First, he always aimed high, personalising the issue. You had to be prominent to be a target for Carver's street-smart insults. No point in abusing people no one's ever heard of. Secondly, he always justified his point of view by claiming to speak for 'the plain people of Ireland'. How the Irish love a rebel. It probably has something to do with centuries of oppression, or shit like that. The little man, sticking it up to the Big Boys.

In a city as small as Dublin, working for the press carries a certain prominence, but it isn't big-time. You can beaver away in print all your life, writing pretty explosive stuff, but you need stronger strings to your bow to become a household name. This axiom isn't lost on media wannabes, past and present. How many kids come out of college, burning to become court reporters for a respectable newspaper? Pretty goddamn few. But they'd all kill to be in front of a TV camera, spouting any old guff, within five seconds of graduating.

The problem with 1980s Ireland, however, was lack of scope. The country had precisely two television channels, RTV1 and RTV2, which was a bit like having a choice between cheap white bread, and cheap white bread lightly toasted. In the digital age, where you can summon up hundreds of different stations with a single button on your remote control, this is not an easy situation to comprehend. It smacks of Stalinist Russia. But RTV, the state broadcaster, enjoyed a complete monopoly of the medium until the late nineties. For decades beforehand, if RTV didn't rate you then you didn't get on television, full stop.

Carver, it seems, made his first bid for TV stardom in 1984. Throughout that summer, his column refers enthusiastically to a pilot programme he was making for RTV, promising 'a politics show with a difference'. He hinted that readers should 'watch this space'. But then, at the end of August, he penned the first of a series of articles that savaged RTV to the core. RTV management was, he declared, 'lazy and stupid'. Their output was 'tripe'. He informed his readers that, more in anger than in sorrow, he had put his boot through his television screen, and advised them to do the same. It didn't take much reading between the lines to guess that his pilot had not been commissioned. When I learned about this, I asked a friend in the RTV archives to try to hunt out any record of this glorious non-debut. But he soon came back saying that a lot of tapes from that period had been re-used to shoot a wildlife series, and of Kevin Carver, there existed not a trace. Pity.

I remember when I first set eyes on him. It was 1991, and I was in my first year as a media student. A Welsh band called the Manic Street Preachers were fast becoming fashionable. They played guitars, which was deeply unfashionable at the time, and mouthed slogans about a long-forgotten fad called 'punk'. I'd only vaguely heard of punk then – we all wanted to be DJs, not punks – but I liked the Manics, because they were boys who looked like girls. And they were loud, and fast, and you just knew it would all end in tears (eventually, it did).

A few of us were strolling up Grafton Street after a Manics concert when we saw this weird old guy, clutching a bottle of champagne and a spliff. He was small, spidery, dressed just about well enough not be mistaken for a wino, and he was dancing around the pavement in front of a busker playing some wretched Beatles song. We hung back to watch and when the tune stopped, the little man started calling the busker a 'fuck-dog', demanding that he play some more. The busker took the hump at being called a fuck-dog and said he wanted money, but the little man had none. So I stepped forward, threw the busker a few coins, and said to play, because we wanted to watch his monkey dance. At that, the little man unleashed a volley of abuse, calling us 'university-educated fucks', before weaving off into the shadows, laughing wildly.

'Do you know who that was?' one of my friends asked me. I told her I hadn't a shagging clue. 'Big columnist on *The Sunday Reporter*. You should have been nice to him.'

'Eh? Why?'

'Could help you get a job.'

'Job, my arse.'

The same girl is now a top presenter with RTV.

I was doomed to spend the next three years writing dummy feature pieces, making mock programmes, and lapping up the wisdom of lecturers who could barely land a job doing death notices for *The Nowhere*

*News*. By time I graduated, which I did by the skin of my teeth, Ireland was beginning to turn the corner, and there was an exciting new scent in the air called 'money'. People were beginning to buy new cars instead of second-hand bangers, they had things called jobs, and, for the first time in living memory, it seemed worth our while to stay in Dublin, instead of pissing off to England or America. I was both lucky and unlucky in that my father was an alcoholic cameraman, a damned accomplished one. And not a bad cameraman, either. I was lucky in the sense that, by the time I turned teen, I'd seen enough of the media to know that the long hours, the wild parties, and the wanton sex were just the thing for me. But I was unlucky, because by the time I went looking for work, my father had degenerated into a burnt-out, lonely wreck, and blatant nepotism, that traditional passport into media employment, was not an option. But I'm tall, with bright green eyes and jet-black hair, and I can smile and kiss ass with the best of them. Plus, I have an endless capacity for work. And for drink. And for most other things, too.

By 1996, I'd managed to crawl my way into a producer's gig in some shitty Dublin radio station. One of those horrendous shoestring operations where the music is picked by a masturbating loser with a computer, and you can win a cordless electric kettle, every hour on the hour, if you're the lucky fifth caller. Occasionally, we even got paid. They gave me the graveyard shift, looking after a madman called Gus Devenny. Back in the mists of time, Augustus

Frederick Devenny had been a big noise in Dublin journalism, but by the late nineties, he was merely a barking curio. However, commercial radio stations are often obliged to include a certain percentage of speech programming in their output, so what they cunningly do is play the same market-researched musical vomit all day long and then lump their quota of talk into the evenings when no one's listening and call it 'current affairs'.

As a production job, it wasn't exactly taxing. Mainly, I would set up second-rate politicians for Gus to knock down, a mutually satisfactory arrangement for all concerned. The politicians got publicity, and Gus got easy meat. The man had been preying on the weak for most of his professional life, and nothing I said or did was about to change that. When we needed a panel, we'd trawl the pubs at the top of Baggot Street, where newspaper hacks hide from their families of an evening. We'd prep the show from a pair of barstools, collaring anyone drunk enough to agree to come on. At a quarter to nine, we'd shepherd our captive contributors over to the station, which was housed in a crumbling, airless Georgian slum just off the main drag. The nerve centre was a studio about the size of a pub toilet, up three flights of dark, rotting stairs.

From an even smaller green room/control booth/ lobby, I'd press the necessary buttons to get the show on air, cue Gus to start slabbering on the dot of 9.00 pm, and then scribble out a few calls from non-existent listeners about the burning issues of the day.

Immigration is always a good one, but you can't do that every night, so I'd sort of rotate house prices, traffic congestion, America, and the state of the health service. The things that drive people mad. Gus would then read the comments out and keep the ball in the air with that week's political-corruption story, whilst we waited for the loopers to start ringing in. Most nights, we wouldn't have long to wait. There's a certain class of person, and thank fuck I don't personally *know* any, who lives entirely for radio phone-in shows. After that, it was a simple matter of patching looper after looper through to the studio, letting them make their dumb-ass point, then leaving Gus plus guests to toy with them on air. When the phones went quiet, I'd either ring my friends and beg them to call in pretending to be irate listeners, or else go and buy Gus plus guests more booze, to get them through the dry patch.

It was one such evening in June, drier than a nun's knickers. The Irish soccer team had a home game during our show, so that was our small constituency of crazies temporarily preoccupied. Gus was cracking up. Only two of our guests had materialised. One was a gossip columnist from *The Sunday Reporter* called Gavin Kelly – an urbane, white-haired semi-alcoholic who was never unavailable. The other was some senile actor with a worn repertoire of luvvy-land anecdotes. The Dublin theatrical scene is of enormous interest, but only to those directly involved in it. Gus was particularly annoyed about the non-appearance of a certain guest, whom he himself had booked. He spluttered at me on talkback during ad breaks that he 'would never give that little fucker another chance', whoever 'that little fucker' was. I had just about exhausted my cast of fake callers, and we still had over an hour to fill. When you have absolutely nothing to say, even thirty seconds is an eternity on radio. I was about to suggest ringing up a few telephone sex-lines and sticking them on air, thus allowing Gus to mouth apoplectic indignation about the filth besetting Mother Ireland, when we hit an ad break and Gus demanded a tray of pints from the pub around the corner.

'Because if I'm going to die, I may as well do it with a drink in my hand! This is *extraordinary!* Extraordinary, I tell you! Gah!' Gus always employed the adjective 'extraordinary' whenever he was in a flap. Which was most of the time.

Anything to get out of that hell-hole. I waited for the break to finish, turned the mikes back on, and as the luvvie launched into yet another of his chronicles, I darted for the stairs, which were unlit as usual. I flew down a short flight, swung around the landing, and crashed straight into something that emitted a fearsome screech, then clung viciously onto me, using me as a cushion, as together we bounced all the way to the ground floor. I landed on my back, with the loathsome creature lying on top of me. It had sour breath – a lifetime of tobacco, booze, and poor oral hygiene. Only then did I shout, as I frantically tried to shove it off me. A nasty demon, from a bad dream!

'Nao! Nao! No, wait! Naaoo!' it skirled.

It was human, then – at least, partly. I stopped kicking, and felt the weight of it shift, as it tried to untangle itself from me. I lay flat, stunned. Then I heard the rasp of a cigarette lighter, which served only to reinforce the darkness except for a bizarre, hovering yellow face. Hanging like a mask it was, illuminated from underneath. A thin, lip-less slit of a mouth, cheeks like knotted rope leading to a splodge of a nose cratered with blackheads, old and new. Overhanging it all, a protruding shelf of a brow, made even more prominent by an uninterrupted shock of thick, matted eyebrow running from one side of the short forehead to the other, which was capped by a flat-combed helmet of brown hair. Charcoal pits for sockets, ridged with wrinkles and lines, at the bottom of which lay a pair of tiny black eyes, bright and hard as gun-barrels. I managed to prop myself up on my elbow, drew a painful breath, then stuck out a hand.

'Dr Livingstone. Who the fuck are *you*?'

The apparition went from surprised anger to confused apology. It took my hand, but put no effort into helping me to my feet.

'Nao, nao ... I'm looking for ... a *radio station*. I must have the wrong place ...' and the eyes darted, trying to penetrate the gloom. It was the first and only time I ever saw him stuck for words.

'*The Gus Devenny Show*?'

'Ehh ... yeah! You know that fucking eejit, do you?'

'I'm that fucking eejit's producer.'

'You've got to be joking! This kip is a radio station?'

'Afraid so. They keep the overheads low.'

121

'They keep the lights low, baby! Still,' and he laughed an infectious, dirty laugh, 'Devenny likes working in the dark. Sunlight cramps his style!'

We held onto each other as we climbed back up the stairs. He slumped into the sofa in the control booth and rubbed a knee. Nondescript green sports jacket. Open-collared Marks and Spencer shirt. Navy trousers, scruffy slip-on shoes. Now that I could actually see him, I remembered him from Grafton Street five years previously, but thank Christ he didn't remember me. He winced. 'Old injury, from my rock-and-roll years!' He did seem genuinely hurt. It would be the following morning before my much-younger body would bruise and completely seize up. Gus spotted the little man from inside the studio. He waved his arm in a beckoning motion.

'And, eh, we've just been joined by our next guest, a former singer in a, gah, *punk rock* band, who went on to be described as Ireland's most irritating columnist. Kevin Carver, welcome to the studio!' Gus beckoned even more frantically.

'Fuck you, Gus! Your producer has just thrown me down a flight of stairs!'

'Soundproof glass.' I rapped the window to show him. In a flash, he was out of the sofa, past me, holding the studio door open.

'I said, "Fuck you, Gus! Your producer has just thrown me down a flight of stairs!"' He looked back, smiling at me. Oh, it went out on air all right – off-mike, but our tiny audience would have heard it, for sure. Carver laughed and dived into the studio.

'Gus Devenny! When I first met you, you were the most highly paid, widely feared newspaperman in Ireland! Folks, you should see the *kip* Gus is working in now. Do you need a few bob? Do you need a sub? I could lend you 50p to put in the electricity meter!'

And that was it. No matter what Devenny said, Carver was straight back at him, laughing and joking, ripping the piss. It was like watching some guy in a pub taking on all comers, getting the place going. When Gus pointed out that nobody was calling the programme because of the match, Carver bawled, 'Well, that might have been the case before *I* arrived, but the action's here now, baby! There's fuck-all happening on that football pitch tonight! It'll be a no-score draw, I promise you! Gus! I promise you! Nao! Some of the lads on the team are great, they play with their hearts, but the manager's a tosser, and we'll always be a second-rate side as long as he's in charge, so fuck that! This is Radio Free Ireland, baby! Don't watch that rubbish! Listen to us!'

That got the phones started, and one of the first calls was from the station manager, a typical Dickie Vaughan type, screaming and panicking. We would lose our licence for foul language on air. What would our advertisers think? Who was that bastard, anyway? What did Devenny think he was doing? I had to put a stop to it *now*, or else I was sacked. I said I'd see what I could do.

The phones were going bananas. It was great. I've never seen anybody set a room, or a switchboard, on fire the way Kevin Carver could, with no more than a bit of vulgar bombast, expertly delivered.

I informed Gus on talkback that our snivelling shit of a manager wasn't happy, and then fed him a few callers to buy time. How dare we say such horrible things about the national squad, blah blah blah. I cut Carver's mike, but you could still hear him shouting wild abuse at the callers. Gus was getting flustered, but I knew, instinctively, that if I went in and tried to grab Carver, there'd be a struggle which I might not win. Anyway, I'm a great believer in the illusion of free speech. Then I had an idea.

To look at me, you'd think Afghani Black wouldn't melt in my mouth, but I'm actually one of the fastest, tidiest spliff-rollers in the world. I got busy with the skins, right in front of the glass, and Carver, who kept looking over, presumably to see if I was going to throw him out, instead saw me smiling and putting one together. I lit up. He made the universal finger-and-thumb circle to his mouth, inquiring whether he could have some. I knew it. I'd guessed right; we druggies can spot each other a mile off. I held the smoke up, offering. Bring it here, he beckoned. No, I grinned. He looked at me. I took another big, long toke. He was out of his chair and through the studio door – that rapid, scurrying, half-crouched way he has of moving. He hung through the doorway, reaching for the spliff. I held it back.

'You wanna smoke shit with me, or talk shit with them?'

'Fuck it, you're right,' he cackled, and sidled over, seizing the spliff and flopping onto the sofa with one swift, ruthless move. He pulled hard. 'Fuck! Yes! Oh, fuck! Jesus, I'd forgotten what good smoke was like, fuck me! Yes! Jesus!' His mouth formed a sort of extended kissing movement, funnelling the lower half of his face out to meet the joint, like a beast feeling the ground for insects. 'I've been living in Donegal. They all drink beer for kicks up there.' I quickly rolled another, as his was burning fast. I could feel his eyes on my hands, taking in the size of the lump I was working from. Suck. Stub. I knew it was coming.

'Can you get me some?'

'When?'

'Tonight?'

'Gimme your cigarettes.' I looked up, keeping my hands low. Gus Devenny glanced nervously at the window, but didn't engage our attention, probably to keep the evil spirit from re-entering his studio. Carver passed me a near-empty packet of high-tar fags, and I ripped some of the paper foil from inside it. 'It's a bit crumbly, but it's good,' I explained. I took a Swiss Army knife from my pocket and split my lump, wrapped his share, then stuffed it into the box. He grinned. Grateful monkey. For the first time.

'How much do I owe you?' He patted the pockets of his sports coat.

'You're all right.'

'Are you sure? I mean, you're just a poor student, and I'm a highly paid journalist! I just don't seem to have ...' He frowned and kept patting his jacket.

'Forget it. Think of it as compo for your injuries, or medicine, whatever. And I'm not a poor student: I'm a highly trained producer.'

'Then you shouldn't be working for this fucking spastic,' he sneered, just as Gus came flying out the studio door. Oops, show's over! I killed the mikes and punched in the ad break.

'That was *extraordinary*! Extraordinary! *Gah!*'

'Gus! You were *great*! Great!' Carver jumped up, glad-handed Gus, and did a miniature dance of joy around the booth with the sheer pleasure of it all. I laughed out loud at his performance, more than a bit stoned. 'We'll go get a drink! I insist! On me! To celebrate the success of your great little show!' Gus shot him a look that would have punched a hole in the wall, had it missed. But Carver caught it and snickered all the more.

# 9

## GETTING TO KNOW YOU

We walked to a plush hotel. 'It's where I stay when I'm in town,' Carver announced, as the doorman nodded. 'Expenses,' and he nudged Devenny in the ribs. 'Remember what they are, Gus?'

My presenter spluttered an extra-large 'Gah!' at that, turned abruptly on his heel, and stormed off down the street, shaking his head, alternately spluttering 'Gah!' and 'Extraordinary!' at random passersby. After a moment's hesitation, the doting actor made a fumbling excuse about the lateness of the hour and ran after him. Carver laughed to see them go.

'Poor Gus,' he chortled, as we hunted out a table. 'How the mighty have fallen! Would you believe that that man was once one of the most feared operators in Dublin journalism? I know people who had nervous breakdowns because of him! Grown men and women, in floods of tears! Really! But now, he's a beaten docket! No credibility in the game!' The other remaining guest from the show eyed Carver speculatively.

'You haven't exactly been around much yourself, Kevin. What brings you to Dublin, anyway?'

The response came with a degree of *froideur*. 'Well, I'm *from* here Gavin, as you know. So I reckon I'm at liberty to come and sniff the air, occasionally. If that's all right with you.'

'Donegal getting a bit quiet for you, then?'

'You know what? I have a nice buzz on me, so I'm not gonna waste it on a poxy gossip-monger!' Carver waved a dismissive paw in Kelly's face and wandered off across the lounge. A pianist tinkled idly at the far end of the lobby. Kelly shrugged at me. What had started out, in my mind anyway, as a bunch of lads going for a genial post-show pint had degenerated within minutes to the two of us standing awkwardly in a crowded hotel bar. I felt mildly pissed at him for driving the object of my curiosity away. I decided to split.

'Hey. There's no free seats. Let's do this some other time.'

But as the words left my mouth, a middle-aged man and a woman, closely followed by a fat, boyish yuppie, jumped up from the table right beside us and scuttled quickly towards the door. They ignored us, but all three watched Carver's back as they fled. Oblivious, he sauntered around the distant piano, waving the stub of my burnt-out joint in time to the music, as if conducting an imaginary orchestra.

'Hello. That's interesting ...' Kelly stared after the departing trio.

'What is?' I reluctantly sat down. That mundane act of sitting, instead of going home, was the fulcrum, the tiny accident of fate, upon which the rest of my life was to tilt.

'Those people who just left. I'm pretty sure that two of them used to play with your friend Kevin.'

'*Play* with him?'

'In his band.'

'He's in a band?'

'Not is. Was.'

'They seemed in a hurry.'

'I think I know why. Carver's taking a case against them.' With this tantalising snippet, Kelly broke off to order drinks from a waiter. I changed my mind about wanting to go home. In Ireland, legal actions are followed with a great deal more interest than sex scandals.

'What kind of case?'

'Spat over royalties. Carver was in this band, about twenty years ago. They had a minor hit, a song about politicians being arseholes or wankers ... no, bastards, that was it. Probably sold about a hundred copies, at the time.'

I tried to mentally digest the notion of Carver as a musician. 'Hardly worth fighting over, I would have thought.'

'Ah. But it's been re-released.'

'I haven't heard it.'

'No, you won't have, because some bunch of kids

in the States covered it. Surprise hit of the year across the pond. They're having an …'

'Election.'

'… exactly.' Kelly nodded. '"All Politicians are Bastards". It must have captured the Zeitgeist.'

'Sounds very Carver, I have to say.'

'Well, this is the thing. I don't know who the fat fellow was, but that couple who just fled out the door, I'm pretty certain that was the O'Gorman twins. Apparently they're credited on the original single, so they get the royalties. But Carver claims he wrote the lyrics.'

'And did he?'

'I don't know, but I'd sure as hell *like* to know. Case is listed for September.'

'How much are we talking about?'

'I've heard three-quarters of a million, and climbing. Dollars, but still, that's a lot of dough.'

'I hope he wins.'

'Do you, really?' Kelly took a large swig from his pint. 'Why?'

'No reason. I kinda like him, I guess. You've got to admit he's good craic. Bloody good talker.'

'Yes,' agreed Kelly, after a moment's hesitation. 'He's that all right.'

'I'd love to get him on the show again.'

'Would you, indeed?'

'But he lives in Donegal?'

'Has done for a couple of years.'

'Not exactly the epicentre of the known universe, is it?'

'He left Dublin in a huff. Had a big falling-out with our editor. Used to be the golden boy, but not any more. He's still under contract, so they have to pay him, but he only contributes the occasional piece now and never shows his face in the building. That's why I was surprised to see him.'

'Sounds like he's having a rough time of it.'

'Nothing he doesn't deserve, believe me.'

'You don't like him.'

'No, I don't.'

'But you came for a drink to get stuff for your column?'

'How very perceptive of you. I'd like to know what he's doing in town.'

'Well, I'm glad he's in town. I enjoyed that, tonight.'

Kelly contemplated his half-empty glass in silence for about thirty seconds, then snatched it, and drained it in one go. He put it back down again, slightly harder than necessary.

'Get involved with that man,' he gestured towards Carver, who now leaned across the piano, greeting passers-by with a big grin on his face, 'and one day, he will fuck you.'

I laughed. 'Excuse me?'

'I said, "Get involved with that man, and one day he will *fuck* you."'

'Fuck me how?' Kelly studied my expression, to see whether I was taking him seriously. I must have wiped my mirth away with appropriate haste, because after another short pause, he continued.

'I'll tell you how. We both started out at *The Daily*

*Enquirer*. At first, we hit it off. He was raw, but good company. He had attitude, you know? Then, one day, completely without warning, the little bastard turned on me, just like that.' Kelly snapped his fingers.

'Why?'

'That's the thing. To this day, I still don't know why. Maybe he just saw me as competition. I take it you've never worked in a newspaper?'

I shook my head.

'You won't know the meaning of back-stabbing until you do.'

'But you're both at *The Reporter* now?'

'I jumped ship in '88, to get away from him. Then they poached him a few years later. When I heard he was coming, I thought, "Jesus, here we go again", and sure enough, for a while he could do no wrong. But it hasn't worked out for him.'

'Why not?'

'Basically, they think he's mad. He falls out with everybody in the end.'

'And is he mad?'

'I think you're about to get an opportunity to judge for yourself ...'

'*Seig Heil!*' Carver's voice boomed from across the lobby. The hotel pianist seemed alarmed by the gnomic figure that had just reached over and stolen his microphone, but played on, nonetheless. Carver repeated the salute towards a throng of foreign tourists, pouring through the hotel door with their suitcases, fresh from the living hell of Dublin airport.

'Good luck, now.' Kelly snorted, stood up, and left. I sat back to watch the show.

'Where you from, you are being from Germany, ja?' Carver addressed the new arrivals in a stage-Nazi accent. A few of them shook their heads, agog. This was obviously the traditional Irish welcome they'd read about in their guidebooks.

'Vot? You are Swedish? Ja? Is goot, I haf played in Sweden many times! I am a professional! Velcome in Ireland! I am singing you a little song, to velcome you in Ireland, ja?' The tourists gawped. 'Vot is der matter? You are no speaking the Irish? Don't worry, I don't speak Irish myself! No one speaks Irish in this country, we just pretend to! So, vot vill you be doing in Ireland, nice Swedish people? Magical, mystical, Ireland! You vill be kissing der Blarney Stone, ja? You vill be having der craic and der Guinness, ja? You vill listen to der fiddle-dee-dee music, played by university-educated fucks in Aran jumpers?'

And, as Carver launched into a Sid Vicious-style rendition of 'My Way', the tourists politely stood around the piano, evidently convinced that in Dublin, this was as good as it got.

When the tourists finally dispersed to their rooms, Carver flung down the microphone and scampered over to my table, demanding 'somewhere with more action'. I was too amused not to follow – young, virgin company, I guess. Dolce Vita was utterly devoid of action, and a bored hostess consigned us to a booth at the back of the club. Carver insisted on buying champagne on his credit card. In exchange, I had to 'roll a couple of numbers, baby'.

'Is it cool?'

'What do ya mean, is it cool? I've been coming in here since the seventies, they know me.'

'It's nice to see they've preserved the décor, in memory of your first visit.'

'Fuck you, baby, I'm wild! Roll a spliff!'

'You can resist everything except temptation, eh? *You* roll a spliff, with that shit I gave you earlier.' He looked at me with suddenly vulnerable eyes, like a child confronted with impossible homework.

'I can't. Would you believe, I can't? Anything I make, it burns too quickly and falls apart in my hands. You do it, would ya? Yeah?'

We sat in that booth, sipping bubbly and smoking hash, surrounded by wallpaper that bore tired testament to three decades of late-night parties. Carver seemed to relax, in that he grew marginally less manic.

'So, what was all that about?' he demanded, sucking on a fresh joint.

'All what?'

'That pox-dog Kelly. Friend of yours, is he?'

'He's a regular on the show.'

'Set yourselves high standards, don't you?'

'Well, I'm here talking to you, aren't I?'

'What did he say about me?'

'What makes you think Kelly said anything about you?'

'Think I came down in the last shower of rain, do ya? He hates my guts. What did he say?'

'He said you were mad and bad.'

Carver chuckled. 'Well, am I? Am I mad and bad?'

'How should I know?'

'You seem a smart enough young fucker: don't pretend you haven't formed an opinion.'

'It's bad journalism to trust a single source.'

At that, Carver smiled, then reached out and half-patted, half-slapped the left side of my face. 'See? I knew you were a smart young fucker.'

'Well, are you?'

'Am I what?'

'Mad and bad?'

'Yes and yes!'

'How bad?'

'Ooh, I am bad, baby. You better believe it, I am sooo *bad.*'

I laughed. 'How bad?'

He pulled heavily on the joint. 'If being honest to the point where it fucks up your career is bad, then I'm bad. If trying to make a difference in this rotten little country is bad, then I'm very bad. And if refusing to take the soup is bad, then I'm awful.' Voice husky, he fixed me with his shiny button eyes. I could see my reflection in their blackness. 'I've never taken the soup, baby. And never will.'

'What the hell are you talking about?'

'Example – that arsehole Kelly. Every freebie, every lig, every poxy wine-and-cheese party … I bet you Gavin Kelly couldn't, if his life depended on it, tell you when he last paid for a meal. Or a drink. Or a holiday. Me, I never accept anything. I never accept invites; if anybody sends me a present, even a bottle of plonk, I send it right back. I've never been on a junket in my entire professional life.'

'You're kidding!'

'A journalist should never be beholden to anybody. Not for one red cent. Accept someone's hospitality, and you're compromised. Do you understand? If I gave you fifty quid every time you met me, how would you feel about me?'

'Like you'd paid me for that hash.'

'I'm being serious here. How would you feel about me?'

'Pretty good, I guess.'

'Exactly. So the day comes when you have to fuck me for a story. When you have to write bad things about me, because they're true. But I'm the nice man who gives you fifty quid every time you meet him. How would you feel then?'

'Not good?'

'Right. On the basis of give-and-take alone, Gavin Kelly is the biggest slag in town. He's been at it for years. Compromised to hell and beyond. Whereas I never accept *anything*! You gotta be impersonal. You gotta be cold. In this game, you can't *have* friends. Only good stories.'

'That's very spartan of you.'

'Where do you think all the pol corrs get their stuff? I mean the really good political stories, not the lazy shit churned out by the party press officers?'

'Sources?'

'Sources! These boys crawl around the corridors

of power, on their hands and knees! They take the feed! I'll tell you about sources! Have you ever set foot in the Dáil bar, deep inside our glorious parliament buildings?'

'No.'

'Well, if you did, all you'd see is politicians and journalists, standing around, feeding each other lines. Have you heard about so-and-so? Guess who's up to such-and-such? Whisper, whisper! Who's screwing who? And off they go and print it! But step outside that charmed little circle, baby, and your sources dry up overnight!'

'And you're outside the circle?'

'I was never inside it. Because I don't take the soup. And they hate me for it!'

He ordered another bottle of champagne from the indifferent hostess. He was jaded, he told me. Tired. Ireland was too small a place, the media scene dominated by cant and mediocrity. Everything was worn-out, limited by a lack of imagination and a resolute unwillingness to tackle the status quo. It was a shitty fucking game. He knew it inside out, knew all the players, and nobody had any intention of rocking the boat. He'd tried himself, tried for years. Tried to tackle the corruption, but nobody took risks any more.

'Those bastards at *The Reporter* don't believe in proper journalism! It's all celebrity gossip and arse-licking nowadays, and I've told them exactly what I think of that! You gotta run your gig by your own lights! But they love straw men like Kelly, who'll write tripe to order!'

'I wouldn't be surprised if he wrote something about you in the very near future.'

Carver flicked channels from deeply indignant to darkly suspicious. 'What do you mean?'

'I take it you didn't see those people who left when we arrived?'

'Arrived where?'

'In the hotel. After the radio.'

'No, who?'

'Three people left in a hurry when they saw you. Kelly said that two of them used to be in a band with you.'

'What did they look like?'

'Man and a woman. The O'Gorman twins?'

'No!' Carver practically squealed in disbelief. 'Nao! Margaret and Vincent were there, tonight? In the hotel?'

'Apparently so.'

'Fuck me!' And he slapped his hands on his forehead. 'Fuck me!'

'Yeah, they seemed anxious to avoid you. They were with some guy ...'

'Who?' His voice developed a sudden, definite edge.

'Dunno. I have no idea who any of these people are.'

'The other man! Describe him to me!' Carver barked, as if the perfidious O'Gormans were somehow my direct responsibility. He cocked his head and skewered me with those eyes. If I'd told him that I was about to reveal the location of a buried treasure chest, he couldn't have listened more closely.

'Fat, ginger yuppie. The town's crawling with them.'

'Brown skin, brown hair, brown eyes, big nose, well-dressed, foreign-looking?'

'No.'

'Are you sure?'

'Not even close.'

'How can you be sure?'

'Because this guy didn't look foreign, he looked like a bogger, okay? Like a country boy, packed into a suit.'

'As long as you're sure.'

'Man, I'm lost.'

'It's just that ... look, it would have been very bad news, very bad news indeed, if the person I described was hanging out with Maggie and Vinnie O'Gorman. I'm taking them to court on a point of artistic principle.'

'"All Politicians are Bastards"?'

'Kelly told you?'

'He said it's worth a few quid.'

'It's not the money. If I win, I'll give every penny to charity. And they better get their chequebooks ready, cos those cunts are in for a surprise!'

'What kind of a surprise?'

'If I told you, then it wouldn't be a surprise, would it?' He stubbed the joint out. By the time he looked up, I was already rolling another. He frowned. 'If you ever tell anybody what I'm about to tell you, I'll cut out your tongue.' The least discreet person I ever met. I passed him the unlit joint. He took his time over lighting it. 'The guy who used to run our record label. He knows the truth. If I can get him into court, the O'Gormans are dead meat.' I felt flattered. My first-ever piece of insider information. Here was a much older man, an experienced operator, who appeared to trust me. Then, flick channels, another change of mood. 'Do you like working for Gus Devenny?'

'It's a job.'

'So, you don't?'

'It's a job.'

'Okay, same question, put another way. Do you see yourself working in that shithole of a radio station for ever and ever?'

'Christ, I hope not!'

'Have you ever considered that working for Gus Devenny might be all you're good for?'

'Fuck you! It's not a bad start!'

'It's not a *great* start, though … is it?' His eyes glittered with amusement.

'Hey! I'm just two years out of college! And I'm already a producer!'

'Big deal! A producer of what? Unadulterated shite!'

And there's me thinking I was Kevin Carver's New Best Friend. 'Listen, you! I've argued black and blue with Gus that we should use our show to try to get good stories, instead of skating superficially over the surface of everything. That we shouldn't settle for second-rate guests with scripted answers. But he doesn't give a shit. Last week, I told him that just once in my life, I'd like to work on the kind of show that I want to listen to. Bastard just ignored me.'

'You're his producer. What's your excuse?'

I was fit to hit the ceiling. 'Bollocks to that! Maybe it was different back at the dawn of history when you started out, but these days, it's all run by marketing men! What you read, what you watch, what you listen to – all decided by greedy little wankers in suits, with their pie charts and their bloody demographics. The media is dumbing down, my man, at the very moment in world history when it needs to smarten up. Everything's a copy of a copy of a copy. Focus groups are in. Original thinking is out. Perhaps,' I added, wanting to hit back, 'that's why your own career isn't going great guns either?'

He threw me a flinty look, but then softened it slightly, with a thin smile. 'Roll me another joint, you young smart-arse. But before you do, write your number down and pray to God that I don't lose it. Then send this champagne back and order more. Tell them it hasn't been properly chilled.'

# 10

## CARPE DIEM

'Just once in my life, I'd like to work on the kind of show that *I'd* like to watch!' The board of TV Ireland shifted in their high-backed leather swivel chairs, whilst Carver threw shapes at them, hands hovering like a kung-fu fighter. 'The kind of show that doesn't settle for scripted answers!' More shifting and a few coughs. 'A show that gets to the bottom of things, instead of skating superficially over the surface!' A rebellious shuffling of paper, now, and someone deliberately clicked a pen. 'My motto is, don't dumb down, dumb up! And if you guys are smart, that will be your motto, too!'

Dickie Vaughan glanced up the long wooden table at his bosses, as if seeking their permission to speak, then settled forward, his podgy fingers forming a steeple. 'Yes. Thank you, Kevin. All very ... *worthwhile*. But our market research shows that our target audience will be the Cs and the Ds. Most of our output will be imported.' By which Dickie meant that TV Ireland would be re-broadcasting English soaps and crappy American films. 'Unfortunately,' he continued, 'the government has forced us to tag on some home-grown stuff ...'

The Chairman of the Board, an urbane, silver-haired sophisticate, cut straight across his underling.

'I think what Dickie means to say is that the terms of the new licence rightly include a definite commitment to a certain quantity of domestic product, particularly in the area of news and current affairs. Naturally, TV Ireland, ah, enthusiastically embraces this requirement and will seek to offer its audience the best domestically made programming possible, bearing in mind our limited resources.'

Vaughan, who had retreated as if slapped, furiously polished his glasses at this, nodding his head so hard I feared that it might fall off and roll across the polished wood. I despised him already. If the board had told Dickie to transmit the entire schedule in Dutch, or to kill his mother, then paint his arse blue, and hang himself upside-down off O'Connell bridge, he would have done it. Much as I disliked him, I couldn't help staring at his hair, blow-dried and dyed glossy black, just like Elvis in his final days. Where the fuck did they get this guy?

The call had come through on my mobile three days after we met. I was in rag order after a weekend of clubbing. My bum was still massively bruised from those stairs. Me and my druggy housemates were curled up on our half-wrecked sofa in our rented, half-wrecked house in Stoneybatter, watching video after video, smoking spliffs, sipping red wine, and necking Diazepam to quell the antsy fear that attacks the system after too many nights on pills.

'What are you doing, ya degenerate young fuck? Am I interrupting a three-ball? A four-ball, maybe?'

'I'm having dinner at my mother's.'

'Oh. Look. I have a meeting with this crowd of fucks out at TV Ireland tomorrow. I want you to come along.'

The TV Ireland consortium had recently won a commercial television licence. They were due on air shortly, but had been rather blasé about hiring. Reading between the lines, they'd had trouble attracting proper talent. None of the established personalities were remotely interested in being poached – why take that kind of risk? A job with public-service broadcaster RTV was a job for life (and, judging by some of their presenters, beyond). Plus, TV Ireland appeared not to be tossing money around, and in television, you need cash to make a splash. Lots of cash.

'TV Ireland? What do you want me for?'

'You're a producer, aren'tcha? Yeah?'

'Yes, but what would I be there to talk about? Give me a clue.'

He sounded irritated. 'You know! Production stuff! How it would work! How we could do a show!'

'Are they giving you a show?'

'Nao! Nao! Well, they are, but they don't *know* that yet! I'll stroke them, don't worry. I've been in this game a long time. I know these boys; I know what buttons to press!'

'But what *kind* of show are you pitching? A news show? A quiz show? Or are you going to dress up as a scarecrow and read bed-time stories to kids?'

'I'll do a fucking gardening show, if they ask me! Listen, you young fuck, we could get a gig out of this! Just back up everything I say, okay? Let *me* do the talking: I know my way round these people; I know how they think! I'll tell them whatever they want to hear, and if we get in the door, we'll just do the kind of show we both want to do, and fuck them! But we gotta get in the door, first! That's the hard part! Swing by for me at half-eight! Yeah?'

We could get a gig out of this. The kind of show we both want to do. Since our first encounter, I'd been replaying Kevin Carver's radio performance in my head, contrasting his verbal pyrotechnics to Gus Devenny's lumbering, pedestrian style. I had wanted to book Carver again immediately, but Devenny overruled me. Now, here was Carver ringing me. I felt like a young bride trapped in a stale marriage being sniffed out for an affair by an exciting, if brutally ugly, older man.

To my young eyes, there was a blunt, rebellious honesty about Carver, a sort of perverse integrity that I'd previously assumed did not exist outside the pages of Raymond Chandler novels. We could get a gig out of this. I staggered off to the computer, knocked up two pages of wishful thinking about an imaginary current-affairs-stroke-chat show, printed them off, then fell into bed. The following morning, I borrowed a suit from one of my housemates, a small-time drug dealer called Ritchie, and picked Carver up ten minutes early from the plush hotel. He became quite excited, nodding frequently and vigorously, as he read my programme proposal in the taxi. Then he showed me his idea, in the form of a longhand scrawl on an A4 notepad. We were both advocating a weekly chat show that went for the jugular, examined issues in depth, and refused to settle for scripted answers. Spooky, huh?

'I can't type,' he smiled ruefully.

'You've never done a day's manual work in your life, have you?'

The TV Ireland building was a deluxe warehouse in the middle of a suburban industrial estate. They had a month to go to air and the interior was a non-deluxe mess of rolled-up carpet, shrink-wrapped office furniture, and kilometres of bunched-up cable. The receptionist allowed us to use her computer, the only one working, and Carver paced up and down, sucking voraciously on a fag, whilst I condensed our words into one document. He stopped jabbering every so often to grab my shoulder and stare at the screen. Talk about doing your homework up the back of the bus on the way to school. The board made us wait twenty minutes before calling us in − standard practice, designed to make you feel small. But for us, the 'fuck you' delay was welcome, because by the end of it we had multiple copies of a proposal we were both half-happy with. The problem was, nobody else was half-happy with it.

In contrast to the chaos engulfing the rest of the building, the boardroom was quiet, clean, and elegant, with incredibly expensive furniture and the very latest in upward lighting. The board itself was a curious mixture of bankers and entertainment industry types, a couple of whom, I could tell by just looking, were no strangers to the night. So, that's how Carver got through the door to make his pitch, I thought. Rock-'n'-rollers. Fellow party-animals. Street kids. Movers and shakers. Guys who rule the world at four o'clock in the morning.

And then there was Dickie Vaughan, Head of Programmes, TV Ireland.

'If you had to take a helicopter view of the changes in the broadcasting landscape in Ireland at present, what would you see?'

'Your stupid fucking hair,' I thought to myself. Then I twigged that Dickie was directing his question at me. I'd said nothing so far, leaving everything to Carver, as instructed. But his pitch was getting us nowhere. Then, Dickie transferred the eyes of the board onto me, so I felt I had to say something. The words just kind of came to me, as if I'd sub-consciously scripted them.

'That's a very good question, Mr Vaughan. I think what we really have to ask ourselves is not how *broadcasting* is changing, but rather how *people* are changing. Broadcasting is about people, not in the sense that we care about people, but in the sense that people consume it. A clever broadcaster holds a mirror up to the customer, one that flatters. Now, Ireland is on the verge of an economic boom – I think we'd all agree on that.' Already, I had two of the bankers nodding. 'During times of wealth, with all respect to your research, people don't want to be a C or a D. Everyone wants to be an A – or, at least, a B. People use their new-found disposable income to upgrade their social status. They stop thinking 'bus' and start thinking 'BMW'. Pasta, not potatoes. Smart becomes the new black. I say give your customers a show that flatters their changing mindset. A show that tells them they are an intelligent, sophisticated audience, no matter what your research shows. You call yourselves TV Ireland? Well, give them a show that reflects the new Ireland!'

Dickie looked baffled. One of the bankers scanned his notes, looking for my name.

'If you don't mind me saying ... Lee ... that sounds ... *expensive*.'

'It doesn't have to be. I see a plain, stripped-down set,' I was on my feet now, 'with simple, modern furniture. Black leather and brushed aluminium. A dark background, with white spotlights, to create an intimate yet austere presence. All you need is a presenter who can hold people's attention, someone who can talk to anyone, be they A, B, C, or D.' Jesus, they were still listening. 'Gentlemen, I've seen this presenter in action. Well – he's not a presenter yet, but he soon will be. You want customers? Well, no one can light up a switchboard quite like him – I've seen that for myself. I am one hundred per cent positive that together we can get this presenter to light up our screens, in a way that will benefit your station and your

148

shareholders. Gentlemen! This presenter is sitting in front of you!' And I flung out my arm towards him. Carver sat perfectly still, watching me with a wicked half-smile, as if I'd just offered everyone in the room a big, fat line of coke. Short silence.

'And, er, what about resources? What sort of resources would this show require?' The banker, again. There would be no resources: we all knew that.

'Creativity and flexibility are the best resources a show can have! You don't need lots of people; you just need the right people, doing the right thing!' That was it. One more question and the board would find that my line in creative, flexible hyperbole was played out.

'You produce Gus Devenny, don't you?' Dickie leapt back in, trying to make himself look important.

'Yes, I do.'

'Then, as his producer, why aren't you pushing Gus Devenny in front of us?'

Get your dirty little hands off my future, Dickie!

'Because in my opinion, Gus wouldn't be right for TV Ireland. I could just as easily ask you why you haven't approached him?' Deft. A swift, smooth denial of the man who'd been my bread and butter for the past two years, plus the ball smashed back into Dickie's teeth. Carver's wicked half-smile turned into a full-blown one. After his faltering start, I'd opened the floodgates, and now he spilled right through them.

'What did I tell you? This is a great young producer, gonna be big in the game!' The board looked at one another, undecided. 'Come on, guys, we're all gonna be big in the game! That's what we want, isn't it? Bums on seats! Numbers! The sweet smell of success! I love what you guys are doing! I'm a commercial animal! I believe in competition! The free market! Live and die by the sword! The kid is right – we don't need resources: there'll be no fat on us! A slim, trim fighting-machine, with the courage to succeed! And if we don't get the numbers, then I'll be the first to throw myself outta here! You won't have to sack me: I'll sack myself, I swear!'

He got a few laughs for that, and so, amidst a lot of fidgeting, Dickie and I were politely invited to go find ourselves a coffee. I was mighty relieved to be put out of the meeting, but Dickie was massively offended. Carver could barely contain his glee. He gave me a hugely indiscreet wink as I closed the door, then fired up a fag and tried to look business-like in front of the now-whispering board.

Dickie blanked me and bustled off down a corridor, pretending that he had more important matters to attend to than the potential deal being discussed in his absence. Out of sheer badness, I ignored the snub and followed him, exuding ersatz sugar.

'I'd love to see your facilities, Dickie.' That stopped him in his tracks. He swung his little bulk around and for a second I thought he was going to tell me to fuck off. Instead he reddened, frowned at the floor, and gestured towards a soundproof door. I smiled sweetly and sashayed on through.

The studio resembled an empty, cavernous warehouse, because that's precisely what it was. I strolled around the dismal expanse, trying to think of nice things to say – things like, 'Um. Very good. At least you have plenty of space …'

Dickie stood in the shadows, arms folded, and stared. No sets, no seating, no lighting rigs, no lights, no cameras, no sound gear – nothing, except for concrete and cables. Christ. Along one wall, a few internal windows, accessed by metal stairs and doors.

'Gallery?'

Dickie nodded. I poked my head into a cramped control booth at ground level, then climbed to the gallery proper. A grudging fluorescent light shone on banks of mixing desks, tape machines, and monitors. They had the basics, then, but not wired up. I came back out to the top of the stairs, overlooking the gloomy void. For the first and only time in my life, I felt a twinge of sympathy for Dickie Vaughan. As my father's child, I'd spent enough time in television studios to be worried on his behalf. Very worried.

I called down. 'Are you sure this will be ready in time?'

'TV Ireland shall go to air at the start of next month, as scheduled.' He pouted and frowned at the floor.

'Er, okay. Lotta work to do, still.'

'Yes. As Head of Programmes, I *am* aware of that.'

I mustered as much false respect into my voice as I possibly could and spoke across the distance. 'I suppose if most of your stuff is on tape, all you really need is a few machines connected up, and you're off.'

'The board has decided that TV Ireland will go to air with a two-hour, live introductory programme, from this very studio, which I shall personally produce.'

I looked around. 'Oh, shit ...' The disbelief was far from false.

'Look,' he retorted, kicking at a small pile of concrete dust. 'I may as well be perfectly clear with you. Wearing my executive producer's hat, I don't think that Kevin Carver is right for this station. His print career has faded. He never made it onto RTV. Have you ever asked yourself why? Wearing my manager's hat, I shall, of course, accept the decision of my board, whatever that may be. But they already have my recommendation.' He stared up at me, finally, his glasses twin circles of white in the shadows. 'I just don't think that you, or he, can do it.'

He turned on his loafer-clad heel and strode away, in the comical, jerking manner that small men deem purposeful. Just as he reached the soundproof door, it flew open and Kevin Carver's head popped through the gap, swivelling from side to side. He wore a grin the size of Texas, which disappeared the instant he identified Dickie in the dark. A visor of hostility snapped into place, hiding his ecstatic face.

'I'm looking for Lee,' he announced in a cold, flat tone. Dickie stepped back to allow him in, gesturing up towards me with a stubby arm, but Carver made a point of holding the door open and staring fiercely at the hapless manager, who took the hint and shuffled past. Carver kept his hate mask on until the door clicked shut. That was the first time I saw him give someone the full flinty-face treatment, and also the first time I saw how quickly he could alter the mood in a room, even one this big, by deploying it.

'Do you two know each other?'

He squinted up towards me, on the gallery steps.

'No. Never met him before in my life. I asked the board where they got him. He came from a shopping channel in London. A fucking shopping channel! They admitted they couldn't find anyone else. I can tell just by looking at him that he's a useless bastard.' Carver's voice remained harsh, as if I was somehow to blame for the very existence of Dickie Vaughan. 'Your first job, as my producer, will be to keep that little prick off my back! I never want to see him, do you understand?'

I slapped the handrail and let out a shout. 'No way! No fucking way!' That hot feeling in your stomach, when, just once in your life, something actually goes right. His grin the size of Texas reappeared.

'They're waiting for you! Get in there! And don't be greedy: remember who's the star here!'

As I tore down the stairs, he launched into this curious sort of disco dance, where he bunched his fists up to his chest, lifted a knee to his stomach, and stuck his tongue out the side out of his mouth. He was still doing it, in the middle of the vast studio floor, as I scrambled through the door.

# 11

## GLITCH

'We'll be the intelligent, rock-and-roll show that doesn't tolerate bullshit!'

For a second, I thought I'd got the wrong room. Several hacks sat on bubble-wrapped office chairs, scribbling into notebooks. Four photographers moved around, letting off flashguns. But it was Carver's voice, for sure. 'We won't insult our audience, the way RTV does, with lazy journalism! We are real people, not effete wankers stuck in ivory towers!' There he was, sitting at the head of a long, cardboard-clad table, sucking on a fag, like a sickly cartoon parody of the Chairman of the Board. As if on cue, he proceeded to name individual members of the TV Ireland directorate, stating how delighted they all were about signing him up. Then he noticed me.

'Lee! Lee!' He leapt up and scuttled over, got an arm round my waist, and pulled me towards the scribbling hacks. 'This is Lee Lovecraft, my brilliant young producer! The secret to any good show is a good producer, so I personally head-hunted Lee to join me here at TV Ireland!' I wore a big, shit-eating grin all over my hunted head. One of the hacks spoke to me directly.

'Tell us, Lee, who will want to watch this new show of yours?'

Carver answered for me. 'We want everybody to watch it, obviously! All our viewers will be very important to us, but we'll be designing the show for a sophisticated audience! This show will reflect the new Ireland! That's why I have a smart, young producer! We want smart, young people who take BMWs to work, not the bus! We want yuppies, with plenty of disposable income, to keep the advertisers happy!'

The hacks chortled at Carver's frankness. Still flush from his praise, I didn't mind when he pointedly asked me to 'set up the next meeting', as he ushered everyone outside for photographs of him, alone, under the TV Ireland logo on the front of the building. There was no next meeting to set up, but I hate having cameras pointed at me, they're worse than guns, so I didn't begrudge Carver his glory. I flopped into a swivel-chair and mentally planned where I'd position my desk, with my back in a far corner and a full view of the room. I lifted a phone. Not working, of course.

We had celebrated our embryonic deal by heading straight into town for a long, boozy lunch at a Dublin restaurant, typical, as I would learn, of the kind

Carver favoured – expensive, shit food served on thick linen tablecloths. We had lashed into the wine and I'd listened to him lashing into Ireland in general, and Dublin in particular. He repeated his rant about the cowardice of the Dublin media, which had signally failed to expose the corrupt heart of the place. I used that as a cue to steer the conversation onto his background, but extracted only one significant fact: that he'd quit school at the age of fourteen. He had educated himself, he claimed, by reading non-stop, always getting ribbed by the other lads in some god-awful workplace for bringing a newspaper to digest over lunch. That's why the DIY sensibility of punk had spoken to him, when it finally came along. The fierce intelligence of the gutter, the need to stand up and scream.

Looking back, it was this aspect of Kevin Carver that awoke in me something other than a mercenary desire to further my own career. Yes, I would stand to gain if my gut instinct about his presenter potential proved correct. But I also felt that there was more to him than the mouthy little motherfucker I'd seen on the radio. Of subjects he didn't care for he had less than the barest knowledge. Fiction, fine art, foreign languages, the classics, the sciences all fell into that category. However, when it came to politics, power, and, most of all, people, he was like a walking encyclopaedia. He read mainly biographies, he said. The global affairs of his lifetime he could recount in vivid detail. He instinctively saw the connections between things, how societies worked, and how human beings clawed their way round inside them.

Describing Ireland's élite, he deployed his talent for finely observed insult, honed by years of carrying chips on both shoulders. We were going to expose the Big Boys, he said. What he wanted more than anything was to humiliate the Irish establishment. A good journalist, he said, was always diametrically opposed to those in power, no matter who they were. We would suck up to nobody. Instead, we'd get a good show up and running, and soon everybody would be sucking up to us.

All this rebel talk was music to my young ears. Carver burned with the self-belief of a Hibernian Hitler, and by the time we finished our third bottle of Margaux, I'd mentally appointed myself his Joseph Goebbels. Of course, I wasn't old enough to stand back and see how he really viewed me. As a hard-nosed young stormtrooper, probably, who knew enough to be of practical help, but not enough to question his primacy. Media slut and sly monkey.

The following morning, we reviewed our plans for world domination with a hangover, no phones, no computers, no cameras, no studio, and no staff.

'Those boys were quick off the mark,' I observed, as Carver scurried back into our office, having seen the press off the premises. 'Who handles the PR here? I'd like to meet them.'

'TV Ireland had nothing to do with this. I rang the papers from home; I invited them here myself. Are those fucking phones working yet?'

157

'No. Shouldn't we have waited for the station to issue a press release? I mean, neither of us has actually signed anything yet.'

'Fuck that,' he snapped, 'I handle my own publicity!' He waved a hand in the general direction of Dickie Vaughan's office. 'You'd be waiting a long time for this shower to get their act together. I wanted our news out before they had a chance to change their minds. Did you notice the way I named specific board members, said how happy they were about hiring us?'

'Yes.'

'Well, that puts them in the frame, see. They'll read their names in print tomorrow morning, linked to mine. Ropes them in, makes it harder for them to go back on anything. I had a pop at the opposition, too.'

'"Effete wankers stuck in ivory towers"? RTV will love you for that.'

'Fuck them! Lesson number one when you're embarking on a new venture: attack your enemy immediately, kick him in the balls! If you don't have an enemy, then make one! Create targets! New ventures need enemies, it's what defines them. *They* are mediocre, *we* are not! *They* are cowards, *we* are not! *They* are boring, *we* are interesting!'

'Two legs bad?'

'Eh?'

'Never mind.'

'Lesson number two. For the time being, I do all the talking to the press. Me, okay? It's not that I don't trust you; I have no ego. It's just that I know how to handle these people. I've been in the game a long time. Understood?' His eyes glinted, anticipating dissent. Prime weapons, lock and load.

I shrugged. 'You're the presenter. It's in both our interests to get your name out there as much as possible.'

'Good.' He nodded, satisfied. 'In that case, you won't mind that I told them our programme would be called *The Kevin Carver Show*. They asked me, and it was the first name that came into my head.'

'Of course it was.' He glanced up sharply, but I kept a straight face.

'This fucking place.' He frowned and slapped a telephone, to change the subject from his non-existent ego. I popped out my mobile. He was far too a-technical to carry one himself.

'I'll ring you a taxi, you go get some rest, and I'll start badgering Dickie for things like phones that work. And computers. And people ...'

'Like a good producer,' he leered. 'Oh, by the way, I've resigned from *The Sunday Reporter*. I gave them a bit of a kicking, too, just before you arrived.'

'You don't hang about, do you?'

'Fuck them. I don't need them any more. A new venture needs enemies.'

'Well, at least we have plenty of something ...'

The next month was a nightmare. A complete, balls-out, full-blown nightmare. We were right about Dickie Vaughan – the man *was* useless. He was actually worse than useless: he was downright dangerous, because, like most petty bureaucrats, he poured all his energy into pretending to get things done, rather than actually doing them. It became quickly evident that Dickie couldn't have run a sweet shop, let alone a TV station. He used a wide battery of ploys to cover his fat arse, principally the old 'coat and keys' technique. This is a trick whereby you leave your office door open, hang a jacket over the back of your chair, put a spare set of car- keys by your phone, and switch off your mobile. Anyone who comes looking for you automatically assumes that you're in an important meeting elsewhere in the building, whereas, chances are, you're relaxing on a far-off golf course. Another Dickie trick, on the rare days when he could be found, was to agree to a number of important measures in one meeting, then completely 'forget' about them in the next. However, Dickie's most irritating manoeuvre was what I came to call his 'helicopter view', in honour of our first encounter. When the going got tough and I had to get pushy about undelivered gear, unhired staff, or unpublished publicity, Dickie would hover off into a cloud of the densest psycho-babble, where it was impossible to follow. I became convinced that he spent his evenings poring over glib tomes of American management-speak, learning pat phrases, like:

'The company will have to take a considered perspective on that.'

'Responsibility is twenty-five per cent given and seventy-five per cent taken.'

'I'd like to park that suggestion.'

'We have to decide what we want from this situation and revert.'

Translated, all of the above mean only one thing – 'I haven't a fucking clue!'

The upshot was that Carver and I ended up doing everything ourselves. To staff our programme, I trawled the campuses and colleges, as the word was now out about TV Ireland around the established workplaces. And the word said that we hadn't got our shit together and probably wouldn't survive. So nobody in the game – nobody any good, anyway – was interested in coming over. Eventually, we recruited a couple of young researchers, Dervla and Elaine, and an assistant producer whom I vaguely knew from university, Kate. I pushed for her because I knew she was capable, quiet, and unlikely to pose a threat.

Charlotte the Charity Case landed in one morning after Carver had been out on the rip. She had big eyes, a big head, and a very small brain. As for Scally – well, Christ only knows where Carver dug up Scally. They were definitely not related, as Carver avoided his relatives at all costs. But he nonetheless loved Scally in the same way that mad old ladies dote on rat-like dogs. Scally hailed from a north-inner-city housing scheme, so perhaps Carver hired him because, unlike the rest of us, he wasn't a university-educated fuck.

Far from having to keep Dickie off Carver's back, as the latter had so emphatically demanded, it became impossible to keep Carver off Dickie's back. As transmission day inexorably approached, Carver became more and more hyper, to the point where the least computer glitch was an excuse to storm into Dickie's

office, screaming, 'You cunt! You *cunt*! You *cunt*!!'
Mind you, whenever I got to the point of no progress
with Dickie on any given matter, which was
frequently, all I had to do was casually mention his
stonewalling in front of Carver and that proved just as
effective as pointing a rocket launcher at the little
tosspot's door.

Then, with about a fortnight to go, we finally had
a couple of cameras and the gallery working, most of
the time. The chippies were nowhere close to building
our set – they were still hammering away at a roofless
wooden box in a far corner of the studio where the
news bulletins would emanate from. But the day
arrived when I finally got to stick a chest mike on
Carver's lapel and a camera on his face, and we
started doing screen tests. And he was shit. Not just a
bit shit, not even worryingly shit, but extremely
fucking shit.

The camera was not kind to him. His eyes
disappeared into the chipped skin of his face, sunk
down the stress-chiselled holes of his sockets, buried
beneath that jutting mound of brow-bone and hair.
Most people appear to gain weight about the face and
body when viewed through a broadcast camera.
Instead, Carver looked even smaller. He resembled an
unwrapped Egyptian mummy propped up in a chair.
Presenting television is no easy task – I'd say maybe
about one in a thousand people could actually do it,
and less than one in ten thousand could do it well.

This happens a lot in the industry. Even the most
experienced radio presenters are prone to discover,

when they get their big TV break, that they look like a rabbit caught in headlamps. Carver looked like a lizard caught in a steel snare. For someone who enjoyed such enormous command of his facial expressions off-camera, he could only summon an unconvincing, vaguely disturbing demeanour when the red light went on. He glared at the autocue as if it had just challenged him to a fight. He couldn't smile, and when he forced himself to do so, he looked horrible.

His speech came out all stumbly, like a drunken Neanderthal reciting The Lord's Prayer. I refused to show our demo tapes to the rest of the team, much less to Dickie and no way in hell to the board. I didn't dare. Dickie, or 'Duster', as the sound-ops had quickly christened him, made frequent sorties into the studio to try to peek at the monitors when we were piloting. But I had asked the crew to create a technical hitch every time Duster hove into view, and they happily obliged. Rule number one about being a producer anywhere, be it radio, film, or TV, is always, always make friends with the people who operate your equipment. That way, you will reap untold rewards. Act the prick, and they will act the prick straight back. That's crew for you.

After yet another disastrous effort, Carver and I would stand together in the gallery, staring at the shrivelled abortion stuttering out of the screen, and hang our heads. Perhaps as a consequence of my early enthusiasm, I regarded his apparent lack of talent as totally my responsibility, and, as nothing could possibly be Carver's fault, so did he. My gut instinct about his presenter potential seemed dreadfully misplaced. Furthermore, with impeccable timing, his court case was listed for hearing the week we went to air. Gradually, Carver's mind seemed to reject the unmitigated chaos of TV Ireland, embracing instead the endless preparatory susurrations of a murder of barristers.

'I don't know what you're gonna do with me, Lee,' he would sigh, and stumble off to yet another legal meeting. I didn't know what I was going to do with him either. In a matter of weeks, I'd gone from playing second fiddle to a joyously power-hungry punk dictator, to propping up a tired old ghost.

# 12

## SKERRIES

I drove out of Dublin in the dark. Rain pelted off the windscreen. Our happy Monday three weeks previously, when the TV Ireland board had so miraculously teetered our way, now seemed like a distant joke. I felt sick. Sick with fear and sick with anger that the hated Duster would soon be proven right. We weren't up to it. I had been practically living in the TV Ireland building, going home only to pass out with fatigue. Then, one evening, with ten days to go to air, I unlocked my office drawer, retrieved the single demo tape that I hadn't wiped in disgust, copied it onto VHS, and headed for Skerries, a fishing village turned overspill town, twelve miles up the coast. When I arrived, I bought a bottle of Powers from a pub in the main street, the kind of place where the women look you over once and the men look you over until you leave.

A mile further north, I pulled into the drive of a nondescript seaside chalet. The lights were out, so I waited. The rain softened into that misty, all-pervasive stuff that will soak you more thoroughly than a winter storm. I never learned to speak Irish, but I only regret this when I study the rain. I fancy that the Irish language must have fifty-seven different words for 'rain', in the same way that Inuit has for 'snow', depending on the type of snow. If, in reality, this is not the case, then I'm really glad I've never bothered to learn Irish. I sat in my battered hatchback, smoked several cigarettes, and tried to imagine what it must be like living in Skerries. I failed.

I couldn't have been asleep for long, because when I heard a car door slam behind me, my mouth had not yet gone totally dry. The car drove off, and footsteps crunched up the drive. I checked my eyes in the mirror (red, not good) and fired up a fag, before he did exactly what I knew he'd do – fumble with the passenger door, tug it open, peer in at me, and exclaim, 'Well, hello! How the hell are *you*? What brings you all the way out *here*?'

'Hello, Maurice.' I can't remember when I last called him 'Dad'.

I insisted that I wanted my whiskey hot, because I knew he'd not only insist on making them, but that he'd also join me, instead of wading into the stuff neat. Hot whiskey made him mellow; neat made him mad.

'I've no lemon, though,' he called from the tiny kitchen.

'Of course you haven't,' I called back.

My father's living-room resembled a rat's nest at the bottom of an arms dump. Ragged piles of books and newspapers occupied most of the floor, and on top of each mound lay the oily guts of either a broken-down camera or a gun. Or a mixture of both, it was hard to tell. Super-8s, SLRs, shotguns, instamatics, automatics, rifles, Brownies, Brownings – Maurice had loved his shooting in more ways than one. That's the upper classes for you. Military pedigree – guns were part of the furniture – and he'd been a champion shot as a teenager. The cameras had come later, along with hippydom and girls. Probably wanted to be David Bailey, or in his case, Lord Snowdon. Anglo-Irish family, on their last financial legs. Decades later, when the drink finally won, Maurice had fallen into the habit of taking his beloved instruments to pieces to clean them, but then leaving them disassembled, as if – a bit like his life – he'd forgotten how to put everything back together again.

The house stank of unwashed laundry, laced with man-sweat and whiskey. A middle scale of scent emanated from the musk of old newspapers, then, above it all, drifted the smell I best remembered, a thin descant of sweet mechanical oil.

Suddenly, I was a child, sitting at the kitchen table of the rectory, watching my father, home on a rare visit, strip and clean his man-toys. First, he would break down his guns, rub the glistening black jigsaw pieces with a rag, rebuild them carefully, and lock them in a strongbox at the back of the boot-room.

Then – the part I loved best – he would get me to spread a little butter on his palms. I laughed every time we did this, and he'd tell me there was nothing better for shifting oil. He'd wash his buttery hands with Fairy liquid, dry them for what seemed ages, then hoist his shoulder-mounted camera onto the table. He'd peel away the plastic rain cover and probe the innards with a watchmaker's screwdriver, abnormally quiet, focused, and happy, barely sipping from a balloon-glass of claret at his elbow. He had long sideburns, and he always wore the same blue suede cowboy jacket, with patches of black sweat below the armpits. My father never allowed my two older brothers to witness this ritual – only I was given the signal honour. If he was in a really good mood, he'd let me stand the shotgun cartridges in a row like soldiers, but mostly I knew just to shut up and watch.

At the time, I pretended not to care about my father leaving my mother – it turned out to be the biggest kindness he ever paid her. She eventually moved on and married the kind of man she should have married in the first place. Neither did I begrudge him his drinking – children can't tell the difference between adults drunk or sober. My father's dissipation did not seriously impinge on my reality until I was fourteen, when we had to move from our rectory on the outskirts of south Dublin into the rectory lodge, then a series of my mother's friends' homes, and ultimately to a corporation flat in Clontarf. Leaving the big house was traumatic, but I'm afraid I blamed my mother as Maurice simply wasn't there, having finally bolted. From country estate, to council estate. But my mum was too decent to embitter me towards him and did not tell me until much later about Maurice drinking his inheritance, as well as everything we owned. Then, I was seriously pissed off.

Of course, my brothers already had that part worked out for themselves and hated his guts. After he left, because I was the only one who would speak to him, Maurice would occasionally send for me, to take me on shoots. That meant flying unaccompanied to Heathrow, magically met by a chauffeur with my name on a sign, and whisked off to Elstree, White City, or perhaps taken on location. And, once again, he would simply let me watch. I'd watch the actors in take after take. I'd watch the directors going slowly insane. I'd watch the crew, how they had their own private language and no-bullshit code. But most of all, I'd watch my father. How he concentrated, turned professional, and became the sober, omnipotent figure I adored. Movies, documentaries, concerts, studio shows, adverts, and, towards the end, corporate videos – it mattered not. To me, every shoot was just as glamorous as the last. Without a doubt, I'd have become a cameraman myself, if only he'd waited a few more years to tutor me before succumbing to the booze.

Now, the wheel had come full circle. My mother had met and married a captain of industry, moved to his mansion in Wexford, and was living happily ever after. Whereas my father inhabited a shitty seaside chalet, knowing no happiness that couldn't be poured from a bottle. I hated seeing him, not because of the past, but because of the future. Or more precisely, because of a possible future. For here in Skerries, available for detailed, agonising inspection any time I cared to look, was a real-time, living mock-up of what awaited me if I fucked up in life. I was terrified of ending up like my father.

'As hot as hell, as sweet as sin, and as strong as a woman's love!' Cue another instant flashback of Maurice dressed in boots, jeans, and his blue suede jacket, handing hot whiskies around a wrap party in Richmond, in 1987. He always said that, whenever he made hot whiskeys. Cheesy, but usually enough to start some young actress giggling.

He handed me my drink, lowered himself into a greasy armchair, and asked about my brothers. But I already had Carver's tape playing on his video and wordlessly sloshed my steaming glass towards the screen.

'Hmm. What have you got *there*?' He took a pair of half-moon glasses from a breast pocket and stared down them towards the TV. 'Oh, *that* little shit! You're not working with *him* now, are you? Have to say, never liked him. Guttersnipe. Mouth. Knows the price of everything and the value of nothing!'

'He's not that bad.'

'Yes, he is!'

'No, I mean, as a person. He's all right, trust me, I know him.'

'You are young and foolish, Lee. But everyone is entitled to make their own mistakes. Our mistakes define our lives. This I know, believe me. But your new friend, his mistake is going near a camera. Big mistake.'

'Come on, I can see that! What can I *do* about it, though?'

'Get a new presenter,' he frowned.

I put my face in my hands and left it there for a minute. I'd rather have wet my pants than cry in front of my father. He must have smelled my tired desperation, because when eventually I looked back up, he was fidgeting with the remote.

'Well, all right, then. Against my better judgement ...'

I lit a fag. He looked at me, desirous. 'I say, you don't have any, ah ...' and he coughed. I nodded and got busy with the skins. For the next five minutes, he wound through the tape. Once again, I had that curious sensation of slipping back in time, watching my focused, visually expert father, as he nursed some neophyte director through a tricky outdoor scene on the Cob at Lyme Regis. Kevin Carver wibbled his head from side to side, his slit mouth opening and closing like a letterbox flapping in a gale. Finally, the tape paused on a pallid, frightening close-up. Freeze-frame.

'Okay.' He turned and glared down his half-moon glasses, the way he used to do at my brothers after they stopped him from using his fists. His eyes were still a piercing emerald green, but gone milky round the edges. Drink had destroyed the very asset by which he made his living, as well as rendering him intolerably canaptious on set. I finished the two spliffs I'd started, lit them, handed one over, then sat up rapt, pen and notebook at the ready.

'Look at that.'

I pondered the monstrous vision, as wide-eyed and innocent as I could muster.

'First thing, the blackheads have to go.'

'*Blackheads?*' This incredulously spluttered in spite of my apt pupil act.

'Yes, *blackheads!*' I shut my mouth. No more interrupting, or all would be lost. 'Are you here to *learn*, or are you here to teach *me?*' I went wide-eyed again and got scribbling. 'His nose and his cheeks are covered in blackheads! They look like the fucking plague, beneath that cheap slap you've used! Got that, Lee?' Scribble. Exude childish respect.

'Now, if you value my advice, you'll get yourself a decent make-up artist. It'll cost, but they'll know how to tone down his nose, give him something resembling a pair of cheeks, smooth out the wrinkles around his eyes, put a bit of flesh on his mouth, and most of all, trim in those horrible eyebrows. He needs very light powder underneath the lower eyelids, to bring those rotten orbs out from the sockets. Small, very small touch of mascara on the upper lashes, just a touch, give them size.' Scribble. 'Ring him first thing in the morning, tell him to start using eyewash, twice a day, and maybe you'll see some whites by the end of the week. Teeth! Nothing you can do about the shape of those gravestones, but send him to the dentist for a good clean and polish; get rid of some of that charming brown. He'll look marginally less like the living dead when he tries to smile.

'Next – posture! Tell him not to sit bolt upright like that: he's too thin and he looks like he has a prick up his arse. Make him lean forward a bit, widens the shoulders and face. Give him a clipboard, something to hold, something that forces him to expand his elbows slightly.

'Chair! Get the smallest chair you can find, to make him look big. A chair with a back no higher than the bottom of his ribcage. On a high-backed chair, he looks like a corpse on a slab. You'll need arms on the chair, low arms. Again, a reason to lean forward. If that fails, get a pencil mike, put it on a table in front of him, and tell him he won't be heard if he can't get close to it. That'll pull him into the camera. You with me?' Nod. Scribble. 'Always, always, always make him wear a black jacket: that green check number is fucking repulsive, reflects up on his face, makes him look even worse! Black won't reflect. Black jacket, off-white shirt. Black trousers, needless to say. Get the fucker fitted for a few decent, roomy suits, nothing tight. No colours. Got that?' Yes, Daddy.

'All of the above, however, is wasted, if you don't get a decent lighting man in. Make them pay for one. He needs up-lighting, gentle, subtle, from two or three weak spotlights, positioned low, about ten feet in front of him. He won't be able to see beyond those lights, but he won't need to. They'll hammer out the down-shadows cast by his brow. With me?' Scribble.

'Next, one single spot at eye-level, back in the audience – keep a couple of seats empty to accommodate that. Put a warm filter on it, make the bastard look human. Then, from the overhead rig, a couple of decent white spots, one left, one right. Give him a bit of a glow. Background, dark. No lights behind him, never, never, never. Any distraction from the back, you'll start to lose him. Needs presence, at all costs! Put his guests close, right of shot, so he listens in profile. Tell him to cross his legs, sit sideways, and keep his hands still when listening. Moving hands make him look nervous.'

'How do I get him to look at the camera like he's not a mental patient?'

'He's scared of the camera. You'll probably find he's okay when he's not addressing it. He hates the autocue, alien device. Make him rehearse, without camera or autocue.'

'How?'

'You, Lee, you. You say you get on with him?' Nod. 'Then make him rehearse reading, with you standing at camera-distance. Write a basic script on a series of large, throwaway cards. Know how they used to do in theatre, those big, silly cue-cards?' Nod. 'Well, you stand there and hold them, throw as you go. Relax him, make him laugh, get him used to staring at one place, reading aloud. It's an artificial situation for anyone to be in, but it's not as intimidating as the full broadcast gear.' Nod. 'And tell him he needs to act at being himself.'

'What?'

'He needs to feel whatever he reads, let it show in his face. Needs to imagine he's in a pub, telling a story to his mates! If it's a sad story, look glum. Happy story, look happy. He has to imagine he's trying to impress someone, and he'll find it easier if he starts off doing it towards a real person, not a machine. One last thing.' Eyes wide. 'Tell him to read aloud at home, every spare minute he's got. Give him Kipling, give him Doctor Seuss, and tell him he has to read aloud for at least an hour a day. Give him *Mein Kampf*; he'll enjoy that, if he hasn't read it already. How's your mum?'

Here endeth the lesson. I stayed for another two hots, gave Maurice all my hash, then drove back into town, even though I shouldn't have been driving. But the only alternative was a night in my father's chalet, and that would have made me feel like I belonged.

'I still think you're making a mistake!' Maurice called from his doorway, as I reversed down the drive.

People used to ask me how I lasted so long with the Monkey Man, given his reputation for falling out with everyone he ever worked with. I would smile and say something smart-arsed about knowing where to get good coke in Dublin. But deep down, the truth was that Kevin Carver reminded me of someone I really looked up to when I was little.

# 13

## FALSE START

'Aaaaow! Aaaaoow! Nao! Get her off me! Make her stop! Aaaaow!'

A funky, middle-aged woman called Liz straddled the Monkey Man as he lay back, helpless, in a reclining chair. She had big hair shoved up in a messy pile that must have taken hours to perfect and wore black leg-warmers above her tiny feet. She bent forwards into Carver's face, as if to kiss him, but instead held his nose between finger and thumb.

'My, my, some of these have been here all your life! Did your mummy never show you how to squeeze?'

Carver emitted a shriek, as Liz extracted yet another recalcitrant blackhead by force and wiped her thumb on a tissue. It was the Friday before launch; we had exactly a week to go. After my trip to see Maurice, without telling Carver, I'd phoned his legal team and informed them that their client was sick. Then, I'd locked him in an edit suite for nearly three solid days and forced him to read from cue cards as I stood ten feet away, as prescribed. The method had borne fruit almost immediately, as the fundamental absurdity of the tableau we presented caused us both to laugh, and so relax a bit. I pulled silly faces to try to corpse him, and he progressed quickly, in amused defiance. He was a fast learner, very human and likeable when in that mode. For his reading-aloud exercises, he chose Kavanagh.

Time may have caught up with us, but it had also caught up with Duster, who was having canaries. The big station launch was almost upon him. He was so lost that he merely nodded absent-mindedly when I told him I was hiring a whiz young lighting guy and Liz the make-up lady. They both worked in film, but did TV gigs on the side. I'd even nailed down an ex-BBC director called Colin to turn up one day a week to do our show. A tiny tingle in my tummy told me that maybe we weren't completely fucked, after all. I left Liz to her grisly task and wandered down the corridor, into the miraculously transformed studio.

Our set was simplicity itself: a low, circular platform with ruthlessly modern chairs and a coffee table procured from one of the many achingly trendy furniture boutiques that had begun springing up around Dublin. I stood and watched as Cathal, the new lighting guy, tried out different combinations of spotlight on Scally, who played stand-in for his master. Colin calmly ordered the cameras around from the gallery, to get a feel for the space. In front of the set, workmen screwed red plastic seats into a tiered audience stand. From a much smaller sky-blue set on the far side of the studio, a prolonged burst of male shouting, followed by female crying, indicated that the news team was also in rehearsals.

'Guests are here!' announced Charlotte, with the kind of slavering joy one associates with red setters.

Liz had done her work. Up close, Carver looked like an octogenarian male impersonator from a vaudeville stage, in his fairy dust and baggy new suit. But on camera, in front of the re-arranged lighting, he looked the business. A little bit of lippy goes a long way, even in this electronic age. As we plugged him up, he laughed and joked with the two guests, both C-list celebrity mates of his who'd come in as a favour to do the dry run. I turfed the news crew off their set and, after a moment's thought, called the rest of the production team over from the office to sit in the front row. We lit the 'On Air' signs, and I made a runner stand outside each of the studio doors, as you'd be amazed at the number of people in broadcasting who don't know what 'On Air' means. I got everyone settled, and then Colin counted us in. He kicked off with a high, wide-angled jib shot, which showed the set as a distant ball of white light, floating in the dark space of the studio. Then he swung in for a profile shot of Carver, still laughing and joking off-mike to the guests. The signature tune ended. Cut to Carver, and he was off, with a grin the size of Texas.

There must have been nearly twenty of us crammed into the gallery afterwards. Carver stood in the middle, loudly maintaining that he hated the sight and sound of himself, but nonetheless wearing a tiny smile. He kept asking for bits to be rewound and played over, staring intently at the monitors through his carefully groomed eyebrows. Scally sneaked off and reappeared plastered in make-up, wearing Carver's old green jacket. He flounced around the gallery, mimicking Carver's voice, and we laughed, Carver loudest of all.

'Fucking Teacher. Ya fuckin' did it, Teach. Ya fuckin' did it. Ya taught an old war-horse how to present.' He half-slapped, half-patted me on the cheek. I couldn't speak, I was so relieved. 'I have an announcement to make! Quiet, please! Scally, stop that prancing around, you dirty little pox! Everybody, shhh! I want to thank you all for your help ... I'd like to thank our director Colin. Colin's from the BBC, and therefore a professional, so I'm obliged to ask you, Colin, what the *fuck* are you doing in a place like TV Ireland?' Cue laughter. 'I'd like to thank Liz, a very brave lady, who performs all kinds of services that I never knew existed, but which I certainly intend to avail of again ...' Cue jeer. 'Liz and Colin have achieved the impossible, which is to make me look human ...' Cue cheer. 'I'd like to thank the crew, and I'd like to thank my team, who should be at their desks making sure that next week's show will have guests on it ...' Cue boo. 'But most of all, I want to thank my producer, without whom I'd be fucked. Well done,

Teach. You're a fucking star.' Cue applause. I stared at the floor and tried not to blush. I failed. I muttered something about him being the star, but it got lost. So I was Teach, now, and Teach I would remain for the next six years.

'I'd also like to announce that I'm going out! I'm taking my team into town for a drink and you're *all* welcome to join us!' Cue cheer. Before we left, I couriered a VHS copy of the dry run out to the Chairman's home, with a note expressing the humble hope that we were on the path towards justifying his confidence and support. Rope them in. I put a second copy into an A4 envelope, without a note, and stuck it to Duster's office door with a dirty great piece of gaffer tape.

That night on the town was my first experience of a particular itinerary that would be retraced many times over the next half-decade. Carver had a formula for piss-ups, which I suspect dated back to the 1970s, when tireless club-hopping was doubtless considered the height of cool. His first port of call was usually The Horseshoe Bar, in the bowels of The Shelbourne Hotel, a Dublin institution where the benevolence of the staff was matched only by the malevolence of the clientele. Carver would greet rings around him, insist on buying precisely two drinks, then chide us back out the revolving door with the urgent refrain of 'I want to sing! I want to sing!' He would then insist on visiting Verdana, where he would murder a few tunes on their crappy piano, whether we wanted to listen to him or not. This kind of behaviour, I suppose, must have been his generation's form of karaoke. After that, things could messy, depending on the amount of champagne consumed. Carver would drag us to four nightclubs in succession, in descending order of seediness. The Terrapin Club, Rosalito's, The Teahouse, then Dolce Vita, always in that order.

Girls and boys would start to do what girls and boys do when they're drunk – talk meaningful shite and develop sudden, unexpected crushes on one another. But God help anyone who tried to pair off, or escape. Like some demented wrangler, Carver would gallop around, herding his entourage this way and that, yelping orders and starting arguments. Then, he'd wander off to dance like a freak, returning at regular intervals to reassert his primacy.

In Ireland, alcohol is the lubricant upon which the engine of society functions. It's practically impossible to achieve anything in this country unless you're a fairly persistent, accomplished drinker. Daytime meetings are rarely taken seriously by any of the parties involved, as sober talk is, by mutual consent, not a medium to be trusted. Real business is done in the evenings, in the pubs, hotels, and restaurants. This is how Irish people weigh one another up; how they decide who is worth taking seriously and who to fob off, with flattery and a shower of friendly smiles. Drink gets things done – slowly, erratically, but according to the unwritten rules. And in those early days of *The Kevin Carver Show*, booze brought our team together and allowed us to gel, in a miasma of ambition-based amity.

The launch of TV Ireland was a wonderful farce. Duster had demanded all hands on deck, although I wouldn't have missed it for the world. We arrived at the station that Monday evening to find that he'd cheated over the weekend. At huge expense, Duster had hired in one of those dinky event-management companies that were springing up in Dublin at an even faster rate than the trendy furniture shops. The place was crawling with out-of-work actors dressed as Celtic warriors with wigs, shields, and spears. Irish dancers leapt, masked creatures cavorted, and half-naked women on stilts threw glitter confetti over everything that moved. About seven hundred guests milled around the studio floor, and what seemed like seven hundred more mobbed the free bar, shouting and waving at the harried staff. In the middle of it all, an enormous, opaque plastic ball stood on a raised dais, surrounded by coloured spotlights.

'What is that for?' I asked Duster, who was tailing the board members around through the deafening madness, sweat pouring from beneath his Elvis hairdo. I had a feeling I already knew.

'That, Lee, is a key factor in the programme I have lined up for this evening. You see, presentation is extremely important in television, so I am going to literally *present* our presenters to the public, in the form of a presentation!' And he proudly patted the outsized Perspex globe.

'Very, uh ... very *Spinal Tap*, Dus ... eh, Dickie.'

'What?'

'It's a very *original prop*. Like nothing anyone's ever seen.'

Duster nodded beatifically. 'That's the idea!' With no small amount of relish, I went off to find Carver.

'I am NOT getting in that thing! What do they think I am, some kind of fucking *reptile*?' Just as he uttered those words, the Chairman of the Board hove into view, with several directors in tow and a phalanx of hacks.

'Lee, how *are* you?' I gave him my capable smile, as he put his arm around Carver's shoulder. 'Ladies and gentlemen of the press, I know that, as one of your own, Kevin Carver needs no introduction, but I *would* like to say that I have had the privilege of previewing his pilot show, and I firmly believe that his new programme, due on air this coming Friday, will sum up everything that TV Ireland stands for! These are exciting times, for Ireland, and for us!' Rope them in.

And with that, Carver was swept off towards the waiting plastic ball. He cast his eyes back at me in an appeal for rescue, but all I could do was shrug, before the hacks engulfed him with questions.

*I'll handle the press, Lee! I have no ego! It's just that I know how to deal with these people!* Tee-fucking-hee.

I watched the rest on TV, with my feet up in our production office, as the cameras went live and the station came on air. A couple of techies, looking for a safe place to skin up, crept in to join me. I took a deep drag of spliff and felt my head lifting, as a pre-recorded TV Ireland trailer replaced the test signal. Then they went live to the studio and the big plastic ball, practically invisible behind a cloud of dry ice and flashing blue strobe lights, surrounded by a throng of waiting luminaries. There was a large crash of tribal-type drumming, followed by wild skirls of souped-up traditional music, as the ball split open, spitting out a thick puff of smoke. Out stumbled a flock of plainly distressed newsreader dolly-birds, followed by a few coughing, lumbering sports hacks, like beasts climbing out of a bog. Then, arms waving wildly, eyes streaming, out dashed Kevin Carver. He collided with Duster, who gasped and went down. Carver stood at the bottom of the ramp, rubbing his eyes. Then came the audible snarl, above the music and the applause, 'Take *that*, you little *fuck*!'

The camera angle cut my presenter off at the waist, but it seemed to me that he kicked Dickie Vaughan, Head of Programmes, TV Ireland, as the man lay helpless on the ground.

# 14

UP

Technically, our first show was a bit of a mess. A taped insert jammed, and Carver addressed the wrong camera twice. I knew that he wasn't exactly going to air a polished professional, so we'd agreed to try humorous self-deprecation in the face of any mistakes, which at least has the effect of getting the audience on your side. It worked for the 150-odd crowd we had in studio, and Carver quickly realised that a bit of well-judged banter towards the audience made him look modest, inclusive, witty, and fallible – all traits which the Irish adore. 'Ah, sure he's one of us,' I heard a man seated close to the edge of the stand remark, as I ushered a guest in. Far from being 'one of us', Carver's greatest talent, as it emerged, would be his ability to play the role of the ordinary man better than any ordinary man possibly could have. His native passionate intensity began to come across on camera, allowing him to deliver amusement, outrage, perplexity, sorrow – every sentiment writ large across that craggy face – as the situation demanded. He learned to act at being himself.

Certainly, his nascent acting ability proved useful, because Carver had lost his legal action less than forty-eight hours before that first show. His entire case had been relying, it emerged, on the testimony of a single witness called Milton McMahon. This would have supported Carver's claim to joint authorship of the contested work, a previously obscure but now commercially successful song called 'All Politicians Are Bastards'.

But Milton didn't show. I sat and watched from the public gallery as a press officer called Martin Pelham took the stand to read a brief statement on behalf of his employer's company, Synsystems International. Mr McMahon, the chairman of Synsystems, was a software publisher with dual Irish/French citizenship and business interests worldwide. Mr McMahon had indeed once owned the small, independent record label to which the defunct act, Carver and the Nutters, had been signed, from 1978 to 1981. He had sold the label with all rights and back catalogue in 1985, and it had subsequently been dissolved by the buyers, a San Francisco-based investment company.

Pelham apologised to the court for Mr McMahon's absence, but, four days previously, during a sales visit to China, Mr McMahon had been involved in a serious car accident and lay in a critical condition in a regional hospital some two hundred miles east of Beijing. Synsystems itself was experiencing a lot of difficulty getting in touch with the hospital and was deeply concerned as a result. The company had not been able to speak directly to Mr McMahon, about this, or indeed any other subject. Beyond that, Pelham regretted that he had no information useful to the court, as both Mr Carver's legal team and Mr McMahon himself had assumed his availability on the day.

At that, the barrister representing the O'Gormans had stood up and declared that his clients had no case to answer. The O'Gormans were not present in court either, as they had been living in London for the past fifteen years and were in the process of moving to New York, where they intended to resume their musical careers.

The judge, an elderly cove more used to doling out traffic fines than dealing with complex copyright issues, had scratched his head and ruled that since the O'Gormans were headed for America, the contested work had been re-issued by a US record label, and the rights now belonged to another US company, any further legal action would have to be brought in that jurisdiction. Each side to pay their own costs. Case closed, in plenty of time for lunch. Incandescent with rage, Carver had cornered Marty Pelham in the corridor outside the courtroom and covered him with abuse.

The story earned about sixty seconds on the main evening news. Carver, in full flow, gave a simmering interview on the steps of the Four Courts, proclaiming the justness of his cause and his undying belief that, in spite of his set-back, all politicians were, more than ever, bastards. Anyone who agreed with that statement was welcome to tune in to TV Ireland at nine o'clock on Friday night, where this and other controversial topics would be aired in a new chat show that did not tolerate the kind of bullshit that had happened in this courtroom today ...

Foolish Duster took this public stance literally and made the enormous error, the following morning, of calling Carver and me into his office to warn us against using TV Ireland to mount an attack on the ruling, which theoretically could have resulted in the station being done for contempt. Instead, Carver mounted a savage attack on Duster, calling him 'a fuck-dog, a wanker, a poser', and worst of all, 'a fucking child'. I sat there and grinned inwardly as Carver once again vented his not inconsiderable frustration, verbally tearing the hapless Duster to shreds. From that day onwards, whenever Duster wanted to check the content of our show, he did so surreptitiously with me, and never in Carver's presence.

The publicity did us no harm at all. From an audience point of view, it was perfect timing. Carver had been canny enough to grasp his only dividend – 'Hey, if you hate politicians and judges, then watch *The Kevin Carver Show*.' Still, as the big night inexorably approached, he sat in his dressing-room with his head in his hands, mourning the money that Milton's absence had cost him.

'It hurts, Teach, but I gotta forget it!' Dripping sympathy, I had agreed. 'It's a lotta dough, but even if I won, it would still cost me thousands to chase those bastards through the States. The game's not worth the candle. We have work to do! The show must go on!' Full of admiration, I had agreed some more.

The critics predicted a short and ignominious life for the station, as they reacted badly to TV Ireland's botched launch and bargain-basement schedule. Duster hadn't been joking about his imported output of soaps and shit films. The TV Ireland news, initially the only strand apart from ours to be made on the premises, was a shambles. One paper snootily forecast 'six episodes, at the most' for our show, before it even started. The state broadcaster, RTV, had been on air for forty years, it opined. How could an upstart hope to match the overwhelming, unshakeable might of this venerable institution?

The answer, of course, was that we never intended to match RTV, merely to undermine it. In his pre-launch press interviews, a fired-up Carver set about this task with all the black magic at his command, dropping razor-sharp insults about RTV's audience. 'The tea-and-buns brigade', he called them. We would be part of the new Ireland, whereas RTV was en-tombed in the old. Things would have to change. We were change. 'The people' wanted change. Therefore they wanted us. We were the armchair revolution, baby, and the armchair was Ikea.

For his first guest, we deliberately booked some up-and-coming Dublin singer-songwriter. The lad played a number, then Carver joked with him to be sure to write his name after all his songs. Then he made a crack about the amount of junk-mail he was getting from solicitors, looking for an easy gig. The studio audience laughed, and for every one of them, there were at least a thousand more out there in punter-land, laughing along with them. I could smell it.

Our second item was a nice little story I'd dug up, aimed squarely at the yuppie audience. Our guest – young, handsome, well-spoken – had been working the night-shift for a major Internet provider, policing their chat-rooms, weeding out obscene stuff, keeping an eye open for kiddie porn. One night, he'd come across a message posted by a woman who said she was about to commit suicide, with sleeping tablets. This sort of stuff crops up in chat-rooms all the time, mostly it's bollocks. But an hour later, she'd come online again, to say goodbye, cruel world. She'd taken the tablets. Whatever it was, our guy sensed something. So he'd checked her customer information and rung her home number. She had answered, sounding awful. Our guy called the cops, who broke into her house in Athlone and rushed her to hospital with less than an hour to spare. When he'd told his boss the story the following morning, expecting a medal, instead he was sacked on the spot. His crime? Disclosing customer information to an outside agency! When he argued that he'd saved a woman's life, his boss said he shouldn't have interfered.

*The Kevin Carver Show* got a sweet hit out of having the hero in studio, sitting alongside the woman he'd saved. Carver listened intently, played them well, then let loose an impressive volley of tart condemnation at the company in question, which had refused to come on and answer questions. He urged people to cancel their accounts. Within minutes, I had the company's regional manager on, screaming blue murder. I offered him the chance to go on air, phone quality, and foolishly, he accepted. Carver chewed him to pieces before dismissing him with sulphurous contempt. Bull's-eye. There's only one thing better than heaping abuse on people, and that is when you provoke them into reacting to it.

I had posted my father a generous lump of hash to thank him for his help, stashed inside a hollowed-out Jeffrey Archer novel. I included tickets for our first night, knowing full well that he wouldn't come. Maurice never did come to see *The Kevin Carver Show*, and somehow, over the next six years, I never quite found the time to drive back out to Skerries, to thank him in person.

Our first reviews were mixed, with one or two commentators prepared to be grudgingly favourable towards us as something, at least, a bit different. But the following week, they skinned us alive. We did an hour with a leading IRA man. At the time, the Northern Ireland peace negotiations were hanging in the balance, and this was a key IRA negotiator. We not only gave him lots of space, but Carver was also polite towards him; friendly, even, and treated him with respect. This was not the done thing, in any medium, at that time. We got our guest talking about his family, about his private habits, about the fact that he made excellent meatballs – and the press made a meatball out of us. There was a torrent of opprobrium, we were accused of sucking up to terrorism, and anyone in the country who hadn't already heard of us knew exactly where to find us after that. Duster practically had a nervous breakdown. We told him to get knotted. As it happened, we called that one exactly right. The peace process, imperfect though it was, subsequently came together in a shambolic sort of way. Yet another feather in the cap of boom Ireland. They still shot each other dead up north, but nowhere near as often, and many former Irish terrorists went on to become media darlings. Of course, in a few years, because of events elsewhere, terrorism was to become deeply unfashionable again.

The late nineties was also the period in Ireland when the rot and corruption of the previous three decades erupted to the surface. For so long, the country had been run like a banana republic, only without the bananas. Then the boom kicked in and there were way too many hard-assed US companies coming over to do business for the Irish to go on being so blatantly Irish. Amusingly, the lid flew off the pot when a certain big Dublin businessman misjudged the strength of American cocaine, during a trip to Florida. More accustomed to the weak, cut-down snort that had begun to trickle into the old country, the poor guy wound up on a very high hotel balcony with a bad case of the heebie-jeebies. He was arrested and then ousted from the family concern back home. The ensuing internecine fight tossed up allegations of payments to politicians, and that was that. Thirty years of sleazy silence had finally been broken. The cracks in the ice spread fast and soon the whole surface began to cave in. There were tribunals, inquiries, and inquiries into inquiries, as public figure after public figure was sucked into the growing mess.

Again, the timing couldn't have been better for us. This new Ireland was going to be a clean, high-minded place where things were done properly – or so the emerging yuppie class pretended to believe. Carver milked the public outrage, demanding all shades of prison and punishment for anyone splattered by the spreading fountain of shit. We stuck billboards up around the country, with a picture of Carver looking stern and the strapline, *Didn't I warn you about politicians?* We became the campaigning programme, the place where you went when you had a grievance, when the system let you down. We had credibility in the game. We didn't tolerate bullshit, even when it might have been better to have done so.

For example, when Lady Di died, Ireland went into a state of sugary, self-indulgent mourning that precisely matched the mood in good old England. You couldn't book a flight from Dublin to London, such was the volume of tragedy-struck traffic heading over for the funeral. I couldn't fucking believe it: what a farce! I remember Carver and me watching the non-stop news coverage in our office, shaking our heads at the flood of lachrymose, sanctimonious nonsense.

Anguish overload, and nobody was saying 'fuck this shit'. So we went on air that week and showed archive footage from 1972, when angry mobs had set fire to the British embassy in Dublin in the wake of Bloody Sunday. Then we cut to pictures of the respectful queues outside the modern consular building, the caught-in-the-moment crowds surrendering flowers and sorry signatures in the glorious sunshine. A candle in our wind. And we asked a lively panel whether this, for a republic like Ireland, represented progress. Don't get me wrong, we weren't anti-English. Hey – some of my best friends are English. We just didn't see what the fuss was all about. The place went mad. We received threatening phone calls, turds sent in the post, how dare we desecrate the memory of the Queen of all our Hearts, sure wasn't she a saint and a martyr, deserving of divine respect and rivers of hot Irish tears?

As well as stirring the shit, we booked all the youngest bands, the best comedy acts, and embraced, with open arms, the new business class. Right was on our side – Left just wasn't fashionable. DIY wealth was the credo, and, if you were a Celtic Tiger cub, we wanted you on. Success, literally, helped breed success. New Irish boys and girls were funny, dirty, had money, and took themselves very seriously indeed. We held a shining mirror up to their eager little faces.

In late 1999, we landed a minor exclusive, a television interview with Ireland's most elusive tech-sector millionaire, the chairman of the now publicly quoted Synsystems International plc, one Milton McMahon. A combination of massive government contracts and foreign licensing had pushed Synsystems into the major league. Every business journalist in the country held Milton up as a symbol of the new economy. His personal fortune was estimated in excess of fifty million, his cachet only enhanced by his aversion to personal publicity. However, as a one-off favour, Milton came on the show to participate in a debate about the Millennium Bug, which Carver was convinced would spell the end of civilisation. Typically indiscreet, Carver had kicked off the interview by recounting the story of his court case, announcing that he 'forgave' Milton for costing him 'a bloody fortune'.

I personally made the arrangements for Milton's appearance, liaising with Marty Pelham, who had thereafter stayed in the background, well out of Carver's way. I got on well with Milton, and, by the time we had navigated the green room, The Terrapin Club, The Teahouse and Dolce Vita, our friendship was cemented. I liked him because he seemed to have a wide streak of decency running through him. I think he liked me because I wasn't deferential towards Carver.

It took a while, but as our audience grew, the more generous the critics became with their praise, which is always the way. We never managed to equal the RTV audience for size, but all their viewers were over forty-five, which meant, in boom Ireland, that they were over, period. The young professionals watched us, and for advertisers, youth is the honey-pot. Cars, property, financial services – the country was awash with cash, and what's the point in having money if you can't use it to run up massive debts? Sure, you can always earn more.

It's no exaggeration to say that our show saved TV Ireland. In terms of revenue, it was hugely valuable. In terms of profile, it was priceless. For the first few years, it was the only one of their programmes that generated either income or headlines. We were all they had, big-time. Apart from large salaries, we demanded something valuable in return – the right to be left alone. Opinions, as we all know, are like arseholes. Everybody's got at least one. In the media, there are two distinct classes of people – those who have no choice but to act upon the opinions of a wide range of arseholes, and those who don't. With the shit-soaked mezzanine of local radio now far beneath me, I only had to listen to one person's opinion. And Carver listened exclusively to mine. When we agreed with one another, which was most of the time, we were fine. When we disagreed, we'd thrash out our differences in private, usually in the empty studio, away from the team. Twenty minutes later it would all be over, forgotten. We'd be friends again, co-conspirators, ready to take over the world. Disagreements, however, were few and far between. I respected his judgement, and he always asked for mine. We were, after all, making the kind of programme we both wanted to watch. His show. My show. Our show.

Our status as an independent republic within TV Ireland kept the job-creationists at bay. A job-creationist is someone who spends their working life pestering other people who have real work to do. Duster was an archetypal model of job-creationism (indeed, most middle managers in any industry tend to fall into this category). As TV Ireland grew fat on our success, so did its complement of functionaries with no discernable function. Carver would scamper into the office, squealing, 'I've just met all these people with suits, in the corridor! They called me by my first name, and I don't know who they are! Who are they, these people?' Christ help any of 'these people' who strayed into our office. At best, they'd be greeted with a roomful of hostile stares. At worst, they'd catch Carver in one of his fits and a face-full of shrapnel, the like of which they'd never caught before. Star monkey, climbing up the tree.

Mercifully, we rarely saw Duster at all. He was too busy playing golf and driving around the country in his beloved yellow Beamer. It tells you everything you need to know about Duster, that a yellow BMW should be his idea of making a statement. He joined every crappy executive institute going and gave after-dinner speeches about the huge success he alone had masterminded at TV Ireland. The helicopter view. They were welcome to it. Everyone who mattered in the game knew the truth, and people laughed behind his back. One of the sales guys told us that Duster cheated at golf, during client ligs. That came as no surprise, I have to say.

Outside the building, we were always at work, too. In a town the size of Dublin, everyone knows what everyone else does before they're introduced. In media circles, we enjoyed a grudging respect (which is the best kind) for having created something new and risky out of nothing. We became automatic names on every guest list, access all areas. During all this time, I was careful to obey Carver's diktat about eschewing personal publicity. I refused to do profiles, never gave quotes, and had my photo published only once, when a glossy magazine wanted a cover of Carver and his 'team'.

However, every so often, he'd take us along to a press interview. He liked to vary the angle; indeed he needed to, because he never turned down a request to talk about himself. When he wanted to play clever monkey, he'd go alone. When he wanted to play danger monkey, he'd bring us. It made him look good, turning up with a pack of young lunatics. He'd arrange to meet a reporter in the evening, always in a hotel or restaurant, never in a pub. We would land in half-cut, and he'd introduce us as his 'marvellous, talented team, without whom there would be no show'. He even went through phases of introducing me as the person who had 'saved his career'. Then, having flattered us, he'd cover us with abuse, which we would gleefully return. That made him look even better, like a great guy who knew how to get it on with the kids. One bemused hack described the experience of meeting *The Kevin Carver Show* as 'akin to watching a pack of wild dogs, who fall on one another at a moment's notice'. That particularly pleased us, because in boom Ireland, it was fashionable to be seen as a smart, voracious creature by day, and as a filthy, rotten animal by night.

# 15

## LOVE YOUR LIFESTYLE

In 1998, I bought a good-sized flat down by the docks
and moved out of the half-wrecked house in Stoneybatter. I gave the keys of my battered hatchback to my
housemates, to show them that I hadn't changed. I
bought my first Alfa Romeo. Silver Alfas were
practically mandatory in pre-millennial Dublin for
young and thrusting types such myself. I parked my
new car underneath my new flat, behind electric
gates, in a space that cost two thousand pounds extra.

'You can always rent it out,' the estate agent
smiled, 'or sell it next year, at a profit. Many of the
tenants own several parking spaces: they're an easily-
managed investment.' In 2001, some commuter
bought one of those spaces for thirty grand. In 1981,
you could have bought an entire street in Dublin for
thirty fucking grand.

I sourced my furniture from the same achingly

trendy emporium that had supplied our set, and filled one of my bedrooms with imported urban clothing, which I flung across my varnished wooden floor. I bought a tall aluminium fridge and filled the freezer full of Stolichnaya vodka. It had an automatic ice machine, which is mankind's most useful invention ever, after the dishwasher. When one day someone invents a machine to automatically stack and un-stack dishwashers, the pinnacle of western civilisation will, in my opinion, have been reached. Somewhere along the line, I acquired the Creature; the perfect household pet that required no feeding, brushing, or worming, just lots of drugs. Someone to sit up all night popping pills and talking shite with, in exchange for a roof over her head. I fell into a routine.

My week always peaked on Friday, for obvious reasons. After every show, high on adrenaline and whatever else was going, Carver would muster his posse into town, bringing guests who were up for it. And plenty of them were. The late nineties saw an influx of celebrities into Ireland, attracted by our Celtic chumminess and the fact that we were temporarily trendy. It was probably inevitable, after so many centuries of being the least chic country on earth, that Ireland would one day be awarded international novelty status, for a short time at least. Doesn't the buzz always seek out the honey? Friday nights followed the Monkey Man itinerary, the set menu, the Grand Tour of media hangouts and VIP lounges. And how he loved dragging fresh celebrity meat along in his wake, to watch him perform some more.

Saturday daytime was for sleeping, preferably alone. I had decided in the early days of TV Ireland to adopt a non-shagging policy at work, an incredibly mature decision, I felt, for one of my tender years. I was probably the only person in Dublin, and almost certainly the only person in Dublin media, to make that conscious decision and stick to it. Let's just say I'd made a few bad calls during my time in local radio. You know what they say about shitting and eating. When you shag a colleague, there's no going back. Everyone knows, and each office affair erodes your position in the poisonous, gleeful mind of the collective. Plus, there's no escaping your lover, nowhere to hide, once the sex is over. In TV Ireland, everyone fucked everyone else, from management through to programming, from sales through to marketing, the latter notoriously available. Even the cleaners were sluts. I reckoned that by staying out of the ring of flesh, I could cement my authority and impart a bit of mystique. There was more than enough casual sex available elsewhere. And as for that someone special in my life – well, I already had someone special, and I saw enough of him at work. The last thing I needed was another emotional sinkhole in the evenings. Oddly enough, the other two station non-shaggers were Duster and Carver. Duster, because no matter how drunk, coked, or pilled-up they got at station parties, the staff still found him repulsive. Carver, because he was too fast and too wild, and everyone was scared of him. Certainly, it wasn't his ugliness, because celebrity has a knack of surmounting even the most shocking bad looks.

Professional duties endured, by five o'clock on a Saturday morning I was invariably in a champagne and cocaine mess, with blackout the only option. Hence, sleep, and lots of it. Saturday nights were different. Friday night was work, that was a given, but Saturday night was when I did what I pleased, with whomsoever pleased me. Ecstasy was my drug of choice. Cocaine, practically unknown in Ireland before the nineties, was everyone else's drug of choice, but most of it was cut-down crap. If you really knew where to look, you could sometimes land quality gear, but market demand grew so fast that most dealers just shrugged and reached for the baking soda.

So Saturday nights, I'd revert to type and stick with pills. If you have decent pills, you don't need anything else, except maybe hash. I'd hook up with the druggy circle that I diligently kept separate from work and we'd gather in someone's flat, usually mine. A few spliffs, then off to the bars along Camden Street. Never, ever Temple Bar, which is exclusively for langers and tourists. Then a nightclub; a proper dark, techie basement with decent DJs, not one of those alcopop knocking-shops for students, PR people, and other needy types. I like to watch on pills, not dance. Watch faces, bodies, skin. Watch all the pretty colours. Party afterwards, more pills, and at that point I'd usually select who I wanted to sleep with, or be selected. Choices could change at a moment's notice, but no one really cared. There was plenty to go around. One night, coming home from a particularly debauched beach party, I crashed the silver Alfa. The following morning, I ordered another.

Sundays, I'd go for a walk at Howth Head. I'd trudge over the summit, admiring the view. There's a lighthouse on Howth Head called The Bailey. I swore to myself that if I ever really made it, I'd buy a lighthouse and live in it. A lighthouse over west, on the Atlantic, beside the real sea. Sunday evening was for pints, spliffs, and maybe a diazepam or two. Carver always rang me Sunday night, to catch up on the weekend's gossip and match notes about Friday. How the show went, how the drinks went afterwards. Who went home with who. Who'd be in for a slagging when we re-convened.

Mondays, I was able to lie in, while most of my friends suffered post-weekend traumatic stress, crouched behind computers in airless offices with a bad case of the horrors. I'd rise about lunchtime and hit the bank, the dry-cleaners, or the beer. Do normal-person stuff. I almost never watched TV – my spare time was far too precious for that.

Tuesday, back to work. Into the office, bright and early, for a day of discussions with Carver, whilst we sorted through the thousand-and-one things we wanted to do on the show. We'd argue the toss, try to anticipate what that week's big story might be, and set about getting to it before the opposition. Wednesdays and Thursdays were spent making it happen, which usually involved staying late at the station, bashing the phones, and going for drinks afterwards. Carver rarely joined these blue-collar nights, which was dandy, because then I could listen to the others bitch and moan about him. The rest of the production team saw me as a benign lieutenant, as one who protected them from their generalissimo's fits of unreasonable spite. I was the go-between, the only person who could reason with Carver, the Assistant Head Keeper. For those first few seasons, I swear I even used to go to bed before midnight on a Thursday, to be fresh for the ensuing twenty-four hours of insanity.

Friday, then, was tension day, try-to-keep-the-monkey-sane day. A frantic build-up; fights, missing pieces, panics, rehearsals, last-minute decisions, guests schmoozed, then that weird sort of calm that descends about an hour before a live show, when everyone suddenly seems to accept their fate. Then, we'd do it. The big buzz, the moment you've all been waiting for. Sometimes we were good, sometimes we were bad, and sometimes we were brilliant.

Over the years, we didn't really change the look of the show that much, keeping the same back-to-basics, black-and-white visuals that we'd started off with. But over the years, Kevin Carver changed a great deal, learning to command the camera, to project himself. He proved particularly adept at lobbing verbal hand-grenades into a bunch of guests, getting a good fight started, then acting the arbiter, the voice of sanity in middle of the explosion he'd just created. Every so often, he would lose his temper, in that luxuriant, snarling manner I knew so well, and many viewers tuned in, week after week, hoping he would do so. Carver always gave the impression that anything could happen, that some fresh madness was just around the corner. Art imitating life.

'I can go nowhere, Teach, nowhere, but people come up to me and wanna talk about our show.' Carver assured me of this reassuring fact at least once a week, and in truth, when I was out with him in Dublin, horns beeped, men shouted from cars, and strange women sashayed up in nightclubs. All thanks to our show.

In the same way that Kevin Carver became an exaggerated version of himself during those last years of the century, so did Dublin. The early nineties had found the city shabby, eccentric, and with an aura of her best days long over – not unlike my presenter, when first we met. But money and glory bring their own irreversible mutations. In the case of Dublin, the city acquired hitherto-undreamed-of components, like a foreign population, obscene property prices, a work ethic, and sushi bars. The narrow streets of the centre, designed for horse and cart, became clogged with shiny German cars going nowhere slowly, as drastic roadworks for naff new office blocks and their concomitant fibre-optic cables erupted on every corner.

Overnight, the smoky little pubs, previously populated by smoky little men hunched over their copies of *The Racing Post*, just seemed to disappear, to be replaced by cavernous 'themed' establishments, thronged with thirsty teenagers and roaming packs of junior executives. I often wondered where the smoky little men went, after their pubs were 'themed'. And on the pub walls, holy pictures of Joyce, Behan,

Kavanagh, and O'Nolan gave way to graven images of foreign footballers and sulky rappers, the trans-cultural idols of the new drinking classes. Guinness, previously consumed at room temperature like a decent red wine, became colder than a penguin's backside, in an effort to wean the kiddies off their alcopops. It became casually possible to eat Cuban, North African, and Pacific Rim, in a city where sweet-and-sour chicken had previously occupied the outer limits of exotic cuisine.

Dublin turned into something out of a travel supplement. Here a Georgian doorway, there a high-speed Internet portal. 'Authentic', yet sophisticated, that's how we felt. Tired of Paris? Bored shitless with Rome? Then why not scoot off to Dublin, where the visitor meets the ghosts of bygone years in quiet, cobbled streets, whilst the city's designer-clad children bathe in the white heat of a vibrant technological boom – that is, when they're not busy banging each other's heads off the vomit-soaked, cobbled streets.

Carver's face featured regularly on magazine covers of the period. We had reinvented him as the epitome of clever cool, so photographers took to side-lighting him dramatically, throwing that craggy surface into stark relief. I remember once seeing a profile shot and thinking that all he needed was a laurel wreath to be Julius Caesar – or maybe Caligula. *I have no ego.* He bought a big old house in some leafy, red-brick suburb, with barristers and diplomats for neighbours. Although he constantly threatened to do so, he never married Anne Stutz. On the surface, she did not appear to mind. It was obvious that she was in it for the long haul, come what may.

The late nineties were the 'baked bean' years. Coming up with a new programme and grabbing a slice of success is the hard part, the frantic part, but it's also the fun part. Once you win the audience over, once you have the critics on your side, once you become another stitch in the social fabric, you tend to fall into a production-line pattern. Like a tin of baked beans, people come to expect the same contents and flavour from a show they enjoy, week in, week out, year after year. And it becomes your job to give it to them. The century turned. The third millennium, A.D.

Looking back, this is when I should have left the Monkey Man, when things were at their best, and I respected him the most. He'd have been horrified had I tried to, and more than likely would have found a way to stop me. But there's a lot to be said for quitting while you're ahead – just because it's a cliché, doesn't mean it's not true. Score a hit, then, as soon as you feel the boredom seeping in, have the balls to walk away and find something else to do. Precisely when I grew bored, precisely when I began to take it all for granted, precisely when the Class As started in earnest … even now, I can't pin it down. It just sort of happened. Needless to say, with the money, the drugs, and the vicarious fame of it all, the thought of leaving the show to go backpacking around Bangladesh never once occurred to me. Carver relied on me – I was the lynchpin, the calm at the centre of the storm. My position as the second amongst equals was never challenged. I demanded, and received, special status.

Everyone else was subject to Carver's nasty little whims, apart from me. By the end of our second year, he had sacked all the others, at least twice. Quietly, I would have the decision reversed, intervening for the unfortunate disciple before our dark little god. The usual forum for sackings was the pre-programme bedlam on Fridays. Someone's guest would drop out, someone else might fail to cower sufficiently before one of his random, incandescent displays. I usually had the victim reinstated by Tuesday or, at worst, would give them a snap holiday to allow the caprice to fall elsewhere, as inevitably it would. Kate, Charlotte, Dervla, and Elaine became used to rotating the rank of least-favoured-chimp amongst themselves, knowing that next week, they'd once again be 'the best little worker in the fucking world'. As long as my position as beta monkey remained secure, it suited me better to keep the troop together, rather than break a constant stream of new recruits into alpha monkey's curious ways.

Scally, like me, was, at first, spared Carver's arbitrary spite, although for different reasons. I was the trouble-shooter, but he was the jester, and his buffoonery seemed to earn him an indulgent protection. It seemed to.

We'd been on air for about a year when Carver finally turned on Scally. Every so often, we'd go for a team dinner, drink buckets of wine, and tell each other how great we were. Unusually, on this particular occasion, Anne was present. Carver rarely brought her anywhere, as she cramped his style. Anne Stutz cramped everyone's style. With her red mullet and pencilled-in eyebrows, she looked downright weird, for a start. She was just as manic and mouthy as Carver but, unlike him, lacked a sense of humour. Frankly, she was a bore. She tended to parrot Carver's themes, but monotonously, with none of his amusing, amoral mischief. She was like a permanent tourist, and when the collective conversation went beyond her, she would pick one of us out and lapse into endless anecdotes about her New York punk days. To listen to her, you'd think she'd been bigger than Debbie Harry. That night, she picked me. We were in some anonymous restaurant, scarfing pasta and red wine. Carver had ordered a pizza, then proceeded to smoke and stub his fags out in the middle of it. The banter was flying as usual, but I was tuned, out of politeness, to Anne's transatlantic whine. Carver ignored her, poking fun at the rest of the table, eliciting laughs, squeals, and sporadic return fire.

I don't know if you've ever been in one of those situations where you temporarily leave a perfectly good-natured gathering and return, moments later, only to wonder if you've stumbled into a parallel universe. The people are exactly where you left them, but atmosphere has, inexplicably, changed beyond all recognition. I had excused myself, to use the bathroom. There was no coke on the go: this was a perfectly legitimate call of nature. Back in those days, I stayed off the Class As Monday to Thursday. We were still finding our feet, and I was still living, eating, and breathing the show.

I remember drying my hands and pondering the range of plausible excuses I could make to leave early. I didn't want to spend the rest of the evening listening to Anne's anecdotes, my eyes wide with feigned interest, my mind adrift on a rising tide of tedium. I returned to the table, reached for my wine, and heard Anne exclaim,'Where does the little creep get off sayin' that sorta shit?'

I thought she was still talking to me and turned resignedly to pick up the thread. It was only then that I realised that both she and Carver were staring across the table at Scally, who was laughing, mouth open, eyes shut, a ribbon of pasta hanging down his chin. But nobody else was laughing. Carver had his flinty, fascist face on. The visor snapped down. One by one, Kate, Charlotte, Dervla, and Elaine fell quiet. An air of utter, abject menace had descended where, minutes earlier, there'd been relaxed, friendly chatter. Jesus. Had I even sat back down at the right table? What was happening? I took a swallow of wine, but didn't taste it. I had that horrible feeling of watching a car crash, but being powerless to stop it. I couldn't reach Scally to kick him under the table, and it wouldn't have made any difference, anyway. What had he *said*?

Bang! The Monkey Man lifted his pizza-ashtray up to face-height and slammed it back down on the table, breaking the thick white plate, causing our wineglasses, and us, to jump. A piece of pineapple flew off his pizza and stuck neatly to the side of a bottle. It's one of those silly things you notice, when you're massively alert to everything around you. Scally shook his head, even more surprised than I at the drastic change in ambience. Diners at other tables stopped eating and stared. I could feel them, rather than see them. Then, quietly, almost calmly, but with an undertone of unmistakable malice: 'Ya think you're such a funny young fuck, don'tcha?'

Carver pursed his mouth like a goat's anus, then, tilting his forehead forward, locked on his victim with the meat-skewer stare. He poised his body forward, leaning on one arm. The hapless Scally exhaled the last of his laugh.

'Wha'?' He sucked the pasta off his chin; his knife and fork twitched like the feelers of some dying insect.

'I asked you, Scally: do you think, in your opinion, that you are a funny young fuck? It's a very simple question! I think everyone else at this table under-stands the question?' Carver rapidly inspected our frozen faces with a grotesquely exaggerated look of inquiry. His voice took on a nasty edge. 'Now, answer the question! Do ya think you're a funny young fuck?'

'Do you have any idea, you little prick, just how lucky you are to be working with this great man?' Anne joined the attack, her face redder than her hair. Carver turned on her, quick as a mongoose biting a snake.

'You shut the fuck up! These are *my* staff!'

Anne's eyes bulged, but she kept them fixed in the direction of the patently confused Scally.

'Now, I'll ask you one final time: do you think you are a funny young fuck? I'd like an answer!'

'But I …'

Carver pushed back his chair and addressed the surrounding tables.

'Folks, this is Scally. He thinks he's a funny young fuck. At least, he *thought* he was a funny fuck, but now he's not so sure.' And, gesturing at his victim, 'I'll tell you what, Scally, make these people laugh, show them how funny you are, and I'll let you keep your job. Go on, funny fucker, make everybody laugh.'

'Please … please …' Scally resorted to pleading. Most of the other diners, acutely embarrassed, pretended to go back to their food.

'Not so handy with your big, fat tongue now, are ya, Scally? Some of the people around this table might be labouring under the impression that you are a funny fuck, but you and me, we both know you're just a stupid fuck, don't we? We both know you're a hitch-hiker, a passenger, along for the ride. This programme doesn't need you. *I* don't need you. You do no work, you're dead fucking wood, and now you're not even funny. Well, there's no free rides around here, baby. So go on, fuck off.'

Scally's face had turned purple, in a combination of anger, humiliation, and surprise.

'Are you s-s-serious?' he managed.

'Which part of "fuck off" do you not understand? Let me put it another way: you're sacked! Do you understand *that*? Now, get out of my sight, Mister Funny Fucker. Go on, make us all laugh now! Tell us

212

a joke!' Scally burst into tears, flung his knife and fork onto his plate, and fled out the door into the street. The rest of us just looked at each other. Carver relaxed back in his seat, smiling, and casually suggested a trip to Verdana. No one disagreed.

Four hours later, I waited for him, drunk, in the narrow, stinking corridor outside the nightclub's toilet. I caught him by surprise, coming through the swing door, and pushed him hard up against the plasterboard wall. I leaned all my weight forward to keep him there, a hand on each shoulder.

'Teach ... Teach ...' he smiled, practically drooling with alcohol. I could feel his old bones beneath my hands. They felt brittle and hollow, like a bird's.

'Why did you do that?' I demanded. 'That poor bloody kid!' In truth, I didn't particularly care about Scally, but the scene in the restaurant had conspired with red wine and countless double vodkas to make me want to prove that I wasn't afraid. Plus, I'd been listening to his girlfriend hissing all evening and felt physically compelled to attack either him or her – it didn't matter which, at this stage. Carver rolled his head from side to side. He was even more smashed than I was.

'Teach ... Teach ... I can't ... you know? I just can't ... let young cunts take the piss. Take the piss. Scally. He's gone. Gone ...'

'If you ever try that on me, I'll kill you, do you understand?'

'Teach! I *never* ... I never would ...'

'I don't care what you do to anyone else! If you

ever turn on me, I'll kill you! I fucking will! Do you hear me?'

'No ... no ...' he started laughing, and, as I unpinned him from the wall, his laughter turned to tears. Not deep sobs, but a silent, wet torrent of slobber from his eyes and mouth. He slumped forward into my arms, and I had to catch him to stop him from falling.

'Please, don't ever leave me ... please. Teach, don't go! Don't go!' And he held onto me, half-hugging, half-slumping, his hot, thick moisture making patterns on my shirt.

'Jesus. I didn't *say* I was going t⸱ ⸱ve you. I just said I'd kill you if you ever tried to fuck me! Come on, don't cry, you're all right!'

'No, Teach ... don't go ... I *need* ya, Teach ... please. Never leave me, Teach, *please!*' Gingerly, I patted his back, as he buried his face in my shoulder, racked with misplaced grief.

Scally rang me a few days later. He was crying, too. He wanted to know what to do. I asked him whether he wanted to stay with the show. He said he did, so I advised him to apologise.

'Apologise for *what?*' Scally raged. 'I didn't *do* anything!'

'Scally, look. You're dealing with a monumental ego, so it doesn't matter about the rights and wrongs of it. If you want to stay, ring him up and apologise. Kiss his arse, and you'll be fine. Do it tonight, I'll prepare the ground for you. I'll make sure he takes the call.' Scally snivelled some more, but had obviously

214

already decided that nobody else was going to pay him three grand a month to surf Internet porn.

'By the way,' I asked, just before I hung up, 'what did you say to him? I missed the whole thing. What did you *say* to set him off like that?'

'Well, that's the thing. I said fuck-all,' Scally whined. 'I only said that if Peter O'Toole cooked his face in a pizza oven and cut his legs off at the knees, he'd be perfect to play Carver in a film about his life!'

I shook my head and got back to work.

# 16

## THE BLUE MOON

"'The past has no existence, except as a succession of present mental states.'"

Her pale blue eyes are level and direct, from under the shadow cast by her hair. I don't know her well enough to suss whether she's being serious or just pulling my chain.

'You think I'm making all this stuff up?' I've spent the guts of an hour giving Therese a potted history of my career-to-date with Kevin Carver.

'That's not what I said. I'm merely observing that how someone describes the past depends entirely on their disposition in the present.'

'Meaning what, exactly?'

'Meaning you're completely fucking horrified by your boss …'

'He's not my boss.'

'... but you play along with all the madness, because you think you'd be nothing without him.'

'But if it wasn't for me, Carver would be nothing either!'

'I bet *he* doesn't see it like that. What you did for him is in the past, and the past has no ..."

'Yes, yes, the wise words of the Maharishi ...'

She snorts and shifts her gaze across the valley. 'It's Hume, actually. Scottish philosopher, eighteenth century. Unless, of course, you think I'm making it up.' Slight smile.

'Ah! "The surprising ease with which the many are governed by the few"?'

She looks back at me, scanning carefully. 'What, you've actually *read* Hume, or was that just a dip from *The Oxford Book of Quotations*?'

I could lie. I could, but I don't, because something tells me I'll get badly caught if I do. 'Neither, I lifted it off the Internet. I pull down the odd quote for Carver, makes him look good in heavyweight interviews.'

'And what crummy show did you lever *that* particular soundbite into?'

'Actually, I suggested it when Bush stole the election ...'

'How frightfully clever.'

'... but Carver didn't use it.'

'Devil-spawn meeja whores, the lot of you ...'

It's Thursday, and, believe it or not, I'm happy. It's been two days since the confrontation over the Archbishop. A burst of even hotter weather has sapped everyone's energy, even Carver's. Yesterday, to placate him, I booked some balding academic to turn up and waffle on about police brutality. Tomorrow night's show, in Duster-speak, does not have a 'bang', but I reckon that a respite from explosions might not do anybody any harm.

I finally called Therese this morning on the mobile number she gave me. I wanted to see her, but have a further motive in that I'm trying very hard to behave. I figured that dinner with a stranger might be a safe way to spend Thursday evening, instead of the usual scenario of Thursday evening spending me. Eat food, not Class As. However, Therese had answered, from the sounds of it outdoors, saying she wasn't up in Dublin but down in Wicklow. It was far too nice a day to be stuck in the production office, so I took an executive decision and offered to drive out to meet her for a bit of fresh air. Therese had drawled that she was getting all the fresh air she needed, but nonetheless agreed to meet me at a pub called The Blue Moon.

Close to Milton's estate, on a twisty little road halfway up a south-facing hillside, The Blue Moon is popular at weekends but early on a Thursday afternoon would be empty except for a few squinting, roll-up-sucking locals. As I pulled up, there she was, sitting across the road from the pub in the sun, a book in her lap and a pint of Guinness balanced beside her on the grass. So this was what she meant about living out of town. I fetched a brace of cold porter and flopped down beside her on the turf. Anxious to make a good impression, I thanked her for her bother, at which she grinned and goaded that it was she who should be humbly grateful for my taking time out of my stratospherically busy schedule to consort with the likes of her. Like a kicked-over bucket, I suddenly found myself pouring forth, in an effort to counter, or at least somehow explain, my devil-spawn media whoredom.

'But hey, enough about me. Let's talk about something *really* interesting and worthwhile … me!'

She arches an eyebrow and sips from her pint. 'You meeja-heads spend so much of your time peering up your own backsides that you often miss what's really going on in the world. A lot of your so-called "news" is just so much lazy rubbish.'

I motion with my glass towards the falling valley, awash with heather, sun, and sky. 'Well, I'm glad I extracted my head from my arse long enough to come and see this.' As if on cue, a pair of speeding meadow pipits zips over us, chirping furiously. Or ecstatically, hard to tell. Therese takes a breath, as if to say something, but then seems to abandon the urge, following instead the bouncing, precipitous passage of the tiny birds. I lift her book – *Tender Is the Night*. Rummaging, I find Tommy Barban's line about how the Divers always make him want to go to war, and she smiles.

'Comfort reading. For when I feel my head getting stuck up my arse.'

'Bastard started *The Beautiful and Damned* when he was twenty-four. Twenty-fucking-four, makes me hellishly jealous. What kind of a mind must you have, to write something like that at the age of twenty-four?'

'Do you write, so?'

I snort. 'Yeah, cheques. Since the age of twenty-four, I've been too tied up with Carver to try anything else. What about you?'

'Oh, I do the odd bit. Start loads, finish nothing.'

'Maybe I could I see some, some time?'

'No.'

'Tell me, how come you're not helping media sluts to buy their Viagra today?'

She shrugs. 'I've taken the week off.'

'Holiday?'

'Things to do.'

'Things to do … but not this afternoon?'

'No, you're my excuse to take an afternoon off, from the things.'

Therese is wearing a knee-length yellow summer dress with a tiny red and green floral pattern, and skimpy leather sandals. No bra. Her arms and legs are surprisingly brown; her moon face has a healthy, outdoor glow. She sits upright on the grass, her thick dollop of hair taking the full brunt of the sun. I'm stretched out beside her, in the shade of a birch, eyes buried in a pair of Diesel sunglasses, trying to be as cool as fuck in a white cotton shirt. Therese does not wear sunglasses. Her toasty skin is offset by the yellow of her dress, which looks as if it was purchased *prêt à porter* from Oxfam.

I really don't want her to think that I'm leching, so I've been fixing my gaze on the tip of her small, pointy nose, which moves minutely, in time with her mouth. That way, I'm hoping she won't sense how sharply aware I am of the rest of her body, which is on the aesthetically pleasing side of voluptuous. She, however, seems utterly unaffected and wears the shabby, revealing frock in the same casually indifferent manner that other girls might wear a sweatshirt and jeans. Fighting to overcome a powerful urge to put my head in her lap, I roll onto my back and stare up at the sky.

'Okay, Lee, you've been on the job for over an hour, admittedly most of which you've spent talking about yourself in the time-honoured tradition of your despicable profession, but what does your research tell us so far? Well, we know that her idea of light reading is F. Scott Fitzgerald. She blithely quotes eighteenth-century philosophers, which is nice; she lives in beautiful Wicklow, yet, paradoxically, chooses to spend her days in a dreary, faraway shopping mall, with her name pinned to her tits.' Slyly, using my glasses to hide my glance, I see her smile to herself.

'I told you before, my job is not my life. And Hume was my doctorate.'

'Your *doctorate*?'

She nods. 'Long ago, I decided what I want written on my grave.'

I sit up, pulling off the shades. 'Go on ...'

'"Therese Woods, Sceptic." Nothing else, not even my sell-by date.'

'Hold on a fucking second, you've got a Ph fucking D, yet you work stacking shelves in a supermarket?'

'Your language is atrocious – has anyone ever told you that?'

'No, wait a minute, Miss High-and-Mighty – there has to be a money-stroke-time equation in everyone's life, even yours. I mean, why aren't you earning twice as much, say, by, uh, lecturing?'

'How do you know *what* I do with my time?'

'Dress up as a bat and fight crime?'

'Actually, mostly I swan around in my silver sports car, necking drugs, and feeling sorry for myself.'

'Ouch!'

'You see? "All our ideas come from impressions."'

'The sceptical Scotsman again?'

'Hume was twenty-eight when he wrote *that*.'

'Would I be right in saying that I'm playing a bit out of my ballpark here?'

'Only a bit?'

'Gimme a break! You'd be a nightmare to interview! Look, you're about the same age as me, right? The big three-o?'

'"A wise man proportions his belief to the evidence,"' and she grins, no longer able to disguise her relish.

'Stop it! You're leading me up yet another of your philosophical garden bloody paths, away from Therese Woods, Person! Share! You're the same age as me, give or take. You're substantially better educated, and yet you work in a ...'

'Lee,' she interrupts, her lilt quickening, 'why does it matter a shit *what* I do?'

'It doesn't!'

'Then why bang on about it?'

'Sorry, I …'

'Are you *so* much a part of the brave new Ireland, where individual worth is measured only in money?'

'I didn't mean to …'

'Okay, so I work in a shop – does that make you a better person than me?'

'No, absolutely not!'

'Does it mean you can patronise me, while you smell me out for a little fling, thinking I'll meekly play along because I'm so hugely fucking impressed by what *you* do?'

'Christ, no!'

'My mum raised six children on a farm, and now that we're all gone, she runs a wee hairdressing business from home. Not for the money, she does it for the company. So that makes her a housewife and a part-time hairdresser. That's what *she* does. Yet my mum is the happiest, cleverest person I know.' She turns her head away, pretending to look down the valley. The silence lasts a while. Then, eventually, 'Can I ask you something?' Her drawl has returned, for which I'm grateful.

'Of course.'

'You don't by any chance pay women to beat you?'

'What?'

'You heard.'

'Beat me how?'

'Beat the crap out of you. Would you pay for that?'

'Maybe. Why?'

Eyes back on me. 'Because I reckon, by now, you owe me the price of a meal in a very good restaurant.' Grin restored.

I pout. 'Only if you promise to let me bleed on the tablecloth. When's good for you?'

'Oh, some time next week. I'll run it up the flagpole with my social secretary and revert when we identify a window in my diary. What's your mobile number?'

She has to wait before punching mine into hers, because she's had her phone turned off. It beeps narkily, two messages. 'Oh, I can't be arsed …' she mutters, switching it off again and tucking it back in her bag.

'Tell me, does your dead Scottish friend have any pithy quotes about the mystery of undying thirst?'

'A few. His best one was: "Hoots, 'tis braw the noo, when a bonny lassie doth stand her shout."'

She picks herself up and walks to the road, carrying our empty pint glasses in one hand and the sunflower bag in the other. Even in the heat, the grass has dampened the back of her dress sufficiently for me to admire a hint of white knicker beneath the fabric, clinging to an admirable bum. I lie back, spark a fag, and deliberately turn to face the view, so as not to be caught staring like an idiot when she re-emerges. The heather is on the turn, a sprinkle of purple dust across the brown and green of the slopes hinting at the glory to come. The smell of it rises, under the sun.

I'm faintly conscious of an engine rattling in the distance, but pay it no heed until the crunching smack of heavy tyres on melting tarmac accompanies the revving sound around the nearest downhill corner. An antique Land Rover that looks like it's spent most of its life transporting dead sheep down muddy lanes roars to an untidy halt between me and the pub, disgorging two guys in scuffy black leather jackets and *Mad Max*-style boots. One of them even sports a red mohican. Cool. And there's me expecting hill-farmers. They peer around for a moment and then disappear into the pub. Thirty seconds later, they re-emerge, with Therese jostled between them, looking harassed. Mohican Guy makes angry noises, but I can't hear the words. His mate jumps in behind the wheel as Mohican Guy shepherds Therese aboard. He crushes in beside her, and the Land Rover reverses back down the road, so fast that I can see Therese through the grimy window, bracing her arm on the dashboard to avoid hitting her face. I think she's looking over at me. By the time I'm on my feet, the vehicle has swung around, its wracking motor heaving it roughly away. I breathe a lungful of black diesel smoke as I stand uselessly in the middle of the road. I can't quite believe what's just happened, so I stride through the pub door, expecting the darkened interior to yield an explanation. I stare around, ready to punch someone, but there's nothing bar a few placid, roll-up-sucking locals gazing into their beer.

'Are these yours?' the barman asks me, gesturing at two freshly pulled pints, glistening on the bar.

'What?'

'I thought you were with the girl in the yellow dress?'

'Fucking hell, pal, so did I!'

# 17

## MORE IS MORE

'Hey! Water baby! Get out of your puddle and come here till you see this! You'll never guess who's on TV!'

The Creature drapes herself around the bathroom door, shouting above the noise of the shower. For a second, I think she's looking to come into the steaming cubicle with me, because she's wearing just her knickers, the rest of her long, willowy body whiter than the bathroom tiles. Stella is tall, only half-a-head shorter than me, flat-chested, with the same jet-black colour of hair. Recently, she's had it cut in a tight, disciplined bob, which accentuates her evil, almond eyes. She has a small Betty Boo mouth, full of sharp teeth. I've taken to showering twice a day now, mornings and evenings, and she tells everyone that I spend so much time in the bathroom, she's taken to pissing off the balcony.

Driving back down into the sauna of the city has done nothing for my mood. I tried ringing Therese on her mobile and got an impersonal message-minder. Boyfriend, has to be. God help her, if she's in that sort of relationship. So much for the hard-nosed, independent sceptic, eh? Now, standing in the shower, I'm replaying our conversation in my mind, viewing it from a number of possible angles and trying hard not to think of her brown skin against that yellow dress. The whole thing doesn't quite play, but then what the fuck do I know, as she herself so stridently pointed out. Now, I have a headache. I feel my old friend, the iron band, tightening around my chest. But as so often seems the case these days, I feel powerless to tackle the cause of my irritation. So instead, I scour myself with Dead Sea salt from one of Stella's tubs, then take forever to rinse it all off. Christ, I'm getting thin.

'It's Mr Ugly!' This is Stella's name for Carver. She's a more prosaic person than I am, in many ways. 'He's on TV!' She walks to the sink, wipes the mirror, and half-heartedly squeezes a no-doubt imaginary blackhead on the side of her alabaster nose. I turn the shower off, and she hurls a bunched-up towel over the cubicle door.

'So what? I see Carver on television quite a lot, you know.'

'No, hun, you don't understand – this is a documentary-type thing: it's *about* him. I think it's nearly over!' She pats water on her cheekbones, then saunters back towards the living-room.

'*What?*'

I sit on the living-room floor, wrapped in towels. Stella pours me a glass of cold vodka from the freezer, adds a dash of water, and gets busy rolling a spliff. If you think I smoke a lot of hash, you should see Stella. About a dozen joints a night, weeknights. I've never even tried to count through a weekend. She is one of these people who will literally start to panic once her personal supply drops below the half-ounce mark. She can hold forth about the quality of every delivery of hash into Dublin over the past decade, which I find an amazing feat for one whose mind is effectively mush. To me, Dublin hash is invariably the same soapy shite, all the time. I smoke it, but can take it or leave it. Stella lives in dread of the big customs busts that very occasionally result in a citywide drought of the rotten stuff. Anyone who says that hash is not addictive has never met the Creature.

'I'm effectively a Buddhist,' Carver is saying, from an armchair in his house. He's wearing a black, open-necked shirt. He has his contrite, sincere face on, the one he saves for the cameras. Nice monkey, eating out of your hand. Or you, out of his. 'My own personal outlook on life is a simple, Buddhist outlook, as defined by, uhh ... Buddha himself. Be nice to people. Do them no harm. Learn humility. And that way, you will reap huge rewards.'

'*What?*' I hear myself squealing. 'He's no more a fucking Buddhist than I am! What channel is this?'

'Uhh, press the remote, it's ... RTV 1.'

'RTV hate us! What's he doing on there?'

The documentary cuts to a shot of our production office, with me not in it. Scally, Dervla, Kate, and Charlotte make like busy little bees, talking into their phones with their best shit-eating grins. Cut to Scally, trying his unconvincing best to look like a person of some depth.

'Yes, he is, he's a *very* spiritual man, in many regards. He's got this kind of calm, I don't know … a sort of *wisdom*. We all feel as if we can turn to him, in our personal lives as well as professional. If anyone has a problem, it's like, he'll always know what to do. He's a father figure, almost. A big brother.' Broad smile, showing rows of crowded teeth. 'And as you know, he's very, very good with people.'

I'm practically choking with disbelief. 'What the … when did they film *this*?'

The closing scene shows Kevin Carver and Anne Stutz, walking hand in hand around the fountain at Powerscourt House, a popular destination for smoochy Dublin day-trippers. Soft focus, sunlight lancing through the branches, sparkling across the rippling water. The closing voice-over ponders how, after a long climb, Kevin Carver seems to have reached a personal peak in his life. How he may have many more peaks to conquer, but the view from this one is beautiful, calm, and serene. Or some fucking thing. The credits roll, and I'm straight on the phone. He always answers after one ring. He keeps a phone on a table beside that armchair in his living-room. Wonder if he's wearing a carefully ironed black shirt or just his usual tatty little home pullover?

'Hello?' That slight hint of suspicion, when he's not expecting a call. Yet he loves unexpected calls, especially gossipy ones.

'Am I through to Siddhartha Gautama?' My mother briefly went Buddhist after my father dumped her, so I know the basics.

'Sid who?'

'Never mind, oh master, perhaps you can enlighten me with one of the four noble truths?'

'Ah! Teach, you big fuck! How the hell are ya?'

'Feeling … better. *Cleansed*, somehow, after tuning into RTV.'

'Watching my little programme, were ya? It was well put together, don'tcha think?'

'I only caught the end of it, because you didn't tell me that it was on. When was it made?'

'Ah, you know what it's like, Teach, I forgot about it myself until Anne reminded me. RTV series about famous people. Filmed it a few weeks ago, did the interview, then forgot all about it.' Is it just me, or is he being a tad over-blithe?

'When did they film in the office?'

'Same day I did the interview, first thing that morning. You had not yet presented yourself for work, Teach.' Is that a little jag at the end of his reply? I no longer come in early because I've been overdoing it at night, admittedly that's true. But I refuse to get involved in this childish 'me here first' competition that the others engage in, just to impress him. In my mind, I don't need to impress him: I've already earned my spurs. Just like him, I'm senior enough to keep my own timetable, as long as the work gets done. 'Don't worry, Teach, your position isn't compromised by missing your cameo appearance,' he continues, and yes, there's definitely a hint of mischief in his voice. 'Everyone knows what a great producer you are, in the game. Anyway, the documentary wasn't about the show – it was about me. They just wanted something to film. Quite exceptional for RTV to do that, admit a rival exists. Shows how much they must respect us. We're part of the mainstream!'

'I was just curious.' I hope I sound breezier than I feel. I move swiftly on to the small talk, to mask my disquiet. Yes, the show's all set up for tomorrow, we're fine. Police brutality, that's right. No, I'm not heading out tonight, this is me home. What? You're taking Anne into town for supper? Well, that's very nice. I'll think of you both holding hands beneath the table in some posh kip. No, of course it won't be a late one – you've got a show to do tomorrow, so it would be deeply unprofessional of you to go on the lash after your meal! See you in the office, Kevin! See you bright and early, Teach! Night-night!

I shake my head and stare at the wooden floor. I take a big swill of vodka and water and stare at the floor some more. Stella respects my silence for about twenty seconds, then hands me the spliff.

'So what's the story, hun?'

'Just a one-off doc. Says he forgot about it himself until tonight; that's why he never mentioned it to me.'

'Pile of shit, no wonder he forgot about it. So no worries, then.'

'No, not no worries.'

'Not no worries? Why not no worries?'

I fetch the vodka from the freezer and resume my lotus position on the floor. I'm not exactly sure what I'm feeling, until I try to spell it out.

'Up until this season, it would have been inconceivable for him to have made a programme like that for RTV and not fucking told me. It just wouldn't have happened. Fair enough, maybe he did forget: he's not exactly Mr Organised.'

'He's Mr Ugly! Imagine him trying to snog you!'

'You'd be surprised.'

'Fucking right I would, I'd be very surprised. God! Imagine waking up with *that* in your bed! Oh, look what I puked up during the night! A hairy baby!'

'I can't decide what bothers me more ...'

'What, the thought of snogging him or waking up beside him?'

'No, I mean him not telling me about the documentary or that garbage he was coming out with. We've spent six bloody years cultivating a clever image for him and here he is, all of a sudden, prattling on about Buddha.'

'He just sounded like a spa.'

'Exactly. Even you saw through it, and you're the most stoned person I know.'

'Thanks. I've got a really good idea.'

'What?'

'Fuck the Ugly Man, fuck everything. Let's have a few more spliffs, welly into that vodka, check and see if we have any Class As, and if we do, let's go out.

It's been ages since you and me got fuckered together.'

'Saturday morning, to be precise.'

'That's what I mean, it's been ages ...'

She's a hound for it, I swear. This is what I'm up against, sharing my flat with a drug fiend. God knows I want to be good, but it's beginning to look like God doesn't want me to be good. So, I can either sit here brooding about not one massive snub, but two – the episode with Therese was confusing enough, but not being told about the documentary is incomprehensible – or, I can get wrecked with the Creature. Take your pick, Lee – get worried, or get wrecked. Ah, fuck it all to high heaven! A quick check of the clothing volcanoes on our respective bedroom floors unearths the arse-end of a wrap of gak and an aluminium strip containing six little blue diamonds, which I'd completely forgotten about. Stella squats beside me, donning a totally unnecessary teen-fit black bra.

'Cool, so that's the Ugly Man's Viagra?'

'What's left of it, yes.'

'I've never tried Viagra, what's it like?'

'I've never tried it either. Let's just do the gak and save the rest for later. Otherwise, we'll never make it out the door – you'll probably end up trying to have sex with the bedside table.'

'And *you'll* probably succeed.'

We're in a place called Mr Blane's. I like Mr Blane's. It's a basement, good DJs play most evenings, it's always packed with people off their faces, you can buy anything and it stays open until three. How good is that? The Creature hits the floor and I hit the vodka, wandering from room to room, watching. I score four pills, speckled Mitsis. Heavy fuckers, cut with something. Speed, it looks like. I do a half, and it kicks straight in, making me sharp, alert, tuned. At times like this, I feel as if I know what everyone within a half-mile radius is thinking, their innermost thoughts. I relax against a pillar, relishing the cold of the metal against my cheek. The bad vibes recede, Therese and the Monkey Man banished to another dimension of far-off fucking pain. That's all it takes – a lock of vodka and a little pill. Ah, me. Why can't it be like this all the time? Why can't I press 'pause' and just stay here forever? Watching, eternally watching, from a position of stress-free, covert superiority.

'Did you get anything?' Stella, bawling in my ear. Sweat lashing off her, smiling, supplicant. She stands real close, so I can drop a pill into her hand.

'I need two, gimme another!'

'That one will fucker you enough! Do it in halves.'

'No, I need two; looks like I could be in with a guy over there!' When on the hunt, Stella always gets what she wants. Chances are, the guy's already choking for her, but the Mitsi will make him love her forever. At least, forever tonight. In the morning, she'll kick him out of bed and give him the wrong mobile number as she shoos him through my flat door.

'All right, but that's all I've got left, okay?' Always lie about the number of pills you have on your person, unless you don't want to have any pills on your person. I find an empty bench at a high, narrow table, and perch, enjoying the view. I get asked to dance, but refuse. I hate dancing on pills: it defeats the purpose. A girl with a blonde crew-cut, charcoal eyes, and a black choker sits and talks to me for quite a long time, but I can barely hear a word she says. She splits abruptly, when Stella, her arm around some bloke, crashes onto the bench, dragging her prey down with her.

'Heyyyy, I want you to meet … uhhh … what did you say your name was?'

The guy has his hands over his face, pushing sweat out of his eyes. His hair is spread flat on his head. He looks up at her. Chubby cheeks, china-blue eyes, and a V-shaped smile, which has developed into more of a gnashing, V-shaped grin, as the pill kicks in.

'Marty. It's Marty.' He puts an arm around Stella's shoulders, chuckling, child-like, into her equally sweaty face. The two of them are coming up fast, Stella obviously having ignored my advice about doing the Mitsis in halves. She's going for it tonight.

'Martin, meet my very best-est friend, and flat-mate, Lee.'

Martin stares at me for second, then lets rip a big laugh. He knocks over an empty beer-bottle, reaching out to hug me with his spare arm. Vastly amused, I let myself be hugged. Marty Pelham, Milton's press officer, is completely off his face.

'Do you come here often?'

Pelham finds my facetiousness egregiously funny. Judging by his outfit, a heavy checked shirt with a button-up vest underneath, I'd say the answer is 'no'.

'First time, but I love it, I love it! Great to see you!' He pats me heavily on the leg. 'And your friend is very beautiful!' He pulls Stella close. She raises her eyes to heaven. The pill has made Pelham all cuddly, released a flood of dopamine into his brain. He wants to touch and be touched. Wrap himself up in the surrounding flesh, skin against skin, warmth against warmth.

'Hey, you two know each other?' Stella catches on fast, I have to give her that.

'Yeah! I know Lee! Lee is great!' He hugs us both. There's no question as to which has the upper hand right now, Pelham or the drug. If the smell of his breath is anything to go by, he must already have been pretty drunk before the Creature laid her chemical nirvana upon him.

'My mouth's as dry as a nun's cunt,' she announces. Like I say, Stella is the prosaic type. 'Huggy Bear, I'm gonna get you a drink,' and she pats Pelham's arm, whilst deftly removing it from her shoulders. 'My, you are fat, aren't you? Beer for you, beer for me, Lee – large one?' I nod. Stella squeezes past Pelham, literally putting her pert jeans-clad bum in his face. She's an expert. She sashays off towards the bar, knowing full well that Pelham's gaze will magnetically follow her divine arse, and it's only when she disappears into the crowd that he turns his attention back to me. He sidles close, very friendly. I feel his sweat through the sleeve of his shirt, on my bare arm.

'Wow, it's not just my first time in here! Believe it or not, this is my first, you know ...'

'Pill?'

Pelham nods, starts laughing again, and squeezes my leg just above the knee. It's almost sweet to think that Mister Smart-Arse Yuppie Press Officer is experiencing something I've known all about since I was fifteen. There's hope for us all, perhaps.

'I take it you're not out with the gorgeous ... what was her name?'

Pelham scrunches up his face and flicks a dismissive wave. 'Catriona. She's just a thing from work, very on-off. And very off at the minute, sure you know yourself. I'm on the rip!' He chews his lower lip. 'Actually, me and her have been off since the night of Milton's party. What a scene. Bit of a major downer for all involved.'

'Tell me about it. I had to get the little fucker back into town. It got worse before it got better.'

'Hey, I'm glad you think he's a little fucker! I'm glad you said that. I don't know how in hell you work with him. I've never met anyone with a temper like his. That one time I had to ... you know, the royalties case ... I don't think he's liked me very much since then.' Pelham clearly feels good about this minor exchange of confidences.

'He doesn't like most people very much. How's Milton?'

'He's all right now, but he was seriously pissed off with Carver that night. He said he was glad we shafted the little bastard when we did.'

Excuse me? Sharp. Alert. Tuned. What the *fuck* did you just say? Take a beat.

'Um … nice. It's not often someone gets one over on him,' I offer, cautiously. But Pelham is too smashed, too eager to please, to notice he's being led.

'Well, we did, big-time!'

'How?'

'I can't tell you – it was a rotten thing to do.'

'Did it have something to do with the O'Gormans?' I'm going on a hunch, here.

Pelham sniggers. 'I don't know the O'Gormans! I just turned up and read my statement, like I was told to!' As is often the case when people are lying, Pelham's denial has confirmed a suspicion. I pretend to laugh and give him a friendly nudge.

'I know, I was in court that day, too. So tell me about the rotten thing, go on!'

'I can't!'

'Does it have something to do with you meeting the O'Gormans for a little chat, months before the hearing?'

Pelham practically falls off the bench. 'How did you know?'

'I saw you with them in a hotel. You were lucky. Carver nearly saw you, too.'

Pelham shakes his head. 'Fuck, yeah! I thought it would be safe … I mean, he lived in Donegal! I nearly died when he walked in!'

'I was with him that night.'

'Seriously? Did you tell him I was there?'

'No. I didn't know you back then, so why would I?

I recognised you at the hearing, but I was up to my bollocks getting our show ready for air, so I said nothing then either. I wanted Carver in my TV studio, not stuck in court.'

'This is weird! Wow! Look, you have to promise never to tell Carver or Milton that you saw me with the O'Gormans. Milton would kill me; he told me never to meet them in public.'

'What does it matter to me? Hey, Marty, we're just a pair of guys, right, who both happen to work our asses off for a pair of much richer guys, yeah?'

'Right!' He hugs me around the shoulders again.

'I mean, we're all the same at the end of the day – you, me, Stella ...'

Pelham nods vigorously and holds me tighter. I'm used to operating in this condition, but he plainly isn't. Beware phantom friendships when on pills.

'Lee, you're a good sort. Milton always said you were. Actually, it's very funny ...' and he laughs. 'You have to promise not to tell anybody. I mean, never, never, never!' I give Pelham a big hug, hating myself. Good sort, my arse. But for people with secrets, a confession is like an orgasm and I've worked Pelham into coming. 'Milton was never in any car accident,' he snickers. 'He wasn't even in China! Ha! Fucking *China*! He was in France, in his mother's place!'

We laugh uproariously. 'Nice one! But why would he do a thing like that?'

'So as the O'Gormans could keep their money, of course!'

'That's mad!'

'This is the good bit,' and Pelham is boasting now, showing off. Just like I want him to. 'The O'Gormans have a brother, Brian. I take it you know who he is? All politicians are …?'

'Shit! Brian O'Gorman was a government minister!'

'A government minister, in charge of procurement. The O'Gormans wanted their money, and their brother wanted them to have their money, so he did a deal with Milton to drop Carver in the shit.'

'And Milton got?'

'A bit of help when he tendered for government contracts.'

'The crafty bugger!'

Pelham hooted. 'Aye, he's that all right!' I give him an extra-big hug.

'Oh-ho! Not interrupting anything, am I?' Stella, bless you for your immaculate timing. She plonks a round of drinks on the table and her catwalk body beside Pelham, who, for obvious reasons, immediately turns his touchy-feely attention back to her. To cement their distraction, I give them my last Mitsi, to split between them.

Well, well, well. Marty Pelham, the blue-eyed fat boy who blabbers to impress. Maybe Carver isn't the least discreet person I know, after all. This juicy snippet requires dissecting. It could have far-reaching implications. It could, for example, mean that Carver isn't a raving paranoiac. At least, not totally. That night at Milton's party – maybe he'd wrestled with his instincts for years, then out it comes, in one rabid, drug-enhanced burst. If Pelham's story is true, how much more will Carver love me … no, how much more will Carver *need* me, when I lay it before him? We'd have to check the dates, but it shouldn't be impossible to establish precisely when Synsystems started winning big government software contracts. As Carver himself would say – in this game, you have no friends, only good stories. I tap a memo into my mobile for the morning, under the pretence of sending a text.

REMEMBER: MILTONSCAM

The club lights are up. We're waiting for Pelham to go to the toilet, so as we can do a runner. Now that she can see him, Stella has changed her mind about wanting him. I can't say I blame her. It's chucking-out time, the bouncers are shouting blue murder, but Pelham sticks to us like glue. He wants to take us to a party in Temple Bar, because he still thinks he's on a direct flight-path into Stella's knickers.

'You have such lovely friends, Lee, really, you do,' he keeps repeating.

Welcome to pills, Marty. Pills make everyone lovely, even the likes of us. Things are at that slippy, blurry stage – Christ, those Mitsis are strong. I'm beginning to wonder if they're not cut with ketamine, as well as speed. It's becoming hard to maintain. Even though we have no intention of letting Pelham drag us to his party, it's as if there's a sudden space-time edit, and the three of us are no longer sitting in Mr Blane's, but standing instead at the door of some trendy block of flats, hanging onto each other so as not to fall over. Pelham is stabbing at a buzzer. There's another jump cut, and now we're sucked from a mirrored elevator, across a beige corridor, and into a small penthouse flat, packed with coked-up bright young things. Bad rock music blares, compounding the noisy claustrophobia. I steal a bottle of Jack Daniels from the kitchen, then sneak Stella away from Pelham, as he bounces like a beachball to his favourite Oasis track. We slip through a set of patio doors, onto the roof of the building. Whoever owns the penthouse grows bamboo in big clay pots – how totally groovy. We hunker in the shadows between the pots, whilst inside the penthouse, Pelham dances through the crowd, roaring with laughter, completely trolleyed.

Even at three in the morning, the air is still warm. The nocturnal chorus drifts up from five floors down, as shouts, screams, and breaking glass herald chucking-out time in Temple Bar. Everyone's wild on drink; the reptilian part of the brain is in command. English stag parties sing and fight; bevies of office girls mock and screech, mingling with the weird mixture of Romanian immigrants, goths, skangers, junkies, skate-kids, beggars, and tourists that will flood the area until dawn. Slurping the neat JD, we contemplate the party through the patio doors. We're weighing up our chances of sneaking back through the apartment and into the lift without Pelham seeing us, when a ripple runs through the gathering.

The crowd parts, and – *what the fuck?* Aw no! Kevin Carver is standing in the middle of the room, with Anne beside him! What in God's name is *he* doing here? The two of them look quite the worse for wear, although I imagine they could easily say the same about us, were we to crawl in from the dark. Carver has his trademark champagne bottle in one hand and glass flute in the other. They went to The Teahouse, I'll bet, after their late supper. Like us, they probably bumped into someone, who invited them here. Small-town Dublin, eh?

'You don't love me, but I love you!'

Pelham surges forward with a roar, locks Carver in a bear hug, and lifts him off the ground. Some gawp, and others giggle, as Carver drops his bottle and glass, wriggling furiously to be put back down. Pelham dumps him to the ground, where he falls, recovers, then lunges forward and head-butts Pelham square on the face. It's a bad one: I can feel the crunch from where I'm sitting. Stella lets out an 'Ooohh!' whilst I wonder precisely where Buddha stands on the noble art of head-butting. Pelham staggers backwards, bounces off the glass doors in front of us, and then flies at Carver, hands outstretched for his throat. With a bestial ferocity which I hitherto suspected in her, but had yet to witness, Anne Stutz flings herself onto Pelham's back and beats him about the head and shoulders, whilst he tries to strangle her monkey. The whole thing degenerates into a scrum, as the other guests step in to break it up.

'Creature, we are *so* out of here! Now, before Pelham remembers about us!'

I pull her upright and we stagger across the roof garden as, inside the penthouse, Pelham spins around with Anne clinging to his shoulders. I hope he breaks her fucking spine. A wooden door admits us down some concrete steps, then we crash through another push-bar emergency door and onto the internal staircase. We run hand in hand, whooping and falling across the cobblestones of Temple Bar, back out into the bustle of Dame Street. It's as if a monster is after us; that delicious game you play as a child – shrieking, joyous terror, fleeing from the beast. By some miracle, we hail a taxi almost immediately, and a panting, laughing Creature not only picks then to remember about the Viagra, but also to insist on having some. The imaginary chase has aroused her, made her bold. She's being a brat, I tell her, as I pop the little blue diamonds from their protective foil, one into each of our mouths. A total brat.

When we finally stumble into our flat, she wants to play a game that we haven't played in ages, called 'standy-uppy'. The rules of 'standy-uppy' are: we have to stand opposite each other in the hallway, each with a hand down the other's pants. We're not allowed to touch, apart from that, not even kiss, and there's strictly no talking. We have to close our eyes and try to make the other come first. Standy-uppy can last for ages, if you concentrate on winning. We keep it up until our legs turn to jelly, and we both fall over, gasping and wet. I win, holding back by imagining that Therese can see what I'm doing.

# 18

## COLLYRE BLEU

I'm in one of my vicious, vicious rages. I feel like killing someone, and I think I know who. The Monkey Man runs ahead of me through the woods, faster than I imagined he'd be able to run. I'm holding a kitchen knife, the blade pointed backwards, my arms pumping, balancing, pushing me onwards. The undergrowth whips against my legs. Silver birches fly by, their luminous lime-green leaves closing overhead. Carver glances over his shoulder, sees I'm gaining, and is that a look of gleeful mockery in his face? What's he gonna do now, scrabble up a tree-trunk and throw stuff down at me, whip up my rage into a blinding, impotent frenzy? Ha-fucking-ha, Teach, you'll never get one over on me! He turns to look ahead, gives it a real spurt, and for a moment it seems he might even escape me. Then, a thick twist of bramble catches him on the lower leg, and he stumbles, barely managing to stay upright. His pace breaks just enough to allow me to catch up, and I'm on him, the knife raised. Bang! I stick it into his back. Straight through his sports jacket, in and out. He gasps, lets out a yowl, turns, raises his hands, and as I slash at them, my momentum carries me into him. We collide. He goes down, hard and backwards, into the leafy mud. The impact bounces him along, but without coming to a stop, he writhes and is up on his feet again, like an animal hit by a car, mortally wounded, racing off at an angle to hide in a ditch and curl up and die. But I'm on him again, and the knife goes in and out and in and out and he's shrieking, shrieking at the sheer unreasonable finality of what I'm doing to his body.

'Nao, Lee, nao! [gasp] No! Lee! Ahh!'

And I'm no longer plunging the knife through Carver's green sports jacket, but through my father's blue suede cowboy coat, and Maurice is screaming and panting and shaking his head like a woman giving birth. I'm crying hot, salty tears at my own unstoppable rage. I feel pity, sorrow, fury, and disgust, but still the knife goes in.

My arm loose and dead from sleep, I crash my fist across Stella's naked back. Without waking, she snarls 'Fuck's sake!' as my errant limb rebounds and flops between us. My pillow and the sheet beneath me are drenched in freezing-cold sweat. It's as if I've been completely immersed in a filthy rockpool whilst sleeping. I moan, push the duvet off my body, and squirm onto the wooden floor. I lie there panting, inert, like the victim of my own stabbing.

My bedroom window is wide open, but no breeze, only heavy, humid sunlight, hotter outdoors than in. I can't breathe; my lungs claw for air through a throat tight from Marlboro Light. If my genitals weren't so sore, I'd probably piss myself. I press my cheek against the varnish, willing my skin to dry, but it won't. I crawl, like a snake, into the shower. I turn it up full cold and rinse my hair, eyes, mouth, down my chest, tummy, back. I try to dry myself, but by the time I reach the balcony doors of my living-room, I'm slick with sweat again, so I pull them open and flop onto the leather lounger. There's a slight movement of air here, just enough to dry my skin, because this side of the flat is over the river.

I dream every night, no matter how smashed I get before keeling over. Mostly, my dreams involve me trying to sort out some unsortable mess. I'll be in studio, working a camera, only the camera will be covered in alien controls – hundreds of tiny, flickering LEDs, fader buttons where there should be a lever or a grip, and Carver and his audience staring silently at me, because I've just knocked the show off-air. Or, the director will cue a taped insert, and I'll be standing there with the tape in my hand, unedited. A tape that I should have cut before the show.

There's a thousand variations, but always the same theme – a situation where I should be in control, and I'm not. A puzzle I should be able to solve, but can't. Important people I urgently have to meet, but they're not there. And 'there' turns out not to be 'there' either: a busy office becomes an empty street of blank Victorian terraced houses, with me alone, standing in the middle of the road, holding aloft the unedited tape, trying to read the unreadable notes, failing to work the unworkable camera.

I've put up with this nocturnal torture all my life, as long as I can remember. As a kid, all the way through school, through every shitty job I've ever done. And what's more, I know why I dream. However, that basic tenet of psychiatry, whereby identifying the root cause of an anxiety helps to dispel it, does not, in my case, apply. Around about the time my father decamped and we had to move out of the rectory, I started to sleep-walk. My mum and my brothers recall those days more clearly than I do, and they all have their favourite 'Lee sleepwalking' yarns. Like the time they found me climbing into the coal bunker at the back of the gate-lodge, because I wanted to go to bed. Or the time I insisted on counting the stitches in the bathroom carpet, screaming and crying because I kept losing count after four thousand. Or the time I hurled scalding hot tea all over myself and the living-room floor, because I'd walked downstairs in my pyjamas and asked for a cup. They only realised I was still asleep when I tried to drink it.

I no longer sleepwalk, but I still dream every night. And here's the problem – my dreams have become more real than reality itself. In this, I suspect, I am far from alone. Colours, textures, smells, sensations, and, in particular, emotions – everything feels much more vivid than it does in real life. Waking reality is like a badly photocopied script in comparison. Like a dreary film with cheap special effects, piss-poor actors, and me, deeply unconvincing, in the leading role. So even on a good day, even on a day when I haven't been up until six in the morning behaving like a beast, that dreadful sense of detachment never quite leaves me.

On a bad day, it feels as if there's a deep layer of insulation between me and everything else, as if I'm a ghost with no function other than to watch. Cursed to watch a pallid waking world, where nothing competes with the scorching, crisis-driven empire inside my sleeping head. And today, I know, will be a bad day, because, sprawled on the lounger, I can still feel where the undergrowth whipped my legs. I can still feel the jarring to my wrist, as the knife went in and in. I can still feel how the fabric resisted the point of the knife, the marginal difference in pressure between garment and flesh. I can still hear the shrieks and the shocked, hysterical begging. I'm still appalled at myself, that I couldn't stop stabbing. I still feel the iron band, locked tightly around my chest.

Beep-beep.

Fuck! It's eleven o'clock! I register the time from the glowing display of my phone, then see that this is my seventh message this morning. I switched the damn thing over to message minder last night, and I bet I know who's been ringing me, like a madman, all morning. It's Friday, folks, and the Assistant Head Keeper is late for work.

I dress lethargically. Doc Marten boots, the grimy combats again, and a drab olive shirt. I look like a soldier, ready to be shot. I give my teeth another furious brush, then gargle and spit with Listerine. Anyone who tells you that vodka doesn't smell the next day is lying. Breakfast is two soluble painkillers, great big hissing horse-tablets churning the water of a tea-encrusted mug. The final touch comes from a small white bottle of Collyre Bleu. It's this stuff like acidic navy ink. Stella turned me onto it when she moved in. It stings, but a few drops in the eyeballs will turn even the most pulsating red into the most blinding white. Collyre Bleu is the ultimate godsend, because no matter how fucked the rest of your face looks, when people check out your eyes, they seem better than fine. So they can't point the finger at you and say, 'You can't cope! You've been up all night; look at you, you're in bits!'

The controls of my car feel mushy and uncertain. My head has electric slime running from temple to temple. Even behind my sunglasses, the light is way too bright. Traffic and buildings seem remote, menacing, and two-dimensional. I stop for a red light, and a huge billboard looms over the road, advertising the boy-band Westlife, all their smiling, airbrushed faces grinning down at me, twenty feet tall. Across the bottom of the poster, someone has sprayed in crude, black graffiti the words, *I simply MUST have one!*

When I walk into the office, no one says 'hello'. Carver is straight on my case.

'You're late! Do you know what day it is? There's no free fucking rides around here, baby!'

It's nearly midday, and he's got a fair point, but the journey to work has done nothing for my mood, and in a way, I don't care. Reality as a pale photocopy that I can't be bothered to read. Therese is right: we're nothing but a bunch of puffed-up twats, pretending that our little meeja world is the be-all and end-all. So I growl at him in passing, 'The only free rides I get are far from this office, and they're a fucking sight more pleasant, I can tell you.'

'It is deeply, *deeply* unprofessional of you to be turning up at this time on programme day!'

Of course, he has a point. But there's no way I'm accepting a lecture in front of 'the team', not after what I witnessed last night. I know they're listening, but the others barely glance up – they're all glued to their phones, tight-faced and ultra-stressed, like disaster call centre co-ordinators in a rotten B-movie. Which, in a sense, I suppose they are. Whatever artificial panic Carver perpetrates, his emergency *du jour*, they will always buy into it. Pretend that broadcasting really *is* a matter of life or death, just to humour him. I fling my car-keys onto my desk, to show that I'm not intimidated, and return the serve with a little probing dig.

'I suppose *you* were here at the crack of dawn, thinking about the show?'

'As a matter of fact, I was!'

I meet the meat-skewer stare and see that he's not lying. His eyes have retreated even further into his head, if such a thing were possible. I must tell him about Collyre Bleu: he sure could use it. The skin on his face has gone parchment yellow apart from a vivid red patch in the middle of his forehead, which has started to blue round the edges. The primary colours, how apt. Liz the make-up lady will need the skill of a mortician tonight. A sideways thought occurs to me: if I could inject his buttocks with Botox, then use a squash racket to bruise them the same shade as his forehead, I probably could send him on caged and naked and pass him off as a baboon. He misinterprets my involuntary smile as cheeky incredulity and begins to yowl.

'I *was* here before all of you! I *was*! Someone has to take responsibility for this show, if the producer won't!'

Ouch. Unprofessional. Not doing my job. How did it get like this? Baby, baby – where did our love go? His breath, even across the office, reeks of fags and sour champagne. Must tell him about mouthwash, too. Actually, I'm dying to know, for sheer gossip value, how the fight at the party ended, because he plainly hasn't been to bed. What a pity Pelham didn't batter the shite out of all of them, then set fire to that poxy penthouse. The poor bastard. When Carver arrived at the party last night, he was only trying to be friendly, huggy-wuggy-woo. And what does he get but a forehead planted in his face?

Beep-beep.

Carver scowls venomously, waiting for me to rise to his bait.

Beep-beep.

Memo note on my phone, set for noon.

REMEMBER: MILTONSCAM

And it all comes flooding back. I can literally feel my adrenaline gland opening, pumping a burst into my system and blowing the fog away. We have a story, a potential biggie, a real blinder! Government corruption! A perversion of justice, uncovered by the victim himself! Live! On his no-bullshit, rock-and-roll TV show! I meet Carver's stare, and try to look business-like.

'Come down to the studio, I want a word.'

He doesn't stand, just writhes in his seat, and snarls up at me. 'Ya still don't get it, do ya? We have a fucking *show* to do tonight!'

'I know! This is important! I think we have a story …'

The snarl becomes a bark. 'You *think* we have a story? You fucking lush! Fuck you and fuck your story! I'll tell *you* what's important! There's a fucking *massive* story breaking out there, a *proper* story, but we can't get at it, because my so-called producer isn't at the races! *That's* what's important!' His mouth is pursed tighter than a camel's hole in a sandstorm, and he has his chin out at me. This is monkey body language for 'attack'. Lush. Me? I'm about to get the Scally treatment here, I can smell it coming. Fuck you and fuck your story. The others are watching surreptitiously, as they pretend to hector into their phones. I feel the iron band slip into position. Worse than that, I think perhaps I'm blushing.

'Aw, fuck it anyway,' whines Scally, slamming down his receiver, 'they won't help us! They won't give us the pictures. They say they've only got ten seconds' worth, and they're keeping it for themselves! RTV bastards!'

'Did you tell them it was *me*?' asks Carver indignantly.

'Of course I did. That was some prick of an editor in the news-room!'

'And did you point out that I have just done RTV the enormous favour of appearing in one of their programmes, broadcast only last night?'

'Yes, yes, I did!'

'And what did he say?'

'He said … he said …'

'Quit stammering, you're meant to be a researcher. What did he say?'

'He said … for you to … for you to … g-go and fuck yourself …'

Carver erupts, screaming. He rises out of his chair and tries to flip his desk over. He doesn't quite manage it all in one move, rather it takes him a few heaves, but eventually he tips the desk, spilling mounds of fan-mail over the floor. Then he starts kicking his swivel chair against a filing cabinet. From the far side of the room, I try to draw Scally's aghast eyes in my direction.

'I thought we were set up for today! What's going on? What pictures?'

Scally looks at me, then back at Carver kicking the chair, howling at the top of his lungs. It's as if he's calculating whether he has time to answer me before the whirlwind hits his position.

'God ... give ... me ... STRENGTH! This ... fucking ... COUNTRY! Aaaaahhh!'

'What pictures?' I repeat, this time to the wider office, as Kate reaches for the television in the corner, bringing up RTV's midday news. The ageing blonde presenter opens solemnly.

'A major disturbance has broken out during a confrontation between police and anti-road protestors in Glen Dara, Co. Wicklow. Reports are still coming in, but allegations are already emerging that police used excessive force to clear a large encampment that was blocking construction of the new M60 motorway, which is several months behind schedule as a result of the campaign.'

Cut to a clip of jolting, unedited footage shot from behind a line of police in heavy riot gear, pressing forward into a shouting throng of demonstrators. The cops push but are repulsed by a mixture of mainly young men and women, shouting and screaming at the cordon. An older man in the crowd raises his arms, as if trying to calm the situation, but then a placard on a stick flies over his head, bouncing off a helmeted cop. As if they've been waiting for precisely such an excuse, the cops pull batons and charge. As they fall on the suddenly shrieking demonstrators, a gloved hand covers the camera-lens, and the clip abruptly ends.

'Details from the scene are still sketchy, but according to RTV's Environment Correspondent, Lisa Hennessy, over a dozen campaigners have been arrested and many more treated for minor injuries ...'

A large, hard-backed desk diary bounces off the television screen, knocking the set off its stand. 'It's police fucking BRUTALITY!' Carver shrieks, as the TV hits the ground with a bang and a blue flash. He kicks at his telephone, lying disarrayed on the floor, and up it flies, shattering against the wall. Kate and Charlotte look ready to cry; Dervla covers her head with her hands.

'I *told* you! I told you *all* that police brutality was a huge fucking issue! You useless *fuckers*!' Bang! Splash! There goes the water cooler. Carver scurries around in frantic, ever-tightening circles, bent double with the effort he's putting into his screams. His face has gone purple, temporarily disguising the bruise on his forehead. He spins around on one spot, shaking his fist in the air. I'm staring at him, without really seeing him. My body has gone suddenly cold and sweaty again, the way it felt when I crawled out of bed this morning.

Therese was in that heaving crowd of protestors.

No mistake, she was close to the front, beside Mohican Guy, whom I distinctly recognised from yesterday outside the pub. He was holding a small camcorder aloft, but what happened when the police charged is impossible to say, the clip ended so abruptly. I realise I'm still clutching my mobile.

REMEMBER: MILTONSCAM.

Milton? What about Therese! Arrested? Injured? I fumble, bringing up my saved numbers. Press 'T'. I go to thumb the 'dial' button, but a savage thump knocks the mobile out of my grasp and sends it spinning across the office floor.

'Look at you, standing there like a great big string of *piss*! This is a *huge* story! And we are nowhere with it, *nowhere*!' Carver, crouched right in front of me, bawling up into my face.

And it's like I'm in a car, spinning, wildly out of control. Milton's crooked. Therese could be hurt. And now, for the very first time in our relationship, the Monkey Man has struck me. We stand, eyeball to eyeball. One of two very different things could happen in this instant. Either my offended hand could pull backwards, bunch into a fist, and fly forward, crunching into Carver's snarling, half-open mouth, hurting my knuckles, but smashing a few of his ancient teeth and splattering his upper lip into a gaping, strawberry-shaped wound. That would be it, all over and done with, right here, right now. Goodbye, fucker – nice working with you.

Or, I could take a beat, raise an index finger, level it in his face like a gun, and say, '*You* … need to chill the fuck out and start thinking like a professional.'

'Professional? Professional? I'm *being* professional! What are ya, big man, are ya? Big fucking man, big fucking man, gonna tell us all how to behave?'

I keep my finger pointed at him, as I crouch to retrieve my mobile phone from the floor. 'Fuck up and calm down. By the way, I want this office tidied by the time I return.'

Carver shakes his head in disbelief, then springs at me, just as I reach the door. The others peer out from behind their monitors, astounded. I slam the door shut and put all my strength into holding it that way, as the handle bucks and judders, under assault from the other side. He calls me all the cunts of the day. Once I'm sure I can hold the door, I thumb my mobile – good, not broken. Summon up Therese again, press 'dial'. Surprisingly, it doesn't go straight to message, but starts ringing. Come on, girl, answer!

No wonder Carver is having hysterics. Allow me to explain. During the week, to indulge his whim about police brutality, I booked some university lecturer, who last year published a paper on crime statistics. That's as good as I could find, because, in truth, the police in Ireland are no different from elsewhere. As an interview, it was set to be pretty lame. But suddenly, the cops have gone mad and smacked what looks like a very middle-class protest around the countryside. On a slow news week, it's an absolute godsend. All afternoon, the radio phone-in shows will be flooded with calls. This will be the lead item on every bulletin, and here we are, due on in nine hours, with no pictures. Nothing. Nada. Just some talking head to bandy figures around and tell us that we must take a balanced view.

Carver doesn't want a balanced view: he wants blood. He couldn't care less about the protestors – here's a heaven-sent opportunity to kick his enemy of the week. In his role as society's self-appointed weathervane, Carver will want to lead the public outrage, demand an inquiry, sack the Chief Constable, clean up the force! Why, ladies and gentlemen, did he himself not spend Saturday morning fighting state oppression from the floor of a lonely prison cell?

The door handle stops trying to jump out of my hand, but I keep a tight hold of it, leaning all my weight into the corridor. The ringing tone continues at the other end of my phone. I have visions of Therese sprawled in the back of an ambulance or a police van, her mobile beeping pointlessly in a far-off ditch.

'And this is Lee Lovecraft, our senior producer. Lee handles *The Kevin Carver Show*.'

Duster, strolling along the corridor, with a bunch of suits. 'Lee, I'm just showing a few of our sponsors around the station. Everything okay for tonight?' The suits fan out around me, smiling, as I hold the door shut with one hand and clamp my phone to my ear with the other. Ring, ring. The suits nod agreeably to one another, in recognition. *The Kevin Carver Show* – of course! How marvellous!

'Yeah, uh, Dickie – hi. We're just having a production meeting.' A hard, heavy object crashes off the far side of the door, making Duster and the suits jump backward in surprise. I grin my best shit-eating grin, as a louder, more metallic impact follows. That last was a waste-paper basket, by the sounds of it. God knows what the first one was, maybe *The Oxford Book of Quotations*.

Carver screams from the other side of the door, 'Let me out of here, you fucking prick! You dirty

259

fucking bastard! I'll kill you! I'll fucking KILL you! Arrghhhhh!'

'Yes. Ah. Um ...' Duster's eyes swivel in their sockets, as he motions the frozen suits to move on. 'Perhaps you'd, uh, care to see our studios?' As the open-mouthed party shuffles off, more banging, crashing, and shrieking emanates from behind the door.

'You fucker! Raaahhhh!' I smile and shrug my shoulders. Just a normal, routine Friday, folks. Remember this charming little tableau, when you return to your normal, routine jobs selling breakfast cereal or soap powder, or whatever it is that you do ...

'Hello?' Woman's voice in my ear.

'Therese? Therese? Are you okay?'

Pause. 'Who is this?'

'Therese! It's me, Lee! Are you okay? I've just seen you on the news!'

'Christ, Lee! Yeah! Right! Look, now is not a good time ...'

'Are you okay? Please tell me! That's all I want to know, if you're okay!'

'Well, ah, nice of you to ask. Quite a few of us got hurt, actually, I'm not the only one ...'

'*What?* You're hurt? How bad?'

'Not as bad as some people. Look, are you ringing about me, or are you ringing on behalf of your programme?'

'I'm ringing about you! I nearly shat myself when I saw you on TV! I've been worried sick! Where are you hurt?'

'It's nothing ...'

'Bollocks, where are you? I'm coming down there!'

'It's chaos down here, they're still arresting people! That's a very bad idea!'

'Have you been arrested?'

'No. A few of us got away …'

'Therese, if you're hurt, I want to be there, and if I have to drive around Wicklow all day, I'm going to find you! So where are you?' And I suppose there must be something peremptory in my voice, because she tells me. In a caravan, up a lane, halfway up a bloody hill somewhere. 'Don't you move, I'll be there in an hour!' I hang up, think everything over carefully for about thirty seconds, then relax my grip on the office door. Nothing happens; it's gone totally quiet within. I give it a few beats, spark up a fag, and push the door open. Potentially, the next few minutes could be the most satisfying of my life.

The room looks like it's been hit by a thousand-pound bomb. Carver stands in middle of the debris field. The others stare at him from behind their desks, shocked and awed. He sags, panting from exertion. The yellow pallor is returning to his face, but the bruise on his forehead remains a furious purple. Everyone turns their eyes towards me when I enter, but I address my words straight at alpha monkey, ignoring the rest.

'I think we have pictures.'

Actually, 'satisfaction' cannot even begin to describe this feeling. Not at the races, eh?

'What, you got RTV to share their stuff?' he croaks, plaintively.

'No. I think we have our own pictures, better than anything RTV has, and I think I can probably get a few of the protestors to come on the show, live, tonight. Wounded protestors. Victims of police brutality.'

'*Whaaaat?*'

'I said I think I have pictures and guests …'

'Eh? What? Who? Where?' and he scampers over, grabs my arm, eyes bright in their red water, like those of some primeval lizard, shining up into mine. 'Who have you got?'

'I've got a contact who was right in the thick of it. I'm going to go and meet them now.'

'A *contact?*'

'Yes. I've just been speaking to someone who was at the front of the crowd when the police charged.'

'Will they do the show?'

'They might, after I've met them.'

'What pictures have they got?'

'Hopefully, pretty good ones, but I won't know until I see them. From the demonstrator's perspective, taken just as the police charged, not shot from behind police lines like the RTV stuff.' Mohican Guy, holding his camcorder above the heaving crowd. Please, don't have got yourself banged up.

'No way! No *fucking* way!' And Carver is grinning his grin the size of Texas. His paws tighten on my arm.

'Yes way. If I handle this right, you'll have all the police brutality you want tonight, bleeding profusely on the studio floor. We're gonna blow RTV into the weeds on this one, but I've got to get down to Wicklow, and fast.'

Carver turns to the rest of the team, still coiled like trapped animals around the devastated office. 'There! What did I tell you?' he inquires, triumphantly. 'What did I tell you useless bastards, eh? I told you, "As soon as a proper producer gets here, we'll have this story cracked," isn't that what I said? Well, isn't it?' The others just stare, wide-eyed and dumb. I shake my head and make to pull away, but he tightens his grip. 'This is Lee Lovecraft, you fucks! This is a true professional, so take a good look! Me and Lee set up this show, just the two of us together, and don't the rest of you forget it! I don't *ever* want to hear any of you say a bad word against him again, because this is *our* show! The rest of you are just … *passengers*! Lee,' and he turns towards me, 'you're a genius. A fucking genius,' and he finally lets go of my arm.

'You'll want to put a call in to the police commissioner's office,' I say, scooping up my car-keys and keeping my tone as flat and nonchalant as possible. I am trying really, really hard not to smile. Oh, the *feeling*. 'Offer the cops a chance to watch our footage before we broadcast it. Act on the assumption that I *will* get the footage. Then, if the cops don't put up a spokesman, we make them look bad. If they do come on, we'll hammer them and make them look even worse. Either way, we win. Try the same thing with the Minister for Justice, why not? It's his fucking police force. Accountability or lack of it. This has all the potential of a political shit-storm, if we play it right. Ring a couple of opposition politicians. Tell them to get here early, so they can view the footage and brief themselves before they go on air.'

'Yes! Absolutely! Thank fuck *someone* is thinking around here!' Carver is all business, now. 'We need to do this comprehensively, get all the elements in place! Scally, you fuck, get on the phone!' And he lifts the shattered remnants of the kicked telephone onto Scally's desk. 'This is a big story, folks, and I want it done right! Proper journalism! The definitive account! Tell the Police Commissioner and the Minister for Justice if they don't do our show, I'm gonna tear them apart! I'll give *them* police brutality!' The team scrabble for their phones, desperate to grab whatever brownie points are left. 'And tidy this office up! It's a disgrace!'

'You should go home and get some sleep,' I tell him, as I leave.

'Can I, Teach? Can I go home and relax, firm in the knowledge that you will deliver? That you have my best interests at heart?' And he gives me a long, steady look that seems completely at odds with his pyrotechnics of only minutes before.

I shrug. 'I'm your producer, aren't I?'

Still, the strange stare. 'And if you can't trust your producer, who can you trust, eh?'

'I dunno, your feng-shui consultant?'

Before I leave, I go to the green room and lift a bottle of whiskey from the bar. Outside, the sun beats down, but even Dublin's cloying traffic seems to momentarily disperse to help me on my way. My head starts to relax some, and only then do I consider the size of the risk I'm taking. If the protestors won't play ball, I'm gonna look pretty goddamn useless, and then what? I turn the aircon up full, to try to stay sharp. I stick on Death in Vegas. The dual carriageway to Wicklow runs by the massive RTV complex on the southern edge of the city. As I pass their transmission mast, I finally allow myself a smile. Lush, eh? Fuck you and fuck your story? Our show. *Our* show.

# 19

# S N O O T

Ireland needs roads, no two ways about it. Iraq has better roads than Ireland; somehow we never got around to building decent ones ourselves. Until now, that is. Many of the big international companies that parachuted in during the boom years complained so bitterly about Ireland's lack of infrastructure that the government embarked on a massive road-improvement scheme to placate them. Now, the boom is petering out, and the work is still far from finished. Every arterial route is a mess of traffic-cones and yellow diggers. By the time it's all sorted, the conglomerates will have relocated to India, in their tireless search for cheap labour. But that's okay, because at least we'll have vast ribbons of smooth, open tarmac to drive on.

The Glen Dara protest has attracted little media attention, because the road-construction programme is in such a state of chaos that one more hold-up hardly seemed to matter. Certainly, there's no shortage of tree-huggers in magical, mystical Ireland, but mostly they're foreign nationals who stay over West, behaving themselves, doing up cottages, knitting yoghurt and stuff. When the government decided to build a new motorway through Wicklow, no one thought anything of routing it through an isolated valley. As work approached the mouth of Glen Dara, the opposition sprang up as if from nowhere, comprising locals, crusties, and various well-meaning middle-class types. A stalemate developed, and the protest camp grew into a regular village of tents and tree-houses, where eco-warriors sang round the campfire by night and engaged in 'passive action' by day. Ho-hum. But suddenly, people are getting hurt, and the media has woken up to the story *en masse*. Conflict sells.

After several wrong turns down Irish country roads direct from central casting, I finally squeeze the Alfa up a long, muddy lane, through a tunnel of hawthorns and briars. Just when I'm starting to curse myself for not having bought a jeep after my last car crash, the lane opens out into a group of derelict stone cottages, some roofless, others with rusty corrugated metal lashed on top. Our ancestral homes – the way we were. My silver sports car looks so out of place, it could be in an advert. Tucked behind the cottages, using the walls as shelter, are two rotten old caravans, streaked green from rain dripping through the trees. The battered Land Rover that snatched Therese away from The Blue Moon is parked randomly at the top of the yard, tailgate hanging open. A couple of black mongrels take more interest in the wheels of my car than they do in me. Mohican Guy appears in the doorway of a caravan, arms folded. He still looks like something off the set of *Mad Max*, all the more so now that he's sporting a livid welt across one cheekbone.

'Oh great,' he intones nasally, in an English accent, 'the cavalry has arrived!'

'Cops do that?' I point to my own face where his is gashed.

'Naw, mate, cut meself shaving.'

'Where the hell am I?'

'About a mile from the camp. Local farmer gave us these wagons as back-up, to store food and stuff. When everyone scattered, some made it here.'

The interior of the caravan is thick with cigarette and hash smoke, emanating from a homogeneous mass of fellow-crusties huddled on benches around a narrow table. One, a teenage girl with spiky purple hair and several kilos of black eyeliner caked around each eyelid, studies me as I enter their space, but the rest are preoccupied with a digital camcorder placed centrally on the beige Formica table, the fold-out screen turned away from me. I refrain from reaching out to snatch it. Instead, I lean carefully over Mascara Girl, ostensibly to place the propitiatory bottle of whiskey on the table, but also just long enough to study the screen. Sure enough, cops in riot gear can be seen lifting their arms against a crowd. One of the watching crusties emits an 'Ooohh!' and crinkles his face, as he watches a baton come down, perhaps on himself.

As I stand upright again, my face close to hers, I notice that Mascara Girl has gone heavy on the make-up to disguise a pair of black eyes from a nasty cut she's taken across the bridge of her pert young nose. Adjusting to the gloom, I see that her companions sport similar injuries: a swollen mouth here, an open forehead there. A blood-caked hand reaches out and offers me a joint. I shake my head.

'Where's Therese?'

'Up there,' and Mohican Guy snatches both the joint and the whiskey, flicking his coiffure at some vague spot beyond the caravan wall. I step outside into the sun. He follows me to the doorway, then stops and cracks open the bottle. I start up the field, and he watches me climb. At the top of the hill, I cross a dry-stone wall and see two things that make my tummy go tickly – Therese and the view. Therese is standing with her back to me, in her red raincoat and a pair of ankle-length boots, hands in her pockets. She's looking down, into a dramatic, steeply sloped valley with a thick floor of trees. The massive natural geometry conducts the eye south towards a distant group of blue peaks, in a prospect that has remained un-changed since the last Ice Age.

Below us, about half a mile away, a wide brown gash in the land is eating its way onto the valley floor. The tip of the gash swarms with diggers, trucks, police vans, and men in helmets, some orange, some blue. The noise of the machines stutters up, slightly out of synch with their movements. As I watch, a big oak comes toppling down, the soft, creaking crash reaching us a couple of seconds after it hits the ground. I cover the few remaining yards to Therese and stand beside her.

Her face is dirty, bar two uneven, vertical streaks where tears have recently trespassed. Her mop of brown hair is even more disarrayed than usual, and her coat carries several muddy, torn patches. She's still wearing her yellow dress beneath it. Her tired eyes seem oblivious to my arrival. I want to hug her, lift her, carry her off somewhere safe and warm, mop her brow and hold hot sweet tea to her lips, then let her sleep for a week between clean, white cotton sheets as I keep armed vigil by her bedside. Instead, I carefully put my arm around her shoulders.

'There it is,' she whispers, 'there's their fucking road.' And her face starts to crumple, so I stand between her and their fucking road. She buries her face in my chest and sobs silent but sore, as if her very heart has been torn open by the earth-movers. I stroke the back of her head. Christ. Did I remember to spray on my smelly stuff this morning? I think I did. Her upset lasts for about a minute or so, then I feel her go still. After a small delay, during which she neither leans her full weight nor withdraws, I sense fingertips fumbling with the tops of my pockets. For a bizarre instant, I think she's doing something else entirely.

'Hanky,' she sniffs, just after I catch on.

'Here. I think it might even be clean.' Keeping her face averted, she dabs, blows her nose, then brings her head up, with a sigh.

'Sorry,' she smiles, wanly. 'I've made a mess of your ...' and her round eyes, pink and weary, widen slightly.

'Don't worry.' But I look down at my shirt when she doesn't finish her sentence. Above the wet patch from her nose and eyes is a scarlet stain. For a silly second, I think it's me that's bleeding somehow, then I reach forward and gently push back her fringe, exposing a nasty, half-coagulated cut just below the hairline on her right temple. It oozes dark red, into her hair.

'Sorry,' she repeats, 'bastard caught me a right smack, I ...'

'Shhh!' I steer her to a soft-looking hummock and make her sit. At first, I persuade her to rest her head on my shoulder, but she says that doesn't help. She straightens and tries to brush the dried mud off the front of her coat. The moment is over – for now.

'So, now you know what I do with my time, when I'm not stacking shelves in a supermarket.'

'Forget that, you're hurt. You should see a ...'

'What, sit for hours in a crowded hospital, so as some overworked nurse can give me a plaster and a few headache tablets then tell me to go home and lie down?'

'Don't be daft, you need stitches, maybe an X-ray; you've probably got concussion.' She shakes her head, then winces and holds her hand up to it. 'Fuck's sake! Please, Therese, let me drive you to a doctor's, at the very least,' and I really have forgotten about the show when I say that. I'd quite happily spend the rest of my life taking care of her, if only she'd let me.

'Never mind about me,' and she seems on the verge of tears again, 'look what they're doing down there.' More trees tumble, as the snarl of powerful engines drifts up from the brown gash.

'Yeah, nice trees. Bloody shame.'

'It's not the trees. I mean, it's a shame about the trees, you're right, but trees grow, you know?'

'I think you have concussion.'

'Why?'

'People say all sorts of shit when they're concussed. Of course you care about the trees. That's why you and all your crusty friends are here, remember? How many fingers am I holding up?'

'No ...'

'Fingers! How many?'

'Lee! I'm not here for the trees, not like Snoot and all his people below!'

'Snoot?'

'Mohican.'

'Him? You're sure his name isn't Snot?'

'You leave him alone, he's a lovely guy. Up front, but okay with it. I've lived outdoors with him for six months; take it from me, he's a good man. The thing is, underneath the ground that they're ripping to pieces is a network of ancient raths, souterrains, graves. Pristine archaeology. People lived down there for about a thousand years, before that forest even existed.' She snorts. 'Then, another thousand years later, some petty bureaucrat runs his pen through a map, so as a bunch of cars and lorries can get where they're going five minutes faster, and God knows how many sites are destroyed!'

Re-jig compass, not for the first time today. 'So, you're not a crusty, you're …'

'An archaeologist, yes! Quite a few of us in the campaign are!'

'But I thought your degree was …'

'No, I told you my *doctorate* was philosophy. My *degree* is archaeology, that's what I *do*, if you really must know!'

'But you work in a shop!'

'Only to earn money for the camp! We all did that: everyone went on a rota, taking shit jobs up in Dublin to put cash in the kitty. The campaign went on for so long that we had to feed ourselves, buy better tents and outdoor gear. I spent most of my wages on sunblock and bottled water for eighty people!'

'You've lived in a tent since the spring?'

'Yes.'

'Flipping hell …'

'We camped across the route and refused to move. There was no other way. But I guess,' and she casts a bitter glance downward, 'we only delayed the inevitable. We were never going to stop them, not really.'

'I think I know how you might stop them.' I gesture towards the diggers.

'You don't understand – the guys that messed us up are still down there. They enjoyed it. Hunted us through the trees, yelling and laughing, beating the shit out of anyone they caught,' and her eyes start to water again at the thought of it. 'I've lived like a beggar for six months, and it's all been for nothing.'

'Do the show. Get in the car with me, come up to Dublin, and come on the show tonight. Tell everybody what happened here today. Embarrass them, shame them into stopping!'

She rounds on me. 'I knew it! I *knew* you weren't here for me! Fuck … crying like a *child* …'

'I *am* here for you! Look! Here I am! Right here. But come on, Therese. Okay, television is a crock of shit, we've had that conversation, remember? But be fair – it can also be handy for exposing stuff like this!'

'Fucking right, mate. I say we stick it to the bastards!' The two of us jump. Behind us, Mohican Guy, leaning on the stone wall, cradling the now half-empty whiskey bottle. Bollocks, how long has *he* been listening? 'Arseholes, fucked us up good and proper, they did! Well, I say we hit them straight back. You can put us on TV, right, mate?'

'That's what I do … mate.'

'Well, come on, T! The war ain't over till it's over, eh?' Snoot, or Snot or whatever his *nom de guerre* is, runs in front of Therese and kneels, taking her hand in his. Goddamn it, on top of everything else, now I feel jealous. 'Come on, babes! We've been crawling around in mud and shit all this time, and what, are you sayin' it was all for nothing?' I wonder did they share a tent, or even a sleeping-bag.

'Snoot,' and I half-cough his name, 'I couldn't help noticing, in the caravan, the digital camera – is that yours?'

Snoot looks up at me. 'Fucking right it is. When the bastards charged, they came after me, but they didn't get it, did they?'

'Well, there you go,' and I address the pair of them. 'If I can use those pictures and put a few of you in a studio, it will stir up a total shit-storm. Of course, Therese, if you don't feel up to it, I'm sure Snoot and a few of the others will be only too …'

'Hold on a minute! What about Carver?' Therese interrupts, hostile and unconvinced. 'Don't forget, I saw what he did to Charlie Morrison on last week's show! Took him to pieces, live on air! The charity industry. People who make a living out of complaining. Called him "a fucker" – how do I know he won't do the same thing to us?' And I see doubt enter Snoot's face, now, in the form of a frown.

'Look, let me share something with you. This week, Kevin Carver hates the police even more than you do. I'll be totally honest – he had a run-in with them himself on Saturday morning, okay? Just before I saw you in the shopping centre – that's where I'd been, down at the station, trying to sort it out. Yes, I'll admit, he doesn't give a fuck about the road, or your protest, but you'll get sympathetic treatment nonetheless, because Kevin Carver is up in Dublin right now, practically shitting himself with glee at the thought of hammering the cops on his show. Believe me, I know this to be true. Different motives, same agenda. I promise you, it can't go wrong!'

'But he *is* a little fucker ...'

'True. But tonight, for one night only, he's *your* little fucker. Come on, please! Trust me, I know what I'm doing.'

'I'm not at all sure about this, Lee ...'

'Fucking hell, I say we do this thing! Come on, T, let's rock on out! Let's hit the bastards where it hurts!' Snoot leaps to his feet, runs to the wall, and bounds over it, striding down the field towards the caravans, waving the whiskey.

'Not the sharpest crusty around the campfire, is he?'

'Lucky for you he's not, eh?'

I pout and make a show of helping her. Blood has formed a thin line down the side of her face. Halfway to the caravans, I stop and carefully clean it off with my shirt-sleeve.

'Let me drive you to a hospital instead. Fuck Carver, fuck the show, fuck the road, fuck Snot ...'

'Snoot.'

'Whatever. I'm worried about you. Let's both of us just drop everything and go and hide somewhere.'

'You've been honest with me, so I'll be honest with you,' and I'm getting the pale blue gaze. 'For the guts of a year, we've been fighting a losing battle. And part of the reason the cops attacked us this morning is that they thought they could get away with it. Why? Because we were just a bunch of isolated protestors. We tried to get the media interested in this issue; we tried hard. But, apart from a few token reports on the radio and in the local press, nobody cared. Then *you* pop up, and suddenly we're catapulted onto national television, but even then only after we've been kicked half to death. It just seems so … so …'

'Therese, you never *told* me!'

'Lee, you never *asked*!'

About half-a-dozen crusties have climbed out of the caravan and are draped around the battered Land Rover. Didn't take long for Snoot to marshal his troops. Without making it look like a premeditated gesture, I hold my car door open for Therese, then give Snoot directions for the station, in the highly likely event that his crusty-wagon becomes separated from my car in the traffic.

'And the camera?'

Snoot raises his arm, waving the treasure in front of my face. 'No worries, man!'

'Don't get too plastered,' and I point to the bottle in his other hand. 'I want you to look like a righteous victim when we go on air tonight, not like someone who's been kicked out of a nightclub.'

'No worries! The revolution starts here!' And his band of crusties cheer. We reach the bottom of the lane in convoy, then head for the main road. As I relax, the satisfaction spreads slowly inside. Therese doesn't speak, so I do.

'"The past has no existence, except as a …" what was it?'

She curls into the red leather seat, facing towards me. Instead of a tattered coat, she could be wearing stockings and a black cocktail dress, and we could be driving home from a party. She yawns.

"'... except as a succession of present mental states.'"

'Right. If that is true, then explain archaeology.'

'Easy. Without archaeology, the past remains buried in the ground, unidentified, uninterpreted, and unknown. It takes people in the present to uncover artefacts and give them meaning – attach their past to them, as it were. Undiscovered, their past, for us, does not exist.'

'Okay, what about a castle, something above ground, something everyone can see? That's from the past, and it exists in the present, doesn't it?'

'Yes, but unless we regard it armed with knowledge, again the castle's past does not exist. It's just a pile of stones, without our present under-standing of it.'

'Damn. What about Ireland, then? What about here? They're still fighting like pigs up north, over the past.'

'And their past will not cease to exist until their present mental state allows it.'

'I'm never going to get the better of you, am I?'

'You just did. I'm sitting in your car, aren't I?'

'We could still run away, you know. Snot would never catch us. I know a brilliant place in Mayo where we could hide for weeks.' She blesses me with a wan smile. 'Seriously, though, I thought the government wasn't allowed to build roads over valuable sites, even in a country like this?'

She'd been part of a team, she explained, that had been given three months to examine Glen Dara before the road went through. No one site was particularly valuable on its own – they hadn't discovered any dead kings buried in golden chariots or anything – but the totality and variety of the material was sufficient, in her opinion, to merit a serious time extension. They'd applied for a year and been given another month. Having previously moved to a nearby village to do the work, she'd fallen in with locals who didn't want the road, either. After several bad-tempered public meetings, the Green Party had become involved, and then things had really snowballed when Snoot and his crusty army arrived, alerted via the Internet. Snoot, she said, had been blocking roads in England since the eighties. It was he who'd introduced the tactics of physical obstruction, of which the camp was a logical extension. Every time the diggers looked like moving, the protestors formed human chains or climbed into trees, and the developer was forced to relent. Over the months, they'd struck up a decent relationship with the workmen, in terms of friendly banter. Things had fallen into a routine, her life given over to the smooth running of the camp. They'd even received generous donations from a wealthy local landowner who had visited the camp regularly, in person, to hand over money and supplies.

'This landowner – his name wasn't Milton McMahon, by any chance?'

'I can't tell you – he said he didn't want any publicity.'

'Brown eyes, foreign-looking, fierce nice chap?'

'What part of "I can't tell you" did you not understand?'

'But Milton's a friend of mine!'

'Well, maybe your friends have the same attitude towards their private lives as I have ... *had* towards mine – does that ever occur to you? Do you tell your friends everything about you?'

'I rarely mention the sliced-up body parts hidden in my wardrobe.'

'Oh, grow up!'

'Okay, it's not important. Milton lives near here, so I'm just asking. Bet it's him, though!'

Protestors of all sorts came and went over time, but she was part of a hard core that had stayed, determined to see things through. The local police had made several desultory attempts to shift them, but with few arrests and no violence. Spring became summer, and summer burned on into September. Then, yesterday afternoon, about a dozen riot vans had appeared amongst the construction equipment. Snoot, unable to raise Therese on her mobile, had raced up to The Blue Moon to find her. She was sorry there'd been no time to explain; she'd been carried away by the panic. Sure enough, by the time they made it back to the camp, a line of armoured police had begun to probe their defences, but a quick mustering of their own forces had led to a stand-off. The police had retreated that night, but returned at daylight with double the numbers and begun picking off individual campaigners with snatch squads. That had led to the ugly confrontation, she said, which had lasted most of the morning and then finally erupted into the full-blown baton-charge. There's a certain class of cop that would view slapping crusties as one of the perks of the job. They had rampaged through the camp, trampling the tents and beating anyone who got in their way. The protest had broken and scattered through the trees. End of story, and the end of something that had dominated a year of her life, all told.

'So what now?'

'Well, what now is I appear to be going to a TV station, when all I want to do is lie in a bath, drink a bottle of red wine, then sleep under a roof for the first time in six months. But I've nowhere to stay. I'll probably end up on the bus home to Tralee, with my tail between my legs.'

We're on the dual carriageway into Dublin, now. I pull a notebook and pen from the door pocket, scribble my address and all my numbers, then make her take the torn-out page.

'What's this for?'

'My flat, there's plenty of space. Three bedrooms, only two taken. You can stay as long as you like. This isn't a pass, it's a genuine offer. But if it doesn't feel right, I'll get the station to pay for a hotel room for you tonight, for the weekend, whatever you want.'

'Why are you doing all this?'

'Because I'm a devil-spawn replicant meeja whore. Because talk is cheap and a single action speaks louder than a thousand blah blah blahs.' And because I want to put out a cracking show tonight, I could add, and prove to that little monkey bollocks that he can't so much as wipe his bum without my help.

'Okay, I'll rephrase that slightly. Why are you doing all this … for me?'

'Are you going to make me say it?'

She stays quiet for a while, and, because I'm staring fixedly ahead, I begin to think that maybe she's fallen asleep. Then, almost in a mutter, 'No, I won't make you say it, because then I might say it, too.' Silence, again. Then, she does fall asleep.

# 20

## THE LONG GAME

Four o'clock; it's getting on. Accompanied by stares
from the receptionists, I usher Therese, Snoot, and
half-a-dozen crusties into the TV Ireland building. I
ensconce them in the green room, summon Charlotte,
and make her write down orders for take-away food. I
tell her to fetch anything that our precious guests
want, apart from too much booze. She leaps to it, like
a good runner. When I ask Snoot for his camera, he
takes me to one side, says he feels tired, and that he
knows from what Therese has told him that I'll
understand. Without saying a word, I return to my car
and siphon off a small amount of gak from a stash I
keep in the glove compartment. I rub a few dabs onto
my gums, then go back inside and make the swap in a
far corner, without Therese noticing.

'It's good that you're doing this, mate; this is a
good thing that you're doing,' Snoot informs me, as

he pockets the wrap. 'When you landed down today, I thought, like, you were bullshitting or trying to exploit the situation. But tonight, I'm really gonna state the case. I'm gonna hammer those pigs, the way they hammered us. The screen is mightier than the sword, right?'

'Tonight, Snoot, you'll look like a proper hero.'

'Absolutely! So, like, if the pigs wanna come and arrest me live on TV, that would mean even more publicity, right?'

'We should be so lucky. Now, the camera ...'

Slight pause. 'Is there, like, a fee?'

My crusty friend learns fast. Sighing, I pull four fifties from my pocket. 'That's all I have on me. I'll get you more, after the show.' Snoot grins and hands over the goods. Mascara Girl watches us from a sofa, her booted feet up on one of the tables. When I ask whether she wants a doctor to check her broken nose, she just looks at me. I study her in return, mentally calculating the merits of putting her on the show alongside Snoot and the rest, her assassinated beauty an eloquent metaphor for all that happened in Wicklow today. Her injury makes up for her apparent inability to speak. I suppose we can always say that she's been traumatised by the assault. Hell, maybe she *has* been traumatised by the assault.

Finally, I sit for a moment beside Therese, to quietly taste the tiny, private kernel of exhilaration that's sprung up between us.

'You all right?' I casually touch her hand, and she gives mine a light squeeze, in return.

'A bit dizzy, but fine, thanks for asking.'

'I have to go to work – will you be okay here?' She nods, and her eyes follow me out the door.

I pop down to the production office. Everyone says 'hello'. Carver has been told the good news; he'll be in around six. Two senior opposition politicians are due in for eight. Kate and Scally have called the Minister for Justice and the Police Commissioner, but they're still stalling, probably because they've been told that we have unseen footage. Keep trying, I say.

And what footage it is; they're right to be afraid. I'm up in one of the edit suites, I've dubbed Snoot's material into the machine, and I'm scrolling through it, cutting the best shots together. Using the zoom facility, individual cops can be clearly identified lashing into the protestors, a few in particular with rabidly ecstatic expressions that would not look out of place in a hard-core porn flick. I ring the station solicitor. He's a bit shirty about it, but he agrees that there's no legal issue over identifying cops, so I don't pixellate their faces. Over the next few hours, I build up a wild three minutes of fast-moving film, cutting frantic scuffles with shots of batons raining down and close-ups of screaming campaigners being dragged away. One long-haired girl cries and wriggles frantically, as the cops bodily carry her off, her jeans practically pulled off her body. In one truly sickening display, an older man lies curled up on the ground, while a cop kneels on top of him, hitting him again and again. Jesus. This will be our best show yet. Carver will have a field day with this, whether the cops put up a spokesman or not. Police brutality, as brought to you by the intelligent, rock-and-roll TV show that doesn't tolerate bullshit!

For effect, I keep in the last few seconds, where the camera is dropped in the undergrowth, followed by much banging and yelling as Snoot is beaten. After that, there's just muffled cursing, mixed with blurred sky and ground, as he obviously broke free, grabbed the camera, and ran like hell. He didn't film Therese being truncheoned, which is a relief. I check the clock. Quarter past seven. I wonder whether the others have the rest of the show in hand. We need to do up a final running order. I'll take a walk down to the office, check the lie of the land, talk through a line of questioning with Carver, then go see Therese. I swivel my chair away from the editing desk.

'JESUS! I didn't know you were there! Don't *do* that!'

Carver stands just a few feet behind me, wearing his black suit and a white cloth tied around his neck like a giant bib, to prevent his ample face make-up from smearing his shirt. He looks at me, eyes glittering. His face bears the puffiness of overdue sleep, but Liz has done a great job on his forehead. He doesn't speak; in fact for an instant, I have the strange impression of confronting a waxwork that someone has soundlessly slipped into the suite, whilst I was engrossed in cutting the footage. I try to still my beating heart.

'Have you been past the office? I was about to go down and see if we've got anyone to come on and defend these boys – I'm telling you, we're gonna kill them if they do. Blood on the floor. Here, let me play this for you, it's fucking dynamite.' I turn back to the desk and hit 'rewind'.

'I think I've seen most of it, already.' His voice has an odd edge, and as I turn to look at him, he smiles. 'I've been watching for quite a while.'

'Good,' and I'm all business now, 'because I think we should pick a few clips to use as a promo and get the station to play it out right away. You can voice it in the studio. We should also ring the papers, to let them know we have something a bit special on tonight, and offer them stills for the morning editions.'

'I don't want to do it,' and he's not looking me in the eye, but rather at a point somewhere behind my left shoulder.

I don't get it at first. 'What, voice a trailer or give it to the papers? I'm just thinking we could do with a bit of positive publicity, after last weekend ...'

'No, Teach, I don't want to do the story. I don't want to run that tape. I don't want those guests on my show.'

'You *whaaaat*?'

He shrugs. 'Every other outlet has been going big on it all day,' and his eyes are on my face now, but I can tell from the way they're dancing around that he's dissembling. As he continues, I realise that I'm witnessing a monkey first – embarrassment. 'I just think it's, er, overdone by now. The story has no more legs; there's nothing I can really bring to it tonight that hasn't already been said.'

I shake my head a few times, before the words come splashing out. It's only as I babble that I grow suspicious.

'Maybe I'm wrong, but I got the distinct impression this morning that you were rather, ah, passionately of the opinion that we needed to cover this story. Well, sit down and watch the tape properly, and you'll see that there's still plenty to be said. The country will go mad when we play this out: we have real live action footage here of the police losing control against a bunch of peaceful protestors. Not only that, we have a selection of their victims, and by the way, they're *great* victims, sitting up in our green room, still caked in blood. Okay, it's not exactly 9/11, but it's the story of the week, and we have it by the balls!'

He smiles ruefully and half-pats, half-slaps me on the face. 'Teach, Teach, you're a great producer, you're the best there is, and you've done an amazing day's work getting hold of this story.'

'Then quit licking my hole and tell me you're okay to do it.'

'I don't want to run with it, Teach.' Fuck me, he's serious.

'I'm not hearing this. Just tell me you're suffering a minor brainstorm or a fucking aneurysm or some-thing, and we'll talk again in a few minutes when you're back to normal! This will be a cracking piece of television, and we're running with it, tonight! Shit, why are we even *having* this conversation? It's ridiculous!'

He studies the floor now, but I can feel him

thicken up. 'I don't want to do this story. You're right – this morning, it felt that way to me, too …'

'And it felt that way to the office furniture!'

'Yeah, but you gotta be flexible in this game, Teach; you gotta be able to make last-minute changes to the show!'

'Enough with telling me my own job, already! Unless George Bush has been caught screwing his daughters in the last half-hour, this is the story of the day, and you know it! Look, what's the problem here, what's gotten into you?'

And he's on me, little monkey paws outstretched, clutching my arms, his puffy, made-up face close to mine. His eyes are gleaming, and he has the trace of a smile about his lips.

'Teach! You're a good producer, and I'm not buttering you up, truly, you are!' He momentarily frees one hand and makes a snaking motion with it, the way he does when he's trying to explain something so incredibly complex, only he can understand it. 'But I've been trying to explain, we gotta think of the future! You see, we're real players now, you and me! We have a strong programme. Respected. Used the right way, it can be a powerful tool for both of us, but we've got to start playing the long game!'

I think I'm beginning to get it. Maybe he's right; maybe I'm *not* sneaky enough. Sometimes. I break free from his clasp, keeping it super-cool, my eyes and voice both flat, betraying nothing.

'The long game, huh? So, the Archbishop last

week, that's what that charade was all about? The long game?'

'Well, *yes*, Teach!' He takes a step back and claps his little paws together, laughing, in delight. 'This stuff with the road protestors, it's just a storm in a teacup! Okay, we can cause a few problems if we broadcast this tonight,' and he waves dismissively in the direction of the editing machine, a frozen picture of a raised, baton-clutching arm static on the monitor. 'We'll make a few headlines – so what? I know how these boys operate! By the end of next week, this story will be over, no matter what we do! Gone! Forgotten!'

'Who contacted you?'

'What do you mean?'

'You want me to play the long game, then you tell me who I'm playing it with. Who contacted you?'

The visor snaps down, his supplication instantly replaced by something much sterner. 'I'm telling you one last time – I run my show by my own lights!'

So, this is where the journey has finally brought me. In 1953, at the annual Press Club dinner in New York, John Swifton, Chief of Staff for *The New York Times*, was asked to toast an independent press. Here's what he stood up and said:

*The business of journalists is to destroy the truth; to lie outright, to pervert, to vilify; to fawn at the feet of Mammon. You know it and I know it, and what folly is this, toasting an independent press? We are the tools and vassals of rich men behind the scenes. We are the jumping jacks, they pull the strings and we dance. Our talents, our*

*possibilities and our lives are the property of other men.*
*We are intellectual prostitutes.*

One can only imagine how that went down. John
Swifton, I toast you. The soup must have stuck in
your throat.

I have Carver up against the wall, my hand around
his chin, his feet off the ground, like the night he
sacked Scally. It's as if I'm standing in another part of
the suite, disembodied, watching myself do this, the
iron band cleaving my chest in half.

'Those fucking people in the green room!' I'm
screaming. I can hear my own voice, shrill, yet strangely
deadened by the soundproof walls. 'What am I
supposed to tell them, eh? They fucking *trusted* me! I've
dragged them all the way in from Wicklow, with their
busted faces, and I told them, I *promised* them, that they
could tell their side of the story on our show tonight!
Whatever happened to police fucking brutality, eh?'

And he's laughing. I can't believe that the little
bastard is still laughing. I'm so taken aback, I relax my
grip and let him down from the wall. I have flesh-
coloured make-up all over my hand.

'I sent the hippies home, Teach, they're already
gone. I sorted them out, said I'd send them a payment
for their trouble. I told them that something else had
come up. I told them it was my decision, that I edit my
own show. Some of them wanted to see you, but they
left when I called security. What the fuck does it
matter? They're only a bunch of hippies!'

I'm lying in my car, upside down, in a field, off my
tits on drugs, with Stella hanging from her seatbelt,

laughing, and two girls in the back squealing, a jumble of arms and legs. After a beach party last summer, the Creature urging me to drive home faster because she wants to teach the girls standy-uppy, and of course I can't wait. Then I hit oil on a bend and the bushes and … bang!

Now, I'm watching Therese drive off in a jeep outside The Blue Moon, without saying goodbye, and I'm standing in the road, comprehending nothing.

Now, my father punches one of my brothers, and my brother punches him back, breaking his glasses.

Everything's worse than in my dreams. Dreams, no matter how bad, are only a dry run for the horrors of real life.

'You sent them away? But that makes me look like a right cunt! And it also means we have no fucking *show*!'

Carver fixes his collar, where I grabbed him. 'Relax, would ya! Take a chill pill! I called the Minister for Finance. He's gonna come on and do an extended interview. I told the team to change the programme around; it's already organised, so don't worry, you don't have to *do* anything. I have it all worked out inside my head!'

'But we had the bastard on last week!'

'I know, I know, but he and I go back a long way; we're great friends, we can talk about horse-racing, he's a big fan of that. This time it'll be really personal, wide-ranging stuff, with no token lefties to get in the way!'

'Shut up, you stupid FUCK!' I roar so loudly, the effort practically blinds me. I have the heavy swivel chair in my hands, ready to smash it in his face. Instead, I fling it behind me against the editing machine, which judders and plays the footage. I storm out the door, leaving Carver alone with the screams and the shouts, the fast-cut film of truncheons raining down on forearms, shoulders, and heads.

I run to the green room. Empty, apart from disposable cups and take-away cartons lying in testament across the tables. I sprint to the production office; I feel tears filling my eyes. No. Not yet. Please, not yet. I burst through the door, and needless to say, no one says 'hello'. They all have their heads down – quietly and mysteriously busy. I grab my car-keys from my desk and I want to leave without saying anything, but I'm so fucking furious that I stop in the doorway and yell, 'Carver is right!' They look up. 'You *are* a bunch of useless cunts! Devil-spawn, replicant … oh, what's the use?'

Therese. Therese. Her mobile diverts to that impersonal minder. Fuck! What would I do, if I were her? The Kerry bus? I jump into my car, completely disregarding the fact that we're due on air in ninety minutes, and drive into town like a madman. Friday rush hour, the traffic is obscene. I'm crying, thumping my steering wheel, and I nearly run over a bunch of tourists on Gardiner Street. I abandon my car outside the bus station and dash inside. Run along the queues, try to take in the faces. Timetable. Next bus for Tralee leaves in ten. If that's her plan, she has to be here. Red coat, across the station. I run over, and it's a Spanish student, about a foot too small to be Therese and her coat the wrong shade of red. I'm back in my car. Okay, stop thinking 'Therese', start thinking 'crusty'. If I were a protestor, what would I do? Where would I go? Back to the shattered camp, for a last look? Back to the caravans? Then maybe up to The Blue Moon, to get properly drunk and roundly curse capitalism.

I head south, onto the dual carriageway out of town, which is clogged with cars. After about ten minutes edging along, ranting and cursing, I rudely pull across two lanes and onto the hard shoulder, where I stick the boot down, racing up the inside, attracting horns, flashing lights, and manual displays of automotive opprobrium. Fuck you and fuck you. I come round a sweeping downhill corner about a mile further on, my temper cooling to the point where I'm beginning to think that maybe the stunt-driving is a bad idea. And there it is, at the bottom of the hill, crawling with everyone else in the slow lane, the scuffed white roof of a battered Land Rover. I storm down the hard shoulder and skid to a stop about forty paces past the target. I leap out of my car and wave. Snoot sees me all right, because he beeps the horn, flashes his lights, and gives me the fingers through his windscreen. The traffic picks up slightly, and he drives on by. Bastard! I can't see Therese, but Mascara Girl hangs out the passenger window and throws me an ironic little wave. I jump back in my car and race past the jeep on the inside again, only this time, I walk out into the road in front of it. Snoot is so surprised, he stomps on the brakes, but still the bull bars strike me on the upper legs and stomach, sending me sprawling onto the tarmac. As I hit the ground, I hear the car behind Snoot rear-end him, a smash of plastic and broken glass. I'm too hurt to move right away. Snoot is standing over me, yelling curses.

'I mean *fuck* maan, whaat the *fuck* maaan, you crazy fucker! I ought to kick your face in!'

'I'm sorry!' is all I can gasp. 'I'm sorry! Where's Therese?'

'Therese don't *ever* wanna see you again. That is one sad lady!'

I try to stand, but I can't quite manage it. I get halfway up and fall dizzily down again, banging my face. By now, there's a lot of horns honking, and the driver of the car behind Snoot has come around, babbling and waving his arms.

'Please! Where's Therese? I need to talk to her!'

Lying sprawled, I watch as Snoot argues with the other driver and the rest of the traffic, yelling at everything and everyone to shut the fuck up. Someone kneels over me. Therese? No, Mascara Girl.

'You're fucking bleeding, dude. Can you sit up?' So she *can* talk, after all.

'I'm bleeding?' I mumble. 'Then that makes two of us. I'm bleeding, you're bleeding, we're all bleeding. Where's Therese?'

'Like, get up off the road, dude!'

I shake my head on the tarmac and yell, 'Where's THERESE?'

'Oh, cool, I get it! You're blocking the road! Direct action! Nice one!' Snoot pushes the other driver away, then turns back to me. 'He's staging a sit-down protest,' Mascara Girl hoots. 'He wants Therese!'

'Well, she's not here, mate, so go on, piss off!'

I grab his filthy jeans, forcing him to help me to my feet. When he does, I shove him away, then hurl myself at the open door of the jeep, scrabbling inside. Half-a-dozen faces return my stare from the rear compartment, none of them Therese. A rough hand tugs my shirt, pulling me backwards into the traffic. As I fall off the footplate, I seize Snoot's leather jacket, using my weight to pull him to the ground on top of me. The screech of tyres, as a car in the fast lane stops inches from our heads. I hold onto Snoot's leather jacket for grim death, keeping his face close to mine.

'Just tell me where she is! Tell me!'

'For the love of fuck, mate – I don't *know*, okay? She wouldn't leave your fucking station until she talked to you! That little dwarf guy who fronts your programme, he called the heavies, and I'm like, I don't need *another* riot, so I dragged her out of there, but she broke loose and legged it down the street! That's the last we saw of her, I swear!'

'I don't believe you!'

He relaxes, stops fighting me. 'All right, so I'm lying. She's been hiding in my back pocket, all this time.'

I let Snoot go and crawl around the front of the jeep to the hard shoulder. I pull myself up onto the bonnet of my car, as the jeep revs and, amidst a cacophony of car horns, pulls away. Through the open window Snoot shouts, 'You fucked us over, man! You fucked us over!'

The iron band, locked around my chest, cutting off oxygen. Or is that where the jeep hit me? I can't breathe.

'But why would I do that?' I gasp. 'Why would I do that? *Why would I fucking DO that?*' The jeep rattles off into the distance, with the now steadily moving traffic.

I've left my fags at the station, and if I ever needed a fag, it's right now. I feel too mangled to drive any distance, so I ease the car about a half a mile down the carriageway and stop at a roadside pub. I buy three large vodkas and a tumbler of water, then limp to a corner table, hitting the vending machine on the way. I get a few looks, for the cut on my face and the state of my shirt, but who cares? With large, vengeful swallows, I start necking the vodka and fill my lungs with hot smoke. In the far corner of the pub, a raised television set soundlessly plays the opening sequence of our show. I have to refrain from flinging my glass at the screen, but even in the state I'm in, I can't help noticing with a tinge of professional pride that Carver addresses the wrong camera during his intro. Cut to the Minister for Finance, looking bemused.

This is the first Friday night in six years that I haven't spent cocooned in that studio, and look – life goes on, in the real world. I try Therese on her mobile again, almost weeping with misplaced hope, knowing full well that it will divert. The vodka numbs my bruises but does little to numb what I'm feeling inside. I order three more doubles, carry them to my lair in the corner, then, having dispatched them, go to the bathroom and clean up as best I can.

Back in the car, I do two generous lines of gak from the glove compartment. I drive to the station and reverse into a far corner of the car-park, killing the engine and lights. I smoke, I wait, and do a bit more coke. Where are you, Therese? Where? Where? Can't you feel me, alone in the dark, reaching out for you, wanting you to call, wanting to fall asleep beside you, chaste, injured, quiet, content to lose everything, if only I can be with you? Apparently not.

Just before midnight, taxis begin to pour through the station gates and queue up at the entrance. After a few minutes, a group of noisy, weaving figures appears, shouting bawdy insults and pulling at the taxi doors. On any other Friday night, that would be me. Carver emerges, his diminutive silhouette clearly discernable at even this distance, sandwiched between Charlotte and Kate. He breaks off from the pair of them to stage a mock fight with Scally, who snatches Carver's standard-issue champagne bottle and dances around with it on his head. Nice to see them feeling so subdued and guilty about what they did today. One by one, the taxis pull away, for yet another night of VIP lounge-lizardry.

I could wait a couple of hours, then follow to exactly where I know they'll be and confront the little bastard before his sodden, helpless troop. Punch him to the floor, put the boot into him, just to see how they react. Instead, I climb out of my car and walk through reception. The security guards watch me pass with mild puzzlement, but say nothing. I make my way to the edit suite. A frozen arm, raising a baton, flickers on the screen. I dub a copy of the riot footage onto VHS, drop it into an A4 envelope with a hastily written note, then drive a mile to *The Sunday Reporter* building. The security guards there promise to give it to Gavin Kelly first thing in the morning, but just to make sure, I send him a text, alerting him to the contents. About halfway home, my phone beeps. Therese?

THANKS – BUT Y U NO USE 2 NITE?

Bollocks, just Kelly, so I don't bother to reply. Back at my apartment building, the coked-up, wish-fulfilling part of me wants to see Therese, waiting, on the sofa in the lobby, but of course she isn't there, so I let myself into my flat, which is as dark and empty as I am. I crack open a bottle of vodka from the freezer and stand on my balcony, trying to calculate whether a jump would carry me as far as the river, which is as black as Carver's heart, with orange lights undulating over the surface. No way. I'd just splatter on the concrete walkway below, maybe hit some railings, and wouldn't that make a pretty picture in the morning?

I do more gak and more vodka. A lot more vodka. When the bottle empties, I fetch another from the fridge. On the wall above the leather lounger is a framed collage of our show's first listings in the TV supplements. Our show. *The Kevin Carver Show*. The rock-'n'-roll TV show that doesn't tolerate bullshit.

Bang! The empty vodka bottle smashes the frame off the wall, onto the wooden floor. Christ! Who the fuck did that?

Uh, you did, Lee!

Did I? No way! Why would I do a thing like that?

Dunno … maybe you're a bit pissed off, because your fancy-woman thinks you're a liar and a creep!

Crash!

Wahey, there goes the television! But that's good, one less outlet for that filthy little ape! By the way, did kicking that screen hurt your foot?

Wallop!

Now hold on there, big boy, the television I can understand, but why the coffee table? Was that strictly necessary? And in case you haven't noticed, you slit your hand open by failing to let go of that ashtray in time …

Crunch!

Okay, so you've had a hard day at work, but I fail to see how the stereo had *anything* to do with it! Or the magazine rack, for that matter!

Smash!

Ah, go on, admit it, you just love the sound of breaking glass, don't you? It's your upper-class paternity. That balcony door will cost a fortune to fix! I'd stop now, if I were you … No! Lee! Not the fucking bookcase!

Blam!

Do you know who you remind me of? Well, do you? That's right! You're doing exactly what *he* does, in one of his tantrums! Hey, maybe you *are* turning into him! No, wait! Microwave ovens cannot fly, repeat after me, microwave ovens cannot … oh, what's the use?

I wake up in the bathroom, wedged between the toilet and the tiled wall. Someone has vomited and bled profusely over me, over the toilet bowl, and the floor. The shower and the taps are belting out water, turned up full, and I know I've been crying, because my eyes are swollen. I can barely see.

'Lee! Lee! Christ! He's hurt!'

Go away. Not interested. Tired now, had enough.

'We've been burgled, fucking burgled! What the fuck? Who *did* this?'

I make an effort. Therese, come to forgive me.

'Lee!' Shake. 'Wake up!'

Not Therese, but Stella. Kneeling over me, shaking me by the shoulder. I try to stand up, but I can't. My head feels like it's been frozen in a pool of clear plastic.

'Lee! What happened?'

'*Regardez!*' My arm flies out, in a demonstrative, bloody sweep. 'Look upon my works, ye mighty, and despair!'

'Did *you* do this?'

'Have you seen Therese?'

'Who?'

'She lives in a tent up a tree, she's a human roadblock …'

'Man, you are *seriously* fucked up!'

'I'm fine and dandy. Pour me a drink, please.'

'Did you do this?'

'Which part of "pour me a drink" did you not understand?'

'LEE! DID ... YOU ... DO ... THIS?'

'Yes! I'll fill out the appropriate forms in the morning! Now, I have work to do, so pretty please, with pink cunting ribbons on it, pour me a fucking drink!' She's on her feet, talking to some guy I don't know, the pair of them standing in the bathroom door, staring down at me. Guy? What's a guy doing in my flat? Snoot? 'You bastards! Where's Therese? What have you done with her body?'

'What the *fuck* have you been taking?'

'Don't trust her!' I yell, at the blur that is the two of them. 'She'll eat you up and give you the wrong mobile number in the morning!'

'I'm, uh, gonna spend the night at Jimmy's, okay?'

Reminds me of a song. 'Jimmy Jimmy! Ooohh!'

'I can't bring my friends home to this fucking shit! I mean, what the fuck?'

Hey. I feel another song coming on ... 'It's my party, and I'll cry if I want to, cry if I want to, yadda yadda fuckin yah ...'

'Jesus H Christ,' she mutters to Jimmy, whoever Jimmy is. 'Sorry, I've never seen him like this before.'

'See ya! Goodnight! Enjoy the ride, Jimmy! Close the door on your way out, and be careful not to break anything!'

The flat door slams. The taps are still pouring, hard and fast. Good. Running water. That means I can cry some more.

# 21

## OUT OF THE LOOP

I walk into the office, and nobody says 'hello'.

They're all here: Scally, Kate, Charlotte, Dervla, Elaine – the whole troop. At the head of the room, half-hidden behind a newspaper, primate number one presides. Not a grunt out of him either, but I can tell by the smell of him that he's tense, alert. As I sit down, Scally glances in my direction, taking in the cut on my forehead and the plaster on my hand, but studies the wall when I nod, as if he hasn't seen me. I switch on my computer, pretending to notice nothing amiss, but I don't need to have shared a room with these people for six years to know that this calm is entirely artificial.

I put out a feeler. 'Anyone have anything booked for this week's show?' Like I say, Tuesday is the day we chuck stuff into the mix, fire ideas around, see what's shaping up. No one answers. They're all fiercely intent on a series of minor tasks. Okay, use someone's name this time. Kate is my direct junior, so I home in on her.

'Kate. Everyone seems very busy. Have we anything booked for this week that I need to be aware of?' And I can't help snorting this bit, 'Any last-minute changes to the show, for example?'

Kate reddens, looks in Carver's direction, and then at a point somewhere close to my shoes. 'I, ah, well … there's nothing …' and Carver turns a page on his upheld newspaper, flicking it taut, so that it makes a small bang. Kate jumps and reverts to her screen without meeting my eyes.

'I'm sorry, I didn't quite catch that – what were you about to say?'

Another snap of the newspaper, as this time Carver folds his barrier down. He coughs and leans forward. The others jerk to attention and turn towards him in a single, collective motion, like a school of fish.

'Okay, everybody,' he begins, in a tone that borders on the prissy. 'I'd like to review the options available to us for this week's show … Scally, put that pen down.' His meat-skewer stare turns on the aforementioned munchkin, who hurriedly drops the offending implement. 'I have to say,' Carver continues, 'that I was less than happy with Friday night's programme. I want to see more effort go into the production side of things, from now on.'

I let out a really loud 'Ha!' at that one. I sit back, plonk my feet up onto my desk, and clasp my hands behind my head. 'May I humbly suggest that if you

304

want a better production effort on this week's programme, then it might help to talk to a producer?' No one moves. For a second, I think I've got him. He purses his mouth, cocks his head downwards, holds the pose, and I'm braced for the explosion, with shrapnel, in my direction. But it doesn't come. Instead, he lifts his face towards the rest of the hyper-attentive team and enquires, 'Has anyone got anything booked for this week's show?'

And they're off. Scally has this; Kate has that. Dervla has a distinct possibility. Elaine's long-standing request for a certain Irish Hollywood actor has borne fruit. Even Charlotte, God help us, has an idea.

'Are we all satisfied,' I call, as loudly as I can without shouting, 'that police brutality is no longer a massive issue?'

Again, I'm ignored, as Carver makes a show of listening to the others. They're like hungry puppies around a kennel-master, all eager to be seen, heard, and acknowledged. I watch this performance for a solid half-hour. A production meeting, happening as if I wasn't in the building, let alone right here in my chair. With more vigour than usual, Carver alternately shakes and nods his head, and it's a mixture of food and slaps for the hungry little puppies.

'Yes, Kate, let's go with that. I think it will develop into a big story as the week progresses ... No, Scally, I don't think so ... Yes, Charlotte? Hmm, well, let's write that down as a possibility, and sit on it for a couple of days ... Dervla, scrap that; Elaine, book your man.' Yessir, yessir, three bags full. And he's up, tucking a few newspapers under his arm, as he heads for the door.

'Okay, team, see you later – Scally, if anything important happens, ring me at home, yeah? Yeah?'

And you can bet Scally will ring him fifteen times in the next hour, just to make himself look important. When Carver leaves, I remain with my feet up, staring each of them in the face, one by one. But not a sinner in the room acknowledges my presence, afraid to disobey the edict of excommunication – because that's obviously what I'm facing – even when Carver is not present to enforce it. No doubt, anyone who talks to me will be informed on by a trusty colleague, aching to curry favour with alpha monkey. My phone goes, internal extension. Duster. Why, my day just keeps getting better!

I climb the stairs and enter the spick-and-span office, wondering whether I should grab the crystal golf trophy down from the shelf and just get this over with here and now. I pull up a chair, not as close to his desk as I usually would, and settle deliberately into it, legs out, hands behind the head. Duster glances at my cut but doesn't ask how I acquired it. Instead, he pushes his glasses back on his nose and leans forward, making the podgy steeple with his fingers, chief-executive-style. He's obviously been rehearsing today's helicopter view for the bulk of the weekend. As usual, I can tell, because there are too many pedantic flourishes, and the whole thing is too smoothly delivered, for that not to be the case.

'I think we should have a formal review of Friday night's programme, Lee.'

'Love to, Dickie.'

'To be perfectly frank with you, it wasn't very good, and several rather important people attached to the station communicated with me during the course of it, as they frequently do, to convey, on this occasion, their disappointment. Wearing my producer's hat, I would always be the first to defend the programme-maker's position against editorialising from inside or outside the station, but I was compelled to admit that in this instance, both as a producer and as head of programmes, that these critical opinions rather tended to echo my own; that is to say, that you were effectively repeating, at great length, an item from the previous week – an item, incidentally, over which you know I had my doubts in the first instance – when there were other, more compelling stories we could have run with on the day. One story in particular, which every other media outlet was making hay with.'

And he glances towards a copy of *The Sunday Reporter*, the front page plastered with stills from Snoot's recording. Police lost control in Glen Dara – shocking, exclusive pictures – full story, by Gavin Kelly.

What Duster is trying to say, via his gush of verbal vomit, is that the Chairman rang him during the show to complain that it was crap. Therefore, Duster is doing what people like Duster do in situations where blame arises – he's covering his fat, hairy ass. But my problem here is that Duster is right. The programme *was* crap, indefensible crap. Even I could tell that, skulking in the corner of some anonymous pub at the edge of a dual carriageway halfway to Wicklow. So, I have two choices. Throughout my entire career at the station, I've treated Duster with the icily polite, thinly veiled contempt that I know he deserves, taking my lead from Carver's out-and-out hostility towards him. The question of breaking rank with Carver, on any issue, before the contemptible Duster has been hitherto inconceivable. Duster is the enemy.

Choice one is to stonewall Duster, fob him off, and deal with this mess in my own way. However, the evidence strongly suggests that Carver has already commenced the process of fucking me over. Therefore, choice two is to admit the truth of what happened on Friday to Duster. If Carver is spiralling that far out of control, surely it's time someone senior stepped in? At first, more out of habit than anything, I go for option one.

'There's been a lot of disagreement about last week's show, all part of the cut and thrust of normal editorial debate.'

And he's straight back with, 'Yes, I've been appraised of this already. On Saturday afternoon, for the first time since he commenced working for TV Ireland, I had the pleasure of a call at home from your celebrity presenter. He was very charming and agreeable for a change, but after a bit of a chat, he told me that he felt he had to warn me about you. He said that you turned up late for work and arbitrarily, against his wishes, dropped a very important, carefully planned item about the road protest from Friday night's show. He said that he was unhappy with your level of professional judgement and that the two of you argued. You then stormed out of the building, an hour before air, and took the rest of the evening off. You left an inexperienced colleague to studio-produce. You also left your team with no other alternative than to book whomever they could, at short notice. Kevin told me that the Minister for Finance agreed to appear again, for the second week running, as a personal favour to him. He even apologised to me for the weakness of the programme, but I am in no doubt as to where the blame lies.'

That dirty, dirty little monkey! Still trying to cope with the enormity of being blanked in my own office, now I'm forced to fend off a pack of lies about Friday night. And like all lies, once uttered, this one will grow legs. The past has no existence, except as a succession of present mental states. History, re-written, in that gnarled little head!

So, option one is no longer an option. I reach for option two. 'Dickie. Carver is fucking with you. *He* pulled the road-protest item on Friday night, not me.'

'Kevin's a highly experienced journalist! Why on earth would he do a thing like that?'

'Because he's off on some self-serving agenda. Because he's decided that the show is his personal vehicle; no more, no less.'

Duster forms a little moue with his porky lips, makes a show of shrugging, and stares out his executive office window. I hope he likes what he sees.

When he turns his eyes back to me, they've gone all beady and hard.

'Okay, let's park that allegation and revert to it at an appropriate juncture.'

'No! Carver has lied to you! Don't park it, deal with it!'

'May I also remind you that, in the light of certain recent gossip stories, I'd asked you to report any disagreements, indeed anything at all unusual in Carver's behaviour, to me, personally. In this instance, from what you yourself have just told me, you signally failed to do that.'

I laugh in his face. 'So, you noticed nothing at all *unusual* when you saw me on Friday morning?'

Cover ass alert. 'Now, wait a minute! I asked you, in front of witnesses, how the show was going! You told me you were having a production meeting!'

'And you didn't get the joke?'

'Look here, Lovecraft, TV Ireland pays you to produce good television ...'

Uh-oh, where have I heard this before?

'... but we also pay you to manage, on an ongoing basis, what I would call a creatively volatile situation ...'

Quick! Cover your ears! Because if that golf trophy starts talking again ...

'... and that, if anything, is your true value to this station ...'

*Pick me up! Grab me! You know you want to do it, my son, so go on!*

'... and I may as well formally notify you that if

there comes a point where it seems you can no longer manage *The Kevin Carver Show* …'

*Kill him! Kill the fat fuck!*

'… then your value to this station, unlike your presenter's enormous value, would be severely diminished.'

*You are such a fucking wuss, Lee! Christ, if I had legs, I'd climb down there and do him myself, on general principles!*

I have to get out of here. This is payback, Duster-style. This is what I get for treating him like an idiot all these years. Of course he knows that Carver is lying. But he doesn't give a shit. Because Duster can't sack Carver, but he can sure as fuck sack me.

*Kill him, Lee, kill him!!!*

'One more thing before you go,' and Duster, blithely unaware just how close to death's door he is, opens *The Sunday Reporter* at an inside page. He turns it primly in my direction.

'Do you know what this about, by any chance?' Gossip column item, no byline.

*Who's been a naughty boy, then? Unchastened by his recent travails at the hands of our country's finest, my Diet Coke-loving friend has, at least, finally taken to using his head. To hit other people with, if the stories I'm hearing from the party circuit are true! You really are incorrigible, you horrible little man!*

I drop the newspaper back onto Duster's super-tidy desk more contemptuously than I should, in present circumstances, and throw my reply over my shoulder, as I leave.

'I have no idea, Dickie, but why don't you ask your new best friend Kevin? I have to say, it sounds like a creatively volatile situation to me.'

The term 'boycott' originated in Loughmask, County Mayo, in September 1880. Captain Charles Cunningham Boycott was a land agent for the absentee Lord Earne. Protesting tenant farmers demanded a rent rebate from him, and when he refused to grant it, everyone in the locality ignored him and his family. He couldn't even buy food in the shop. Quite why they didn't just shoot him, in the traditional manner, is uncertain. It would have been kinder.

In the workplace, boycotting is the most refined form of bullying imaginable, and therefore quite common in media circles. If you ever make it through the hallowed portals of some newspaper, radio, or TV station, you'll notice that there are quite a few individuals who won't talk to you at all. Ever. But don't be confused – this isn't boycotting, and it's not personal. You have to *be* a person before things get personal. Ignoring lowly newcomers has more to do with displaying status and is non-verbal language for: 'I'm somebody, and you're nobody – are we clear on that?'

Boycotting, or blanking, denotes another level of sophistication altogether. It is an exquisite, subtle, and highly effective technique that has, ironically, been encouraged by increasingly progressive employment legislation. In this highly pressured environment, technically you can no longer call someone a cunt, a fucker, a stupid bastard, a dumb bitch, an idiot, an ignoramus, a moron, or any of the other epithets that spring to mind when someone makes a mistake or when you just don't like them. There are laws against using such terminology, and an unguarded volley of abuse can risk turning the unfortunate victim into an instant winner. All he or she has to do is knock on a manager's door, and if remedial action is not instantly taken, then the employer could be looking down both barrels of a court case. But cold-shouldering is much harder to pin down, extremely difficult to prove, and impossible to stop, once it begins. It's not easy to knock on a manager's door and say, 'Excuse me, but, ah … nobody will speak to me …'

So, blanking tends to be the bullying instrument of choice in large, properly run organisations. However, in shabby shoestring outfits like TV Ireland, pretty much any behaviour still goes, which is why Carver has been able to act like a madman with impunity for so long. As his celebrity increased, so did the frequency and violence of his tantrums. But now I'm being blanked, not because Carver is afraid of employment legislation (I mean, who's gonna wave the rule book at him – Dickie Vaughan?), but because he knows that tantrums don't work with me.

Being ignored is tough, on many levels. Mainly because it's such a ridiculous situation to be in, as an adult. There's the sheer cowardice of those who collectively blank someone at another's command – it's extremely disheartening when the people you've worked with, drank with, laughed with, and, in some cases, trained, don't have the fibre to approach you, even privately, to try to establish what's really happening for themselves. Instead, they become sheep, at the bully's command. Then, there's the utter impracticality of trying to function alongside colleagues who pretend they can't hear you. Even simple questions like, 'Is the printer working?' assume a sort of silent, doom-laden, irresolvable significance. There's the inevitable sense of isolation, the feeling of uselessness that the entire exercise is designed to instil. Blank faces – one becomes a blank, a non-entity. There's the sense of pride, the desire to show the bastards they're not winning. Absurdly, you end up collaborating in the wider pretence that nothing is, in fact, going on. And then there's the anger.

It's Thursday evening, dusk. I'm lying on the leather lounger, before my broken balcony doors, watching the water. Behind me, my flat is a mess of shattered glass and tossed furniture. The place looks like it's been ransacked by crack-hungry gibbons. I think my cleaner came round, took one look, and left again, because I haven't heard from her. I haven't heard from the Creature either; she's probably curled up in some ravishingly alternative drug-den with Jimmy or whoever, where she'll doubtless stay until she gets bored. I just phoned Therese – message minder. There goes my chance to be good. I can't remember the last time I ate anything. I've replenished the freezer with vodka, and I've had a few spliffs, but nothing can stop my brain from racing like the engine of my car. What can I do? Go to Carver and apologise, just as I once advised Scally to do, to regain a place in the troop?

Out of the fucking question! Apologise for what? Thing called 'pride', Lee!

Maybe I could confront Carver in front of 'the team'? Argue the whole thing out in public?

No chance, they've already decided which side their bread is buttered on.

Maybe I could go back to Duster and try to reason with him?

Oh, *please*!

What about the board?

Lee – they don't care, as long as they're making money.

I lie perfectly still, willing my impotent rage to go away, but impotence just makes it so much worse. The Monkey Man doesn't love me, I can see that now. I *am* the cuckold in a faithless relationship; I *am* the nagging housewife. I am no more Carver's partner than Scally or Charlotte or any of the rest. Equality was a chimera that he cultivated when he needed me to kick-start his TV career. Cunningly, he'd conjured up the illusion of rebellious, collegial respect, sensing immediately that, as a gawping twenty-four-year-old, I'd respond with total loyalty. He read me like a book. But six years on, we've entered the comfort zone of assured celebrity. The good fight is long over, and the beta-monkey status I earned in battle has been reduced to a mere honorific, in the gift of a capricious master. I was just too stupid, too vain, and too much of a meeja whore to see it.

The message is clear – if I want to hold onto my position, to my salary, I'll have to lie down and take a good fucking from time to time, just like everyone else. Do as I'm told. Become a twisted, second-hand version of Carver himself, just to keep a place in his pecking order. If I want to stay in the tribe, I'll have to be fucked monkey, submissive monkey, because at long last it's my turn. I realise all this, as I lie here alone.

It's the end of my third day as a non-person. This week's programme has been set up entirely without any input from me; I've only been able to establish what's on it by listening to Scally's breathless reports to Carver's home number. Ungrateful monkey – he wouldn't *have* a show if it wasn't for me. Our show. *His* show. We did it together, but now I can see that this is really all about the greater glory of him. I take another swig of vodka.

If you ever try to fuck me over, I'll kill you.

Hold on … *what* did you just say?

You heard me.

No, I didn't.

Want me to repeat it?

Oh Jesus, look at you! You suddenly discover that the world is a cruel place, and your first response is to … *kill?*

Why not? Happens every day in America! The Travis Bickle Technique! The Columbine Solution!

Why, you big, soft pussy …

Shut up, or I'll kill you!

Oh, ha fucking ha.

316

It's amazing how a few drinks can render the answer to a consuming conundrum so blindingly obvious, a course of action so refreshingly clear. In the media, when you're being shafted, people move away from you. Nobody wants to be standing beside you when you finally get shot. I'm about to be shot, and nobody will help me. I'm the only person who can – who *will* – help me. Not to get shot. Carver has hit me with an opening salvo, but it's more of a warning, a clear demonstration of what will happen if I don't fall into line, and fast. If I'm going to survive, I have to neuter the shooter.

I unravel myself from the leather lounger and stand under the shower for twenty minutes, going over the answer in my head. I think through the angles, review the possible pitfalls. Eventually, I come to the conclusion that everything depends on certain people's movements remaining true to form for a Thursday night. But old men are nothing if not predictable.

I do a small line of gak. A sharpener, enough to boot the system but not impair judgement. Could be a long night, so I tuck the wrap in my hip pocket. I toss my mobile on my unmade bed, switched on, fetch a sponge from the bathroom, and take the lift down to the underground car-park. Before I set off, I use the sponge to collect some of the oily gunge that coats the underside of the engine and smear the mess onto my number-plates, front and rear. I dab it on carefully, not obliterating the entire plate, just enough to confuse the issue for anyone who might be bothered to look.

Now that I'm on my way out to Skerries, I feel calmer. The iron band has stopped tightening – it's as if the pressure across my chest has suddenly become an aid, not an impediment. I know what I have to do. Producers are paid to come up with immediate solutions to pressing problems. I'm not excited, because I don't need the likes of Carver to tell me that I'm good at my job. If anything, I feel a quiet sense of professional pride. Why should he have it, if I can't? Why should I go back to the shit-soaked mezzanine of local radio? No reason whatsoever! How dare he take everything I've done for him and try to sneak off with it, my only thanks a huge slap in the face? I'm not going to let him: it's as simple as that. He's spent the last week showing me that I'm expendable. Well, he's got such a big fucking ego, it won't have occurred to him that I might think he's expendable, too.

The black combats, black polo-neck, black cap, the black leather driving gloves, and the black twelve-hole Doc Marten boots are, I'll admit, perhaps a tad OTT, but they feel right for the job; tight, practical, comfortable, and, when the lights are out, pretty much invisible. The universal uniform of the television élite. I have a less-dramatic change of clothing beside me on the passenger seat. I pull into a petrol station halfway to Skerries, taking care to avoid the forecourt and therefore the security cameras that might record my car's registration, dirtied-up as it is. I use my cap to hide my face from the garage shop camera. I buy a public call-box phonecard, some fags, and a large rubber-clad torch, paying cash. Then, I make a detour into Rush, a few miles from Skerries, and use the card to ring Carver's home number from a booth on the main street. After several rings, Anne Stutz answers. Good. If he was there himself, he'd have lifted after one ring. I hang up immediately, without saying anything.

I drive past my father's chalet, to confirm what I already know – that there's no way in hell he'll be at home on a Thursday night either, as long as the pub up the road is still open. Scabby local bar, scabby VIP lounge – they're not that different, the Monkey Man and Maurice. Of course, isn't that how I lasted so long with Carver, because he reminded me of my father? Isn't that what attracted me to him, in the first place? I take the precaution of tucking my car into the shadows at the side of the house. I don't want any of my dad's mates, scooting down the road for last orders, asking him about the Dublin-reg sports car parked in his driveway. He'd know it was me and hurry back in delight at the highly unusual prospect of a visiting child, no matter how mercenary.

Surprisingly, Maurice has remembered to lock the back door, but his kitchen window quickly gives way to the wheel wrench from my car. I break the smallest pane and reach in to open the window proper. Then I'm in, through the kitchen, through the narrow hallway, and I'm standing in my father's living-room. I draw the curtains, then risk switching the lights on. The place smells of him, more so than the last time I was here, over half-a-decade ago. However, still drifting above the combined essence of unwashed

319

clothes, whiskey, and despair, is the tinge of sweet, mechanical oil. This emanates from the jumble of delicate yet purposeful metal parts scattered across his much-augmented pile of old books and newspapers. Camera parts. Gun parts. Machines for shooting, amongst other things, dirty little monkeys. For was it not here, in this very room, that my father revealed the alchemic formula that turned base metal into gold, the spell that enabled me to put Kevin Carver on the path to celebrity and success? Well, on that occasion I was keenly interested in the workings of one shooting instrument. Tonight, the principle remains the same. It's just a matter of finding the right tool for the job.

I spread a few sheets of newspaper in the centre of the floor and permit myself a smile, as I sort through the parts. This is all so deliciously appropriate. I like to watch. I liked watching my father when he was working, the way he was when he stood behind a camera. And, although I was young, I liked watching him strip and clean his guns. The drawers of a heavy commode in the corner yield a set of screwdrivers wrapped in rags; wrapped with them are springs and numerous fiddly bits of firing mechanism. Also in the commode are several tatty boxes of bullets, of a variety of shapes and calibres.

Even wearing the gloves, it doesn't take me long to assemble a really old army-issue Webley revolver – the parts are obvious matches, crudely fashioned and easily put together. Bastard weighs a ton. I point it and try to pull the trigger with one hand. It's a struggle,

320

better use two. Thunk. The hammer falls, and the chambers rotate. Good. I hoke through the bullet boxes for the bluntest samples. Sure enough, they fit. I can find only four, but I reckon that one would be enough to put a sizeable hole in any target. That's if the bloody thing doesn't blow my hands off instead.

The hunting rifle takes quite a bit longer. The mechanism is more complex, and I make a few incorrect choices of part before I settle on the right ones. It's a bolt-action, single-shot affair, which takes long brass bullets that look as if they'd fell a giraffe, let alone a dirty little monkey. There's a fitting above the breech to receive a telescopic sight, and if I search around, I might find the thing. But I wouldn't know how to calibrate it, I don't have the time, and anyway, I don't intend to be that far away when I pull the trigger.

Christ, you're joking, Lee!

Prepare to die laughing, baby.

I stuff the bullets for both guns into my pockets, then tidy everything back more or less the way it was. I let myself out through the kitchen door, hoping that my father will be pissed enough when he returns to think that he neglected to bolt it. Who knows, if he's on a mission with the whiskey, it could well be a couple of days before he sobers up enough to clock the broken window. Placing the guns across the back seat, I drive down the coast road a few miles, to where it passes within yards of a long shingle beach. You hear about these endeavours going wrong all the time, because nobody bothered to test the gear. So, I carry the guns down onto the beach and, after stumbling around with the torch for a few minutes, settle on a weathered wooden sign that warns:

NOTICE TO BATHERS:
DANGEROUS CURRENTS
AT ALL TIMES.

How very true.

I prop the torch pointing up at the board, so as not to lose it in the dark, and walk thirty paces up the shingle to a point where the stones are banked slightly, and I can lie easily behind the rifle. I slip one of the evil brass bullets into the breech, settle down, line the metal sights up, breathe out, and squeeze gently. The butt of the rifle kicks at my shoulder, as an impressive tongue of reddish-blue flame spits from the end of the barrel, accompanied by a sharp crack. I miss the sign altogether, shooting high. I walk back to the torch, adjust the rear sight on the gun, then set myself up again, as before. This time, the sign vibrates and drops a small shower of dust into the upturned cone of light. An inspection reveals that I've drilled a large, neat hole through the 'E' of 'DANGEROUS', which is as close to the centre as I reckon I'm going to get without a lot more bullets and a few days of practice. But the sign itself is about the width of a man's shoulders, so I should be safe enough. Pity I don't have the equipment and skill to make doctored bullets, like Edward Fox in *The Day of the Jackal*. Brilliant scene, where he calmly blows the shit out of a melon, and you think, 'Wow, he's going to do that to De Gaulle's head!'

With some trepidation, I pick the old Webley up from the pebbles beside the torch. This bugger, I'm not so sure about.

You're right, Lee, don't do it!

Fuck up.

I smell it, to try to tell whether it's been fired during my lifetime, but Maurice has kept the revolver so well-oiled, it's impossible to know. The fact that he's cared for it gives me some cause for optimism, but still, leaving the chambers empty, I pull the trigger again a few times, just to make sure that the single effort back in the house wasn't a fluke. It works just fine. However, I've heard about people using these things, and the ammo is so old it blows up, shattering the gun, the hand, and the face. And wouldn't I look a right fuckwit if I were to do that in front of the Monkey Man?

'Excuse me, your life is now over … Bang! Ouch! Shit! Err … would you mind calling an ambulance, please?'

I don't think so. It would be the wrong time to lose my reputation for casual efficiency. I press one of the heavy old slugs into a chamber, line it up, hold the gun with both hands, as far from my head as possible, and point it at the sign, less than five feet away. I avert my face, then watch out of the corner of my eye as the revolver erupts with a dreadful roar, jetting a halo of yellow flame from the muzzle, and the centre of the sign explodes and disappears into the night. Jesus, shit! I lift the torch. The sign now reads:

Edward Fox, eat your heart out! I study one of the old Webley slugs from my pocket. The tip is rounded, almost flat. The bullet must be made from something really soft, to spread on impact like that. They took no chances back in those days.

Aware that by now, anyone living within a mile of here must be wondering what the hell is going on, I gather the guns quickly, stash them in the boot of the car, and head back into town, towards leafy south Dublin. On my way through the city centre, I pull up beside a call box and dial Carver's number again. The phone lifts after three rings, and I'm thinking 'shit, it's him,' when Anne's voice answers, 'Kevin? Is that you?' in a tone of exasperated enquiry. Good, he's still out on the razz, and she thinks I'm him, ringing for a lift home. I hang up, and five minutes later, I'm parked at the end of their street.

It's one in the morning, and this is a quiet, respectable part of the city, with no pubs or take-aways close by, so there's no one around. The street itself comprises two tall, unbroken red-brick terraces of substantial Victorian houses, set back, in typical Dublin fashion, from the pavement by the width of a tiny front garden, up the middle of which runs a set of wide, shallow stone steps, leading to a decorative front door, elevated half-a-floor above the road. The houses don't look particularly impressive, but they're spacious inside and, Dublin being the massive rip-off that it is, they cost an absolute fortune. Mature trees are spaced at various intervals along the street, although, thankfully, my memory has served me well, and there are none close to Carver's house. I park the car tight up against the back garden wall of the end-of-terrace house opposite Carver's side. It's a bit of a gasping, scrabbling climb, especially with a pistol stuffed down my combats and a rifle strapped to my back, but I'm able to jump from the top of the vehicle onto the garden wall and, using a fire-escape to scale the back of the building, emerge triumphant onto the roof. The façade parapet is flat and wide enough to walk on, so within ninety seconds, I'm directly across the street from, and some thirty feet above, Kevin Carver's front door. I fish out my wrap, do a line of gak off the parapet, light a fag, and settle down to wait.

I go over everything in my head. I should only need the rifle; two shots, three at the most. I inspect the front door between the metal sights, savouring the smell of the gun. Plenty of light from the sodium street-lamps – I bet I could pop one through the letterbox from up here. Message for you, boss! I decide that I *will* go for the head shot first. I've been debating the notion for most of the drive in. A body shot – which I couldn't miss – would fell him for sure, giving me time to re-load and finish him off. But a head shot would be infinitely more satisfying – just the thought of seeing his face down the length of a rifle barrel is enough to make me smile with pure, unadulterated pleasure. I reckon that if I miss the head shot, by the time he knows what's happening, I'll have reloaded, then the default option will be to make the second a body shot, and take it from there.

Oh, Monkey Man, you *so* have this coming to you. I hate you, you wee bastard! I hate the way I've prostituted myself towards you, put up with your ego, your madness, your pretensions, and your hypocrisy for so long. I hate the way I was starting to *become* you. This is a very clean thing I'm doing; I'll get so much of myself back again, when this bullet goes cracking across the street. You deserve it. If you ever try to fuck me, Monkey Man, I'll fucking kill you. Sorry, but that's how I feel. Maybe it's my father's vicious temper; maybe it's been there all along, bubbling under the surface. Maybe it's love, turned to hate. Maybe this is the law of the jungle, Monkey Man, the natural corollary of the chaos, of the utter disregard for people that lies at the very heart of your being. Or maybe this is just what you get when you humiliate me and try to steal everything I've worked for.

Wait. I'm drifting. I need to think this through to the end. When I take the shot, or shots, I reckon I can be back down to the car and away, into the traffic, before anyone in the street even opens their front door. I can be at Howth Head less than twenty minutes after that. The guns, the gloves, and the black clothing will go into the heaving sea, and I'll be home again well within the hour. And, for a change, I'll be up bright and early, listening to the morning news!

So what if they ask me a few questions? I'd be surprised if they didn't. When the cops start digging for a motive, they'll realise that they'll have to question half the fucking town! Jesus, officer, plenty of people in the media hate each other's guts, but if we went around literally *killing* each other – well, there'd be nobody left, would there? No one except for the millions of media wannabes, waiting to scrabble their way onto the oily, over-crowded rock. And what will 'the team' say about me, when they're asked? Yes, officer, we'd been told to *ignore* Lee, but we're not sure why – we were just following orders. So Carver and I had had a spat. But it was nothing. Sure wasn't I the first person to be called to a police station only two weeks ago, when little Kevin had a spot of bother? That's what good pals we were! Go on, you can check that out, just ask Guard Anthony O'Mahony down at Store Street.

And then there's my father. I doubt if Maurice will even notice, let alone report, his missing guns. But in the unlikely event that he does, there's nothing to connect us, right away. It would take a pretty sharp cop to spot that Kevin Carver's producer bore the same surname as some petty crime victim out in Skerries. Okay, 'Lovecraft' may be an unusual surname, but nobody knows anything about Maurice; I never discuss him with anyone apart from Stella, not even she has met him, and he's never been to see the show. I haven't seen him myself for six years, and counting.

But let's just say, for the sake of argument, that Maurice turns on his radio in the morning and somehow makes the connection – would he tell anybody? Shooting some bastard of a presenter is exactly the kind of thing he would have done himself – in fact, now that I think about it, I'm surprised he never has. I rather think that Daddy would endorse what's happening here!

What's the worse-case scenario? Let's say every piece of luck runs against me. Let's say Maurice *does* make the connection between his missing weapons and a dead monkey. What if he blabs through drink, shock, or annoyance, and the police arrest me on that basis? They'd still have to find the weapon and prove something forensically, and there's not a snowball's chance in hell they'll be able to do that. The waters around Howth Head run deep. I can picture it now: 'Sorry, Officer, my dad … well, we don't like to *talk* about it, but my dad's been an alcoholic for years, estranged from the family – he used to beat us, you know – and … I hate to say this, but I haven't been to *see* him since 1996. If anything, Officer, he disapproved of my career – he told me as much the last time I saw him. I was kind of offended, that's why I hadn't been back. That, and various family shit, you know how it is. And as for *guns* … I didn't know he kept guns! What *was* he getting up to, in that horrible little house, all by himself?'

And so what if the Monkey Man's home number took two anonymous calls that night, one of them from Rush? What's *that* got to do with me? Not sneaky enough, eh?

Therese, where are you when I need you?

There's a taxi rounding the street corner. Here it comes, this has to be him. Christ knows, two a.m. is late enough when you have a show to do … Yes! It *is* him. The taxi stops just short of his house, and he's out like a shot, clutching a champagne bottle and a lit cigarette, calling the driver a fuck-dog and a pox, flinging bank-notes into the back seat, slamming the door … and please, please don't let the driver follow him out of the car and beat his lights out on the pavement … No, the taxi's away with a squeal of the tyres, and Carver is laughing, staggering, and – what the fuck – he sits himself slowly down, on his front steps. He takes a swig from the bottle, which he places carefully at his feet on the pavement, before throwing his butt away, fumbling in his pocket, fishing out another fag. Still cackling, he lights it up. I don't believe it – this is too perfect to be true! I'm up on my haunches, I have the hunting rifle resting on the edge of the parapet, I have everything lined up, I take a deep breath, I let it out, I relax, and I pull …

Wait. There's something wrong … no! Lee! You fucking idiot! Too immersed in detail, you've missed the big picture! *Where's the satisfaction, if he doesn't know that it's you?*

Mmm, you've got a point …

He'll die, out like a light, without knowing what's coming, why it's coming, and, most importantly, from whom! *I* told you *I* would kill you, Monkey Man! Me! I want my name on the closing credits! I drop the hunting rifle behind the parapet, and I'm running along it, thirty feet above the street, diving for the fire escape, practically falling down the metal steps, in a mad scramble. I'm onto the garden wall; I land with a thud on the roof of my car, bending it. I'm on the ground, running, tugging the revolver from the waistband of my combats. I'm round the corner, dashing along the pavement, waving the gun. He's across the road from me now, about four doors up, still sprawled on the steps, chuckling to himself. You'll be laughing on the other side of your face, Carver – literally – when I'm through with you! Famous last words, come on, come on, what will I say? Knock the celebrity dead on his ass with a killer line!

'I told you I'd kill you, Monkey Man, if you tried to fuck me over! Oh, and by the way, that's how I've always thought of you, Kevin, "Monkey Man" is my pet name for you, but you're not my pet any more, are you?'

Bollocks, far too long. I need pith. How about putting the gun to his head and saying, 'Kevin! This is your greatest hit!'

No, *our* greatest hit, this is *our* greatest hit. Not yours.

Ah, fuck it … I sidle around a parked car directly across the street from him, gun ready, and he still hasn't seen me when … no! His front door opens, and there's Anne Stutz, standing framed in the hallway light! I throw myself sideways, falling behind the parked car, banging my elbows and knees on the pavement, and nearly crying out loud with the pain.

'Get your ass in here, now! Whaddya think ya doin', lyin' like a bum out here in the street?' Anne's voice – sharp, angry, shrewish. I peek up, over the car bonnet. She's still standing in the doorway, arms

330

folded. She's made no move to grab him or usher him inside. Christ, I don't have the balls to do them both. Plus, what did Anne ever do to me, except bore me rigid?

'Fuck *you!*' Carver bellows, tossing the champagne bottle towards her, and it must be nearly empty, because it bounces off the door, then clatters back down the steps, without breaking.

'No, fuck *you!*' Anne shrieks at him and slams the door shut, leaving Carver half-sprawled, cackling, waving his little arms, as if conducting an imaginary orchestra. I stand upright, quietly move a couple of yards away from the pool of light cast by the street-lamp, and gather myself in the dark. I have the gun in my right hand, held close to my leg, pointed at the ground. Carver's laughter subsides to a nasty, guttural chuckle, and he rocks back and forward on the step, shaking his head at a joke only he can understand. Then he stops, suddenly, cocks his head, and peers across the street towards me. I swear the little bastard always knows where I am, on his monkey radar. He stops chuckling – alert now, moving his head slightly from side to side, like an animal suspicious of a bush that could be hiding something big and hungry.

'Who's there?' he calls across the road. 'I know someone's there!' I don't move a muscle. 'Who are ya, ya fuck? What the fuck do ya want?'

I stand in the dark watching him as he slumps, peering in my direction, unable to see who I am.

But I can see him, objectively and dispassionately,

for the first time in our relationship. I don't know how long I stand like that, stock still, my gun-hand hanging relaxed, just watching, as he half-dozes, starting awake every so often to growl a curse in my direction. Five, maybe ten minutes? If only everyone could see him as I see him now. If only everyone else could see that this is all there is to it – a pathetic little monkey, sprawled across stone steps.

I walk away from him, up the far side of the street. He detects the movement and shakes himself fully awake, but I'm moving too fast, with my back turned, for him to see that it's me.

'Ah, go on, ya bastard!' he shouts after me. 'Go on, ya pox!' I keep walking. 'If ya wanna watch me,' he roars down the street, 'why don'tcha watch TV poxy fucking Ireland?'

# 22

## EXEGESIS

I have such a rush on me, there's little chance of sleep.
It's not just the intermittent dabbing at the coke –
you've got to admit, it's not every night you come
within a whisker of blowing someone's brains out with
a bloody big gun. I feel exactly the way I did after my
car crash – alert, hyper, visually aware, yet oddly
disembodied. I wonder whether I've done the right
thing. But the hunting rifle still lies where I dropped
it, ready for use over the weekend, if all else fails. And
there's always the comforting weight of the old
revolver, which I place in the glove compartment,
ready for later.

At this time of the morning, when there's no
traffic, you begin to appreciate just how small Dublin
really is. I make Stoneybatter in less than ten minutes
and pull up outside the half-wrecked rented house. I
knock on the door and experience that ghost-like

sensation that accompanies return visits to former abodes. It takes a while, but eventually Ritchie answers.

'Heyyy, Leeee! Excellent!

Ritchie (or Witchie to his customers, because of his lisp) is the last remaining member of my old household. Everyone else has grown up and got a proper job. Ritchie, as a drug dealer, saw no reason to alter his lifestyle, knowing full well that a portion of our respective incomes would continue to come his way. My two a.m. visit is a perfectly normal part of that lifestyle. The man rarely wakens before dusk.

The air in the living-room is so thick, I feel stoned just breathing it. Ritchie has been decorating – two enormous sofas take up most of the floorspace, and the biggest plasma TV I've ever seen occupies the rest. Two guys I don't know are killing each other on Playstation. Just like Ritchie, they have grey skin, bulging cow-like eyes, and long, greasy hair. And there's me worried about my drug intake.

'Bit of a wekking session planned, then?' Ritchie enquires, as he bags me up four grammes of coke and two dozen pills.

'Wrecking session? You could say that, yes. Do you have anything else?'

Ritchie studies me with the cow-likes. 'What d'you have in mind?'

'Any trips?'

He grins. The two combatants laugh and continue with their digital murder. Ritchie shows me into the kitchen, where the table is covered with hundreds of magic mushrooms, drying on two sheets of newspaper. You can barely see the front-page photos of police beating protestors, so bountiful is the harvest.

'Fweshly picked! Today's dwugs today, that's my motto.'

Of course – we're in season, and the fields of Kildare and Wicklow will be crawling with people like Ritchie and his mates, studying the grass with forensic interest. Ten years ago, I would have been out there with them.

'May I?'

'Take what you want, totally fwee.' I wrap about fifty in a piece of tissue and add them to my stash. 'Last thing – would you by any chance have a syringe I could borrow?'

Ritchie smiles crookedly and opens a kitchen drawer, full of clinically wrapped plastic syringes, from which he extracts a handful. I pick a large one, without a needle.

'You gettin' into the sewious shit, man? Who sold it to you? Is it good stuff?'

'I only buy from you, Ritchie, you know that. My ears are blocked. Just wanna clean them with warm water, that's all.'

'Ugh! You awe one sewiously fucked-up individual, my fweind …'

As I drive home, I idly wonder how Witchie will cope if he ever starts selling wocks of quack. I stop at a twenty-four-hour garage and buy three tubes of superglue. I don't bother avoiding the forecourt cameras this time. No need. The mobile on my bed has registered no calls. Funny how people instinctively know when you're on the way out. I lie down, forcing myself to rest. I stare at the ceiling, my heart beating like fuck.

My father sits on a rock on the beach near his chalet. I'm trying to walk across the shingle, to warn him about the tide, which is already lapping around his feet. I'm carrying the revolver, only it's silver-plated, like a toy gun. Maurice is fully clothed, but he doesn't react as the wash hisses across the pebbles, soaking his shoes. He's wearing his blue suede cowboy jacket, and I don't want him to get that wet. The salt water will ruin it, cover it with big, dark stains like the ones he already has under his arms, from the sweat. The sea snatches at my feet, as I stumble on the pebbles, cursing. I shout his name, but he doesn't acknowledge me. Then, as I reach out to grab his shoulder, we're no longer on the beach, but far away out to sea, and Maurice is still perched on his rock, but suddenly I'm flailing in the sucking, bottomless water at his feet, and I've nothing to stand on, nothing to hold on to, no way of saving myself. I go under, take a mouthful, and resurface. Therese sits on the rock beside my father, her yellow dress damp from the brine. My father stares off into the distance, oblivious to me drowning, and Therese huddles up beside him, talking into her mobile …

Beep-beep.

… and I'm swallowing half the fucking sea, and no one reaches down to help me.

Beep-beep.

Thank Christ, that'll be my mobile, set to alarm, telling me I don't have to drown.

Beep-beep.

I raise my hand from the water: sure enough I'm holding my mobile where I thought I had a revolver, and it's glowing and throbbing and going beep-beep, but no matter how hard I stab at the button with my thumb, I can't answer her call.

I'm up like a shot, slippy with sweat, at 6.55 a.m., precisely five minutes before my mobile is timed to go off. I spend half an hour in the shower, trying to wash the dream away. I use lashings of Collyre Bleu on my eyes, and, as I do, I catch a good look at myself in the mirror. All this stress has done wonders for my figure. I dress in the black combats, a black nylon shirt, and the twelve-hole Doc Martens. Hell, why not? I take a last look around the flat. Still a mess, still no Stella. I check her room and observe a minute's silence beside her empty bed, piled high with crumpled clothing.

To business. I put the kettle on, stuff the magic mushrooms into a steel vacuum flask, and pour half-a-cup of boiling water in on top of them. That should brew nicely. I have a laptop that I never use, and I evict it from the smart leather bag it lives in, replacing it with the revolver, the vacuum flask, the Class As, Ritchie's syringe, and the tubes of superglue. I drive to TV Ireland, arriving just after eight a.m., long before even the most eager of the monkey troop will have made it in. I dump my bag in the office, then go on the prowl around the building, stopping first in the basement, where the techies have a hideaway crammed with junk. I take a roll of black gaffer tape, then go to the studio, where I make the necessary adjustments. When I finish, I climb to the top of the gallery steps, the exact spot where I stood the day the board hired us. Even with the tiers of audience seating, the lighting rigs, the cameras, and the set, from up here the space still seems large and lonely, as it did on that first day.

Kate arrives just before nine. She's startled to see me sitting at my desk, gazing into my computer screen. I look up at her and fix her with my own version of the Monkey Man's meat-skewer stare. This comes with a bland smile, which I like to think makes it worse. Kate goes completely puce, mutters something about needing a coffee, and disappears back out the office door. I can understand why it might be uncomfortable for her to be alone with me – the unkindest thing I ever did to her was give her a job. She's a decent, middle-class girl who probably, on one level, is appalled by recent events. But it's always the decent, middle-class types who do exactly as they're told, who follow orders. Eventually, one by one, the rest of the troop arrives for work. They settle uneasily and contemplate their computers, silent, waiting for alpha monkey to show. This is meant to be a busy production office on programme day, but nobody says a word. As the awkward silence drags on, I feel my spirits lifting, knowing that I am the cause of it.

I know lots of things these ciphers don't. I know that Milton fucked the Monkey Man, but I see no percentage in sharing that particular story – yet. I know about the Monkey Man being kept in a cell overnight; I know about him head-butting Marty Pelham. I know that the Monkey Man is selling out. I know that I had a hunting rifle pointed at his head last night. I feel great knowing that I could have pulled that trigger, and that I still might. I know that I have a revolver in my laptop bag, and, best of all, I know what's going to happen next.

And here he is, at last, at the crack of midday, hung-over to Jesus, with a head on him like a wasp's nest, minus the honey. The first thing Carver does upon arrival is to tear a chunk out of Scally over some minor detail to do with tonight's show. This is the monkey method of asserting authority – bite a member of the troop, hard, for no reason, so that the others will be meek and submissive for the rest of the day. He must have had a filthy row with Anne last night, about her defiance at the entrance to his lair.

When the dust from his attack on Scally settles, I cough, pick myself up, and approach Carver's desk, meek and submissive. I can feel the others, watching my back. I am the banished one, the untouchable – how dare I approach the feet of their little god, unless it is to grovel? I let my lower lip tremble, allow my eyes to water slightly. I slump my back, try to shrink my height, and turn my face towards the floor.

'Can I talk to you … please?'

Carver fixes me with his meat-skewer stare. 'Talk to me about what?' he asks, louder than necessary.

'I just want to talk to you, that's all.'

'Well, go on then. Talk.'

'Not here. In private, down in the studio,' I wheedle, 'please.' This is as close to begging as I can possibly manage. If he pushes me any further, I'll go back to my desk, unzip the laptop bag, and, in full view of his acolytes, splatter his ugly head across the wall behind him. For an instant, I'm tempted, but a bit like last night, it would be too simple, too prosaic. Justice must be poetic, must it not? His eyes strip-search me for any sign of insincerity. But I must look pretty crushed, so eventually, he barks, 'Go on then. I'll follow you down when I've finalised tonight's programme with the team here.'

Ignoring the calculated insult, I quietly leave the room, looking neither left nor right. I can feel the smirks, as I go. I make my way to the studio and park myself in one of the guest chairs on the set. He takes forever to come, as I knew he would. It's the tired old make-'em-wait trick. I fetch a wrap from my pocket, spill a small mound of coke onto the back of my hand, snort it, and slouch forward dejectedly in the seat, my head in my hands. I'm sweating, yet feel cold. That's how he finds me, in the cavernous dark, with only a few white spots beaming down on the set. He walks straight across the floor, into the light, and assumes his throne. To a casual observer, we could be live on air, interviewer and interviewee. He purses his mouth, sits back, and looks me over with an impersonal, hostile gaze.

'Right. What do you want?'

I take my face from my hands, revealing an expression of tearful, wounded loyalty.

'What did I do?' I practically blub. '*What did I do?*'

He puts a little paw up to his mouth to hide what I know, from the twinkle in his eyes, is a nascent smile. Ha-ha, tough-ass producer Lee, didn't take long to crack! Victory monkey, got you licked. Still, he can't resist twisting the knife.

'What did you *do?*'

'What did I do to deserve this? Why are you treating me like shit?'

And the flickering smile disappears. 'You're not a fucking child! You're such a smart guy, you go figure it out! And when you figure it out, have the good grace to leave! Or else convince me why I should keep you, but I warn you – it'll be an uphill task!' And he's up out of the chair, ready to go. The hard word delivered. The stiletto firmly in place.

And I'm practically crying. 'You're a *cunt*. That's what you are, a fucking *cunt!*'

He stops, turns. I bury my face in my hands again. He moves slowly and deliberately back to his seat. He settles into it and draws himself up, leaning slightly forward, the way I taught him to sit when the cameras are pointing.

'You're right, son. I *am* a cunt. That's what I am, I'm a fucking *cunt!* I've been around too long *not* to be a cunt!' And his features contort with contempt. 'Who did you think you were dealing with – some sort of *beginner?*'

'I seem to remember a time when you *were* a beginner, yes!'

'But only in this particular medium!' and he

gestures at a nearby camera. 'And the medium doesn't matter, because the principle's the same!'

'What fucking principles?' and I allow myself to shout at him. 'I haven't seen any principles, lately!'

He throws me a sardonic glare, then shakes his head. 'Come on, you know that's not what I meant by 'principle'. But now that we're on the subject, are you trying to tell me that you, personally, give half-a-fuck what *anyone* thinks out there in punter-land? They're there to be *entertained*,' and he waves towards the camera again. 'What are we gonna do, solve the problems of the world with a TV show?' He puts on a fey, self-important face, deepens his voice in mockery, and addresses a camera, as if doing an intro.

'Hey, folks – do we have a great show for you tonight! Ten million people have Aids! We ask – why? And does Aids hurt? Also on the programme, corruption tackled, the venal vanquished, and world hunger – the final solution! Accept no substitute – Kevin Carver, the presenter with principles!' He slumps back into his seat, re-adopting his sneer. 'Come on! Gimme a fucking break! No one gives a shit about any of that stuff! Principles, my arse!'

'Fuck you!' and this isn't play-acting, this is coming from the heart now. The anger's coming through, I can feel it welling. 'We made our reputation as the no-bullshit show! That's how we built our audience; that's how we earned our credibility in the game! And now you're pissing it all away with your own self-serving agenda! People are starting to notice!'

'FUCK PEOPLE!' he screams, and he's on his feet now, jumping up and down on the set. 'Fuck what people think! What matters on this programme is what *I* think! The audience wants to see *me*!' And he gestures at the camera again. '*That's* the principle that remains the same, you stupid young fuck! *That's* what I'm talking about! *That's* the rule that applies from newspapers to radio to TV, across the board! The people buy *me*! It doesn't matter *what* I say, as long as I say it!' He jumps towards the camera, beating his hand off his chest. 'I *am* the product! It's all about *me*!'

'Objectivity was never your strong point, was it?' Now I'm sneering, too.

'Consistency and objectivity are the hobgoblins of the second-rate mind!'

'That's just another way of saying that your fucking ass is for sale!'

'My ass is *not* for sale, baby!'

'The Archbishop! Scrapping the protestors! The Minister for Finance! What the fuck do you call that?'

'I call that the real fucking world! I hate to break it to you, Lee, but this is how it works!'

'"He who helps the prince to power, is himself condemned to ruin."'

'What?'

'Machiavelli.'

'I don't *do* opera ... baby!'

'Oh ... never mind, let me try you with something closer to home!' And I lean forward, as if addressing an imaginary audience. He's pretty surprised at how well I imitate his voice but, as the words come out, not half as surprised as I am. 'We are the intelligent, rock-and-roll show that doesn't tolerate bullshit!'

'What the … why the fuck do you keep *saying* that? What's *that* go to do with anything?'

'You said it yourself, at our first press conference, in that very office, six years ago.'

He laughs. 'Did I, really?' And he tosses it around: 'The intelligent, rock-and-roll show … that doesn't tolerate bullshit … hey, I like that! Do you mind if I use it tonight?'

'Feel free, they're your words!'

He addresses the camera, with his Dick Van Dyke parody strut. 'Hello, and welcome to the intelligent, rock-and-roll show that doesn't tolerate bullshit! My producer here, a young gobshite called Lee, thinks I should be bursting with integrity, a real big man about town. Prove Lee wrong by tuning in no matter what I say, because you love me, because I'm your fucking hero, so I can say what the fuck I like! You … love … me!

And I'm on my feet, now. 'That's your problem: you don't believe in anything, except for yourself!'

'Oh, that's my *problem*, is it? Well, oh me oh my, what a terrible problem! Look at all the misfortune it's brought crashing down on my poor little head! Let me see now … my beautiful house, my burgeoning celebrity, my money in the bank, the politicians who suck my cock because they're afraid of my show! I don't have to listen to anybody; I just look into that camera and it's Abra-fucking-cadabra! But, now that I think about it, you're right! I *am* kinda fucked! I've got absolutely nothing going for me! Whereas you … you have everything!' He mock-clutches his heart. 'Tell me, Lee … please tell me … where did I go *wrong*?'

And I mock-clap my hands in return. 'You were wonderful, Kevin. *Love* your show.'

The anger returns to him. 'Fuck you! You're not exactly charity material yourself! What makes *you* so superior? Eh? You turn up late, your head's away with it … what the fuck do *you* believe in?'

'You!' and I fire that back before I can stop myself. To my surprise, I actually *am* crying, now. 'I used to believe in *you!*' And he's stopped for moment, unsure, hands on hips. 'All those lectures about what a shit society we lived in, how there was no integrity, how everything was mediocre, second-rate, and how you and me were gonna be different! Christ help me, I *believed* you!'

And through my tears, through the shadow cast by the spotlight, I can't see his eyes, only his chiselled features, cast in stark relief. And when he talks, his tone is flat, matter-of-fact, the play-acting over.

'Well, that was pretty stupid of you, wasn't it? Stop crying, and stop pretending you have principles, Lee, because *you* don't believe in anything, either. You young people have no principles: you all want the same thing – money, drugs, sex, and an easy fucking life. You're just like me, only I'm better than you'll ever be, because I understand how the levers work. But you *are* right about one thing – I *do* only believe in me! Fuck everybody else! I'm the only person I can trust! I'm gonna give you some advice as a parting present, just to prove what a nice guy I am. What I'm about to say is more valuable than any gold watch, so listen up!' I wipe my eyes, annoyed that I let myself go, and try to return his basilisk stare. He continues, neutral, impersonal. 'I've been sitting where you are now. If you think that journalism is a whore-house, you should try the music industry. I've been fucked over in my time. And it hurts, but that's how you learn. So here it is – fuck, or get fucked. It's that simple. In my case, son, you didn't stand a chance. I've had my eye on you for quite some time. I've decided you're not loyal.'

'Fuck loyal, what about equal?'

His tone doesn't change. 'You were never that. You really *are* stupider than I thought, if you ever imagined for a single second that you and I were equal.'

'Much better a troop of snivelling chimpanzees, for you to lord it over, eh?'

'They're smart enough to do exactly as they're told. No more, no less. Now, you may recall that on Fridays, I have my show to do. *My* show, Lee, not *our* show, *my* show. *The Kevin Carver Show.* You've helped me reach a decision, with this little conversation. It hasn't been a complete waste of time. I've decided that there *is* no way back for you, Lee, no matter how much you cry. You'd be sullen and resentful if I let you stay, and I can't trust you. Kate can produce tonight; you're off the team, effective immediately.' He gives me his toothy, malevolent grin. 'You have until Monday to hand in your resignation to Dickie; he's waiting for it.' And I shoot him a look. 'Oh yes,' he continues, 'Dickie is totally across this one. He's delighted to be rid of you – he thinks you're a prick. He wanted to sack you, but I said no, a resignation won't look so bad for the show. It won't look so bad for you either, when you're applying for your job back in local radio. And if you say anything to the press, I'll fall on you so hard, you'll never work in this town again.'

'Oh, so it's Dickie now, is it? Well, the two of you make a great pair! You *know* he's a useless bastard!'

'Not so much a useless bastard, more a useful idiot. Just as you've been. Just as they all are. Now, if you'll excuse me, I have a show to do.' And he turns, scurrying off into the gloom.

'Cunt!' I shout, after him.

'It's too late for compliments! You've been used, get used to it!' and he's through the soundproof door, his hunched form briefly silhouetted in the light from the corridor.

# 23

## SHOW TIME

I'm holding the revolver in Duster's face, about three inches from those stupid black-rimmed glasses. Dickie Vaughan, Head of Programmes, TV Ireland. This isn't one of my sick little fantasies – I really *am* holding a gun in Duster's face, and it feels great. The gun is highly necessary, because Duster needs some persuading to swallow the four tabs of E.

After my fuck-you chat with Carver, I hung back for ten minutes in the studio, alone. Then, I flounced into the programme office, head held high. Looking neither left or right, I made straight for my corner, lifted my laptop bag, and stormed out the door again, slamming it behind me, every inch the angry exile. I was conscious of the troop watching my back, but Carver didn't so much as glance up from his newspaper. This conversation is over, baby.

However, instead of leaving the building, I locked myself in an edit suite, chopped out a few lines, and settled down to make the final preparations.

Exactly an hour before the show, at 8 p.m., I stride into Duster's office without knocking and plonk my laptop bag down in front of him, on his gorgeous, gleaming, competition-standard desk. It is time to act. As Duster watches, I give him a thin smile, unzip the bag, don my black leather driving gloves, then methodically retrieve the Class As, the syringe, a few tubes of superglue, the vacuum flask, and, finally, the revolver.

At first, I say nothing. Just stand there, in my black uniform, with the gun, flagrant. Duster's expression is priceless – dumb disbelief, transforming slowly to confusion, then horror, when he studies the hand-cannon long enough to see that it's real and my face long enough to see that I'm for real, too. Long enough to see that an executive decision appears to have backfired, badly. His eyes flicker from his phone, to the door, and back to his too-tidy desk again, searching for help or anything he can use as a weapon or a shield, but it's at times like these when a tidy desk is no shagging good to you. Then, he blubbers some bullshit about the need for calm, but I guess no *How to Be a Better Middle Manager* handbook is going to be any good to you in a situation like this, either.

I ignore his pleas. I'm busy arranging four pills from my stash nice and neatly on the desk in front of him. They're the speckled Mitsis, mighty fuckers.

Meantime, I keep the gun levelled at his podgy nose, which, I notice for the first time when I look back up at him, has reddish hair growing out of the nostrils.

'Eat them,' I command.

Duster looks down at the pills and shakes his head.

'Fucking eat them.'

Duster shakes his head again, this time with his eyes closed, like a plump, spoiled child refusing his greens. He folds his arms.

'You're not going to eat them?' As he shakes his head some more, I redirect the gun towards his display of golf trophies and aim at the big one that played such a central role in an earlier, unfulfilled fantasy.

*Go for it, Lee!*

I'm going for it, golf trophy. See you in another life. I pull the trigger. The roar is deafening in the enclosed space, as the trophy disintegrates in a spray of cheap crystal. A hole about the size of Duster's head appears in the plasterboard wall behind where the trophy stood. When I point the smoking gun back at him, he's gone all white, his piggy eyes have doubled in size, and he's clutching the edge of his desk, staring at the glittering fragments that lie strewn where once there had been order. Bits of glass sprinkle his bouffant hair and his shoulders, like a fatal case of dandruff.

'Eat the pills, Duster!'

I wonder how long it's been since he was called that to his face? Thirty years, at least. He looks even more rattled by my using his school nickname than he did by the gunshot. He cowers and nods violently, the way he's wont to do at board meetings. One by one, he lifts the pills and chews them. Christ, who *chews* pills? Another bloody amateur.

'Open your mouth, I want to take a helicopter view of the broadcasting landscape in Ireland.' He looks genuinely puzzled. A bit obscure, granted. 'Oh never mind,' I sigh, and tap him on the cheek with the tip of the revolver. 'Say ahh.' He reddens, but obeys. It's not a pleasant sight, but he's definitely swallowed all four pills. There's still the odd fleck of white sticking to his teeth and the back of his tongue, but they'll work faster that way. I order him to give me his wallet, which he fetches from his pocket. I extract a twenty-euro note, roll it up like a cigarette, and then hold it up to his right nostril. Once again, his face flashes rebellion, but once again, I rap the gun on his cheek and he succumbs. I push the tubed note firmly home, twist it around, and drop it on his desk. Then, I lock him in his own stationery cupboard. It's a tough squeeze, but with a bit of swearing and gun-waving, we manage.

With Duster safely out of the way, I take a wrap of cocaine and empty it over his desk. It looks quite pretty, mingled with the glass. With a gloved fingertip, I rub the rolled-up twenty around in the scattered gak. I stash two more wraps in Duster's briefcase, along with twenty pills in a plastic baggie. I put the gun and the gloves in one of his desk drawers, for the time being. I open the vacuum flask, drive the syringe plunger down, tip the flask, and suck the syringe full of warm, brown liquid. Mushroom tea, the way we used to make it as students. Only much more concentrated. I slip the syringe and the superglue into separate pockets.

If anybody else in the building heard anything amiss, they've ignored it. Upstairs, at management level, the corridors are empty and quiet. But on the ground floor, it's all noise, crowds, and chaos, as the security guards conduct the audience to their seats, the techies test their gear, the floor managers shout, and the monkeys dash from office, to studio, to green-room, to make-up, checking on the guests. I take the back staircase to the basement, unnoticed, and squeeze three whole tubes of superglue into the lock of the plant room. The plant room is where all the power switches for a TV station are located, along with the equipment that relays the signal to the transmitter. The techies keep it locked, because you don't want some fool wandering in and knocking the entire operation off air. Tonight, I want to ensure that nobody can knock the station off air, not even the techies.

Then, I ascend to the ground floor and walk around to the corridor with all the dressing-rooms off it. Elaine sees me pass, but she's busy fawning over the Hollywood actor and is probably still under strict orders to ignore me. Why would anyone want to talk to a dead man? Off the far end of the corridor is a small kitchen. I reach it without incident. I close the door behind me and extract from the fridge the box of microwavable pork ribs that I know will be lurking within. The revolting snack that Carver insists on consuming prior to the show. Every Friday, it's Charlotte's sacred duty to bung his ribs in the microwave, then bring them up to his dressing-room, with precisely half-an-hour to go to air. He goes mental if he doesn't get his ribs, piping hot and bang on time.

I slip the plastic box from the cardboard sleeve. The gruesome reality of the pork ribs bears no relation whatsoever to the glossy product photo. Instead, they look like carrion, immersed in sticky, blood-like sauce. Hungry monkey, chewing on a bone. Using my Swiss Army knife, I carefully slit a tiny hole in one corner of the microwavable film, leaving the main body of it taut. I squirt the entire contents of the syringe over the ribs. Then, I give the box a shake, slide it back in its cardboard sleeve, and return this veritable food of the gods to the fridge. The great thing about magic mushroom tea is that, apart from a certain earthy quality, it doesn't taste of very much. Certainly, the lurid scarlet sauce should overpower any tell-tale flavour.

I use the back stairs to Duster's office. Of course, he's banging like crazy on the cupboard door, but he stops when I smack it a few times with the butt of the revolver and tell him to shut the fuck up, or I'll use the door for target practice. It's twenty past eight. I take my time to roll a nice, juicy spliff, then I pull Duster's high-backed, executive-issue swivel chair up to the cupboard door. I light the spiff. Calmly, without anger, but in a voice that I know he can hear, I start telling Duster how useless he is.

I tell him everything the Monkey Man's ever said about him, how he's dead wood, how he was just another dork, working for a shopping channel, before he somehow struck it lucky with TV Ireland. I laugh at his hair. I tell him that nobody in the building respects him, that they all laugh behind his back, Carver in particular. I assure him that, one day, Carver will fuck him over, just as he's doing to me now. I also tell Duster that he has a reputation for cheating at golf. At this point, he starts to moan and bang the door again. I'm told, by those who play the game, that this is the worst possible thing you can say to a golfer. Accuse a man of rape, of child-molestation, of not being able to drive very well, but *never* say he cheats at golf. Hold on, though; captains of industry play golf. Politicians play golf. Journalists play golf. Every chief executive, middle manager, lawyer, and marketing man in the world plays golf. And what, are you seriously telling me that all these people somehow miraculously dispense with the very traits that make them what they are, just before they tee off? That golf is the one clean, honest thing they all have in common? Duster seems unconvinced by this thesis, judging by the quickening ratio of moans and knocks emanating from the cupboard door.

Avoiding the glass, I dab a bit of the spilt coke from Duster's desk onto my gums and switch on the wide-screen television at the far end of the office, wheeling myself all the way over on Duster's deluxe swivel chair. I must have been torturing my prisoner for longer than I thought – the show's about to start.

Not *our* show; *the* show. I spark up a fag and watch the adverts, the life-blood of all media.

Roll VT. The sig tune plays over a wide shot of the studio, then the jib camera homes in on the white ball of light that is the set – the darkened, expectant audience just visible right of shot. Cut to Carver's camera, and he's off, perched upright, looking pale and tense. His intro goes okay, but already I notice he's not flashing his habitual conspiratorial smile, the one that draws the viewers in, gets them on his side. He looks nervous and unconvincing, as if he's not sure what he's doing. Tut-tut, Kevin, you're forgetting everything I taught you.

His first guest is the Irish film star, who, like every other Irish film star, spends ninety-nine per cent of his time as far away from Ireland as possible. There's a bit of the usual swill about how great it is to be back on the old sod, but by the time Carver gets around to plugging the film – some epic, action-packed pile of crap – the cracks in his performance are starting to show. He asks the poor bastard three times what the film is actually *about*, looking more sceptical and confused each time he puts the question. The actor shifts uncomfortably in his seat, delivering marginally different doses of more or less the same waffle, then eventually realises that Carver is no longer listening but instead staring intently off-set. The actor stops talking and pouts. After a definite pause, Carver shakes his head and refers to his clip-board. He seems mildly alarmed by the clip-board, and shakes it.

'Look at that!' he exclaims. The actor leans forward, face quizzical. 'It's gone all spongy!'

'Excuse me?'

'This ... thing here,' and Carver waves the clipboard, holding it away from himself, 'it's gone all ... soft!' He tosses it away, staring after it in disgust. 'Bloody stupid thing. Went all soft.' He gathers himself, or at least tries to. 'So. Yeah. You've made an action movie. But tell me ... was there any action ... *off* the set?'

Puzzlement and a polite smile. 'Sorry?'

Carver laughs, a bit too hard. 'Action! You know what I mean! Any three-balls? Any four-balls, maybe? It wasn't *all* just for the cameras, come on now, was it? Get it on, baby!'

The actor, now looking very much as if he's dealing with a bit-player who has totally forgotten his lines, launches into an anecdote about how *utterly* married his female co-star is, but Carver interrupts him with a big peal of laughter, reaches over, and half-pats, half-slaps his face. The actor looks horrified.

'Truly, folks, truly ... this man is a hero! Not just an action hero, but a proper fucking hero! A *hugely* talented individual! One of these days, God willing, he'll get a film that's worthy of his talents! But in the meantime, bring him a drink, because he's a brave bastard, appearing in this stuff! Brave. Yes.'

We're way off-script, now. The studio audience murmur, shifting round in their seats in sympathy with the actor's discomfiture. The poor fellow waves his hand, in a motion of combined modesty-stroke-rejection, but Carver is leaning over the back of his chair, away from camera, gesturing off-set, presumably at the floor manager.

'Hey, you! Bring us some booze! Fucking shaken, not stirred! How do you expect us to do a chat show without booze? This man may not *look* like much, but he's an A-list celebrity, so get your act together! I want shampoo! Cold shampoo, on ice! And a roast suckling pig!'

At this, Carver dissolves in hysterics, and the actor gives the camera an exaggerated shrug. What a pro. Knows exactly which one to address, because when a broadcast camera is live, a red light activates close to the lens. Unless, of course, someone has stuck gaffer tape over the red light, but thank goodness I remembered to remove it all after our little meeting, eh? Carver shouts across the studio, 'Scally! Scally, you pox! Organise some booze here, send up to the green room, move your skinny ass, what is this, Saudi fucking Arabia?' And he turns, looking for the live camera. After a wrong try, he finds it. His face is turning purple; he wipes moisture from those pits of eyes with the back of his sleeve. 'I'm sorry, folks,' he addresses the nation, 'but TV Ireland is a disaster. Really, how is any self-respecting celebrity supposed to work in these conditions?' He starts laughing again, uncontrollably, as if at some private joke that's so incredibly funny only he can understand it.

Duster's desk phone starts ringing. I run across the office and lift it. It's the Chairman of the Board, TV Ireland.

'Dickie,' and his voice is more of a bark, rather than the usual feline purr, 'what precisely is *going on* down there? Is your man drunk?'

I pinch my nose and raise the pitch of my voice. I may not sound exactly like Duster, but I definitely don't sound like me.

'Mister Chairman! Go fuck yourself!'

I slam the receiver down again. Time to move, fast. I reach into the laptop bag and fetch out a tape. I deliberately place the revolver at the corner of Duster's desk, where he'll plainly see it when I release him. I bang on the cupboard door.

'Okay, Duster, shut the fuck up and listen carefully. Are you listening?'

And a sort of 'Vaaaaaaaa' sound comes from within the cupboard.

'I have in my hand a broadcast tape, which is *not* part of the schedule. This tape was recorded in studio this afternoon, with the unwitting co-operation of your star presenter. This tape shows Kevin Carver being very honest, an increasingly rare commodity on television these days, I'm sure you'll agree. By the way, that was your chairman on the phone! He wants to know what's going on down here at this shit-hole of a station, because frankly, tonight's programme is already a bit of a mess. You haven't seen it, locked in there, but believe me, it's real car-crash stuff! Kevin is acting strangely!'

'Vaaaaaaa…'

'Shut up, you moron! Listen to me! I'm taking this tape down to the studio, right now – believe me, anybody watching TV Ireland tonight, they ain't seen nothing yet! I'm going to play it out, because I don't like you! This tape could mean your job! Do you understand?'

'Vaaaaaaaa...'

'Okay, I'm gonna prove to myself that you really *are* the useless bastard that everyone says you are. I reckon there's nothing you can do to stop me, are you ready?'

I unlock the cupboard door and dash for the far side of the office, where Carver sits doubled up in his seat, laughing wildly, on the screen behind my head. Christ, he must have scarfed that food down in a hurry.

The cupboard door bursts open, and with an extra-large 'Vaaaaaaaaaaaaa!' Duster tumbles out, his glasses falling from his face. He clutches the edge of his desk, to prevent himself from falling over, and steps on the glasses, breaking them. He raises his head, like a bull in an abattoir, spots me across the room, spots the gun on the desk, reaches for it, and knocks it to the floor. He falls to his knees, retrieves the pistol, and barely manages to stand up again. Bloody hell, I could roll another spliff and smoke it in the time he's taking to get his shit together.

'Carver was right! You *are* useless!' And I hold the tape up, where he can see it. 'Kiss goodbye to your career!'

This is where things could get tricky, but fortunately Duster is so panicked that he raises the revolver and fires. Bang! The widescreen television sports a gaping, smoking hole where the screen was, but already I'm halfway out the door.

'Catch me if you can!'

He stumbles after me, as I leg it down the corridor. I stop at the top of the stairs and hold the tape up again. With another 'Vaaaaaaaa', Duster lurches forward, but already I'm leaping down the stairs. It's like luring a half-blind but potentially lethal dog with a piece of raw meat – I have to stay close enough for him to see me, but far away enough not to get minced. Duster cascades down the stairs, somehow contriving not to fall. He comes at me, pointing the gun, as I dive through the studio door. Once inside, I take care to skirt around behind the cameras, along the edge of the audience. They're still pinned to their chairs, watching as Carver staggers from his seat to wrestle a bottle of champagne from the arms of a burly floor manager called Franco. I notice from the monitors that the programme is still live – Kate hasn't had the sense to run an extended ad break, and use the time to try to sort her presenter out. Of course, Kate has no way of knowing just how badly her presenter *needs* sorting out.

As I reach the bottom of the metal staircase leading up to the gallery, Duster comes charging into the studio and reels right across the set, in full view of the cameras, waving the gun and shouting nonsensically. His eyes are crazed, his shirt half-open, and white flecks of spittle fill the corners of his mouth. Some women in the audience start shrieking. The actor dives from his chair onto the set floor and wriggles under the prop table with the kind of amazing speed that I'd have dismissed as a special effect, had I seen it in one of his films. Carver stands swaying, clutching his bottle, staring at Duster, even more confused by this latest development.

I'm at the top of the gallery stairs. Now, the entire studio erupts in shouts and screams, the delayed reaction to Duster and his gun. I tuck the tape into my waistband and burst through the door. The gallery crew are screaming, too – the director roars at the vision mixer to 'hit a fucking ad break', which she's just about to do when I fly into the room and throw myself across the control desk, knocking the poor woman from her seat as I go.

'Hide! Hide! The bastard's got a gun!'

Obligingly, Duster appears in the gallery door, brandishing the pistol. I duck down behind the desk as he looses off another ear-splitting shot. Bang! I feel the machinery judder, and splinters of plastic and metal fly over my head. Jesus! If he's put us off-air, I'll kill him! Gallantly, the director sneaks out the door behind Duster, who advances across the room, pointing the pistol. To my relief, the monitors still show Carver standing on the set, but now he's leaning forward, being violently sick all over himself and the table under which actor is hiding. Streams of reddish-brown carrion goo, like a vulture disgorging food for her young. I don't know how he eats that stuff – it can't be good for him.

'I'll show *you* who's a useless bastard!' howls Duster. One of the broadcast assistants crouches up against a wall, gibbering. The vision mixer crawls across the floor, trying to get away, and of course Duster falls over her, trying to get at me. An unholy burst of squealing ensues, a mini-mayhem to echo the riot developing down in the studio, as the panicked audience scrambles for the exits. I suppose, what with strange men waving guns around and Kevin Carver regurgitating his ribs live on TV, everyone assumes he's been shot. Goddamn, they could be next! The War on Terror! Such an uncertain world we live in, these days! Duster thrashes around the floor with the hysterical vision mixer in a seething mess of limbs, giving me plenty of time to pop my special tape into the machine, open the correct fader on the mixing desk, press 'play', and close the camera fader.

Roll VT.

Tight shot of the Monkey Man perched on his seat.

'I *am* a cunt,' the recording begins. 'That's what I am, a fucking *cunt!*'

From a different angle, Carver repeats this statement. Then, back to the tight shot, this time a teensy bit out of focus because obviously I had no one physically operating the cameras, just black gaffer tape stuck over the red lights, so Carver wouldn't twig that they were all live, recording him from six different angles. The sound isn't great, because I couldn't exactly have asked him to use a chest mike, but he's still plainly audible through the pencil mikes on the table, which I'd left fully open.

'Are you trying to tell me that you, personally, give half-a-fuck what *anyone* thinks out there in punter-land? They're there to be entertained!' And again, in a wide shot: 'They're there to be entertained! [blip] ... entertained! [blip] ... entertained!'

Okay, crap editing, I admit, but I think the message carries, nonetheless. Cut to Carver's fey little speech, straight to camera. This came out perfect. Even my father would have been proud.

'Hey, folks – do we have a great show for you tonight! Ten million people have Aids! We ask – why? And does Aids hurt? Also on the programme, corruption tackled, the venal vanquished, and world hunger – the final solution! Accept no substitute – Kevin Carver, the presenter with principles!' And he slumps back in his seat, re-adopting his sneer. 'Come on! Gimme a fucking break! No one gives a shit about any of that stuff! Principles, my arse! [blip] Principles, my arse! [blip] Principles, my arse!'

Duster has finally managed to disentangle himself from the vision mixer. He stands upright and takes aim. As he does so, the vision mixer and the broadcast assistant follow the director out the gallery door on their hands and knees, before hurtling down the steps as if their lives depend on it. Which, in fairness, they believe to be the case. I look Duster in the eyes, as he pulls the trigger. Click. I only had four bullets for the revolver – I used one at the beach, another on Duster's golf trophy, and he's used two on me. And missed. Duster advances. Click, click, click, goes the hammer on the gun. Whoo, freaky, he really *would* kill me, if he could! It's an odd moment, when you watch someone try to kill you. It's as if my own murderous

363

spite towards Carver has turned the tables and hunted me down. Duster hollers with frustration, then holds the gun by the barrel, using it as a club. Meanwhile, Carver is telling his viewers, from a variety of angles, 'FUCK PEOPLE! FUCK PEOPLE! Fuck what people think! What matters on this programme is what I think! The audience wants to see *me*! You love me! I *am* the product! It's all about *me*! [blip] It's all about *me*! [blip] I *am* the product! [blip] It's all about me!'

Duster hits me with the pistol, harder than I thought his fat ass would be capable. I block his first blow with my left arm, but it connects straight with the bone, and the feeling goes out of my limb from the elbow down. The second swipe is for my face. I move my head, but not fast enough, and the corner of the butt takes a lump out of my cheek.

'Hello, and welcome to the intelligent, rock-and-roll show that doesn't tolerate bullshit!' Carver continues. 'My beautiful house, my burgeoning celebrity, my money in the bank, the politicians who suck my cock because they're afraid of my show! [blip] … afraid of my show! [blip] … afraid of my show!'

Duster makes a lunge for the tape machine, but I lean back on it, raise my boot to his chest, and kick him good and hard, sending him flailing backwards across the gallery. As he recovers his balance, I lift the vision mixer's chair with my right arm and throw it at his head.

'Consistency and objectivity are the hobgoblins of the second-rate mind!' Carver declares, as the chair connects and Duster roars in pain. He reels out of the gallery to the top of the stairs.

'Get this station off air!' he yells at the milling throng below. 'GET IT OFF!' It's at this point that Duster's staff-relations policy backfires on him – he doesn't know any of the techies' names, so he starts banging the gun against the metal banister to attract their attention. 'Get to the plant room!' he hollers. 'Kill the signal! Get off the air! Call the police!'

The sight of a plump, insane-sounding person with a gun and an elevated view of the studio floor generates a new wave of panic amongst the fleeing audience. Carver shares a taped insight, 'I *am* the product! It's all about me! [blip] It's all about me! [Cut to close-up] IT'S ALL ABOUT ME!'

Press 'stop'.

I re-open the camera fader. Amazingly, they're all live: none of the boys and girls bothered to switch them off before escaping – indeed, the autocue camera is still focused on the Monkey Man, sitting dazed and puke-stained at the edge of his set. The sticky red vomit on his chest does, indeed, resemble a Peckinpah-esque gunshot wound. The actor has long since fled for the safety of his dressing-room, and in the back of shot, Duster can be seen gesticulating wildly at Franco the floor manager, who punches him in the mouth, laying him out flat. Franco kicks the revolver from Duster's flaccid hand. I press 'eject' on the tape machine and tuck the tape under my waistband again, but this time at my back, with the tail of my shirt hanging over it. I leave the equipment in 'transmit' mode.

I have that empty, down feeling I get at the end of every show, when the rush is over and my work is done. I climb to the lighting desk, which Cathal has abandoned, and close all the faders. The studio goes dark. I descend the gallery steps and join the remains of the studio audience, pushing through the doors. Thank you, and goodnight.

'I've gone blind!' Carver yowls, from somewhere behind me. His words, still going out live, reverberate through the blackness. 'I'm dying, I tell you! I can't see! You useless bastards! I'm fucking dying, live on air!'

Once out of the studio, I slip along the empty corridor, up the stairs to Duster's office, where I retrieve my laptop bag, vacuum flask, syringe, and driving gloves. I return to crime scene number two, the little kitchen, where I wash the flask and the syringe in hot water. I put the flask in a crockery cabinet, pull the fridge out from its niche, throw the laptop bag into the gap, and push the fridge home again. I stuff the syringe well down into the bin, beneath the rest of the rubbish. I walk up to the station lobby, where a couple of nervous security guards shoo the last remaining guests out into the car-park, the latter needing little encouragement. The guards obviously feel safer evacuating people than venturing into the studio to confront whatever nightmare is on the loose in there. Word has obviously not yet reached them that Duster has been neutralised.

No one pays any attention to me as I leave the building. I stumble through the throng in the car-park, as if in a daze. I'm not sure to what extent the security cameras cover the car-park, so I want my movements to seem as random as possible. I appear to trip to the ground – behind Duster's yellow Beamer, as it happens. Lying prone, out of sight, I take the tape from my waistband, clean it with my shirt tail, and lodge it in the gap between the exhaust pipe and the chassis. It will fall out eventually, more than likely unnoticed, when the car is in motion. Or maybe the police will find it, should they for some reason decide to give Duster's car a good going-over. Suits me, either way. Staying down, I roll under the car next to Duster's and stuff my driving gloves into a similar position. They won't fall out until they burn.

I stand up again, clutching my left arm, which is no act, as it's starting to hurt like hell, then mingle with the disgorged, gawping audience. I triple-check my pockets for any further evidence, coming up with a small ball of hash and the remains of a wrap. Both are dropped in the crowd. Then, I return to the front of the building and sit on a low wall below the TV Ireland logo, beside the entrance doors, nursing my damaged flipper. Blood from the cut on my cheek drips onto my shirt, but I do nothing to stop it. Neither injury was planned – indeed, I'm still quite taken aback by the strength and speed of Duster's final onslaught, but I view them as a positive development. It takes ages for the police to arrive, so I smoke a fag while I wait.

# 24

## NOMEN EST OMEN

I must have slept forever. The hospital is deadly quiet, so it must be night-time. I'm in a private room. I'm propped half-upright on pillows, with a raging thirst and a stabbing pain in my face. The hangover from hell. A figure sits by my bed, peering up at me from behind a magazine. Therese? No, not Therese, but a uniformed cop. Through blurry eyes, I think for a moment that it's Guard Anthony O'Mahony and almost greet him as such, but as I focus, the face and shoulders become much slighter, the hair fairer and quite trendily cut for … a female cop, younger than me. Christ, they must be keen, if they're waiting for me to wake up. I try to touch my face with my left hand, but it won't lift. I look down. My arm is covered in plaster as far as the elbow and doesn't feel part of me. I use my right hand and find there's a substantial bump where the pain in my cheek is. My fingertips touch paper. The female cop stands and pours a glass of water from a plastic jug. She hands it to me.

'How are you feeling?'

'Like I've been beaten up,' I try to smile, but it hurts. 'Is my face bad?'

'You have two paper stitches, and it's swollen, but I see a lot worse most Friday nights. How did it happen?' Now, there's an odd fucking question to be asking, under the circumstances. I lie back and close my eyes.

'Someone shoved a gun in my face. Like you say, it could have been worse.' A cop, waiting for me to wake up, who doesn't know how I ended up in hospital? Ah! They're trying to question me when I'm woozy and off-guard! Sneaky cops ... I pretend to drift back off to sleep, and the thing is, after about a minute, I do.

I sat on the low wall and watched. It was highly entertaining, in spite of the agony unleashing itself in my arm, that level of discomfort that tells you something is broken. The crowd milled around the car-park, staying well clear of the station entrance but close enough to see what might happen next. There was a sort of weird hiatus, during which the three-hundred-odd evacuees gave one another their versions of what they'd witnessed inside. A mad gunman, on the loose. Kevin Carver had been shot, that much was for sure. Shot dead, live, on television. Then, the gunman had climbed some stairs and taken more victims. He was still in there, holding hostages.

He'd fired into the fleeing crowd. He'd be sending someone out, any minute, with a list of his demands. No, stupid, he didn't need to – sure that's why he took over a TV station, to broadcast his threats. He's an international terrorist; he was heard calling for everything to be shut down. Shut down what? The neighbourhood? The city? Western civilisation? Our very way of life? Shit. Maybe he has a bomb. He has a bomb, did I hear you say? No, I said … hey, apparently your man in there has a dirty bomb. Al-Qaeda, is he?

A few of the bystanders looked over at me, sitting beside the station entrance, obviously hurt. But no one approached to ask if I was okay – perhaps because I was perched too close to the dangerous doorway, or perhaps because I was smoking. I mean, if you can light a fag, you must be coping, right? A TV Ireland news crew ran out of the building and started shooting. One of the reporters, a girl of about twenty-three, tried several takes to camera but kept goofing up, so the cameraman wandered off to gather footage instead, as she cursed, hissed her lines to herself, and adjusted her hair. The cameraman spotted me. 'What happened in there, Lee?'

'Therese. Please call me.'

He went elsewhere. It occurred to me that if I had died in that place, the world would have kept on turning. That fat, coiffed woman with the ridiculous ear-rings would still have been standing, clutching her little husband's arm, staring at the building with her eyebrows raised and her mouth in an 'o'. That group of teenage girls, awkward, lanky, with their fingers in their mouths, would still be half-shrieking, half-laughing, frightened but chuffed that something had actually happened to *them*. 'It's like being on TV!' they kept telling one another.

The crowd stood around, doing exactly what it would have done if I'd been lying dead in the gallery or on Duster's office floor. I was like a disembodied spirit – it was as if I really had been killed. The coke, the shock, and the adrenaline wearing off no doubt contributed to this state of dream-like detachment, but detached was now good. I no longer felt burdened; I no longer felt as if I had to urgently do something, without knowing what it was. The insoluble puzzle had been solved; the impossible task performed. I no longer felt the iron band, squeezing around my chest. For the first time in weeks, that was totally gone. Whatever happened next, justice had been done. That's what you get, Monkey Man, for betraying me. That's what you get for not being half the man I thought you were. Everyone has had a good look behind your monkey mask.

After about ten minutes, distant sirens could be heard above the chatter in the car-park, then three squad cars arrived in quick succession, driving almost right up to the station door. When the cops jumped out, and had it confirmed to them that a man with a gun had indeed been loose inside the building and that it wasn't just *The Kevin Carver Show* messing around, instead of going in, they pulled their cars back and herded the crowd further away from the entrance. I kept my seat until one of them, a tall young fellow, came over and asked me to move. I refused.

'I'm hurt,' I said quietly. The cop reached for my sore arm, and I yelped, recoiling. He jumped back too, then recovered himself and knelt in front of me.

'Have you been shot? Are you hit?' he asked.

'He shot at me twice, but missed both times, so he smashed me on the arm and the face with the butt of his gun. I feel dizzy, and I want to stay sitting down.'

The cop frowned and rubbed his nose at that, but the noisy arrival of two navy-blue transit vans with smoked-glass windows gave him cause to stand and stride off towards his colleagues. The back doors of the vans opened and spilled out about a dozen cops in matching navy-blue boiler-suits, carrying guns – stubby little Heckler & Koch machine pistols, if I wasn't mistaken – clutched tightly to their chests. The armed cops ran towards the entrance, and some round the sides of the building. One of them crouched down beside me and pointed his weapon at the door. A wire led to a big black earpiece on the side of his head. The teenage girls were right. This *was* like being on TV.

'How're ya?' I nodded at him.

He paused, then nodded back. 'How're ya?' He re-focused his attention on the door.

'I think your man is out of bullets,' I informed him. That got his attention back.

'How's that then?' he asked.

'The guy with the gun. He hit me with his pistol, like a hammer, because he ran out of bullets. Then a floor manager floored him, if you know what I mean. I think it's safe to go in.'

A few things happened at once. My police marksman began to talk into his radio, just as two of the ordinary uniformed cops came forward and tried to move me from the wall again. 'There'll be bullets flyin',' one of them sagely informed me. They were so careful and considerate, I wondered whether either of them had been on duty at the Glen Dara protest last Friday. Then, two station security guards emerged from the lobby, into the waiting marksmen. They were wrestled onto the ground at gunpoint and made to lie with their hands behind their heads, amidst angry protestations of innocence. My cops laid off trying to move me and joined in watching, nice and close to the action. Franco, the floor manager who'd hit Duster, came out next and leaned on a metal pillar beside my seat. He watched the security guards being manhandled for a minute, then began explaining to the unarmed cops that Duster had been disarmed and was being pinned to the studio floor by a few techies, so it was safe to come in. Duster was also engaging in angry protestations of innocence, according to Franco.

'Did he shoot you, so?' Franco asked me, as casually as he might have asked whether I had the common cold.

'He tried, but he missed.'

'Jayz. That's gas.'

'Were you not afraid he might have shot *you*?' I knew rightly Duster couldn't have.

'Yeah, that's why I hit him.'

Over much effing and blinding, the armed police released the security guards and piled through the door, into the building. Franco snorted, then followed them inside. Two ambulances arrived, and I allowed the unarmed cops to walk me away from my perch into the back of one of the blue-flashing vehicles. A paramedic tried to make me lie flat, but I sat slightly upright, looking back out the door. Now that I was officially injured, part of the crowd came over to stare at me. Carver was amongst the first to emerge from the building, after the police went in. He was half-walking, half being carried by Scally and Charlotte. A phalanx of station staff followed behind, anxious to share the drama. The red goo vomit still looked quite splendid down the front of Carver's shirt. The paramedics ran forward with a stretcher, but he recoiled, and a scuffle broke out as the paramedics tried to guide him towards my vehicle.

'Get off me, you fucks! Nao! Nao! Go away! I'm fine! Scally, you dog! Call a limo! We're going out, okay? We're going into town! We're going to Dolce Vita, okay? Get away from me! No autographs! Scally, you pox! Get everyone together, I want to sing!' The ambulance rocked, as a paramedic bundled him onto the bench across from me. 'Nao! Nao!' Carver cried, 'You can't arrest me, I'm a fucking star! Don't put me in the van! Teach! Teach!' He lunged across and poked my sore arm, hard. I cried out. 'Tell them to let me go – this is police fucking brutality! Police brutality, you hear? Make a few calls, Teach, and let's get some …'

He drew his hand across his nose and made a violent sniffing sound. 'Teach! Get up off your backside and order some coke, or you're fired! Over! Gone! Beaten docket! I demand my fucking rights!'

'Your colleague has been injured,' a paramedic informed him, extending an oxygen mask towards my face. Carver snatched it off him and took a deep draw, as the doors slammed shut, and we sped away, in a whoop of sirens.

'Teach!' Carver squeaked, his voice high from the oxygen. 'What are you doing in my limo, you big fuck? I've just remembered, I fired you already!' He turned to the medic, waving the mask. 'Fuck me, this is good stuff, what is it?'

I genuinely did pass out then and woke up in a bright room on a trolley. A bespectacled doctor informed me that I had a green-stick fracture across the bones in my left forearm, and that the injection he was about to give me would put me to sleep while they 'sorted it out'. As the needle went in, I could see Carver on a bed across the room. Anne Stutz had arrived. She'd been crying, and the streaks of black mascara down her face served to compound her freakish, alien demeanour. Along with one of the doctors, she was trying to hold Carver still, while a second doctor tried to unbutton his shirt. The three of them weren't having much luck, as he wriggled furiously.

'Get off me, you pox-dogs! Take your rubber gloves and shove them up your own ass! University-educated cunts, the lotta ya! Don't you know who I *am*? Anne! Tell them who I am! This is police brutality!

Give me back that mask, or you're all sacked! I want my mask, I want it here, and I want it now!'

Then that was it, over. Gone. Beaten docket.

I wake up again, dry and sore. The woman cop is not by my bedside. I reach out with my good arm for the plastic jug of hospital water, but I drop the damn thing and it bounces across the dark floor, splashing liquid everywhere. A nurse comes through the illuminated rectangle of the doorway, flicks switches on the wall, and the room is bathed in white light. Like every other hospital in the world, the place is too damn warm. I bury my face sideways in the pillow and ask her to turn the light back off, but she refuses, saying she'll have to mop the water up, and anyway, someone wants to see me. She goes off to fetch her mop, and my visitor. Aw fuck, here we go, it was too much to hope that the cops would wait until morning to let me get my head together. By now, they'll have questioned Duster, and that means they'll be gagging to question me. The female cop from earlier follows the nurse back into the room and sits on the far side of my bed, away from the spilt water. She looks like she's been sleeping.

'I found out what happened to you.' She has a gentle voice. 'You've had a bit of a time of it. How are you feeling?'

'Like I've been pistol-whipped by a mad gunman,' and I try to sound as pistol-whipped as possible.

'Look,' she continues, and her tone changes, for the worse. Here we go … 'This may seem like a bad time,

376

but there isn't going to *be* a good time to do this,' and she straightens her back, eyes serious. I say nothing. 'Are you Lee Lovecraft, of 69 Morgan Quay Court?'

Jesus, you'd think they'd let me wake up, brush my teeth, and use the toilet before cautioning me. 'Yes. You know I am.'

'I have to formally check, before I … well … it's your father, Lee. I'm really sorry to have to tell you this, but he was found dead at his home in Skerries last night. You're the only immediate relative we could trace, which is why we were anxious to talk to you right away. I know this will be very hard for you to take in, but he's downstairs, and we need you for a formal identification. Not right now – take your time, have a cup of tea first – but the sooner the better. Is there any other family you'd like us to notify, or would you rather get in touch with them yourself?'

# 25

## CONFITEOR

I spend a lot of my time watching the water these days.

I used to enjoy watching the water, but now it's an exquisite torture that I mete out to myself. My front door overlooks the Irish Sea, which is more of a large, flaccid puddle than a proper sea. Like my life, like the inside of my head, it's featureless and utterly depressing. The Atlantic – now, that would be different. The Atlantic is the real sea. That had actually been part of the plan, to sell my flat at a huge profit and rent a cottage or even a lighthouse somewhere savage and remote, then spend the winter watching storms crash into the land. Woolly jumpers, walks along cliffs, and reading by oil-lamp – all that psychic healing sort of shit.

Instead, I'm picking my scabs in Maurice's chalet up in Skerries, close enough to Dublin to sense the presence of the old whore, yet far enough away to be forgotten by my bosom druggy friends and my dazzling meeja contacts. Far from being savage and remote, Skerries is practically a suburb, an in-between place for in-between people. In both senses, my dreams are finished: my ambitions, for obvious reasons, but I've also stopped dreaming at night. It would seem that there's no need, now that I've inherited my worst nightmare. Literally, I've ended up like my father.

Everything in my life, even the police investigation into what happened at TV Ireland, has fallen into a stagnant limbo. And the thing is, I don't care. As far as the cops go, I'm sticking to my story out of sheer perversity. If they can work out what really happened, then well and good, I'll take what's coming, embrace it, even. The cops would dearly love to make Duster's version of events stand up, because they can sense that he's telling the truth, and I'm not. Their problem is, they have no proof. The weight of evidence, if anything, is very much against Duster, which is probably why I haven't been arrested and charged. I mean, I wasn't the one captured on live television waving a loaded gun around. Many witnesses agree that Duster tried to kill me. Technically, I am a victim. Still, they've questioned me at length, trying to pick holes in my account, but my pride, my monstrous fucking pride, won't let me concede. All the cops can do, for the time being, is request that I notify them if I intend to change address or leave the country. But I have absolutely no intention of doing either. My place is here, amidst the tattered mementoes of Maurice's wasted life, his legacy as good as mine, his failure my only meaningful possession. Like my father before me, I'm a burnt-out nobody, at the age of thirty. Jesus, at least he made it into his fifties before he became unemployable.

Maybe the cops *will* figure it out, eventually. Maybe they'll come for me, but somehow I doubt it. The courts, a short prison sentence – that, at least, would be a relief. Who knows, if I confessed and took the hit, maybe I could write a crappy book about it – *The Producer's Revenge*. Some great books have been written in jail. I could tell all, become another D-list celebrity, a person with a past and, therefore, a future. Instead, it's like, 'hello from hell'. I'm not going to lift a finger to end my true punishment, which is far more fitting and severe than anything the authorities could conceivably inflict upon me for fucking up the Friday-night schedule of some cheap, shitty television station. My real prison is here.

Maurice was found dead, sprawled on the concrete yard behind his chalet, about an hour after I unleashed my televised vengeance that Friday evening. One of his drinking cronies had called by to collect him for last orders and checked the back door when he got no answer at the front. A doctor summoned to the scene said my father hadn't died instantly, when he'd fallen off the rickety wooden chair he'd been standing on. He'd taken a bad tumble, hit the back of his head, then drifted in and out of consciousness as he tried to move, suffering a series of heart attacks, which gradually paralysed then finally killed him. They could tell this from the patterns his blood made on the concrete. Small pools, where he'd lain still, interspersed with drag marks from when he had woken up and tried to help himself, then a slightly larger pool where he'd finally succumbed. The doctor reckoned he'd died minutes before he was found.

As to why he was standing on a rickety wooden chair in his backyard – well, it appeared he'd been trying to repair his kitchen window. The window I had smashed, to break into his house. So, a poor, lonely man had suffered a poor, lonely death, lying helpless on the ground here in the real world, whilst I vented my precious rage on some celebrity gobshite over in loo-la television land. I'd had my moment of white-hot glory, but my father had paid for it.

The thing is, Maurice would have understood my fury – I mean, where else did I inherit my temper, if not from him? He may even have approved of my methods. The more I think about it, the more I'm convinced that when I was a kid watching him clean his cameras and his guns, half the time he was entertaining fantasies of blowing the shit out of some director, producer, or arsehole of an actor.

The strange thing was, when the police had entered the house looking for ways to contact his relatives, they hadn't found any gun parts. Neither did I, when I arrived – and I even checked the attic, which I doubt if the police did. Forever after, I must live with the distinct possibility that Maurice had guessed that I was the thief and so disposed of his deadly detritus, just in case. Perhaps he'd even been watching television and put two and two together. He hadn't reported the theft; instead he'd quietly set about fixing his window.

He may have assumed that local yobbos were responsible – but why wouldn't they steal his TV and his whiskey, while they were at it? Who would break in, assemble two guns from practically unrecognisable parts scattered around the floor, and disappear, leaving everything else untouched? No, I believe that Maurice knew much more about his youngest child than I gave him credit for. I also believe that I killed him, just as surely as if I'd stolen the guns and used them on him, instead of Duster's golf trophy. That's why my place is here. It's my torment, no less than I deserve.

The female cop conducted me downstairs to identify my father's body. Yes, we even ended up in the same north Dublin hospital. People who suffer heart attacks look like they're sleeping, and as Maurice lay there in his drawer with his red face and white beard, I half-expected him to wake up, demand whiskey, and start calling me all the cunts of the day. I couldn't bear the thought of him stuck in that bloody sterile place, so, after an argument with the nurse, I discharged myself. The cop kindly drove me out to Skerries, whence I made the funeral arrangements first thing the following morning.

I'm not religious – far from it – but when they released the body that Saturday, I got the local undertaker to lay him out in his living-room, in the traditional Catholic style. Maurice came from a long line of mad Protestants, but gave no more a toss about religion than I do. When the undertaker had suggested a home wake as one of the options, it seemed like a good idea, better than leaving him in some anonymous stained-glass parlour overnight, or worse still, in that hospital morgue.

Half of Skerries turned up to pay their respects. I had no idea my dad was so popular, down the local boozer. By the time the last well-meaning old codger went home, I'd drunk more whiskey and tea in one night than I had in my whole life – I was obliged to send out twice, for fear of running out. When I phoned my mother to break the news, she said she would attend the funeral, but not the wake. She'd called back a few hours later – my brothers would not be returning from their respective homes in London or France to attend either.

That Sunday, alone with Maurice stretched out in the corner, I sat by him on a wooden chair – *the* wooden chair, I think – and told him everything that had happened since I'd last bothered to pay him a visit. Everything, since that night he helped me with the Monkey Man. I told him about the success I'd enjoyed, of which I'm sure he was aware, and tried to explain how messy it can get when people start betraying one another, how quickly treachery breeds more treachery and spirals out of control. I showed him my arm in plaster, hanging in a sling. I cried a lot when I confessed to killing him with my break-in.

I'd turned my mobile off before my showdown with Carver that Friday, to ready myself for battle. When I turned it back on the following day, to call the undertaker, it beeped like a mad thing, with countless text messages from journalists chasing the TV Ireland story and queries from Stella. For some time afterwards, it was quite a sensation. Viewers had been riveted by the spectacle of Carver losing it with the actor, only to be interrupted by a gunman, followed by the even more bizarre exhibition of his egotistical preening, which few realised at the time was a pre-recorded tape. Now that's entertainment for you, a lovely bit of reality TV.

There were different theories as to what had actually happened. The first news stories said that Carver had been shot. His outburst was some sort of hideous swansong – a shock-induced, televised rant. Those who knew television well enough to know an edited tape when they saw it said that the gunman had burst in with the express purpose of playing the thing out. By the following morning, this was the version the papers were running with. A TV Ireland executive, who had hated Carver for years, had held the staff at gunpoint and forced them to play the recording. *The Sunday Reporter* ran the headline IT'S ALL ABOUT ME! with a big picture of a spew-stained Carver as their front page. Byline, Gavin Kelly. Then, there was the conspiracy brigade, who claimed that the show was in league with the gunman, that the whole thing was a publicity-seeking ploy.

Beep-beep.

RU SHOT?

Beep-beep.

RUOK, HUN? SAW U ON NEWS, U LOOKED LIKE SHIT

Beep-beep.

PLEASE RING ME AT THE DAILY TRIBUNE, MY NO. IS …

Beep-beep.

IS TRUE CARVER DEAD?

Beep-beep.

LEE, GAVIN HERE AGAIN, W.T.F WENT DOWN IN THERE? RING ME!

Beep-beep.

… TELL THE STORY IN YOUR OWN WORDS, FOR A GENEROUS FEE …

Beep-beep.

U FAMOUS! FANCY A PINT?

None of the texts were from Therese. So, a childish thing to do, perhaps, because all of my contact numbers were in that mobile, but I walked across the road down to the sea and threw the bastard thing as far as I could, into the waves.

The Dublin cops finally tracked me down around midday on Monday, their internal systems having taken a day or two to connect. There wasn't much they could say, for they arrived just as the undertakers were carrying my father out to the hearse. They were a pair of strapping city detectives, a far cry from the friendly female cop, but they left when I promised to attend a formal interview in Dublin the following day.

We planted Maurice in his family plot, in a tiny old churchyard in leafy south Dublin. Me, my mum and her man, Stella, a few of our druggy mates, and about half-a-dozen of the Skerries codgers – what a glamorous send-off. No one from the world of TV or film to lend glitter to the occasion. We didn't bother with a service, just a few words by the grave. My mother didn't cry. She and her husband offered to take me home with them, back to their mansion in Wexford, but I declined. She wanted to know what had happened in work, and I mumbled something about maybe taking a career break. She told me I'd lost too much weight. I told her not to worry. When she realised she was getting nowhere, she didn't push it – the woman has her own happy life to lead, after all. What was I going to tell her, that I'd killed the man she'd had three children by? And gosh, Mummy, you'd be so proud – I nearly murdered *two* people, instead of just the one!

After the funeral drinks, I made a point of returning to Skerries alone, to commence my exile. Maurice's bathroom was like a slum, compared to mine, but I cleaned the bath and lay in it, smoking fags, drinking whiskey, and rewinding the last three weeks in my head. I considered my body, white in the water. There wasn't a pick of flesh on me. All I'd eaten in five days was a box of bloody vol-au-vents someone brought to the wake. I had totally stopped it with the Class As, though. Their presence was no longer required – it was time to face the big, long downer. I've read that coke and pill users always hit depression when they stop, because they've burned up supplies of dopamine and serotonin to the brain. They become organically incapable of being happy.

The Tuesday after Maurice's funeral started humid and close, and by the time I reached Dublin the rain was pelting down. I had to take a taxi, because of my arm.

They opened the interview with a few platitudes about my father's death and a solicitous inquiry about my own battle-scars. My face was still bruised, and I agreed with the cops that I'd had an unfortunate few days. Detective Ramsey asked the questions. There was nothing brisk about the occasion – Ramsey had a slow, tendentious manner about everything he did, which is how I knew that they had their suspicions, in spite of my injuries. By now, they'd have had plenty of time to straighten Duster out and hear his side of the story. They'd also doubtless have talked to Carver – fuck knows what *he* thought happened – and they'd have interviewed witnesses from the studio, as well as watching back tapes of the fateful show. Like everyone else, the cops were struggling to make sense of it all. Something bad had happened – they just weren't sure what.

In the name of 'getting it right' and 'just making certain', Ramsey asked a number of seemingly innocent questions several times, appearing to labour over his writing pad as he did so. The other cop, a plump woman in her mid-forties, sat off to my right, perfectly still, hands on her lap. Had it not been for her hard grey eyes, Detective Boland could have almost been maternal. Placing someone on the edge of your vision field is a tactic designed to make you slightly nervous, so they can watch you without the interview appearing overtly accusatory or aggressive. After taking endless personal details, Ramsey asked whether I knew of any connection between my father's death and events at the station on Friday night. I feigned surprise and said no, that I could see no connection between my father accidentally falling off a chair and some lunatic going mad with a gun in a TV studio twelve miles away. As if slightly frightened by the thought, I turned the question around and asked it of him. Ramsey said no, that they did not regard my father's death as suspicious, for the time being.

That's when the shame hit me. I had killed my father, and now I was betraying him by not explaining how. This was a sour, cowardly betrayal, which carried none of the quiet, delicious pleasures of my previous efforts. My eyes watered with self-loathing. I rubbed the cut on my face and shed a little tear for my poor old dear dead dad.

So, Ramsey asked quietly, no one was 'after' me, I had no enemies who would do such a thing?

I said no, I certainly hoped not.

Then, they led me through a meticulous step-by-step account. I'd had an altercation with Kevin Carver during the afternoon, they knew about that. What had been the problem? I said that Carver had threatened to sack me every Friday for six years, usually for failing to kiss his ass with sufficient enthusiasm. Friday is show time, and he loves a good fight on a Friday, does Carver. I said it was no biggie, that it went with the territory, that he pulled the same celebrity bullshit all the time. Ramsey and Boland allowed themselves discreet little smirks. Not everyone in punter-land, I guessed, swallowed Carver's hero-of-the-people guff, least of all the cops.

However, I admitted to them that I'd been sufficiently irritated by the argument to report it to my manager, Dickie Vaughan, Head of Programmes, TV Ireland. Carver had been behaving strangely of late, I explained, and I was obeying orders by referring assiduously back to my immediate superior when our celebrity presenter acted the maggot. Dickie had specifically demanded that I keep him posted about any problems, no matter how minor. So, I'd climbed the stairs to Dickie's office, walked in without knocking, and found him snorting cocaine off his desk.

'Sorry ... he was ... *what*?'

'It wasn't quite Al Pacino in *Scarface*, but because Dickie's desk was normally so tidy, I noticed the lines straight away. Plus, Dickie was in mid-snort with a twenty-euro note jammed in his face when I walked in, so there was no avoiding the issue.'

'Go on.'

'Well, I was taken aback to say the least, because everyone had Dickie down for a total square.'

'So what happened then?'

'I didn't know whether to laugh or be embarrassed, so I made to leave again, but Dickie yelled after me to sit down – he was very definite about it. He pointed at the seat in front of his desk and told me to sit down. So, I sat down.'

'Why did you do that?'

'That's a very good question, and if I'd known the bastard was about pull a gun on me, I would have run away instead. I guess I was so stunned that I just, like, obeyed. This man had been my boss for six years, don't forget. But on another level, I was never *afraid* of Dickie – he wasn't exactly a threatening figure. So, half not thinking, half amusement, half having no idea what was coming next. Oh. That's three halves. You know what I mean.'

'I think I do. Your relationship with Mr Vaughan had been like what, up until then?'

'Normal, low-key working relationship, really. Dickie tended not to interfere much with the programme: he and the Monkey Man had never seen eye-to-eye.'

'The Monkey Man?'

'Shit. Sorry, that's my private nickname for Kevin Carver.'

'Why?'

'Because he looks like one, I suppose.'

'Uh, go on …'

'Well, Carver and Dickie totally hated one another – ask anybody – so I was the go-between. I'd see Dickie alone maybe once a week, just what's-on-the-programme kinda talk. He'd mix with the guests after the show in the green room – he loved doing that, getting his little photo taken with whoever was in town

– and not much else to say, really. He spent a lot of time on the golf course. At least, that's where we *assumed* he was. Now you're going to tell me he was running a terrorist cell from his home, instead.'

'Excuse me?'

'Sorry, a poor attempt at humour. What I'm trying to say is, Detective Ramsey, that this was the first abnormal thing I'd ever seen Dickie do. We all thought he was totally straight. Golf, management bullshit, the yellow BMW, the whole shebang.'

'I see. So you sit down in front of your manager, even though you claim he's consuming an illegal substance – what then?'

'What then is, Dickie starts talking all sorts of weird shit. He stands up and paces around behind his desk, babbling about Carver. About how much he despises him. About how he's 'made an executive decision'. He kept using that phrase over and over, 'an executive decision'. What the specific problem was, I don't know. I mean, I go to Dus ... Dickie's office with a minor complaint about Carver, and instead I end up listening to a truckload of major bitching coming back the other way! Dickie had been on edge about Carver for quite some time; he was nervous about all the shit getting into the papers. Maybe the TV Ireland board had been giving him a hard time over that, who knows? Or maybe it was about money – these things frequently are.'

'What did he do then?'

'Well, Dickie sits down and stands up a few times, then he finally sits down and I think by this time I'm beginning to realise that he's got much more on board than just a few lines of gak. I mean, cocaine.'

'How so?'

'Well, he's sweating like a pig, and his eyes are like piss-holes in the snow. Dark pinpoints, crazy-looking. I get up to leave, but he gets all flustered, tells me to stay, then chops me a line of cocaine from a bag in his briefcase.'

'From his briefcase, you say?'

'Yes. That's where he had his drugs. I refused, so he offered me a pill.'

'A pill?'

'Yeah, a pill. He offered me one, and when I didn't take it, he swallowed it.'

'What sort of a pill?'

'Small, round, and speckled. I don't think it was a headache tablet.'

'What did you think it was?'

'I had no idea. Look, all I know is that Dickie had all these little bags of white powder and pills, that he tried to get me to take some, that I said 'no' and wanted to leave.'

'Why didn't you?'

'Because Dickie said he had something else to show me. He reaches into his drawer and takes out this gun, like a cowboy pistol. Then, he points it right at me, and he's like, "What do you think of that, Lee?"'

'He pointed the gun at you? Are you sure about that?'

'What do you mean, am I sure about that?'

'I mean, are you sure about what you're saying

here, that your immediate superior pointed a gun at you?'

'Have you ever had a gun pointed at you, Detective Ramsey?'

'No, I haven't.'

'Well, let me share something with you. It's just like in the movies, only for real. Dickie Vaughan pointed a dirty great gun in my face and said something like, "Sit down, you're my employee, and you're going nowhere!" The gun was pointed at me, by him. It was scary. I didn't like it. He didn't seem in control, and that made it worse. Sitting there, at his desk, off his knickers on drugs. With a gun.'

'So you say he pointed this gun at you; what did you do?'

'Well, I nearly shat myself, frankly. I think maybe my heart stopped beating for a few seconds, and then I decided to call his bluff and stood up to leave.'

'You left the room?'

'No, I didn't say that, I said I stood up to leave. I stood up and was making to back off slowly then run for it – he has a big, long office, does Du ... Dickie – when he stands up too, and he fires the gun at the wall.'

'He fires the gun at the wall?'

'He fires the gun at the wall. Well, *on* the wall is a bunch of shelves and these ornaments and shit, and he hits one of them, a big glass vase thing, and it breaks fucking everywhere, man, like, it just *explodes*, you know, all over me, all over him, all over the floor, and the noise is terrifying, so I sit back down again.'

'You sit back down again?'

'Jesus! Why do you keep repeating everything I say? Man, you must have had your people in his office by now and seen for yourselves what that gun did to the wall! Well, I was *closer* to Duster than the wall – think of the mess he'd have made, if he'd hit me instead!'

'Duster?'

'Sorry, station nickname for Dickie.'

'Why Duster?'

'Dunno. The techies started that off and it kinda caught on.'

'Is it because he took … dust, like powder, you know, cocaine?'

'Maybe the techies knew something the rest of us didn't. But Duster and coke, that was news to *me*.'

'So Dus … so Dickie Vaughan shoots at the wall. What then?'

'I sit down again, pdq, and Dickie waves the gun around, talking complete shite. This is when it got really, really scary.'

'He threatened you with this gun again?'

'Yeah! I mean, come on! I'm sitting there and he's standing there and the whole place is covered in glass from this vase he shot, and the room smells of, I dunno, fireworks, you know, and this fucker is waving a gun around, saying shit like how he's gonna make us all pay, how nobody respects him, how everybody's always laughing at him behind his back. He says that I'm as bad as all the rest, I'm as bad as Carver, and if I try to get away, he's going to blow my fucking head off. And I'm sitting there, like, pinned to this chair, and I'm kinda thinking now I might actually die. If you call that "threatening" then yes, Detective Ramsey, I guess I felt threatened, all right.'

'So how did you get away?'

'Well, this roaring and shouting and gun-waving goes on for some time, but eventually Duster sort of calms down a bit and flicks on this gargantuan TV set at the far end of his office with a remote control. He says the show's about to start, and we should watch it, because Carver is in for a bit of a surprise.'

'A surprise, you say? What kind of a surprise?'

'He didn't say what kind of a surprise, but it actually occurred to me that he might have dynamite strapped around his body under his shirt – maybe *that* was his surprise, y'know? Take us all out.'

'Why did nobody else know this was happening? Why didn't your colleagues try to find you before the programme started? You are the producer, aren't you?'

'Good fucking question, shower of dopey bastards! You know, the same thing occurred to me, but not until much later. I guess they thought I'd stormed off home after my row with Carver. Plus he probably told them to ignore me – he has a habit of huffing with people, that's what he does. But in fairness, how was anyone to know that I was being held hostage upstairs, by the Head of Programmes, TV Ireland? I guess it just goes to show you can work with someone for years and yet have no idea what they're really like. The man must have serious problems. I'd say by this stage you people must have some idea what was eating him. Paranoid delusions. A closet coke habit. Tell me you have him under arrest, by the way. Is it safe?'

'Mr Vaughan is helping us with our enquiries. So you're both watching television, *The Kevin Carver Show*, right?'

'Right.'

'Did Mister Carver's behaviour strike you as any way odd?'

'Do you know what, I was too worried about the gun Dickie had aimed at my head to pay attention to Carver. I just wanted out of there alive.'

'And what happened next?'

'Well, about ten minutes after the show starts, Dickie chops out more coke from his plastic bag. I'm pretending to watch the screen, but obviously I'm watching him. I figure if he relaxes a bit, he might not shoot me right away. So, he chops out more lines and says it's time to get ready for the surprise. He goes to snort, and there's a split-second when the gun goes down, and he's not watching on me. That's when I run for it. That's when I dive out of the chair and make a dash for the door. Duster shouts something like "hey", and I hear another shot. Bastard just misses my head; I could feel the bullet whiz past me, and I run down the corridor.'

'You mean, you got away from him?'

'No! He came after me, shouting and screaming. I could hear him on the stairs behind me, moving fast for a drugged-up little fat man. When I hit the ground floor, I dived through the studio door, looking for somewhere to hide. And you know the rest.'

'Tell us the rest, in your own words.'

'For chrissakes, Duster follows me into the studio, so I run for the gallery, which is up a flight of stairs, thinking if I can get behind the door, maybe I can block it, or maybe someone will call the shagging cops … sorry, but you know what I mean … it's like the fucking *Terminator* at this stage – he just won't stop coming, and to be honest I'm kinda hoping he'll pick on someone else, or maybe someone will wrestle him to the floor, but he follows me into the gallery and tries to shoot me again.'

'He tries to shoot you again?'

'No, he says he's sorry and gives me a great big hug! Yes, he tries to shoot me again, only I duck down behind a machine: that was the only thing that saved me. Then … then … [and at this point I deliberately think of killing my father, and I start to cry a bit] … then he f-fucking buh-buh-beats me with his guh-gun …'

Detective Boland stood up, offered a tissue from a box at one end of the desk, which I accepted. She sat down again, without saying anything.

That was over two months ago. They called me back to go over it again. Ramsey even came out here to Skerries with a gaunt young sidekick whom he didn't introduce and sat in Maurice's living-room, cross-referencing several of my answers, but as yet they haven't challenged me, contradicted me or hit me with Duster's version of events. Like I say, the whole thing's stalled, gone into stasis. Duster and their hearts are telling them one thing, whilst myself and their forensic evidence tell them the exact opposite. If only they knew me. If only they knew the true dynamics of betrayal, what a wondrous, delicate game it is, when you can smell treachery coming and you step out to meet it with a few weapons of your own.

You see, I'd always known that one day, Kevin Carver would try to fuck me. Hadn't I been well-warned, and hadn't I the evidence of my own eyes, the way he treated other people? It had never been a question of 'if', only of 'when'. And I knew that 'when' was coming fast over the horizon the night of the Archbishop programme. Carver had never gone on a solo run like that before, and I realised immediately that if I didn't clip his wings, I'd be screwed, because he'd do it again. If I let him away with undermining me, it would be the death of a thousand cuts. His ego had swollen to the point where I was no longer to be consulted, as he made his play to be accepted by the very establishment he had hitherto professed to despise. Of course, he only despised the establishment because he wasn't part of it. I guess at the heart of every ageing rebel is a raving power-monger who just wants to be loved.

So, I had counter-attacked, hard and fast. Rewind, to that night in late September. There's me, standing on the pavement outside The Terrapin Club, immediately after the Archbishop programme, ostensibly hanging back from the posse to order up egregious quantities of coke. As I wait for Ritchie to swing past on his Vespa, I make another call, to Gavin Kelly of *The Sunday Reporter*. I tell him that if he can get himself up to Milton McMahon's party in the Wicklow Hills, he'll witness Kevin Carver make a complete fool of himself, guaranteed. Gavin Kelly, who would travel to Mongolia, let alone Wicklow, to see Carver brought low.

And there's me, five minutes later, in the toilets at The Terrapin Club, locked in a cubicle, preparing my special wraps for Carver. I grind four tabs of E into the coke, and two of the requisitioned Viagra. Chop chop chop goes the Visa card. Get that up your nose, Monkey Man! Spiking drinks is one thing, but nobody ever expects to have their drugs spiked, do they? Carver was well-used to coke, but pills and Viagra were new to him, and he was about to experience an unwitting baptism of fire.

Forward-wind through an evening of madness, and there's me, leaving the police station, early the following morning. I wish I could say I'd planned to get Carver locked up, but that was just luck – an unexpected bonus. The perfect icing on Kelly's nasty little gossip item, as I put it when I call him from outside the cop-shop. Add this to your piece, Gavin: Kevin Carver has just spent a night in the cells, screaming his head off. Then, still operating under drug logic, I feel suddenly dirty, so I jump in a taxi to go seek divine retribution from a total stranger called Therese. *'Doesn't it bother you, some of the things you get up to in television?'* Baby, you don't know the half of it.

I had figured – and you'll just have to believe me on this score – that a combination of a thumping comedown, the bad reviews for the Archbishop programme, and Gavin Kelly's pointed gossip story would have been enough to give Carver pause for thought. Warning shot across the bows, Kevin. A little reminder that there are things in life that can damage even powerful men. I certainly wasn't seeking to destroy him – I mean, Carver was my bread, butter, and platinum credit card. I just wanted to scare him, put him back in his box.

With anyone else, it might have worked. Instead, I only made matters worse. Carver had smelled my betrayal. He couldn't put a name to it, but his sharp animal instincts had alerted him, just as surely as if I'd bared my rear and sprayed musk in his face. A bit like Milton's betrayal of him in the royalties case, Carver *knew*, without needing proof. Wild beasts don't wait for proof: they completely trust their senses. So, as soon as he recovered from the party, Carver was watching me. The dance of treachery had begun, and it was merely a question of who would be first to show the dagger clutched behind his back. For what is it that they say? If your producer betrays you once, it's his fault, but if he betrays you twice, it's your fault.

I think the Monkey Man stopped loving me, I think he stopped trusting me, the day *after* I fetched his Viagra. Love, in his emotional running order, is entirely predicated on usefulness. If I couldn't be trusted to do his bidding, then I was no longer of any use. That same morning, perched high above the sea at Howth Head, totally in bits but never more lucid, was also when I realised that I no longer loved the Monkey Man. Fucker was eating my soul.

No doubt it was then that he teed the others up against me. Looking back, I can see it all now. The office door is closed, and I'm late, as usual. They're all in there, the Monkey God presiding. 'Okay, here's the plot,' he's saying; 'I want rid of Teach. I want your full co-operation, for which you will be well rewarded. You'll get more money, because you'll all move one space up the pecking order. Kate, when Teach is gone, you'll be my producer, because I know you'll do exactly as you're told. Dervla, Elaine – I'll have you promoted to assistant producers. Scally and Charlotte, you are now researchers. We'll get a couple of new monkeys in, and you can lord it over them, just as I lord it over all of you. How does that sound? Good, when I give the word, we're gonna start freezing Teach out. When that happens, I'll have told Duster that I want him gone from my show. My show, monkey troop, and don't any of you ever forget that!'

Forward-wind to the morning Carver butted Marty Pelham in the face, and there's me driving into work, in a total mess. But not so messed up that I can't pull over and place a call to my favourite gossip columnist. How about this for Sunday, Gavin? Another little thrust between the shoulder blades, because once you start stabbing, it's impossible to stop.

# 26

## EXEUNT

Skerries is named after a couple of little offshore islands, one of which sports a Martello tower that Joyce didn't live in. The towers were built when fear was rife that Napoleon might invade Ireland as a springboard for England, and this historical non-event is without doubt the most interesting thing that has ever happened in the area. The coastline is flat, and I walk for hours without distraction.

It will soon be Christmas, and the winter weather has finally arrived in earnest, which is some consolation. No more sweaty Irish-Indian summer days; how nice to wear a coat again, turn the collar up, hide my face, and walk back to my father's chalet in the gathering dark. There's nowhere else to go around here, except for the bloody beach, so I tread the same five-mile route twice a day, just to get out of that miserable little shack. And every time I round that final bend in the coast road, I allow myself to see Therese standing in the driveway, wearing her red coat. I don't want to see anybody, apart from her. And so, of course, Therese is never there.

Yesterday, the Creature was waiting for me. Her escort sat outside in his Subaru, while we sat in Maurice's living-room. At first, I had nothing to say to her. There were no bad feelings, but now that I was no longer living off Class As, there were no good feelings, either. I'm a very boring person when not on drugs. She upbraided me a little for cutting myself off, feigning concern. However, I knew that the real purpose of her visit was to suss out how long she could stay in my flat, so I told her that I'd decided to sell. Maybe some time after Christmas, I'd summon up the energy to ring an estate agent and get it all sorted. If I didn't, the bank would repossess it anyway. She would have to move on, but I told her that she could take whatever designer furniture I hadn't destroyed.

'But it took me ages to tidy that place up!'

'Don't take this the wrong way, but I don't care. I won't be back, so do as you please in the meantime.'

'How can you just abandon your pet?'

'Creature, you are an unbridled force of nature, and definitely no one's pet.'

She seemed pleased at that. 'Fucking right. Hey, some woman called for you the other day. I was in the shower and Jimmy let her in 'cos he thought she was a friend of yours.'

'What woman?'

'She said to tell you her name was Hume, you'd know who she was.'

'*Hume?* What did she look like?'

'Brown hair, older than me, not as slim. Ordinary.'

'What did she want?'

'Well, it was a bit fucking odd, 'cos even though she said she knew you, it turned out she wasn't very clued up about the shit that went down.'

'What d'you mean?'

'Well, the TV Ireland story was all over the papers for weeks, right, but she kept asking me for details. What happened to you and that sort of thing. Then, she didn't know about your father dying, so I thought maybe she was some sneaky bitch of a tabloid journalist. She wanted to know where to find you.'

'So you told her?'

'Course not, hun, you know you can always count on me!'

'Ah, *bollocks*! That was Therese! Did she leave a message or her number or anything?'

'No.'

'Nothing at all?'

'No! Is that Therese who you smashed the place up over?'

'Yes! No! Well, actually …'

'Good. I'm glad I told her fuck-all, then. Cow.'

'I … ah, for fuck's sake …'

'Have I done a bad thing, hun?'

'Ach … you weren't to know. Just do me a favour, if she ever comes back, tell her where I am – you have my permission, okay?'

'I don't think she'll be back, 'cos I got snotty with her and told her to leave.'

'Well, that's just great ...'

A bit of a pause, then, 'She's not as pretty as me.'

Deep sigh. 'No, she's not as pretty as you.'

'And I bet she's useless in bed.'

'Look, Stella. Jimmy's waiting. See you around, okay?'

'That's not Jimmy, that's his mate Darren. I'm with him now. Bye, hun. What are you going to do with yourself?'

'Go for another hugely exciting walk along the hugely exciting beach.'

'No, I meant "do" as in with the rest of your life?'

'I just told you.'

So I'm on my way home from my evening exercise period, and I round the bend in the coast road. There's a black Merc limo parked across the mouth of the driveway. Therese? A limo would hardly be her style. Maybe it's the bailiffs, come to repossess the extremely filthy, dented silver sports car languishing at the side of the chalet, but bailiffs don't drive big black Mercs either, do they? The parking lights are on, and the exhaust is puffing lightly, as the engine ticks over. I'm half-inclined to turn on my heel and walk back towards the beach again, because whoever it is, I don't want to talk to them. But then the tinted rear widow hums down, spy-movie style, and Milton's face appears. Smooth, rich Milton. Well, well. He opens the door, and I climb in beside him.

'How are you?' and he smiles his smooth, rich smile.

REMEMBER: MILTONSCAM

'I'd invite you in, but my home isn't as nice as yours, and I'd be a bit embarrassed. Come to think of it, my home isn't as nice as your car, so let's just sit here.'

'Do you mind if we drive around for a bit?' Milton leans forward, taps the closed glass partition, and his driver, the same guy from the night of the party, moves off slowly.

'What, you'd prefer not to be seen with me?'

'Sorry about your father, Lee. My condolences.'

'Thanks. Shall we go for a pint in some charming seaside pub, so I can tell you what a great guy he was?'

Milton smiles reprovingly, then glances out the window. 'Nice part of the world.'

'If you like your world utterly barren, I suppose it is. Look, I don't mean to be rude, but I'm not much company these days. In fact, I don't see anybody any more.' Milton doesn't look at me, just peers out the window. Eventually, 'He knows you did it, you know.'

I force myself to relax into the beige leather of the seat. 'Who is "he", and what am I supposed to have done?'

'You know, you'd make a good press officer, if you ever decided to give up broadcasting.'

'Oh, but I *have* given up broadcasting, very much so. Not only that, but I've shat on it from a great height. What, are you here to offer me a vacancy at your firm? Sacked anyone lately? Marty Pelham, perhaps?'

'No, he's still with us, just about.'

And I concentrate on the dark beyond the window, for a good thirty seconds. 'You can't sack him, can you? He knows too much.' Milton glances over, his expression hard to read, but I barge on. 'Look, I know why you're here. Pelham has obviously told you that he blabbed to me that night in the club. You've come to do a deal, because doing deals is what you're good at. It probably goes a bit like this: you're here to promise me that you'll get that monkey off my back about certain events in TV Ireland. Of course he knows I did it, and he's probably mouthing off around town that if the cops won't do me, he will. How I'll never work again, yadda yadda. I'd say the little bastard is livid. But you, you're worried that if I'm busted, I might just squeal about the royalties case, go to the press, write a book, go down all guns blazing, and that would be the kind of publicity you don't need. Would I be right?' Milton keeps his eyes on me. 'In fact, I wouldn't be surprised if you have a rather generous banker's draft in your pocket, just a little something to help me through my rough patch. That, plus the reassurance that not only can you smooth Carver out, but you could probably smooth the cops out as well, because smooth is what you do, isn't it? "Don't worry, Lee, take this untraceable, tax-free gift, maybe go away for a while, and in a year or two, the investigation will be over, inconclusive, and we can all get on with our happy, happy lives." Is that the plan?'

Milton looks out his window again, but this time, when he replies, there's a definite note of humour in his voice, as if he's stifling a laugh, which rather irritates me.

'Without confirming anything, Lee, I repeat – you'd make great press officer. You're very plausible.'

'Look, you can tell Carver from me – tell him yes, I did it. I *want* him to know. Tell him that I royally fucked him over, although obviously not nearly as professionally and profitably as you did. But tell him I've already paid a high price for my revenge, more than anything he can do to me, and that if he ever annoys me again, what I did at TV Ireland will look like a gesture of peace and reconciliation. Tell him that I'm brooding and unstable, and that if he doesn't let it lie, then one night he'll meet me in a dark street, where it'll just be the two of us. And this time, when I'm finished, I'll be honest with the cops, because this time, my name will most definitely be on the closing credits.'

'I'm sure there's no need for …'

'*Tell him!*' I roar, and the car swerves as Milton's driver looks round, my voice having penetrated the glass. The driver brakes and makes for the side of the road, but Milton leans forward, raps the partition, and indicates for him to keep moving. After a filthy glance at me, the driver does as he is told. Milton sits back with his arms folded. A silence ensues, as the car enters Skerries village, down the wide main street, once a market venue, where hard men did hard deals over horses on fair day and children on hiring day. I ask Milton to pull over. He complies, but makes no move to say goodbye.

'Don't worry, I've no intention of squealing about the case, okay? Why would I do that? It would only make Carver look like a hero, and that's the last thing I want. More to the point, why would I screw a friend, even if he is a rich bastard?'

Milton reaches into his suit pocket and withdraws a white envelope.

'I don't want your money.'

'You ought to take this.'

'I don't want your pity, either.'

'Take it anyway.'

'No!'

'Lee. If you don't mind me saying, you need to get over yourself and stop taking everything bad that happens in life as one big, personal insult. You have a vastly exaggerated sense of your importance in the scheme of things, and a feverish imagination, to boot.' Bastard's still smiling, pulling my chain.

'Remind you of someone, do I?'

'Actually, yes!'

'So what has that little monkey fuck been saying about me?'

'To anyone who will listen, that he knows you did it. To me personally, nothing – I haven't seen him since the pair of you were so rude at my party.'

'I'm sorry, that was my fault, too. Think of it as a dry run for what happened at TV Ireland. As penance, I promise on my dead father's grave never to tell anyone about the royalties case, cross my heart and hope to die, so help me Jesus. Happy now?'

Milton opens his belt and the top of his trousers and unbuttons his shirt. For a bizarre instant, I completely misinterpret what he's doing.

'Uh ... look, Milton, I'm flattered, but I'm not your type, believe me!'

Saying nothing, Milton reaches up and turns on an internal light. He pulls his jacket and shirt back. The right side of his body – his ribcage, stomach, and upper hip – is a mass of scar tissue, as if someone's poured melted wax over his body.

'Car crash. China, September 1996.'

'Jesus, I ...'

He tucks himself in again, rebuttons his shirt, closes his belt. 'Let me tell you about Marty Pelham. His real name is Connor O'Dowd. He's my half-brother, on my father's side. Some writer, my dad published one of her novels, but he never acknowledged Connor, and she got nothing from our family until after my dad died. When things started to go well for me, I gave him a job, because my mother asked me to.'

'You're kidding! Sorry, the pun wasn't ...'

'Like a lot of new-Ireland yuppies,' and Milton throws me a reproachful look, 'Connor likes to exaggerate his own importance. He's jealous, insecure, and re-invents himself constantly. I'd crucify any paper stupid enough to print the rubbish he spun you, and I can assure you that your source would be the first person rushing forward to deny it.'

'But I saw him in the hotel! With the O'Gormans!'

'So what? I've just told you: Connor thinks he's a player, but he's not. He thought he was helping.'

I give it a few beats, because I'm not at all sure how to take this.

'Dads – they can fairly fuck you up, eh?'

'They don't mean to, but they do.'

'Milton, no disrespect, but I don't trust anybody any more, not even myself. That damage to your body – I only have your word that it happened how you say it did. And I've only your word that Marty, or Connor, or whatever his name is, is your idiot half-brother. Most of all, whatever the truth about the accident, you survived. So why has Carver never used you to take a case in the States?'

And Milton starts laughing, a smooth, polished laugh. 'Carver has a bit of money now, but you need more than a bit to buy justice in America! Look, I don't care what you believe. I'm already late for dinner, in town. Take the envelope. You don't deserve it, but I really think you should see what's inside. I promise you'll forget everything else as soon as you open it.'

Baffled, I ungraciously snatch the missive out of his hand and rip it open with more violence than the quality of the stationery deserves. It contains a folded letter on matching paper, and not the cheque or banker's draft I had envisaged. The writing is small and rounded, in black fountain pen.

*Lee,*

*They say you can judge a person by the company they keep. I've been to your flat, and if the occupants are typical friends of yours, then you're*

411

*in more trouble than I thought. I'm not at all sure that I'm doing the right thing, but your phone doesn't answer, and TV Ireland say you don't work there any more. Damn your shallow heart, but in spite of myself, I'm concerned.*

*As you correctly guessed, Milton McMahon was our kind benefactor on the road protest. He agrees that you're a frightful brat, but he also says he can find you, so once again, I'm relying on his generosity.*

*I'm very sorry to hear about your father, truly, I am. I know my condolences are rather belated, but I've been in hospital since our last encounter and completely out of touch. A badly fractured skull; I suppose I should have listened to you on the mountain, because I collapsed when I ran away from that ghastly TV station. Intensive care for a week, then my mum took me home. I'm afraid I was obnoxious to Kevin Carver in your absence, but I imagine that hardly matters, in the light of subsequent events. You don't do things by halves, do you?*

*I'm back down in Wicklow for a bit, salvaging what I can from the cursed motorway. You'll be delighted to hear that certain photographs published by a Sunday newspaper caused enough political embarrassment to stall construction for another six months. Not much, but to borrow your expression, I guess I owe you one. So, in my capacity as the patron saint of lost causes, I'd like to know:*

*1) Are you all right? (No one seems to know!)*

*2) Are you still a devil-spawn meeja whore?*

*3) Do you agree with Hume's assertion that*

*'The most unhappy of all men is he who believes himself to be so'?*

*Love,*

*Therese.*

I jump out of the car, in case I cry in front of Milton, and I'd rather wet my pants than cry in front of Milton. It's cold, but cold is good. I pull my coat about me and re-read the letter. The car window hums down. Milton grins like a wolf.

'Well?'

'You're such a fucking wind-up merchant, Milton.'

'Don't tell me; and what's annoying is that I'm extremely good at it?'

'Interrupting the purity of my exile to take the piss. I'm not meant to have a sense of humour right now – it's not aesthetically appropriate.'

'Quite. And Therese?'

'Tell her … thank her for her note and tell her that the answer to all three questions is "maybe". Tell her that I'm still in the process of excavating my head from my arse, but it's not been easy and I may require some … uh, archaeological expertise.'

'You can't be helped, if you can't be found.'

'Then please tell her exactly where to dig.'

'Fine. And a spot of free advice – I know quality when I see it, so don't fuck about.'

'How did you find me?'

'Lee. I'm ten times smarter than you and approximately fifty-four point seven million times richer. Get back in the car, and I'll drop you home.'

'No thanks, I'll walk. The movement helps work my head loose.'

'I'll tell Therese that a breakthrough is imminent, so. You might even give me a call when it pops, and we can all go for a pint in town to celebrate.'

'What's wrong with Skerries?'

Milton wrinkles his nose. 'Everything.' And his window hums up, as the Merc rolls off down the street.

On my way back towards the coast road, I pass the display of an electrical goods shop. Several televisions blaze, showing a close-up of the Monkey Man, sitting back, relaxed, looking good, laughing at the words of yet another celebrity guest. I'd forgotten it was Friday night. Show time. His show, not mine. No doubt his audience figures will have climbed dramatically, as people tune in, attracted by the publicity, all hoping that one day, something as insane as my farewell performance might happen again. Hell. I've probably done him more good than harm.

Last night, amongst one of the many tottering piles of books in my father's living-room, I noticed a set of encyclopaedias from the 1920s, those marvellous days when Britain still ruled the world, or most of it. I picked out the one with a gold-leaf 'M' embossed on the faded blue leather spine. Apparently, the in-habitants of the East Indies used to worship a monkey with a black face, called the hanuman. It could never be touched, because it was sacred to Hanuman, the monkey-god. So, if one of these little fellows climbed through the window of your hut, pissed on the floor, bit your wife, made your children cry, then ran off with your supply of mangoes, there was nothing you could do about it. On the contrary, you were meant feel favoured by such a divine visitation.

I guess we're not unique, much as we in this great little country love to think we are. Every society worships its share of jumped-up parasites, purely because they reflect our most venal desires, writ large. The selfish, howling ego in its most naked form. The higher the monkey climbs, the more he shows his arse, eh? Kevin Carver is an official court jester – no more, no less. It was my mistake to imagine that he could ever be anything else. Just remember, the next time you find yourself gazing in wonder at a celebrity – all you're looking at is a pampered ape.

Where the pavement and the street lights end and the coast road begins, some drunk has been sick, leaving a miasma of Chinese take-away and curdled beer splattered across the concrete slabs. A huge white seagull pecks hungrily at the mess, barely moving aside as I walk on by – into the darkness, into the night.